Praise for the novels of JUDITH KELMAN . . .

Hush Little Darlings

"JUDITH KELMAN FURTHER CONSOLIDATES HER PLACE among the best of the suspense writers publishing today . . . a finely wrought story of chilling suspense."

—Thomas Chastain

Where Shadows Fall

"GRIPPING . . . it swept me along to the shocking climax."

—Mary Higgins Clark

"SEDUCTIVE . . . SHOCKING . . . PAGE-TURNING SUSPENSE."

—Greenwich Time

"FASCINATING . . . Marvelously grim wit."

—Publishers Weekly

Berkley Books by Judith Kelman

PRIME EVIL
WHERE SHADOWS FALL
WHILE ANGELS SLEEP
HUSH LITTLE DARLINGS

WHILE ANGELS SLEEP

JUDITH KELMAN

BERKLEY BOOKS, NEW YORK

WHILE ANGELS SLEEP

A Berkley Book / published by arrangement with
the author

PRINTING HISTORY
Berkley edition / December 1988

For information address: The Berkley Publishing Group,
200 Madison Avenue, New York, New York 10016.

ISBN: 0-425-11093-1

BERKLEY®
Berkley Books are published by The Berkley Publishing Group,
200 Madison Avenue, New York, New York 10016.
BERKLEY and the "B" design
are trademarks belonging to Berkley Publishing Corporation.

PRINTED IN THE UNITED STATES OF AMERICA

10 9 8 7 6 5

To Flora and George on their fiftieth,
with love and thanks.

Special thanks to Natalee Rosenstein,
my editor.

WHILE ANGELS SLEEP

CHAPTER

1

THEY CALLED IT the hanging tree. Overblown, important name for a clumsy old swamp maple with gnarled, obese branches and bark gone dry and patchy from a century of raging tree ailments. It stood, in all its dubious arthritic splendor, at the entrance to the Thornwood Foundation, the artists' colony my father had founded and run for over thirty years until he died last spring.

Driving past it, I felt a remembered tug of the terrified respect I used to bear for the fearsome legend of the tree. It had magical harming powers, I was told in malicious whispers by the older, more knowing children who came around to amuse themselves at my ignorant expense. If you got too close, you risked incurring its woody wrath and causing consequences too hideous to describe to someone of my obvious innocence and tender sensibilities. Terrible things had happened on account of that tree, they told me. There was even a body-shaped bloodstain on the bark. You could see it if you looked just so and knew the way to hold your head.

I was too young to hear the rest, they said. Maybe

someday I'd be old and strong enough to take it all in. But even then I'd have to be prepared to learn about the devastating powers of the hanging tree the hard way.

Lacking hard information, I had conjured a grisly, surreal scene of milk-pale dead bodies dangling from the rigid limbs on bright loops of grosgrain ribbon like so many tree ornaments. I could envision the tree's victims in great, horrific detail: necks cracked like dried wishbones so the heads bobbled and swayed in the wind, bloody blue tongues swollen through tight rubber smiles, vacant eyes bulged round with shock, dead hair floating on unseen currents like long, filmy silk scarves drying on a line.

Most often, when I was at the colony for a rare visit home from boarding school, I'd stayed as far away from the hanging tree as possible. I would climb the fence halfway down the road rather than risk the use of the regular entrance to Thornwood where I might come near enough to the piebald trunk to inflict some disastrous, unintentional insult.

But once, driven to reckless foolishness by a dare, I climbed in a terrified sweat to the top tier of branches and promptly fell like a stupid stone to the rock-hard ground below, breaking my wrist in several important places in the process. The pain was a hot metal stab between my eyes, worse because I knew it was self-inflicted and well-deserved. After the cast came off, I vowed never to mess around with cranky, vindictive spirits again.

So why was I back in this place I had left so many years ago? Why was I upending my reasonable life, bringing my reluctant family to this place that had not been my home for what seemed like a thousand years?

A dozen times in the past week I'd tried to explain

my reasons to my husband, Will, but the whole thing was beyond his understanding. Coming as he had from a textbook normal family, he could not imagine how the ragged scraps of my ruined childhood littered the corners of my life. Soon Thornwood would be out of my hands, turned over to an independent arts organization. I saw this visit as a chance to say a final good-bye, a last chance to set aside my ancient nightmares: my mother's sudden, tragic death; my father's terrible descent to madness; the way he had pushed me out of his life, driven me away from everything I knew and cared about.

To Will, I was simply looking for trouble. "Your father's dead, Em. Why can't you just forget all that?"

If only I could. Especially now when the rest of my life was going almost suspiciously well. The children, all three of them, were in a rare state of calm, most incredible for eleven-year-old Rachel whose emotional development had been chaotic enough to track on the Richter scale. Will, who'd done some painful job-hopping, had finally settled in a comfortable, satisfying position with an import-export firm. He loved the travel, the title, all of it. And I loved the freedom his hard-won career contentment gave me to fully enjoy my own. At the end of the spring term I had been granted tenure on the English faculty at Columbia and a chance to teach the coveted senior humanities seminar in the fall. Teaching suited me perfectly. So did contentment. Contrary to Will's furious, tight-lipped assertions, I had not come back to Thornwood to look for trouble. I was trying to put the past behind me, where it belonged.

As Will turned the Jeep in through the pocked wooden gate to the colony, I was infected by his uneasy silence and the children's. Rachel was leaning against the filmy window, mouth settled in a determined pout, slim elastic arms folded over the hint of an impending bosom. Her wide, charcoal eyes were blazing fury. She hadn't spoken a word since we crossed the Connecticut line half an hour earlier into Sharon, Massachusetts. And her last ones were not encouraging. "I don't want to go to that dumb place," she said with a careful drape of control drawn down over her rage. "I'm not going." She edged the tip of her long, black satin ponytail in the corner seam of her mouth and began to chew.

"M'not gowin'," Adam echoed, with all his four-year-old determination. His pudgy legs swung to the rhythm of the nervous currents pulsing in the car. I felt the firm thwack as the toes of his little red Nikes pummeled the upholstery behind my back.

"Stop it, Addie."

David was off in one of his dreamy two-year-old trances. Webs of deliberate distance clouded his wide, ice-blue eyes and the soft circle of his lips, corked by a chubby thumb, seemed the critical center of his universe. The moist heat of the car had turned his unruly halo of lemon curls into a dark mass of clinging worms.

Will did nothing to lighten the mood. He was furious with my unthinkable failure to see things his way. Though he had insisted on driving us to the colony, "to help you get settled," he said, he spent the entire ride muttering under his breath, tapping impatient fingers against the steering wheel, making supercilious faces until I could not help but wonder how it would feel to coil my fingers around his neck and squeeze.

We bumped and jarred over the narrow access road to the main house. I wanted to break the gloom by pointing out the hanging tree and several of Thornwood's other more intriguing features: the peaked red tile roofs of the tiny cottages poking through the trees, the slick, polished black surface of the swimming pond winking in the distance, the cedar copse where an angry or frightened child could pass long, healing hours amid the dense thickets of her own imagination. I wanted to say something to draw the children into this unwelcome adventure. But a painful catch in my throat blocked the words.

Will wrenched the Jeep to a stop in front of the wide gray veranda. The farmhouse had seen better days. Paint peeled from the dark green shutters, and the clapboard facade had faded from stark white to the discouraging yellow of neglected teeth. A splintered rail wobbled as we trudged up the broad stairs to the porch, and a loose riser squealed under the unwelcome weight of our mass arrival. I'd hoped to find Aunt Lizzie, my father's ancient housekeeper, waiting. She wasn't.

"What a dump," Rachel said with obvious satisfaction.

Will placed a broad, reassuring hand on her shoulder. "Are you absolutely sure about this, Emily? We could still forget the whole thing and be back in the city by dinnertime."

"I'm sure." I hoisted David on my hip, took Adam by a moist, chunky wrist, and forced a note of artificial cheer into my voice. "Come on, Rach. Aunt Lizzie's probably inside fixing lunch. You're going to love her. She's a real character."

"This place is gross," Rachel said. "Sick."

"You haven't even seen the inside yet. Give it a chance."

She flashed a desperate, pleading look at Will. "Can't I go back home with you, Daddy? I won't be any trouble. I promise."

"You know that's impossible, baby. My meetings in

London start at the end of the week. I'm leaving in a couple of days, and I have to work on my presentations in the meantime.''

''So let me come with you to London. I wouldn't be any—''

He shook his head. ''Sorry, honey. It's just impossible without your mom around. I won't have any time to entertain you over there.''

''Well, I'm not staying in this dump. And that's final.''

Will stroked her hair. ''I'm sorry, Rach. Mom thinks she has to do this. Try to understand, will you? You know how it is.''

I tried to murder him, but my look was loaded with blanks. He kept crooning and fussing over Rachel, making things worse as he often did with such brilliant ease.

The front door was unlocked as it had always been, and I peered into the dim, musty foyer, hoping. ''Aunt Lizzie?'' I called. ''We're here.''

Silence.

''Aunt Liz?''

David popped his forgotten thumb back in his mouth. I kissed his spongy cheek and tried to sound reassuring. I had painted a careful picture of the lovely time we were going to have in the country, and Lizzie was part of the sales pitch. ''She's probably out shopping, sweetie. I didn't say exactly what time we expected to get here. I didn't want her to be worried in case we were held up.''

With spare, fluid motions, Will emptied the trunk, making several trips to fill the shadow-striped foyer with a motley array of suitcases, toy-laden shopping bags, and a collection of small, child-powered vehicles. Finished, he slammed the rear hatch of the Jeep and passed a sleeve of his faded blue work shirt over the beads of sweat freckling his forehead. He arranged his mouth in a careful, unconvincing smile. "All set, now. How about some hugs to tide me over?"

He crouched down, caught a giggling trio of assorted bodies in the wide circle of his arms, and gave them a dramatic squeeze. "You guys be good, now. Listen to your mom."

"Please, Daddy," Rachel said in a shrill whisper. "Please don't make me stay here—with her."

Five years and I was still the wicked stepmother. I bared my fangs in an understanding smile. "It'll be fine, Will. I'll take care of it."

He flashed a meaningful look at his impossible daughter. "I'm counting on you, Rach. Remember our talk? Don't let me down."

"I love you, Daddy. Please let me come home with you." Performing to the last, she bit her pout-swollen lip and managed to squeeze out a solitary, oversized tear. It traced a long, lazy path down her cheek and left a large, damp freckle on the padded shoulder of her giant pink polka-dotted T-shirt.

Will motioned for me to follow him outside. "You guys wait here a minute, okay? I have to talk to Mom alone."

The sun was climbing in the late morning sky, using my head as a stepladder. Will was reduced to a lanky shadow by the glare.

"She'll be fine," I told him. "No child has ever perished from a couple of weeks in the country. She might, heaven forbid, even forget herself and manage to have a good time."

He made a sound like a tire deflating and shook his head. "I doubt it, Em. You can see how miserable she is over this. She was looking forward to the summer she had planned: day camp, art lessons. There are no kids here for her, nothing to do. And the little guys are going to miss their things, their routine. It makes no sense to drag them all to this godforsaken place."

"We've been all through it. It makes perfect sense—to me. This is something I have to do, Will. I told you—"

His voice dripped sarcasm. "Perfect sense. Right. For years your old man treats you like dirt, he's too important or too busy or too sick in the head most of the time to even let you visit his precious colony. And you still feel some crazy connection to him and this place. I don't get it."

Someone was excavating my insides, leaving a cold, empty void. "It'll only take me a couple of weeks to sort through his things and straighten out things with the Berkshire Federation. Once they take the colony over for good, I'll be done with it. For good."

"You'll never be done with it."

We were separated by the wall of glare. And more. "I'm trying to be done with it. That's the whole point. Why can't you at least try to understand?"

"I understand perfectly. Business as usual. You do what you please and damn everybody else. Especially Rachel."

"That is a world class crock, William Archer. I have all but stood on my head to please that child, and it doesn't make a damned bit of difference."

An angry scowl twisted his face. "You can get along with her if you make the effort."

"You're absolutely right, Will. The child doesn't want anything unreasonable, after all. If I would just fall off the edge of the earth, she'd be ecstatic. No problem. I'll get right on it."

"She's going through a difficult stage, that's all. It hasn't been easy on her, losing her mother, trying to get used to our marriage and the little guys. Give the kid a chance."

I bit back the words. We'd been over this territory enough times to leave permanent, hazardous ruts in an otherwise very fortunate marriage. "Why don't you stay for a day or two? Give her some time to get used to the place. She always has an easier time adjusting when you're around."

"Be reasonable, Emily. I happen to have my own obligations. I can't pick up and forget everything just because you want it that way."

"Well, go on then. Go back to your everything. We'll be just fine here. All of us will be fine, including Rachel." I squinted at my watch. "Go ahead. I wouldn't want you to waste any more of your precious time."

I stormed back into the sweet, musty coolness of the farmhouse and began hauling the bags upstairs. The boys trailed me up and down the creaky flight with its threadbare green runner. Rachel went out through the squeaky screen to register her final desperate pleas with Will. I could hear her insistent whining and the steady slap of his boat shoes as he paced the veranda, waiting for his cab.

"Please, Daddy. Please, please, please don't make me stay here. I'm gonna die in this awful, ugly place."

"That's enough, Rachel. Stop it."

I peeked out through the window of the boys' room as a chunky lemon Checker veered in through the distant gate. It lurched over the narrow access road, raising cloud puffs of burnished dust as it approached the house.

There was a sharp squeal of brakes followed by Will's determined stride on the porch steps and his voice, booming a final, relieved farewell. "Take care, troops. See you in a couple of weeks."

"Bye, Daddy."

"Bye, Rachel, Adam, David." He ducked his head and folded his long, lanky self into the rear of the taxi. "Bye, Em."

I snapped open the first of the suitcases and started depositing piles of overalls, striped T-shirts and elastic waist shorts in the paper-lined drawers of an old maple dresser. The car door smacked shut with a satisfied rush, and the air filled with exhaust fumes and the churning roar of the engine.

"Good-bye, Will," I whispered, swallowing back a sour lump. "Good. Bye."

"Bye, bye, Daddy," David chanted as he rolled a red matchbox TransAm back and forth across the bare plank floor near my feet. "Bye, bye. Daddy awgone."

Out of the mouths of babes.

CHAPTER 2

I STARED OUT through the filmy dining room window until my eyes ached, willing Aunt Lizzie's vintage red Oldsmobile to turn through the colony gate. This was not like her. Elizabeth Agnes Margaret McGrail was as certain and predictable as house dust. When I was growing up, she was the sole constant in my slippery, irrational world. Always there when I needed her. Which was often.

Even now, I could conjure the plump, girdled body, the steel-gray waves lacquered in firm order around the square canvas of her face, the underbite that sent her considerable jaw jutting out in front of her to take on the world. Her lemon garlic scent.

When I was a child, that granite-willed woman had stood between me and disaster—real or imagined. "You'll be over that bug before you know it, Emmy Lee," she would say, her voice strident and commanding as a tuba, and my fever would surrender in a torrent of cowardly perspiration. "Do not worry, Emmy. Just put that thought right out of your mind." And I would manage to climb over whatever juvenile torment I was facing at the time. ''Everything is taken care of,'' she would assure when nothing seemed certain. And so it was.

So where was she? Adam and David were chasing each other through the unbroken circle of common rooms on their respective Big Wheels. Kitchen, dining room, living room, den. ''Roarrrrr . . . I'm gonna get you . . . roarrrr.''

''Addie no getchoo,'' David screamed in terrified delight. ''No getchoo!''

Rachel was sprawled in front of the primitive color console in the den, reflections of some syndicated drivel danced across her polished brow. ''Shut up, you two dummy idiots. I'm trying to watch this.''

The boys were revving up to the sort of impossible frenzy guaranteed to end in disaster. ''Calm down, you guys.''

''You're a dead dummy duck,'' Adam screeched.

''No duck duck! Daybit no duck.''

''Ssh,'' I said. ''Take it easy, boys, please. Don't be wild.''

''Shut up, you stupid little jerks,'' Rachel screeched in frustration. ''Shut the hell up.''

''Watch your language,'' I said in a leftover reflex of response. The child loved the shock value of forbidden words. Ignoring her was the best defense.

''I said you shut your goddamned stupid little mouths.''

I could feel the tension building, threatening to boil over. ''Addie, David. Please calm down.''

Where was that woman? My eyes blurred with the effort of staring through the dying afternoon. Come on, Aunt Lizzie. Having you here was part of the bargain.

"I'm gonna get you, David Bavid Pavid."

"No getchoo!"

I replayed the call from her two weeks ago that had cemented my decision to make this trip. I could still hear her voice, stretched reed thin with fretful apology. The Berkshire Federation was threatening to renege on their promise to take over the management of the colony. Yes, they had seemed enthusiastic about the project at first. But, for some reason, they were having second thoughts. Maybe if I talked to them myself?

"But what seems to be the problem? I thought things were all settled. They all seemed thrilled with the idea."

"Wish I knew, Emmy. I ask but all they do is talk around in circles. Best I can figure, one of their board members has been away. He's back now and dead set against getting involved with Thornwood. So now they're all having a change of heart. I suppose they might be willing to tell you more, seeing as you're the one who inherited the place. . . . Don't suppose you can make the trip on such short notice though."

"I don't see why not. Rachel's school is out for the summer and I'm about finished grading the last of my exam papers. I was planning to take the summer session off anyway, to be with the kids."

". . . Oh now, if you've got plans with the children and all, that's the way it is. I don't want you to fret about things here. They'll work out exactly the way they're intended."

"No, I didn't mean that. There's nothing that can't be arranged. I'll bring the children. It'll be good for them. They can breathe real air for a change. See what real grass looks like. I bet the three of them think vegetables and milk grow in the supermarket bins. . . . The more I think about it, the more I like the idea. To be honest, I think I should see the place one last time before it's taken over. I've been arguing with myself about it since Daddy died, and this settles it. I'll be there.''

''. . . Why don't you take a few days and think it over, Emmy? It's not a decision you have to make right this minute. Course, I'd love to see you, but I can imagine how tough it'd be for you to change everything around at the last minute. That's how it goes with a young family and all.''

''No. It's settled. There are a few things to clear up around here, and then I'll be there. How does next Thursday sound?''

''. . . Sounds fine. If you're sure. I suppose it'll give you a chance to go through your father's papers and all. Suppose it's only right for you to be the one to see what he left. To tell you the truth, I'd be grateful not to have to take that on.'' Was that a shiver of frailty in her tone? Impossible. The Aunt Lizzie frozen in my memory was stone strong, hard-edged, and invulnerable.

But . . .

A blade of a scream sliced through my mind. I turned to a tangle of flailing limbs and frenzied faces. Rachel had one arm drawn across Adam's neck, the other coiled around David's plump middle like a murderous snake. Her face was contorted with rage, hands blanched white and trembling.

David's horrified scream was constricted to a pathetic whimper. Adam was mute with shock, his face purpling with the effort to breathe.

''Rachel! Let go of them!''

She was caught in a spasm of fury. I tried in vain to pry her loose. The force behind her rage was incredible. ''Let them go!''

There was a hideous coldness in her eyes, as if her

insides had been stolen. I slapped her cheek to shock her back to sense. "Let them go!"

Her body went rag limp. She blinked hard as if to dislodge a speck in her eye and stared through me. Her fingers fluttered up toward the vague pink imprint of my palm on her cheek, then seemed to lose their way. She reached back with both slender hands and tugged the thick clump of hair beneath the elastic band holding her long, flowing ponytail. An odd smile warped the edges of her mouth. "Stupid babies."

I studied her eyes, stared into the cold, black marbles, and caught the reflection of my own shock. "They were just playing, Rachel. What in God's name happened to you?"

"I was trying to watch the damned show."

David's whimpers had dimmed to an occasional sniffle of indignation. He climbed onto the worn chintz living room couch and stroked one of Aunt Lizzie's crocheted cotton afghans. Adam cowered behind me, using my oversized shirt as a shield.

"It's okay now, sweetie. Rachel lost her temper, that's all. Come. I'll give you a snack." I could feel her fury, boring into me like a hot metal bit. "Go to your room, Rachel."

"Why the hell should I? I'm not tired." The side of her lip peaked in that way that suggested I had just failed an intelligence test. She dismissed me with a look and flopped back down in front of the television. I registered my silent disapproval and left the room. No point locking horns with her when it wasn't absolutely necessary.

I took the boys into the kitchen and found some of Aunt Lizzie's chunky oatmeal raisin cookies in the old red ceramic cow canister and a fresh bottle of milk from Minkus Farms in the antique Frigidaire. That would keep them busy for a few minutes. I closed the door to the den behind me and wished for Ruth Messenger, Rachel's psychiatrist, to be somewhere near her phone. Ruth had a way with Rachel. At times, she had stepped in at the first rumbles of trouble and managed to avert an emotional avalanche.

There was a desolate bleating at her number, and the syrupy lilt of her voice on the answering machine. "You have reached the office of Dr. Ruth Messenger. . . ."

I dialed again, hoping she wasn't off for two weeks on a chartered sailboat in the Caribbean as I knew full well she was. ". . . I will be unavailable until the fifteenth of the month. If your call is an emergency, please dial Dr. Ralph Sorley at . . ."

So Ruth's gone. No big deal, I told myself. There's no emergency here. No reason to assume Rachel was sinking into one of her impossible troughs. It was probably nothing more than an isolated fit of temper.

In fact, Ruth had been upbeat and optimistic about this trip. She had even hinted that this might be the best way for me to get through to my impossible child after all these years of futile trying. Off together, without Will and the destructive force of his well-intentioned meddling, we might be jarred out of our set pattern of stupid anger. Maybe this was nothing more than the beginning of a permanent improvement. The storm before the calm.

I walked back through the kitchen. The boys sported foamy milk moustaches and cookie-induced mumps. Adam's feet drummed the claw-footed pedestal of the old oak table. David was humming as he chewed. Typical David melody: part nursery rhyme, part air raid. The incident was done and forgotten as far as they were concerned.

Maybe they had the right idea. Chalk it off to an

acute, insignificant attack of sibling fury. As an only child, I could not imagine the full force of that primal hatred. Will had often told me what a joy it was to grow up with four brothers: there was never a glut of boring peace, always someone around you ached to dismember. No reason to think it was anything more than that. Rachel was a difficult child. Hot-tempered. Impulsive. Surly. Nothing new there.

She tossed me a quick, bothered look as I stepped into the room. "They're a pain, those two."

"Brothers can be a pain," I said.

"Well, they are a giant pain . . . in the ass."

"You can feel any way you like, Rachel. But you may not hurt them. Hands off. Understood?"

"Pain in the ass," she muttered, savoring the word.

Back to her normal, nasty self. Crisis over. I was about to return to my vigil at the window when the doorbell rang.

A large, thick-boned old woman stood framed in the bug-freckled porch light. Her hair was a great mass of whipped vanilla frosting topping ash-toned eyes caught in wide circles of permanent surprise. Her makeup was harsh and heavy-handed. Oblique stripes of crimson rouge settled on the pudding puffs of her cheeks, and her eyebrows were crisp, penciled quotation marks. Her top lip was a pair of sharp, scarlet hillocks; the bottom a deep red sling. Her slim, patrician nose and cupcake chin were powdered into near disappearance. Jeweled half-glasses were suspended from a heavy gilt chain around her neck.

Defying the heat, she wore a shabby beige Chesterfield spring coat and had a tiny brown-netted hat pinned in the center of her head. Her body ballooned from a pair of trim, well-turned ankles set off by rakish, stiletto-heeled, patent leather pumps. The legs and the rest of her were distant acquaintances at best. Spare parts from a pair of mismatched vehicles. She cradled a large, foil-wrapped casserole against her pillowy chest.

"For your dinner," she said. "I'm Alma Prom. You must be Emily. Every bit as pretty and trim as your Aunt Lizzie said you were. Nothing like dark hair and big blue eyes. Nice fair skin, too. Bet you avoid the sun. Smart. We girls have to think about our looks, after all."

She was like an old, rusty bucket, leaking words. "Do you know where Lizzie is? I've been waiting for her."

"And worried to death, I bet." She clacked her hefty tongue. "Well, it's all my fault, I admit it. Didn't mean to be so late. Your Aunt Lizzie asked me to come over early as I could and explain things, but I got all tied up at home. You know how it gets some days. So many chores to do, and the phone just keeps on ringing."

"Where is she?" I took the casserole. Beef and bricks.

She brushed past me into the farmhouse, peeling her outer clothes as she went. "Called away to look after her sister. Poor thing had a fainting spell, took a nasty fall and broke her hip. You know how it is when they get to that age." She batted the air. "Terrible. I'll tell you, I've got no plans to get old and crochety myself. Hanged if I will."

"That's too bad. Which sister?"

"The oldest. Down in Florida."

"Did she leave a number? I'd like to see how things are going."

"Now, see there. Just what Lizzie said you'd say. Woman isn't long on looks but smart as a tack, I'll tell you. Fact is, she said it'd be near impossible to get hold of her what with running back and forth to the hospital and all. Said she'd call you soon as everything settles down a bit.''

''That's a shame. I was looking forward to seeing her again, having her get to know the children.''

''And she was surely dying to see all of you. Believe me. Your coming was about all she could talk about. Isn't that always the way? Not to worry, though. I promised her I'd take real good care of things here while she's gone.''

With a flourish, she hung her coat in the hall closet, set her little velvet cap on the shelf, and peeled off the worn, white kid gloves, one foot-long finger at a time. There was a thin, dented gold band inset with a tiny diamond chip on her ring finger. She positioned it in the square center of her finger and angled the chip to catch a spark of light from the window.

Finished, she arranged her face in a mask of prim contentment and caged my hand between her considerable pair. ''It's so good to meet you at long, long last, Emily. I've been a friend and neighbor to the folks at the Thornwood Colony for a long time. My place is right up the road. Been real close to your Aunt Lizzie. And like family to your dear father. Rest his soul. Don't know what Lizzie would have done without me at the end. Bet she told you all about me and what a help I was.''

She reminded me of a strong, cold, noxious breeze. Blow in. Take over. ''Not really, Miss Prom. Aunt Lizzie and I only spoke once in a while.''

Her face fell. ''I know, dearie. I know how hard it must've been for you with your father so sick and all. Bet it was a real trial with you being so young and him not wanting you around, poor thing. I can just imagine being how I'm one of those people with a talent for telling how other folks feel.''

I hoped she also had a talent for disappearing. ''Did Lizzie say when she'd be back?''

'' 'Fraid not, dearie.'' She patted my arm. ''There, there. I know. Things around here aren't the same without her, but I'm planning to do my best to take her place. You just leave everything to me.''

Fat chance. ''That's very kind of you, Miss Prom, but it's not necessary. Really.''

''Now, not a word of that. I promised your Aunt Lizzie I'd come in every day to help with the cooking and cleaning. You have your work cut out for you just getting through your father's things like Lizzie said you were planning to do. Quite a mess that man collected.''

Pack rat syndrome. Lizzie had despaired over his compulsive collecting. ''I'll manage, Miss Prom. Thanks anyway.''

''Oh, now, you needn't thank me, dearie. My pleasure.'' She waved me away like so much dust and worked her eyes around, surveying the room. ''What a god-awful mess. I'm afraid poor Lizzie didn't have the heart to see to it all. If you don't mind my saying, that woman's got a decent brain but not much intestinal fortitude.''

''Lizzie is one of the strongest women I know, Miss Prom.''

''Oh, sure, sure she is,'' she said without a snip of feeling. ''Guess it just came as a terrible shock to her when you decided to turn the colony over to the Berkshire Federation. Really threw her for a loop.''

I felt a sudden pang of unreasonable guilt. Lizzie's preferences had necessarily been beside the point in this. Anyway, she'd been talking about retirement for years. ''I didn't have any choice. There's no way I could afford to keep the colony going on my own. I thought she understood—''

She flapped a hand at me. ''Oh, now. Don't give it another thought. Your Aunt Lizzie's getting on. You know how those old folks can be. It can take quite some time for them to get used to things changing.''

''That's not easy at any age.''

''Now, then.'' She clapped her palms together. ''I'll see to the house, the meals. And, of course, I'll be glad to help out with the children in my free time. Nothing like children.''

''I told you that won't be necessary, Miss Prom. Absolutely not necessary.''

She held up a hand. ''Now, not a word of it. It's all arranged. You wouldn't want your Aunt Lizzie to be any more upset than she already is, now would you?''

Stubborn, infuriating woman. ''I'm sure Aunt Lizzie will understand, Miss Prom. We'll be fine. And if we need anything, I'll be sure to call you. First thing.''

''Now, now dearie. I insist. It's done, decided. And call me Granny, will you? Everyone does.''

Rachel appeared at the door to the den, half hidden in shadow. ''Who's that?''

''This is Granny Prom, a neighbor. Say a quick hello because Miss Prom is very busy, and I'm sure she'll have to be going.''

Alma Prom extended a meaty hand in Rachel's direction. ''My, my, what a young beauty you are. Come here, dearie. Let Granny have a look at you.''

The Rachel I knew would have snarled and stormed out of the room. This very convincing imposter assumed a shy, pleasure-flushed expression and did as she was told.

Granny Prom placed a thick finger on each side of the

pointy dimpled chin and surveyed Rachel's face from several angles. She sucked in a noisy breath, let it out on a whistle. "Would you look at those cheekbones. And that complexion. Like the finest French porcelain, I swear it. Why, you'll be able to do without makeup altogether if you've a mind to, lucky girl."

Rachel beamed and dropped her voice to a conspiratorial whisper. "There's this kid in my class, Julie Morris? She wears so much pink lipstick it looks like she's got bubble gum stuck all over her mouth, and all this thick black mascara so you'd think she's got spiders sitting on her eyes. It's gross." She was leaning toward Granny as if the woman were embedded in a powerful magnetic field.

"Well, sad to tell, dearie, but some girls need all that or you'd think they had no features to speak of. Even I use a touch now and then. Not a lot, mind you. But not everyone can be a natural beauty like you. One in a million. Believe me, I know. Used to do hair and makeup for the biggest stars. You ever hear of Betty Grable? Joan Crawford?"

"I . . . think so."

"Well, no matter. They were hot box office in their day. You can take my word. Had men falling all over them, pictures all over the news. Sex symbols, they were called. Goddesses." She rolled her eyes. "Truth was, first thing in the morning most of those so-called goddesses could've hired on to go haunting. Most all the ones I worked on were like that. I had to paint on all those bones and the like. Took hours."

"You did makeup for movie stars?" Rachel said.

"And hair." She placed a meaty palm under Rachel's ponytail and gave it a tentative boost. "Blessed in that department, too, aren't you now? Good shine, plenty of body. We can try it different ways, if you like. Bet you'd look great in most any style. French braid, pageboy fluff.''

''That'd be fun.''

That odd look on the child's face was excitement, the strange quality in her voice: enthusiasm. I couldn't, for the life of me, imagine the attraction.

Adam galloped in from the kitchen. David trailed a step behind. Each of them claimed a side and clamped themselves to me like barnacles.

''Whoozat lady?'' Adam said, pointing an accusing finger in Granny's direction.

''That's Granny Prom, Addie. Granny, this is Adam and David. If you'll excuse us, it's time for the boys to have a bath. Thanks for the casserole.''

She hiked the skirt of her shabby brown linen dress and crouched to their level. Her knees crackled like a heap of kindling. ''Well would you look at the pair of you. Regular cherubs right out of a church painting. Aunt Lizzie said to be sure and give you both a big squeeze.''

Adam retreated to his customary refuge behind my kneecaps. David angled right over to the stooped stranger and poked a finger in the silvery swell of her hair. ''Ah boom.''

She pinched his cheek and giggled. ''Now isn't he a stitch? 'Ah boom' indeed.'' With a mock serious expression, she turned to Rachel. ''I bet you take real good care of these little fellas. Now don't you, darling?''

''I guess,'' she said. ''They can be a giant pain.''

''Ah, yes.'' Granny's forehead settled in a mesh of pleats. ''I imagine that's true. Well, not to fret. Granny's here now. Everything's going to be hunky-dory.''

Rachel wove her fingers into Granny's square-tipped, sturdy set. "I like you."

The crinkled lips stretched in a studied grin. "Now isn't that a happy coincidence, missy? I just happen to like you, too. Nothing like a little girl."

"You really know how to do a French braid? Could you do one on me right now?"

"We have unpacking to do, Rachel, and I'm sure Granny has things to do herself," I said, anxious to see Granny from the rear view as she made her exit. "Maybe another time."

She held up a manicured hand to stop my words. "Now's fine, Emily. I can help the child unpack afterwards." She patted Rachel's cheek. "Be my pleasure, dearie. Let me go pop the casserole in to warm and I'll be right with you."

"I'll take care of it," I said.

"Now, now, Emily. You just relax yourself, why don't you? Seems to me you're one of those, whatchamacallems? Type A's, isn't it?" She bustled past me and into the kitchen. I heard the oven door open and bang shut. The grating shrill of her voice pursued me like a blood-starved mosquito. "You young people today don't know how to take it easy, now do you? It's no wonder what happens: heart attacks, ulcers, premature wrinkles. Terrible."

I took several slow, deep, deliberate breaths. Calm determination seeped in to replace the bristle of annoyance. I was ready for her as she burst back through the kitchen door. "You'll have to excuse us, Miss Prom. We've had a long trip and I think it's best for the children if we spend a quiet evening. Just the family."

Her head cocked like a curious dog. "Well, now," she sniffed. "I certainly never meant to intrude, Emily.

All's I was doing was what your Aunt Lizzie asked. Far be it from me to step in where I'm not wanted."

Rachel shot me a poison look, crossed over to Granny, and snaked an arm around the old woman's considerable waistline. "Don't leave, Granny. Please. You said you'd make me a French braid."

"Sorry, dearie. One thing about me is I can take a hint. Your mother wants me to go, I'll go."

"Please stay." Rachel's voice was shrill with desperation, her face tight with pleading. "Come on, Emily. Please can't Granny stay? Please."

Was I being unreasonable, selfish? What was the big deal if it would keep Rachel happy, even for a few minutes? So what if the woman was overbearing, tactless, and had the physical presence of Mount St. Helens? Nobody's perfect. ". . . I guess it's all right for a few minutes."

Granny rubbed her meaty palms together and smacked her scarlet lips. "Fine. Come along then, dearie. We'll get started on that braid right away." Her eyes ping-ponged around the room, and she seemed to be making a mental list. "I'll start in on the housework first thing tomorrow, Emily. Don't you worry yourself about a thing."

"Look. It's really nice of you to offer. But I'd rather take care of things myself."

She flapped a winglike palm at me. "Just rest yourself, Emily. I'll see to everything."

I had known walls more yielding and flexible than this woman. And far less intrusive. "We don't need the help, Granny. Thank you, anyway."

Rachel set her face and shot a blind load of hatred in my direction.

Granny caught her eye and winked. "Come along,

dearie. Let's go see to that French braid. Bet you're going to look just stunning when I get through.''

Rachel looped a proprietary hand around Granny's cocked elbow and steered her toward the kitchen. Adam and David trailed at a cautious distance. The strange sight of their sister enjoying herself was enough to make them wary.

''Get lost, you dumb little jerks,'' she hissed over her shoulder.

''Now, now,'' Granny said. ''I don't see as they'll be any bother. Not with the both of us to look after them.''

Rachel softened like warmed butter. ''I guess.''

''That's the girl,'' Granny said and batted open the kitchen door. ''You're going to have the time of your life here at Thornwood, dearie. I'll make sure of that. You just wait and see.''

CHAPTER 3

THE NIGHT WAS torn into small, useless fragments. Uncountable times, I was jolted awake by a phantom voice; tossed up from a warm, lovely sea of oblivion by a teasing, menacing image. I was assailed by sharpened scraps of events that played over and again in the bizarre theater of my unconsciousness: *I am stark still in a pit of perfect darkness; a chilling electric silence pulses in my bones. There is a frozen eternity of waiting. Screams. Then the crisp, certain, metallic sound of a single, startling hand-clap. The paralysis of expectancy slips around me again like slick ropes of chains . . . steals my breath. I'm caught, held, waiting . . . waiting.* No!

It was sometime after dawn when a fresh feeling of unease prodded me fully awake. My eyes were grainy, my body sore and battered from the night's mental exertions. I worked to shake the fog of fatigue and the persistent sense of menace.

There was a clatter of activity downstairs. Must be the boys, I told myself. It had to be the boys.

Who else?

I slipped on my white cotton robe and tried to move in a soundless shuffle across the worn plank floor. A tortuous step at a time. Testing for telltale squeaks and crackles as I went.

Out in the hall now. Past the KEEP OUT sign scrawled in blood-red marker over a mean-faced skull and crossbones on Rachel's closed door. She was getting to the age where sleep tended to slop over into the afternoon.

I peeked into the boys' room, hoping. But as I had feared, they were both still fast asleep in their beds. Adam was sprawled across the width of his mattress, pink, pudgy feet lolling in midair; David's face was scrunched hard in the pillow, his rear end puffed skyward like a lump of risen dough.

Someone was in the house.

I instructed myself to remain calm, but raw terror punched holes in the surface of my resolve. Our apartment had been robbed six months ago. We had taken the children to visit family friends in Riverdale and come home to find the door ajar, our things pulled apart, drawers dumped out, furniture slashed so the foam-rubber clumps oozed out like the guts of a dismembered animal. The sense of violation was overwhelming. I had been stripped, invaded, turned into a true big city paranoid. Out here in East Noplace, I had thought we would be safe. Safe from greedy strangers, anyway.

I grabbed Adam's undernourished Louisville Slugger from behind the bedroom door and slithered my silent way down the endless flight of stairs.

Please be my imagination. Crazy Emily. Always hearing things. Always expecting the worst.

A shadow shifted in the kitchen.

"Who's there," I called in a sorry tremor of a voice.

"You'd better get the hell out of here. I have a gun."

The shadow grew and edged toward the front hallway where I stood. My throat closed.

In the spare glimmer of fresh morning light, the figure softened and took human shape. "Oh, my, I am sorry, Emily. Silly me. I should have warned you I'd be coming by early today. Must've scared you half to death, you poor thing."

"Granny? . . . I thought . . ." I dangled the bat behind my legs, trying to look nonchalant. Dimwit on deck.

She wiped her hands on a flowered, pink cobbler apron, plucked her ring from a saucer on the windowsill, and wiggled it over a thick knuckle. Her hair today was rope-colored, scored down the center, and angled chinward in a taut, lacquered pageboy. A thin wisp of gray poked out from underneath like a trail of smoke.

"Silly me. All my fault. I should've thought to warn you I like to get an early start. What must you have been thinking? Hearing all this commotion and not expecting anybody. You must have been scared senseless."

Senseless. Yes. "I didn't expect you, Granny. I told you, I can manage things by myself."

She waved me away like a gnat. "Now, mustn't be stubborn, Emily."

A second shadow approached. Rachel.

"You trying out for Little League, Emily, or what?" she said and burst out laughing. "She scares easy," the child told Granny between waves of mirth. "When Daddy's not home, she sleeps with the phone on her pillow and leaves a light on in the hall."

"Now, missy, that's not such a bad idea when you think of it. After all, things do happen. You read about such awful, crazy . . ."

Rachel's face drooped.

"Oh, but not here," Granny said, trying to repair the damage. "Nothing ever happens around this dull old town. Biggest news we had here in years was when Mabel Biggar had her eyes done last fall. Foolish girl took all the money her father left when he passed on and went to some Doctor Hotshot plastic surgeon in Boston. Made her look like a scared raccoon, if you want to know. Still the *Gazette* treated it like the biggest thing since D-day. Interviews, pictures. The works. Canceled my subscription after that."

The eight-burner stove was cluttered with heavy, commercial stewpots and saucepans. Granny had a basket of fresh vegetables in ready position on the butcher block rolling cart. There was a hill of shredded lettuce and a hefty pile of carrot shavings beside the double, scarred ceramic sink. My eyes puddled from the cloying scent of baking bread mingled with the fumes from a power-mad onion.

"You didn't have to do all this, Granny. I told you."

She squinted at me and frowned as if I were written in fine print. "Lord, Emily. Let's not get into all that again. I don't mind in the least. It's my pleasure to help out."

"Right," Rachel said. "Anyway, Granny's only doing what she promised your Aunt Lizzie. You wouldn't want her to break her word."

"That's not the issue here, Rachel."

Granny squinted at her watch. "No point wasting any more breath on the subject, dearies. I'm here to help and that's that. Meanwhile, I'd best be running along home now. Make my beds and the like." She flipped off the stove burners in rapid succession and herded the raw vegetables into a large wooden bowl with the edge of her spatulate hand. "I'll be back to tidy up the house in a bit. Soon as these pots cool, you can pop them in the fridge. And the timer will go off when the bread's ready. I always like to get my cooking done early, before the heat comes. Lunch is all set to go. And dinner. So you people can just relax yourselves. Settle in."

In overdrive, she shed her apron, rinsed and wiped her hands on a soggy, plaid dish towel, and retrieved her worn Chesterfield from the hall closet. "Time does manage to get away from me," she said. "Blink and it's gone."

Rachel positioned herself between Granny and the door. "Can't I come, please? I could help you."

"Oh my, no, dearie. My place is hot as an oven, even first thing in the morning. And small as a doll's house. Hardly big enough for me to get around in without bumping into myself. You have a nice time here, and I'll be back before you know it."

"Please?"

"Now, now. Mustn't put on a sad face, dearie. Those pretty features could freeze that way, you know. That'd be a sin."

Rachel surrendered in record time. Sporting a compliant little grin, she escorted Granny to the front door and out onto the veranda where she stood watching until her industrial-sized idol was swallowed by glare and distance.

"Granny is so neat," Rachel said to no one in particular. "I just love her." She sank cross-legged on the floor in front of the TV and started flipping the channels.

"I can see you like her, Rachel, but we're here to spend time together, just the family. It's not necessary for her to come around here all the time."

She looked back at me, eyes dripping venom. "It's necessary to me, Emily. She wants to come and I want her. She's the only good thing about this dump."

"I'm sorry you feel that way."

"Well I do." Her expression changed, a hint of desperate sadness crept into her tone. "Please, Emily. Please don't tell Granny not to come. I don't know why, but she makes me feel better."

How could I ignore the child's pleadings? She asked for so little, after all: a couple of pints of blood now and then, my guts in a slipknot—nothing unreasonable. "All right. We'll give it a try. But no promises."

Her lip curled in a satisfied little smirk. "Thanks, Emily." Her face settled as I watched into a cautious neutral. "Really, thanks. I mean it."

"No promises."

I took a cup of cinnamon-laced coffee from the old-fashioned, bubble-capped percolator and unrolled the morning edition of the *Ashby Gazette*. Aunt Lizzie treasured the local tabloid and paid a premium to have it delivered to the farmhouse door, the unfortunate feature on Mabel Biggar's eye job notwithstanding.

Leafing through it, I was impressed by the sheer eventlessness of local existence. Dull old Ashby. The lead story was about the truck way station at the town line that remained closed for repairs despite a promised June opening. There was some hint of mismanagement in the road department. Destined to be a major scandal, no doubt.

The school board, in its monthly meeting, had voted a five percent raise for Marvin Teasdale, custodian at the regional junior high, whose daughter, Marvella, needed orthodontia. The annual Fourth of July box social and fireworks display, sponsored by the benevolent Order of Ashby Elks, had brought in a whopping three-hundred-eighty-seven dollars to benefit the town's less fortunate.

There was a midsummer sale on swimwear at Smitty's Discount. A thrill a minute.

Then the chamber of commerce did boast that Ashby was the tranquillity capital of the world. And from the boom in tourist trade, plenty of people were in the market for tranquillity, no matter what its price in yawns.

I heard the syncopated crunch of descending feet. Adam led the procession, rubbing away persistent traces of sleep from his eyes with the back of his chubby fist. David trailed behind, toting his favorite blanket: navy gingham on one side, yolk yellow on the other with an appliquéd red circus elephant in the center.

"David, honey. You know the blanket stays in bed."

"Daybit menkie." He hugged the precious rag to his chest and faced me down.

"I know it's your menkie." (At last I was fluent in a foreign tongue.) "But it's for night-night only."

His lower lip slid forward and curled.

"Put it away," I said. "Now."

He shuffled out of the room, trailing his precious menkie like a bridal train. I was not going to make the same mistakes with him or Adam that I had with Rachel, always forgiving, making excuses. Poor child, I kept telling myself when she was at her impossible worst: struggling with her parents' divorce, her mother's sudden death in a traffic accident, on the way to a custody hearing no less.

And then I come along and she's asked to adjust to a new mother. New family. New life. I couldn't expect the child to be anything but angry and impossible, now could I? And if I was looking for angry and impossible, Rachel was more than happy to oblige. Those things came easily to her, after all.

"Eat," I told Adam who was attempting to drown his

Cheerios, an O at a time, in the puddle of milk at the bottom of his bowl. David returned without his menkie and climbed on the ladderback chair between me and Adam.

I sipped my coffee and turned the page. Arts and Entertainment had the usual ads for concerts at the nearby Tanglewood Summer Music Festival in Lenox and dance recitals at Jacob's Pillow. The Berkshire Shakespeare Theatre was in rehearsals for *Hamlet* and the local summer stock company was featuring a new comedy in pre-Broadway trials.

An item on the back page made me stop and read again. "Locals Warn of Danger From New Home For Mentally Handicapped." The column took less than an inch, sandwiched between the weekly listings of traffic violations and house closings.

The newly formed Concerned Citizens' Alliance met last night in the Regional High School auditorium to protest the scheduled August opening of the Edmund House for the Mentally Handicapped. Mayor Strachan was on hand to assure the group that the patients slated to live in the home present no danger to the community. But Mrs. Parker Hollings, CCA president, says the group intends to seek an injunction against the facility which Mrs. Hollings says will serve, "unstable individuals who cannot be trusted. Ashby's children will not be safe," Mrs. Hollings warns.

I read the paragraph again. I had a vague memory of a halfway house the state had opened many years earlier in Ashby for inmates on work release from the state penitentiary. After that, everything that happened in the town, including a serious flu epidemic, was blamed on the convicts. There was such an uproar, the state finally gave up and closed the facility. It was one of the rare times I saw my imperturbable Aunt Lizzie outraged. ''Everyone's got to be somewhere, Emmy Lee. It can't always be somewhere else.''

''What's so interesting?'' Rachel was behind me, fingers coiled around the top rung of my chair.

''Nothing. Nothing at all.'' The last thing I needed was for her to have more ammunition in her arsenal of complaints about this town. Before she could read the piece, I flipped over to the society page and scanned the ''News and Views'' column. ''. . . Usual Ashby excitement. Listen to this one: 'Sophie and Leonard Larned celebrated their fiftieth wedding anniversary last Saturday night at a party for sixty guests given at the home of Mrs. Peter Stepanhauer, a longtime friend of the Larneds and president of the Ashby Senior Women's Club. Dinner was Beef Wellington and—''

''Stupid paper.''

I folded it in thirds and deposited the *Gazette* in the covered trash barrel under the sink. ''Small towns have their advantages,'' I said. ''And disadvantages.''

''Ashby stinks.''

The pots were cool enough to be stored in the refrigerator. I straightened the kitchen, went up to shower and dress, and offered the kids a walking tour of Thornwood. Rachel declined. She had more important ''stuff'' to do.

I filled the utility bag on David's stroller with a snack for the children and one for the ducks and started out toward the pond.

The morning was soggy and serene. There was no sound larger than the strident cawing of a dyspeptic blackbird hidden in the copse of scraggly cedars. Adam struggled to keep up as I gained momentum on the downgrade, fueled by meager scraps of ancient memory.

For a second, I caught and held a vague picture of my

mother walking beside me, powdery pale and delicate. Features pinched with worry. Nervous, fretful gestures. The voice desperate and shrill. Not at all the precious image I had struggled so long to recapture. I felt a breath of relief when it dimmed and faded away.

The pond appeared over a grassy rise in the distance, vivid black lacquer edged with green moss and a broad, irregular circle of polished stones. ''See, Addie. That's where I learned to swim when I was a little girl.''

Feathers of weed poked through the surface near the shore. In better days, my father had hired a giant harvester twice a season to churn its noisy way through the water, ridding the murky bottom of all but its fundamental slime.

''It's giant big,'' he said in a deep, respectful voice. ''Big as an ocean.''

''I'll take you swimming here. And fishing, too, if you like. We used to catch sunnies and a catfish once in a while.''

''Daybit bitchin?''

''Sure, sweetie. You'll go fishing, too.'' I smoothed a sweat streak from his velvet neck and spotted a naked pink foot, tiny bubble toes wiggling in delight at their accidental freedom. ''David, what happened to your sneaker?''

''Neekuh awgone.'' He hitched his shoulders in a dramatic shrug and changed the subject. ''Daybit go wimmin?''

''No swimming now, Davey. I have to look for your shoe.'' I started searching through the shaggy, sun-scorched grass. The pristine meadow had been given over to spiky scrub grasses and stubborn clumps of weed. The ground was littered with cigarette butts and crushed aluminum blossoms from the ubiquitous Budweiser bush. Once, my father had taken great pride in the land, fussed over the pH content of the soil and the precise blend of seed, fertilizer, and weed killer to insure that Thornwood's rolling acres looked more painted than grown.

"Go wimmin?" His voice crackled its way toward tantrum level. "Daybit go wimmin!"

"Not now," I said in my firmest voice and kept my eyes trained to the sweep of discouraging land.

Sifting through the thatch, I found black patches of powdery fungus, mole trails, and swarming anthills. Everything I could and couldn't imagine except the single, size three-and-a-half, blue and white Muppet sneaker I had purchased for an outrageous sum less than two weeks earlier.

"Go wimmin!" David stiffened in frustration and started to howl. "Lookit Addie wimmin."

I followed his pointing finger to the horrifying sight of Adam crouched at the edge of the steep embankment at the far end of the pond. He leaned out to grab at something, lost his footing on the slippery moss, and slid in a frantic tumble into the water.

"Adam!" I ran toward him, afraid to blink. His arms were flailing in a wild, useless frenzy to keep his face above the surface. The motion was dragging him further and further from the edge.

"Adam!" My lungs were scorched, eyes scraped raw. "Hold on."

"Mommy!" His screams were lost in a fit of gargled choking.

As I reached the far edge of the embankment, his arms churned in a desperate windmill and the blond head was drawn down and lost beneath the surface.

"Hold on!" I plunged for the water and swam toward

the empty space he left. "Addie!" My voice caught in a blade of terror, heart lashing at my throat.

I stopped at the spot where he had disappeared and stared through the murky water. Nothing but a stingy swell of lazy bubbles. I gulped a greedy breath and went under, reaching. Searching until my lungs threatened to burst, and my scalp bulged with an excruciating white hot pressure.

I would have to take a breath, try again. Every second a loss. How many seconds before . . . ?

My hand brushed something. I reached in desperation, praying.

Yes. I grabbed a lifeless, rubbery limb and yanked upward with a surge of anguished strength. There was resistance, a foot caught in the weed-choked muck at the bottom. But I tugged with the full force of my terror, and he came loose with a sick thwacking suction.

Arm around his chest, I drew him to the surface and ferried him in a clumsy, interminable struggle toward the shore. His body was lead, weighted with unconsciousness and the sodden tangle of his clothing.

I dragged him out onto the slippery embankment and made my tortuous way up the incline toward safe footing, raking my trembling fingers into the spongy ground as I pulled his inert little body alongside. His skin was dusky pale, blue as a bruise around the mouth.

David's shrieks bumped off the edge of my horror. Not now.

I set Adam down on a level grassy span, tipped his head back, checked for obstructions in his mouth, and started resuscitation: sharp chest compressions followed by mouth-to-mouth breathing. I could still taste the bitter plastic of the doll I had practiced on in the beginning of my CPR course at the university, the giggled breaths pulsing up from my student-partner during the final exam.

"One one thousand . . . two one thousand." Come on, Adam. Please. One breath, two. The little chest rising in a hopeful arc only to collapse in a useless heap like pumped air wasted on a leaky balloon.

Three one thousand. Four . . . I felt a churning under his rib cage and he began to cough. A blessed convulsive cough shook his body and, as I flipped him on a side, he spewed a murky rush of pond water and began to cry.

"That's it, sweetie. That's it."

David had scrambled out of his stroller and was crouching beside us, face tight with worry, patting his brother's back for comfort. "Addie seepin?"

I gave him a quick, calming hug. "No, he's not sleeping, honey. He just swallowed too much water and we had to get it out. He's all right now."

"Addie no wimmin," he said and shook his head for emphasis. "No wimmin, Addie."

"No," I said, stifling a bubble of hysterical laughter. "No more wimmin today."

Adam seemed shaken but otherwise unharmed. I kept a careful eye on him as we plodded back up the long, unreasonable slope toward the house. He chattered on in a tremulous voice about the "giant ocean pond" and the "big pond man" who pulled him under. Imagination intact. Breathing and color fine. So why did I feel as if I'd just had a memorable little collision with a nuclear submarine? I was soaked to the bone, graced by the incomparable aroma of acute terror and rotted fish. Emotional exhaustion had turned my bones to latex.

Dull old Ashby. Tranquillity capital of the world. Maybe I'd write a strong letter to the chamber of commerce.

CHAPTER

4

I WAS RINSING the pond out of my hair when I heard the thump and slam of angry voices.

More trouble.

I hurried downstairs and found Granny in the dining room, facing off with a sallow, midsized, beagle-faced stranger with a dense black slash of eyebrow and coarse-cut features. He wore a brown bowler hat and a pristine three-piece navy blue suit garnished with an ornate, antique pocket watch on a heavy chain. He was bound in a white-on-white razor starched shirt topped with a dotted red bow tie. A matching dotted silk hankie was propped in his breast pocket like a fresh-cut flower. He wielded a plaid suitcase in one hand and what appeared to be a deceased typewriter in a body bag in the other.

Granny's oversized hands were balled into fists, her face narrowed to a sneer, her body hunched like a mugger on the prowl. "I said you better get your stubborn self right out of here, mister. Right this very minute."

"And I said I have no intention of leaving, madam.

I've been accepted for a stay at this colony. I have the letter.''

''Well, now. You can just take your precious letter and file it somewhere personal, mister. The colony's closed. Shut. Period!''

''Easy,'' I said. ''What's going on here?''

The children were watching from the living room, flushed with excitement.

Granny sputtered and ran an outsized palm over her dense cinnamon chignon. ''Sorry for all the commotion, dearie. This crazy old coot seems to have a problem with his hearing is all. I told him the colony is closed but he doesn't hear me. Now, didn't I tell him that, Rachel? Didn't I tell him real nice and polite?''

''Granny's right,'' Rachel said. ''I think he's a nut case, Emily. You'd better call the police or somebody to make him leave.''

The man set down his luggage and turned in my direction. He tugged up the twitching corners of his mouth, took off his hat, hugged it to his chest like a mendicant, and made a little bow. ''I can assure you that won't be necessary, Miss . . . ?''

''Archer. Emily Archer.''

''You seem to be a reasonable, intelligent person, Miss Archer. Unlike some.'' He rolled his slack-lidded eyes in Granny's direction. ''Please allow me to explain. My name is Augustus Lynch, Deputy Chief of Detectives, Chicago force—retired. I'm here to work on the completion of a book. I applied last fall for a month at the colony to get away from, shall we say, distractions. Several months ago, I received a very gracious letter of acceptance.''

''I understand, but—''

He held up a traffic-stopping hand. ''Please, Miss Archer, I've traveled a considerable distance to get here. Made very difficult arrangements. And now this . . . this person, if I may use the term so loosely, tells me I'm not welcome. That the colony is not in operation. There must be some mistake.''

''Unfortunately, it's true, Chief Lynch. My father died a couple of months ago. The colony has been closed temporarily, until new management takes over. Didn't you get the notice?''

''Notice?''

''A letter was sent out explaining things to all the prospective colonists. I can't imagine how they missed you.''

He slumped down on an upholstered side chair, stared down at his typewriter, studied his hands. His voice wilted. ''I know how. This is dreadful. Terrible. I've been away for several months, traveling. I came directly.''

Granny blew out a snootful of air and made broad flapping motions. ''Away is right. Far, far away.''

My look stopped her but not before the children had taken up the pantomime. ''I'm sorry,'' I said. ''I know you must be very disappointed. Why don't I call around to other colonies in the area? See if they have any openings.''

He scratched his forehead, ran a knobby hand through his sparse, cement-toned hair, and sucked in a tortuous breath. ''No, Miss Archer. It's kind of you to offer but that's not the solution. It must be Thornwood.''

''How about Strassdale? It's only twenty minutes from here. Let me try them.''

He shook his head in slow, discouraged sweeps. ''It's no use. This is the only colony I want to attend. There are reasons. Personal reasons.'' He looked up at me, sighed, and forced a sorry little smile. "I suppose it's impossible then. I won't trouble you any longer." He dragged himself up like a mound of soggy towels, took up his cases, and trudged toward the door. "Good-bye, Miss Archer. Children."

"Good riddance," Granny murmured.

"Good Driddins," David echoed, and the four of them dissolved in a spasm of malicious laughter.

The back hunched lower as Lynch set a heavy hand on the doorknob. He looked like someone hauling an impossible load.

"Please wait, Chief Lynch. I don't see why you can't stay. The cottages are empty. And one more for meals is no big thing."

"Well now," Granny sputtered. "Closed is closed."

I gave her a killing look. "Under the circumstance, I've decided to make an exception."

"Makes no sense, Emily," she sniffed. "The colony's operating or it's not. Period."

The man radiated something that felt solid, comforting. "Please stay, Chief Lynch."

"If you're certain it's all right," Lynch said.

"I'm certain. It's fine."

A twinkle lightened the hangdog look. "Thank you, Miss Archer. Being here means a great deal to me."

Granny chin-butted the air and turned to vent her frustrations on the tabletop with angry shots of spray wax and the sweep of a furious dustcloth. "Closed—hah," she said under her angry breath. "Closed, closed, closed. Comes to closed, open."

"It's all set then," I said, drawing warmth from the kind brown eyes. "Welcome to the Thornwood Colony, Chief Lynch. Sorry for the confusion. I hope your work here goes well."

Lynch set down his cases and caged my hand between his warm, olive pair. His gaze was steady, earnest. "You won't regret this, Miss Archer. I can promise you that."

"I'm sure I won't. Come with me, Chief. I'll show you where you're going to stay."

He followed me out and across the broad expanse of rolling green lawn toward the cottages. We walked in tandem, casting broad, fun-house shadows in the spare remnants of the dying daylight.

He drew in a loud chestful of clear, pungent air and released it in a contented whoosh. "You don't know how much this means to me, Miss Archer. I am eternally grateful for your understanding."

"There are certain things a person has to do, Chief. Anyone would understand that."

"Not anyone, I'm afraid. Only those who've felt the inexorable draw of inner obligation themselves."

"I guess."

He gave me a curious look. ". . . If ever there is a way I can return the favor, please don't hesitate to ask."

I opened the door to Easthoven cottage and flipped on the light. There was a spacious main room furnished with spare essentials: metal frame bed, shabby flowered armchair, pocked pine desk, and a matching chair with a blue corduroy cushion tied to the back. Slim panels of flowered blue chintz hung at the window, and a faded blue plaid spread was folded at the end of the thin, lumpy mattress. Beside the bed was a rickety nightstand fitted with a dime store, yellow, ginger jar lamp. The names of past colonists were etched in a long, scraggly column on the scarred off-white wall. Flimsy bifold doors led to the slim, single closet. And there was a no-frills bathroom with a rust-freckled stall shower and a bare bulb dangling from a broken light fixture. "Not very fancy, I'm afraid,'' I said.

''It's perfect, Miss Archer. Exactly what I'd hoped to find.''

''I'm glad. We'll see you for dinner at seven.''

''I look forward to it. And please remember, Miss Archer. If ever there's any way I can be of assistance . . .''

I made my way back toward the main house, stumbling twice in tangled thickets of scrub. A dense blanket of exhaustion was weighing on me. Too little sleep, too many painful memories.

Granny and the children were in the dining room, their backlit silhouettes played in jerky chorus against the gathering darkness. I hesitated, not ready to face any of them until I had a little time to repair the cracks forming in my careful facade.

The Jeep was parked at an odd angle, left in too big a hurry. I fought back a strong urge to shut myself inside and drive off into the beckoning darkness. Maybe Will was right. Maybe I shouldn't have come. Now, I felt trapped here, nailed to this painful place by a metal rash of sharp, dangerous questions. I was beginning to doubt Aunt Lizzie's tidy explanations about the tragic undoing of my family, running out of places to hide from the vicious truth.

I slipped around to the back of the house, ducked in through the kitchen door, and climbed the little used, narrow rear staircase, making my way slowly up the column of warped wooden risers.

At the top, I exited through a heat-jammed door and walked down the short corridor toward my father's bedroom.

I stood staring at the tarnished brass knob, paralyzed by a sudden, terrible rush of fear. My breath came in sharp, burning pulses. My blood settled in a cold, useless sludge that left me slack and dizzy.

Easy, Emily.

I forced a slow, deep, tortured inhalation. Wiped the clammy slick of sweat off my face with one trembling hand. The other was planted hard against a cold undulating wall.

What was happening to me? Odd, incomprehensible images. Nothing I could bring close enough to get in focus. Trying made my head thunder and threatened to unleash another wave of dizziness.

Turning away, I made my unsteady way to my room and shut the door against the invisible threats. I knew I would have to pry loose the ancient secrets buried in this place. Sooner or later, I would have to face all of it, no matter how terrifying; no matter how ugly.

But not now. Not yet. I paced my breathing, listened to the steady, insistent pulsing in my chest, worked to still the persistent trembling in my bones. The children's voices rose in clamorous chorus. Their laughter seemed so far away.

CHAPTER 5

NOW THERE WERE two Rachels. The one who shadowed Granny like a determined federal agent was sweet, charming, and so unfailingly agreeable it made my eyes water. I worked at memorizing this inscrutable stranger, the melodic purr of the voice, the gentled features, the love-warped grin. Even with Will, whom she adored, she had always been a Rachel I could recognize. Fury simmered so close to the surface, there was a warning trace of heat that held me at a careful distance.

As soon as Granny prepared to leave, that familiar Rachel came back: surly, hostile. The transformation was instant. Fast as a screen door slamming. Fast as a pair of size eleven spike-heeled patent leather pumps clacking in an awkward hobble down the farmhouse stairs.

Adam and David were bewildered. I was torn. Part of me had resolved to put up with Granny for the sake of Rachel's temporary good humor. But another, very vocal part, resented nearly everything about Alma Prom except her absences. How could Rachel be so drawn to this officious, bullheaded typhoon of a woman? What magic did Granny have that I so sorely lacked? No matter how I tried, I could not manage to raise any feelings in this child other than the flashes of mindless anger I was so quick to inspire. Maybe if I learned to do French braids? Or took up compulsive talking?

"There now, dearie. Let me have a look at you." Granny popped her jeweled glasses on the spare bridge of her nose, took several baby steps in reverse, and squinted at her handiwork. Rachel was perched on a high, backless wooden stool, slim legs coiled around the side bars of the gunmetal frame. Her spine was frozen straight, chin tipped toward the ceiling as if she were a mannequin suspended from a set of strong, invisible wires. Her hair was slicked back in a fat, dizzying coil. It looked like a drunken snake had curled up to sleep it off atop her head. Granny poked another pin into the army of matte black hairpins holding the thing in position. She fussed over an invisible stray strand, fired a final shot of spray net from an ancient aluminum can, and plucked a plastic hand mirror from the oversized black canvas tote she used to ferry her beauty supplies back and forth from her tiny house next door to the colony.

"Nice," Rachel said, contorting face and body to catch a peek at the rear view. "Very fancy."

"Well now, dearie. I'm tickled you like it. Did one just like it for Marilyn once, but I can't say it was as dramatic on her. Course, she didn't have your eyes."

"Marilyn Monroe?" I said. Not star-struck. Curious.

She made a face. "Oh, now. You'll forgive me if I don't say, Emily. Nothing worse in my book than a name dropper."

"Right."

"So." She fussed with her ring, rubbed the discussion off her hands, and raked them through the thick side wings on her wig. The one for today was cropped short and tinted bright white with random beige streaks and a dry sheen like overcooked meringue. We had yet to see her wear the same hairpiece twice. This, she told us in a tossaway remark, was one she had designed for "Hedda." She paused in midsentence and fretted at the wall clock. "Oh, my. Time for me to be running along now. See you all later on."

The slide show was getting all too familiar. Granny announced her imminent departure, and Rachel's face lurched through a predictable series of postured stills. Wince. Pucker. Frown. Scowl. Seethe.

Granny put on her coat. Rachel's face darkened, teeth clenched, hands balled into angry, frustrated fists.

The tension was contagious. Of all the myriad things about Granny I found irritating, her uncanny ability to come and go at precisely the wrong times had fast risen to the top of the lengthy list. Her tyrannical, inscrutable schedule hung over me like a malodorous cloud. There was no end to it: the chores that could not be postponed, the thousand unnamed obligations that she bustled off to dispatch, leaving me to deal with Rachel and her raging bull imitations.

". . . I was hoping you could stay a little longer this morning," I said, trying to defuse Rachel's mounting pique. "I have to take care of a few things and it would really be a big help if you could keep an eye on the children."

Her tongue made a ticking sound. "Wish I could, dearie. But I'm afraid that's impossible right now. Certain things need tending. You know how it is. But I'll be back later on. Soon as I can, like always. Be happy to watch them for you then, if you like.''

Rachel was on my side for a breathless change. ''Please, Granny. Can't you stay a little while longer? Or can't I come with you? Just this once?''

''Now, missy. You know I'd be with you every minute of the day if I could. But a body has her responsibilities to see to. You're a big girl. You understand.''

''Sure.'' The word died of natural causes. Next stage—Rachel staring at the ground, muttering.

''There, now, I'll be back before you know it. Goodbye, dearies.''

Slam. Heels clicking on the porch. Day turning dark in an ominous flash like a sudden storm gathering.

''Granny?'' I called through the screen. ''We'll be going downtown after lunch. Anything I can get for you besides those cleaning supplies you wanted?''

She shrugged her shoulders, put up a hand, kept walking.

I tried to work past the sense of impending doom. ''I have an idea,'' I said. ''Why don't we make something for tonight's dessert, Rach? I used to love baking with my Aunt Lizzie.''

''Nah.''

''Chocolate, Mommy?'' Adam said. ''A chocolate cake?''

''Sounds good to me. Come on, Rachel. It'll be fun.''

''Whoopee,'' she said in a grim monotone, twirling a finger in the air.

''Daybit cake?''

''Yes, Monkey. Everyone can help.'' I managed to nudge her as far as the kitchen door. A step inside. Two. Aunt Lizzie's recipes were jammed in alphabetical order in a dented, white-metal file box on the counter. I found a chocolate concoction that sounded manageable, even for two overeager infants, a junior misanthrope, and a devout disciple of Sara Lee. I handed it to Rachel to read and began poking through the refrigerator and cupboards, searching for ingredients.

"Can I break the eggs, Mommy? Can I please?"

Adam smashed the required four into a worn, wooden bowl. I fished out the clumps of battered shell and let David stir the sugar into the eggs and onto the pebbled linoleum floor with a mixing spoon. Rachel recited the instructions in a bored mechanical drone. "Add the chocolate chips. Bake for an hour at three-fifty. Cool before frosting. Frost. I've had enough excitement for now, Emily. . . . I'm going to watch my soaps."

"Come on, Rachel. We're not finished yet. Licking the bowl is the best part."

"M'on, Rayshoe," David said.

"You are such a stupid little dimwit," she spat through a vicious smirk.

David giggled.

"Dumb little creep," she said. "Stupid baby doesn't even know when he's being told off."

"Stop it, Rachel. Leave him alone."

"Tell you what. I'll leave you all alone and get the hell out of this disgusting place. I'll run the hell away." Hot blotches of fury climbed her neck as she charged out of the room. Granny's curly python hairdo surrendered in a shower of black pins behind her.

"Goddammit!" she screamed, grabbing at her head as she ran in a mad clump out the front door. "God the hell dammit!"

I sent Adam and David to play in the small treed yard separating the rear of the farmhouse from the sway-roofed, mud-colored barn. With the back door open so I could keep an ear on them, I walked around the house to confront the last angry child.

The sky was dull, life sounds muted to a lazy hum. Training my ears to catch a hint of her, I picked up the low rush of an occasional car passing on the distant road and the persistent thrum of a power mower gobbling the excess of some neighbor's lawn.

There was a crackle of movement under the porch. "Rach?"

Thick silence.

I sat on the bottom riser and spoke to the empty air. "I'm sorry you're upset Granny had to leave, but there's no reason to take it out on your brothers. Or me."

A puff of disdain.

"Granny really likes you, Rach. She just can't be here all the time."

Tiny voice, trembling fury. "You don't know that. You don't know a goddamned thing about her. Or me, either."

"I'm trying. I'm trying to know you. You don't make it easy."

"Why don't you just go away? Go away and leave me the hell alone."

Odd coincidence that she should pick one of my favorite old hiding places. A long forgotten piece of me could still duck down and scoot under the thick, splintery frame of the stairs. Kneel beside her in the inky darkness. Crouch on my heels. Feet tingling numb, thighs cramping. Head stuffed with the sweet, rotten aroma of mold and sun-starved earth.

For an instant, I was back there, locked in the taut, uncomfortable skin of a lost, angry child, my mind lurching over hurts too sharp to ignore and too large to hide in the back of my life.

Under the porch was where I tried to escape from the inexplicable horror of my mother's sudden death and the first of my father's wild ravings. Where I ran when I was frightened by the impossible sight of him, the sick, funny ramblings of his derailed mind. But there was no real hiding. His words found me in the darkness and stabbed me like a swarm of vindictive bees.

"Emmy Lee. Eh mill lee! Where is that child? Where'd she go? Somebody better find that girl, get her away from here before it's too late. Get away, Emily. Leave this terrible place, girl. Run. You don't go, I'll have to make you. I'll make you go, Emily. I swear to God I will."

I remembered crouching in the cool, black emptiness, pressing my fingers against the triangle flaps in my ears. His words dimmed and ran together. I tried to think of something, anything else. To escape.

But there was nothing.

Nowhere.

Aunt Lizzie had tried, too. She had taken me away on what she had nimbly called a vacation, filled my head with reassuring false hopes. Things would calm down at home, she told me. My father would get over it. Such a shock to him how my mother got sick all of a sudden like that, she said. But he'd be back to himself. All he needed was time, lots of healing time. And so we had wandered for months from place to place, pretending all the world of time could make a difference.

Nothing had changed. There was still no escape from the harshest realities. I couldn't reach this child of

Will's, my child who would never be mine. I had never been able to reach her. From the first time we met, there was something off-key between us. Using everything I knew, every scrap of human understanding, I had never been able to get past the stone walls girdling her affections.

"Rachel?"

No answer.

I knelt down in the shadows beside the porch stairs and peered into the darkness.

"Rach?"

Nothing. She had managed to slip away. I remembered how that was done, too. There was a small hole in the latticework near the foundation at the far end of the porch. You had to squeeze through, shoulders at a slant, breath sucked in, flesh pressed burning hard against sorry bones. I was as small as Rachel in those days. And nearly as pained and desperate.

Where was she? A spider of fear crawled up my neck at the thought of her sneaking around back, taking her fury out on the little ones.

I raced to the backyard, heart leaping like an eager puppy. I couldn't trust her alone with them. She was not to be trusted.

With a rush of relief, I spotted Adam, then David, tossing twigs and pebbles at the boarded barn. Where was Rachel?

The voice was a low growl. Startled, I spun around and saw her sitting on the ground in the speckled shade of a pin oak. Her knees were drawn to her chest, lean muscled calves wrapped in the determined circle of her arms. The dead coldness had crept back into her expression. "I hate you," she said in a hollow voice. "I wish you'd drop dead."

"That's enough." The flat, hollow look in her eyes made me shiver. I turned away. "Come on, you guys. It's time for lunch."

"All of you can drop dead."

Adam made a wide circle around her and into the house. David followed, one anxious eye trained on her, sucking his thumb. I waited for the screen door to close behind them.

"Acting ugly and obnoxious is no answer, Rachel. You're not going to accomplish anything that way."

"I . . . hate . . . you."

I went into the dim coolness of the kitchen and set out the shriveled baked chicken sandwiches and over-salted potato salad Granny had fixed. There was a pitcher of fresh, pulpy lemonade and a green salad. I tucked a large paper napkin in the round knit collar of David's red He-man T-shirt.

"Lunch, Rachel," I called, not expecting or wanting her to answer. It was not the first time I harbored a guilty wish that my darling daughter would miraculously cease to exist. It was all so infuriating and impossible. The harder I tried to get close to her, the worse things got.

If only I could find the reason. Was it something about me? This time in her life? Was it hormones, heredity, chemical imbalance, storms of random electrical current surging through her brain? It was a puzzle full of sharp edges that refused to come together. And I had the dread feeling that if I failed to solve this particular one, it could cost me a great deal.

CHAPTER

6

I DROVE THE ten minutes over the narrow, twisted back roads connecting Thornwood to the center of town and maneuvered the Jeep into a tight spot in front of Southside Sundries and Stationery. I had managed to convince Rachel to come along, but now she insisted on waiting in the car while I took the boys inside to pick up the mail at the post office counter in the rear of the cluttered shop.

"It's too hot to stay here. Please come with us."

Her expression slammed shut like a door in a wind, arms locked out the threat of my intrusion. Case closed.

The clerk, a pock-faced ageless man with spiky blond hair and flat features, gave me a suspicious look when I mentioned Thornwood's box number. "Where's Lizzie McGrail?"

"Visiting a sick sister. I'm looking after things for a while," I said and rebuked myself for feeling the need to explain. "Is there any mail for the colony?"

"Any mail?" he huffed. "You bet there is. Giant pile of stuff. Mostly circulars and the like, couple of bills.

And you got one of them strange ones. A dead letter. Weird how those things turn up every so often. Makes you wonder. I'll tell you.''

He disappeared behind an ancient bank of lock boxes and returned with two soiled, canvas bags stuffed with letters.

''You want to keep up with it, you'd best come by every day. Every other at the least. Lizzie always does.''

He moved in the maddening slow motion Aunt Lizzie had long since dubbed the Ashby two-step, setting the sacks on the stained Formica counter, transferring the rubber-banded mail packets to a pair of paper grocery bags from the I.G.A., ruffling through the tidy stacks of forms in his desk drawer for the proper receipt.

''Rules,'' he said with a mournful shake of his flaxen spikes. ''Have to get the signature of the receiving party on a form ten-eighty. Federal regulation number fifty-three seventy-eight. Whole world's one big rule.''

My eyes ping-ponged between him and the boys who were idling suspiciously near the wooden candy bins at the check out.

''No touching,'' I said as pudgy little fingers strained toward the beckoning stacks of gum and penny candies. I stared at the clerk, trying to hurry him along with my mind.

With great deliberation, he plucked out the correct form and offered it to me with a clumsy flourish. ''There, sign right there, at the x.''

I scratched an illegible signature. ''Thanks.'' I hurried to the front of the store, peeled two packs of sugarless bubble gum from Adam's determined grasp, and frisked David who had sprouted odd lumps in the pockets of his denim shorts.

Outside, the air shimmered with oily currents. Rachel

had rolled up the windows in the Jeep. The last of the morning's do had come undone and her glossy hair swayed to the lazy beat of an imaginary tune. She pretended not to hear when I called for her to give up the mule imitation and leave the oven of a car.

Fingers coiled around a pair of pudgy wrists, I crossed South Avenue toward Fiske's Hardware. Puffs of dried dirt rose from the sunbaked pavement. ''You boys listening? Addie? David? This is not a touching store, it's a looking store only.''

''Yes, Em-ly.''

''Yeth, Emwy.''

''Call me Mommy, will you? I like that much better.''

''Okay, Mommy Em-ly. No touching. No touching.''

A motorcycle whizzed past. So close, I felt the angry trail of hot fumes belch from the straining engine. I drew my pair of sweaty little charges closer and raced them to the safety of the curb.

''Rachel!'' I called again, worried about the furnace of heat that must be building in the airless car. But she kept her eyes straight ahead, pitting her considerable powers to ignore against my unwelcome interference. After a brief, silent struggle, I declared her the winner by default. ''Mule.''

The hardware store was musty cool, redolent of wood shavings and paint thinner. With all the tempting, hazardous tins and boxes, I kept the little ones on a tight rein as I worked my way up and down the cluttered aisles, filling my dented shopping cart with the assorted polishes and cleansers Granny had asked me to get. ''If you're so all-fired anxious for that bunch from the arts federation to change their minds about the place, I'd best get busy fixing things up,'' she said. ''Not that they're worth much trouble if you ask me.'' Puckering her slick, scarlet lips, she passed her eyes in a dramatic sweep across the living room. "Your father was very sick, you know, 'specially at the end. Lizzie tried to keep up the house and all, but it was all she could do to look after him, keep him out of trouble."

I tried not to dwell on that. Very sick. An all-consuming illness that took him over, spread in a pox of decay that consumed his reason, his life, moved him to discard me along the way. Aunt Lizzie had tried to convince me I was better off not seeing him the way he was at the end. If only better off felt better than it did.

I recognized Freddie Fiske himself perched behind the counter on a round metal stool, moving his thin, parched lips as he studied the social page of the *Gazette*. The years had done nothing more than stretch him into a larger version of the dull-witted, unflappable little boy whose sole distinction was his annual victory in the soap box derby at the Ashby Fair. Give Fast Freddie Fiske a hammer and a chunk of wood, Ashbyites liked to say in those days, and you've got something.

When I cleared my throat, he looked up through a sparse fringe of salted mahogany hair. His eyes were tarnished aluminum, teeth reduced to a few brown-edged splinters like a forest after a devastating fire.

I extended a hand. "Mr. Fiske? I'm Emily Archer. Emily Fowler was my name. Remember?"

Blinking hard, he tipped his head and checked me from a different angle. Tufts of kinky brown hair were stuck in his ears like plugs. "Nope. Can't say as I do."

"Hillard Fowler's daughter."

He seemed to come slowly awake. "Oh, yeah. My, my, it has been a pile of years. Last I remember, you were a chubby little thing who cried easy. Turned out real pretty, didn't you? Nice and slim, no more sausage links for arms. Then Wild Hill was good-looking. No one can take that away.''

I felt a flush of anger. To Ashby natives, my father's craziness had always been more interesting and understandable than his art. In their view, his massive abstract steel sculptures, which now graced several major museums and culture centers, were nothing but hard evidence of his progressive mental decline. ''You ever see such a thing?'' I heard one say after viewing a piece my father donated to the Berkshire Theatre Society many years ago. ''Looks like a month of bad dreams.''

They saw it as no particular loss that he soaked his talent to ruin in a sea of delusions and cheap gin. As one of Ashby's self-styled philosophers put it, ''Wild Hill's better off in his cups than off hammering out more of those monstrosities.''

Most of the townspeople were no kinder about the colony. ''Never heard anything so foolish. Three hundred acres and all they grow in a whole season is a couple of highbrow books, paintings of nothing in particular, and plays full of people shouting dirty words at one another.''

They found his craziness far more interesting and acceptable. For that, ''Wild Hill'' had been embraced as a legend, an Ashby landmark. Considered public property like the library or the ancient bandstand on the village green. No one had ever thought to step around any sensitivities I might have on the subject.

''That be cash or charge?''

''Charge.''

He was filling in the slip when I remembered a certain brand of sudsy ammonia Granny had mentioned as an afterthought. I asked Fast Freddie for a bottle, and he lumbered off the stool and disappeared in the rear storeroom, searching through his stock.

"I'm hungry," Adam said.

"Be patient a few minutes, and I'll take you for ice cream."

"M'hungwy, too, Mommy."

"Just a few minutes, baby."

Freddie Fiske was checking his inventory, whistling an off-key rendition of "Dinah Won't You Blow" and "I've Been Working on the Railroad." I was catching the children's impatience. "Mr. Fiske? Why don't I come back for that another time?"

More whistling. "If I knew you were coming, I'd have baked a cake. . . ."

"Mr. Fiske?"

I caught Adam in the middle of a clumsy spin that threatened to end in a light bulb display. "Stop."

"Daybit dance, too, Mommy. Watch."

He hurtled around in mad imitation of his brother. I made a grab for him, but before I could manage a firm hold, he fell with a sick thud on the dusty wood floor.

I scooped him up and held him to my chest, his pudgy legs twined around my middle like a swimming tube as he sobbed and screamed his indignation. I made a quick survey of the damage: one raw, bloodied knee and a budding, scarlet goose egg in the smooth center of his forehead that gave him the look of a sad, baby unicorn. His face was streaked with muddy tears. "That's okay, sweetie. You're okay."

Fast Freddie ambled out of the storeroom with his empty palms tipped up. "Seem to be all out of Parker's sudsy lemon. Want me to call when we get some in?"

"I guess." I wiped David's sloppy damp face with the bottom of his shirt and signed the charge slip.

The sound of the horn crept into my mind as I helped

Fast Freddie bag the supplies.

"What the hay?" He looked stunned as the rude blast tore through the careful fabric of Ashby's peace.

Anxious, I peered out the window. "Rachel?" My heart started a vicious throbbing at the sight of her slumped against the wheel. I grabbed the boys and pulled them squealing in protest across the street to the Jeep. Rachel was splayed across the front seat; head dangling at an odd, impossible angle. Her face was a dangerous dusky pink, swollen with the heat.

The horn kept up its relentless blaring as I tried to pull open the door. Locked. All four buttons were down, and as I tugged in useless struggle against the scorching metal handle, I spotted the keys dangling from the ignition slot.

"Rachel!" Her mouth was hung open in a weird grimace of a smile; the slim arms dangled like boneless strings. "God no!" I bashed my useless fists against the window.

Freddie Fiske was beside me, wiggling an uncoiled wire hanger through the door gasket, angling the hook toward the button lock. "Almost there now. Jeez, can't stand that blasted noise!"

The relentless wail of the horn mingled with the boys' frightened weeping.

"Please hurry!"

A small nattering crowd had gathered to watch. As soon as Fast Freddie managed to wrench open the door, I pushed past him and into the car. A startling oven blast of heat left me breathless. Cradling Rachel's limp body, I hurried to the shade of the giant striped awning fronting the Episcopalian church and set her down on a smooth patch of cool grass. Crackles of fear erupted in my head as I watched for the slim chest to rise and fall and searched her neck for a pulse. I peered under one reluctant eyelid. Her pupil shrank to a pinpoint. "Rachel? Are you okay? Can you hear me? Rachel?"

A powder blue Ashby patrol car screamed and flashed its way down the street and lurched to a squealing stop beside the Jeep. Two dour, potbellied cops lumbered out, moved me out of the way, and took over.

"Heat prostration," one said. "Second case this week. Damned weather." The other ran the garden spigot from the church, saturated his wadded cotton hankie with cold water, and sponged her down.

As an icy trail of water trickled down her neck, the ink black eyes fluttered open and registered shocked protest. "Who are you? You get the hell away from me."

"Ma'am?" The police backed off, happy to leave the remaining unpleasantness to me.

"I'll see to her. It's all right."

I knelt beside her and smoothed a stray sodden curl back from her damp forehead. "You passed out from the heat, Rach. The water was to cool you off."

She stiffened and spoke in a tight whisper. "It wasn't the heat. . . . He was coming to get me."

"What are you talking about?"

The strength crept back into her voice. Her eyes bulged. "This ugly, disgusting monster came to the car and tried to get in. He was going to take me away and kill me. I was rushing to lock him out, and I banged my head on the steering wheel. I must've been knocked out."

Her color had paled to near normal. "Come on, Rach. It doesn't make sense to tell stories. I asked you to come with us. I told you it was too hot to stay in the car."

She leaned on an elbow and spoke through clenched teeth. "It is not a goddamned story, Emily. There was an ugly, creepy monster with crazy eyes and bumps all over, and it happened like I said. I don't give a damn if you believe me or not. I'm not staying around here. I'm calling Daddy to come and get me out of this disgusting place before somebody kills me."

One cop was talking on the car radio. He peered at me over a pair of round, mirrored sunglasses. "The little girl all right now, ma'am? Or you want me to have the ambulance come?"

"No, she's fine. That's not necessary."

". . . I mean it. I'm calling Daddy. You don't care if I get killed, but he does. I'm not staying around this crummy place. It's dangerous."

"Please, Rachel. Get a hold of yourself." I caught the stray comments from the crowd.

"Leaves a child locked in the car like that . . . tsk, tsk."

"What kind of a mother?"

"That's Wild Hill's girl."

"Oh."

Rachel straightened the rolled bottoms of her soiled white jumpsuit and stood facing me with folded arms and a spite-ridden face. Her voice was a hiss. ". . . There was a monster. He was fat, and he had dirty teeth and googly eyes, and he grunted like a pig. I should have let him take me off someplace and kill me and cut me up in little pieces. You'd like it if I died, wouldn't you? Then all you'd have left are your stupid, precious little babies."

"That's enough, Rachel. Stop it."

Anxious to leave the scene and the knots of curious onlookers, I herded the three of them into the Jeep and drove off toward the colony. Adam and David started clamoring at once for the forgotten ice cream.

"Another day," I said. "Rachel needs to rest."

"I do not. I'm fine."

"I'm sure you are, but a run-in with a fat, ugly, googly-eyed monster like that can take a lot out of a person."

I could feel the acid heat of her fury burning into my neck. "You don't believe me."

"Yes, I do," I said, keeping my voice dead even, "when you tell the truth."

With a flourish, she leaned over the seat, flipped the radio on to full volume, and tuned to some nice, upbeat migraine music.

After a few head-splitting seconds, she relented and reached over to lower the volume as we made the turn into Thornwood. I felt a vague tug of menace as we passed the hanging tree. And a lull of superstitious relief as we left the gnarled, ugly thing behind and drove down the ribbon of dirt road toward the farmhouse.

"You'll be happy when I'm dead. Won't you, Emily?"

"Stop it, Rachel. That's a mean, foolish thing to say."

"Well, you will. Admit it. You never wanted me around in the first place. All you wanted was my father, and you got stuck having to take me, too."

I spotted her grim face in the rearview mirror. She was chewing on her bottom lip, twirling a stiff hank of lacquered hair between two slim, nervous fingers. A hint of sadness softened the cold, ebony eyes. I felt a pull of sympathetic sorrow. "That's not true. None of it. I wanted you to be my daughter. I want that still."

"You don't care about me, or you'd let me get the hell away from this place. I hate it here."

"You know we're only going to stay a little while,

Rach. And what about Granny? You like being with her, don't you?''

She tensed as if to argue, then settled in a grim, tight-lipped silence, staring at the farmhouse.

Leaving was not the answer, I knew. The things she didn't want to deal with would follow us, wherever we went. Maybe this was the time, and place, for us to confront them together. Maybe this visit would settle a number of things.

For better or worse.

CHAPTER 7

THERE WAS A note from Lynch taped to the farmhouse door, an invitation to "Miss Archer" to join him for cocktails on the Easthoven cottage terrace at 5 P.M. The favor of my reply was unnecessary, he assured. Sweet, appealing old man. I felt the first tug of a genuine smile in days.

The imaginary monster had taken its toll. While I was unpacking the car, the little ones had trudged upstairs for a rare, voluntary nap. Rachel was settled on a webbed chaise in the backyard, plugged into a Walkman and a prepubescent potboiler with a lurid cover and a title suggestive enough to catch her reluctant interest. Her hair was fanned out in a long, lacy span across the back of the chaise, and she shaded her eyes with a visor of pale, delicate fingers. One slim leg was crossed over the other, the bare foot tapping a vague rhythm in the torpid air.

I had put off the necessary task of going through my father's things. It was something I knew I had to do for Aunt Lizzie, who had never turned down a request of mine. And for myself. I knew his papers might reveal something about my past. That terrifying possibility had sparked my talent for procrastination. Now, out of excuses, I forced myself to sit in his cracked, black leather swivel chair and begin.

My mind filled with his scent, stale tobacco and sweat. My trembling fingers traced the embedded grit on the padded armrests, the flecks of marble dust, metal shavings, and dried clay that clung to his clothing after work. I was buffeted by harsh, bitter feelings: grief, remorse, fury. What impossible force had stolen the dear, funny, brilliant father from my most distant recollections and replaced him with that stooped, muttering, wild-eyed stranger? Could I ever wrap those awful events in understanding so they could be safely stored away? Or would the truth, if I ever came upon it, be even worse than my most dreadful imaginings?

I felt a dangerous rumbling in my gut as I opened the first of the drawers.

Reflections of a disjointed mind. There was no sense in the jumble of papers and things. Each gilt-edged, mahogany drawer was jammed so full I had to wrench it open, crumpling the things on top, causing others to slip out of sight behind the wooden dividers. In one, I found hundreds of old expired trading stamps clumped together, matted with hair and dust. In another, pocket change was tossed and forgotten in a huge tangled chain of paper clips. There were banded packets of torn, yellowed clippings with no clear significance and used envelopes scrawled with bold, illegible scribbles. Underneath were dirty scraps of stale chewing gum and crushed cigarettes spewing dried trails of tobacco, their papers faded to the color of weak tea. A bitter lump of sorrow burned in my throat as I pictured my father hoarding these improbable treasures, pulling them from his stuffed pockets at night to hide here in these drawers, out of view of the hordes of imaginary thieves that trailed him in relentless pursuit, aching to get their mean fingers on some of his crucial possessions.

"It got so bad at the end," Aunt Lizzie had told me after he died. "So bad you can't imagine. Poor man was so sick. It's like someone was pushing him, Emmy," she said. "I kept looking for the hands."

The hands. If only it were that simple. If only there were something you could see. Grasp. Find a way to stop.

I went through the rest of the desk drawers, dumping the discouraging mess into a large plastic trash bag. There was no end to it. In the study alone, there were dozens of cartons piled beside the couch. Dozens more were stacked beneath ceiling-high bookshelves crammed with bent-edged paperback novels, leaflets explaining every conceivable human malady, ancient brochures from hotels around the world, old magazines. Under the windows, dented metal files bulged with papers, stored in no particular order. It was almost as bad in the living and dining rooms. And I had not yet managed to bring myself to look in the bedroom at the back of the house where he spent his final years hiding from the imaginary menace that had grown fierce and formidable enough to render him a tortured captive in his own skin. I couldn't face the magnitude of it—the huge, sorry, insane mess.

I felt the eyes. Rachel was standing there, pressed against the doorway in an odd, troubling pose. Her body was curved against the wall like a passionate lover yielding to an insistent caress. One hand stroked the cool painted surface in lewd rhythm. The other was pressed hard against the small swell at the base of her belly. Her unblinking eyes cut through me like a scalpel.

"I didn't hear you come in, Rach. What's up?"

She was a statue. Staring at nothing.

"Rachel? What is it?" Her face was cold rubber, expressionless.

Now what? I walked toward her, a cautious step at a time. She was sliced in half by the shadow of the door. One unblinking eye was fixed straight ahead, held fast by some private fascination. The other was a hollow gleam in the hazy darkness. Her mouth was a tight slash. Not a flicker of emotion. Nothing.

"Rach? What's wrong?"

I was a few steps away, but there was still no reaction. My heart was squirming like a beached fish, mouth dry as chalk. It was as if I could walk through her, as if nothing was left but an air-filled shell.

I passed my fingers in front of her eyes, snapped to make her blink. The thick-lashed lids fluttered, but there was no change in her expression. She was wax.

I put a hand on her shoulder, tried to keep the terror out of my voice. "Rachel? Listen to me. I'm going to call someone—a doctor. They can help you, give you medicine to make you feel better."

The corner of her mouth twitched. She made a wet, sputtering sound and bent over in a fit of giggles. It was several minutes before she could get the words out, and then she forced them through loud bursts of malicious laughter.

"I sure got you that time, didn't I, Emily? Admit it. I really had you going there for a minute. You should've seen the look on your face. 'I'm going to call someone,' " she mimicked in a shrill, panicky voice. " 'They'll give you medicine.' "

She was seized by manufactured mirth, the laugh a

dry, hacking cough. She was enjoying every minute of it. Having a grand, old time. I felt the heat of an angry flush as I waited for her to play herself out.

The laughter stilled to a flutter, a syncopated pulse, and was done. She refused to look at me, stared down at her grass-stained feet. "It was just a goddamned joke."

"Sorry, friend, I didn't find it the slightest bit funny."

There was an edge of defensive fury in the voice. "You're just mad because I fooled you. I put one over on you, Emily. Admit it."

Fury made my voice tremble. "If that's your idea of an accomplishment, Rachel, I admit it. You put one over on me."

"Well, you don't have to be such a lousy, rotten sport about it. It wasn't such a goddamned big deal."

I took several cautious, controlled breaths until my muscles started to uncoil. "No. I suppose it wasn't." She would not get to me. I would not let her get to me.

Ruth Messenger's impossible advice reverberated in my head—ignore the child when she acts like that, pay no attention or you reward the behavior you want to stop. Easy for Ruth to say. She shared her apartment with three declawed cats, a good-natured goldfish, and a collection of porcelain thimbles. Ruth had precious few reasons to wonder, as I was beginning to do, whether the food was better at Bellevue or Creedmor.

Still brittle with anger, I retrieved the bags full of mail from the foyer and set them on the kitchen counter to sort. Rachel followed me into the room, humming a strained little melody. I started separating the letters in piles: ads, bills, applications for the colony. I would ignore her. Somehow, I would manage to ignore her. Nothing to it. No more difficult than ignoring any poisonous reptile that happened to be crawling up your neck.

She tugged open the refrigerator, ducked her head inside, and spent a long, exasperating time peering in at the contents. I felt the cold air escaping and, from the corner of my eye, saw a dense misty haze wafting out from the open freezer inside. The humming was replaced by a melody she clicked in harsh rhythm with her tongue.

Ignore her, pay no attention . . .

I studied the mail. It was eerie seeing all these letters addressed to my father, his name typed, printed, scratched in absentminded script, rendered in artful calligraphy. There were postcards from ancient acquaintances abroad. A few stray letters from diehard fans. The news of his death hadn't spread that far, I supposed. Then he had left detailed instructions in the will he made before his mind was too far gone for such matters: no funeral, no obituaries, no announcements in art or trade publications. The only formal notices about his dying had been sent to prospective colonists, stiff letters from Thornwood's lawyer expressing regrets that the colony would be closed until further notice.

No observers. Even I was barred by his written edict. At first, I felt wounded, cheated. Then I realized there was no simple, ritual way to say good-bye to my father. How can you give up what isn't yours?

At his request, Aunt Lizzie had arranged that he be cremated as soon as possible at the local mortuary. After it was done, she waited for a gusty day so she could stand at the entrance to the colony as he'd asked and let the wind claim his ashes

Rachel rose and slammed the refrigerator door. When I failed to react, she started opening and slamming the cabinet doors in turn. Click—smack. I held my tongue, hard.

In a fit of mounting pique, she threw over one and then another of the ladderback chairs and stood back, waiting for the expected storm of temper.

I ran my thumbnail under the flap of an envelope and tuned my rapt attention to a reduced price offer for carpet steam cleaning from Stratton Home Cleaners, proudly serving Ashby's windows and floors since 1952.

"You hate me." Her voice was tiny, lost.

I looked up. There was a tremor in her bottom lip, the charcoal eyes were floating in pools of sorrow. "No, I don't, Rachel. I love you. Sometimes you drive me stark raving mad, but I still love you, and I always will."

"No, you don't. You don't love me because I'm not your real kid. You only adopted me because of Daddy."

"That's not true. I came into your life because of your dad. But I adopted you because I wanted to. There was nothing I wanted more than for you to be my real daughter. I still want that more than you can imagine."

Her face twisted in anguish, and a slick of tears spilled over. "Then you're sorry, aren't you? You wish you never did adopt me. You wish I'd drop dead."

"No." Overcome by a swell of feelings, I tried to wrap her in a hug but she was stone stiff and unyielding. Bitten hard by her coldness, I backed away. "I'm not sorry I adopted you. The only thing I'm sorry about is that we don't get along better. I don't know how to get through to you, Rach. I don't know what you want."

She looked up at me from under her dense fringe of dark lashes, now bound in spidery clumps by the tears. Her nose was running. "It's all my fault. I know it. I stink."

I put a hand over hers. She let me hold her for a spare

second. Her hand was soft and jittery as a trapped bird. "No, you don't. And the fault isn't important. What matters is that we find a way to straighten things out between us. That's all."

She rubbed a crumpled napkin over her face and sniffled. "I get so damned mad sometimes. I don't know what the hell to do with myself."

"Me, too."

She took a deep breath and pressed her lips together. Looking away, she tossed the napkin at the trash can. It bumped against the plastic rim and fell to the floor. She crossed her arms over her chest, took a deep, sniffled breath, and set her face in a mask of defiance. ". . . So is there anything interesting in the mail?"

It was a beginning, as much as I could expect for now. More. She had opened up a precious inch. I knew better than to push it.

". . . This looks interesting. Must be the dead letter the postal clerk mentioned." The envelope was old ivory linen paper faded with time and handling. I squinted at the smudged circular postmark: Colombia, South America. I couldn't make out the city. The date was hard to decipher, too, looked like nineteen fifty something. "Every so often, a piece of mail winds up in a dead letter bin for years and years. Then, it's found by someone on cleanup detail or some ambitious new clerk in the post office and forwarded. This one looks like it's been kicking around since the fifties."

"Who's it from?" She pulled the wooden stool closer to the counter, climbed to sit, and propped her chin on an uptilted palm.

The flap refused to yield. I took a butter knife from the drawer and slit open the top. There was a gossamer sheet of yellowed paper inside, crispy dry as a dead leaf.

It had a stale, desolate smell.

"So?"

"Give me a second, Rach. The writing is so tiny. Looks like it was done under a magnifying glass." My eyes worked to adjust to the spare black scratches. "I once heard about a man who could write the whole Gettysburg Address on the back of a postage stamp. Pretty amazing, huh?"

"What does it say, Emily?" She was the impatient taskmaster of a teacher, I was the dopey kid caught staring out the window. Everything back to normal.

I struggled to make out the words. " 'Dearest Friend . . . I am in terrible need. Destitute. My child suffers and may not survive. I am too ill to carry on alone. You are my last hope. My only. I come to you in this desperate hour knowing you are my sole salvation. Help me, my dearest. Help me or suffer as I do. Suffer the torment of my stricken child for all eternity. You must not deny me if you value your future or the future of your children and their children in turn. You must not discard me or this desperate plea for help. Hold fast to this letter and thoughts of my plight. I await your reply, my dearest.' " I could not make out the signature. "That's it."

Rachel pressed a flat palm over her heart, stuck the other arm out like a flagpole, and eyed the ceiling. "Help me, my friend. Help me or suffer the torment."

"Pretty melodramatic. You're right." Of course, it was. But something about the letter had worked its way under my skin. The tone? The threat? I dropped it on the counter, wanting it out of my hands.

Rachel picked it up. Held it this way and that to examine, peered through it at the fluorescent fixture.

"Makes no sense, you know. If this lady was so

damned poor, how come she had money for fancy stationery and stamps?'' She made a snorting sound.

I tried to shake the shiver of fear creeping up my spine. Forced a smile. ''Good point.''

''And if she was so sick and in all this terrible trouble, how could she manage such neat, little handwriting?''

''That, too. I guess we don't have to worry about anyone trying to put one over on you, Rach.''

''I know you can't just believe everything you read, Emily.''

''True.'' I took the dead letter from her and folded it back in the envelope. Dumb thing gave me the creeps.

Finished, I dumped the stacks of ads and circulars in the trash. The new colony applications had to be set aside for the time being. And the bills. Nothing could be resolved until I found a way to work things out with the Berkshire Federation.

I shut the cabinet doors and set the chairs back upright at the table. Rachel had drifted out to the backyard to read another chapter in her book.

Upstairs, the boys were stirring. There was the squeal of bedsprings and the light slap of bare feet on the wooden floor. I was halfway to the stairs to greet them when I remembered the dead letter still lying on the kitchen counter. I hurried back to stuff it in a drawer, out of sight, where Adam and David couldn't touch or be touched by it.

Silly superstition, I thought. Senseless. But I was moved by something stronger than sense.

Danger had a way of arriving unannounced. And in the most unexpected forms.

CHAPTER 8

WHEN GRANNY CAME back later that afternoon, I took a quick walk over the broad expanse of meadow toward Lynch's cottage. I was hungry for distance, desperate for a breath of sanity.

Approaching, I heard the steady clack of the typewriter from inside and hesitated. The man was here to work, after all. I waited a few seconds, hoping for the pause that did not come, then turned to leave.

His voice caught me halfway across the tiny terrace. "Miss Archer? How kind of you to come. Please wait one moment. I'll be right with you."

"I don't want to disturb you if you're working, Chief. We can make it another time."

"No, please." He followed his voice out onto the postage stamp of a flagstone terrace, bearing a tray laden with artful canapés and a bottle of fine, chilled champagne in a lead crystal ice bucket. He set out a pair of fluted glasses on a painted tray table and worked out the cork. "You're not disturbing me in the least. Quite the contrary. I feel most fortunate to have such delightful company to join me in celebration.''

I took the glass he offered, tapped it against his, and took a nose-tickling sip. ''What are we celebrating?''

''Anything you like, Miss Archer. I'm open to suggestions.''

I sat on one of the webbed lawn chairs and stared out at the fading afternoon. ''. . . I'm afraid I don't have any. It's your champagne, you get to name the occasion.''

A cloud crossed his expression as he studied my face. ''My apologies, Miss Archer. I can see you aren't in the mood for celebrating.''

I shrugged off the comment and forced a smile. ''Just a little tired. Strange bed and all. You know how it is.''

''Yes, I do. . . . And how it isn't. If you'll forgive me, Miss Archer, I sense that you are troubled by something far deeper than lost sleep.''

''I'm fine.''

''Certainly you are. Better than fine in my humble estimation. Forgive me. I don't mean to pry. But sometimes it helps to talk. And these ears were clearly constructed for listening.''

Large, generous, dog-tongue ears. Settled and comfortable like everything about the man. ''Am I that transparent?''

''No, not at all. I tend to look harder than most. My training, I suppose.''

I felt the truth bubbling up and the threatening swell of bitter emotions trapped behind it. ''It's nothing important. I'll get over it.''

''Certainly you will.'' He fixed his gaze on the distant cedar copse; his eyes went vague. ''We almost always do.''

I drew a careful breath. ''So, Chief. How's the book going?''

"Coming along," he said. He recrossed his legs, wove his fingers together, settled his gaze on the distant horizon. His voice was a salve. "And your visit? How is that going?"

"The same."

I could feel his eyes on me, piercing my flimsy armor like an X ray. ". . . Tell me, Miss Archer. How was it to be your father's child?"

Sad, difficult question. "That's hard to say. I didn't have much contact with him. After my mother died, I became a suitcase kid. Boarding school in the winter. Summer camp. Paid vacations with faculty members who traded their hospitality for the extra cash. I came back here once in a great while. By default. And then I felt like I was knocking around in some foreign country where I couldn't quite understand the rules or speak the language.

". . . I used to wish I could have parents like my friend, Joan. Her mother called at school three times a day to warn her about germs, kidnappers, cold weather, wet feet, eyestrain, reckless drivers, crooked politicians, boys who only had one thing on their minds. It made Joan crazy. I was so jealous my teeth ached."

"Is it easier now? Now that he's gone?"

I sat back and sipped the champagne. It etched a path through the sharp-edged lump in my throat. "Getting easier. I think."

Chalk scribbles of cloud had drifted over the sky, blurring the borders of the dying afternoon. My gaze was drawn from infinity to Lynch. The man had a way of cutting to the bone, a way that did not make me at all as uneasy as I thought I should be.

"My turn," I said before he could ask another surgical steel question. "How was it to be a detective?"

His voice put on weight. "A job, Miss Archer. Had its ups and downs. The usual."

"You must have had some exciting cases."

"Yes, some." He stared at the sky awhile, a dreamy look on his face. ". . . I handled the God's Messenger case. Ever hear of that one? We had seventeen murders in two months. All young, suburban women strangled with their own nylons. All killed within a ten-block radius in the Loop. We worked for months trying to find a link between them, but we hit wall after wall. They seemed to be a bunch of nice, normal, unlucky women. You should have seen the background sketches: a kindergarten teacher who volunteered at the hospital gift shop on Saturdays, a private duty nurse with a house full of handicapped foster kids, a librarian, president of the town historical society. They had good marriages, nice kids, mothers they called once a week."

"Sad," I said.

"That case stuck in my throat like a bone, Miss Archer. I used to get like that about some of them. Couldn't let go for a minute, not until the thing was solved. Put my life on hold for weeks. Months, sometimes. I lost sight of everything else.

". . . That's the way I got on this one. I was like a fixture in that neighborhood. I got to know every shopkeeper in that ten-block radius, every resident. Delivery boys. Street peddlers. I interviewed the husbands, kids, grandparents, dogs. You name it. And nothing. You know what finally broke the case?"

"Do I get three guesses?"

"All you want."

"I give up."

He nodded his approval. "Smart. We all but gave up ourselves. Then one day I'm at one of the victim's houses, interviewing the babysitter who'd been out of town for a couple of weeks, and I notice this catalog for black lacy underwear that had just come in the day's mail. Real sleazy stuff for a Sunday School teacher, I'll tell you: cutouts, tassels, little red hearts in the oddest places.

". . . On a hunch, I call the mail order house and, *voilá*, all the victims were customers. Remember I said nylons? Not panty hose? That should have given it away right there, but we were all too busy looking for normal clues: hair, blood, dead bodies, that sort of thing."

He sipped his champagne and gave a sorry little shake of his head. "Nylons should have been a dead giveaway. All of them with seams, no less. Turns out the nice suburban ladies were turning tricks for pin money and a little excitement on the side. They were all hooked up with a pimp known around town as Big Louie. I found out that when Big Louie wasn't pimping for bored suburban ladies, he was playing minister. In church, he was known as Father Lucas. A real fire and brimstone fundamentalist, delivered hellfire and high voltage sermons. Scared his congregation out of their wits and life savings the way he carried on about the wrath of the Lord. Turned out Big Louie really knew about wrath. Delivered it with his own two hands." He blotted his forehead with a starched, stark-white handkerchief.

"There must have been some satisfaction in solving a case like that, Chief Lynch."

He rocked back in his chair, tipping his head up as if he were angling for a moon tan. "I used to think so, Miss Archer. I used to think it was the best job in the world. The thrill of the chase. Good winning out over evil. Liberty and justice for all but the really bad guys."

I followed his gaze toward the stand of cedars shimmering in the settling stream of daylight. "What changed your mind?"

He took a deep, difficult breath. "I found out that right and wrong are not all that far apart, Miss Archer. It's too easy to mistake one for the other. I found out that liberty and justice can cost more than they're worth." He blinked and sighed. "Way more."

"But you were able to search for truth, get to the bottom of things."

He turned to look at me, through me. "Yes. But remember, Miss Archer, once you get to the bottom of things, there you are. At the bottom."

I forced myself to meet his pained, weary eyes. "Maybe that's the only real place to begin, Chief. . . . For me."

He tipped forward and stood. Fixed me with a hard, steady gaze. "Are you saying you want my help in getting to this bottom of yours, Miss Archer?"

"You're here to work on your book, not to waste your time on my problems."

He offered a hand to help me up. "That doesn't answer my question. I have an excess of time. You'd be doing me a favor if you'd be kind enough to take some of it off my hands. May I be of help, Miss Archer?"

". . . Yes. I think you can."

He bowed and touched his hand to the brow of an imaginary hat. "I'm at your disposal then. We'll meet again at this time tomorrow. And we'll start at the beginning. Or at the bottom, if need be. You make a list of your questions, we'll find the answers together and settle things, once and for all."

CHAPTER 9

LYNCH'S ASSURANCES DID nothing to exorcise the night demons. My sleep was invaded by dark, horrific images; sharp-edged fragments of a lost, unfocused reality. In one I saw my father's face, drawn on a rubber membrane, stretched and contorted, pulsing like a distended vein as each grotesque grimace yielded to the next. The face was so full of pain, accusation. The eyes, glazed with insanity, worked through me like a sharp, metal spear.

At first light, I dragged myself up and into an icy shower, trying to shock away the drugged paralysis of fatigue and my mounting sense of desperation. I had to be done with this place. And soon.

After breakfast, I left to pay a personal visit to the Berkshire Federation for the Arts. The organization was headquartered at the far opposite end of Ashby. I drove through the bustling downtown section and out along Route 23, a bumpy, two-lane country highway that once served to connect local farmers to the city markets. Now the road was dotted with antique shops, produce stands, used car dealerships, and restaurants.

The federation had relocated in the past year to an out-of-use regional schoolhouse, a squat, brick, horseshoe-shaped building with a riot of solar panels on the roof. Spray-painted graffiti graced the front: "Slam lives" and "For a good time, call Mr. Armbruster—555-9280." Over a cornerstone dated a mere fifteen years earlier, a wag had sprayed, "Your tax dollars hard at work."

I found an unlocked side door near the parking lot and made my way down a deserted green-tiled corridor scented with strong disinfectant and the indelible aroma of lunchroom gravy. The walls were pale celery muted to a watery yellow by a broad wash of pink fluorescent light. Banks of lockers in bold primaries ran between the classroom doors. Most of the locks had been broken off, leaving sorry black holes like empty eye sockets.

Through the bubbled glass panels over the classroom doors, I saw a number of makeshift studios. The low, wooden desks had been pushed aside to make room for easels and stools or shoved together in awkward clumps to serve as pedestals for the sculpture classes. Work in progress lined the radiators: lumpy clay pieces, clumsy sketches on broad sheets of grain newsprint, unfired ceramics with fat walls and irregular bubbled surfaces.

I followed as the hall bent into the center span of the horseshoe. Halfway through the curve was a glass-fronted main office now used to administer federation business and funds.

From what I had heard, the funding was considerable. Many ex-students, wealthy no-talents in their own right, saw fit to remember the Berkshire Federation in their wills or when the frequent need arose for tax deductions. Enabling everyone to enjoy their creative abilities, whether they had any or not, appeared to be an excellent way for an organization to thrive. Recognizing that, the federation had shifted its emphasis in recent years from the support of promising, young artists to the far more profitable support of affluent, overblown egos.

There was a large, shmoo-shaped man seated behind the main desk. From an oily skullcap of brown curls on a tiny head, he expanded to a narrow set of sloped shoulders, a formidable midsection, and a pair of stereophonic hips. The thighs, wedged in the meager kneehole like a pair of bottle corks, were massive Corinthian columns festooned with yards and yards of milk chocolate polyester. He wore a bold chocolate and rust plaid jacket and a string tie, a shirt the color and consistency of beaten egg white. The little head bobbled as he spoke on the phone in a birdlike voice.

As he chirped on, he raised a curly brow at me, squinted up through a set of coffee bean eyes, and motioned me to sit. The chair he indicated was molded green metal, small. About fourth grade size, I estimated as I settled in and worked to shed that degrading Alice in Wonderland feeling. I looked around while he talked about pigments and canvases, placing an order for supplies.

Behind him was a row of blotchy watercolors, all titled variations on the same still life though they might have served as skin rash specimens for a dermatology class. There was a line of ceramic busts on the shelf below, likenesses of some unfortunate, genderless individual whose features appeared to have melted in the sun.

"Now, then." He plunked the phone down, folded his pink, porcine hands, and offered me a political smile. "And what can I do for you today? Miss?"

I extended a hand. "My name is Emily Archer. I'm here about the Thornwood Colony. Mr.?"

He ignored the hand, frowning. "Brindley. Ralph Brindley Junior. Federation Vee Pee in charge of administration. Did you have an appointment, Miss Archer?"

"I've called several times over the past two weeks, Mr. Brindley. There seemed to be some confusion about which officer I should see and who might be free when, if ever. My time in Ashby is limited. I thought it would be best to come in person and try to clear things up."

He twiddled the chunky thumbs and cleared his throat in a grainy mezzo soprano. "I . . . I must be honest with you, Miss Archer. There has been quite a bit of . . . shall we say, discussion, here on the question of our taking over Thornwood as we had planned. Tempers have flared."

Serious business. "I'm sorry to hear that. Please, let me reassure you, I've had a tax attorney do a thorough analysis of the colony's books, and it can definitely be self-supporting in a short while if it's taken over by a nonprofit organization like yours."

The pinhead cocked to the side. "You misunderstand. Money is not what we're worried about at the moment. Certain members of the board are simply reluctant to get involved after . . ."

"After what?"

He flushed. "I really shouldn't get into that. I can assure you, we'll continue to give the project all due consideration before we make our final decision, Miss Archer. The board will look at all the pros and cons. The will of a single member shall not prevail.''

''Please, Mr. Brindley. This is very important to me. I can't respond to your concerns if I don't know what they are.''

A wry little chuckle. ''Forget about it. There's probably nothing behind any of it but fluff and air. Usual small town chitter-chatter. Anyway, it's all ancient history, you know.''

I chuckled back. ''No. I don't know.''

He leaned toward me, dropping his voice to a shrill whisper. ''Don't you worry, young lady. Off the record, I'm rooting for you on this one. Art for everyone is fine and dandy for most people, but I'm afraid it's not enough for me.'' The pudgy hand made a grand sweep over the watercolor collection. ''Some folks here have lost sight of the facts. Ugly is ugly and art's art. At the last board meeting I proposed we change our name to the Berkshire Federation for the Pits. Taking over the colony would give us a chance to deal with real art again, get behind people with real ability. That's why this organization was founded, after all.''

''I'm glad you're interested in Thornwood,'' I said. ''Let me help you clear things up. Tell me what the board is worried about. What's the problem?''

''You want my opinion? The problem is trying to get things done by committee, that's what. Committees are molasses in the gears of progress. Ten people deciding means ten mouths, twenty ears, and only a brain or two. Mucks things up. People get derailed over rumors and nonsense. Or certain individuals try to take us all along on their little power trips."

"What sort of rumors? Please be frank with me, Mr. Brindley. Does all of this have anything to do with my father's emotional illness?"

He puffed his cheeks like a bullfrog and let out a long stream of air. "It's complicated. Legends grow about a man like Wild Hill Fowler. Rumors. I'm sure you know that in his day, your father was considered about the world's finest living sculptor. Man had incredible vision, technique. Truth is, he was decades ahead of his time but so good he was forgiven. Accepted. Put Ashby on the map, I'll tell you."

"But?"

"But nothing. It was a tragedy what happened to him. A sin. The whole mess was a terrible, terrible tragedy. But there are always those who'll see it differently, that it was all his fault. Or that the system was at fault for not putting a stop to it before it ever started. Me, I think genius has its privileges."

There was something odd between the words. "I don't understand. Are you saying people believe my father should have been blamed for being sick? I thought that attitude went out with the dark ages."

He stood and loped around the office. "Look. I've said enough already. Too much. I know you haven't been in Ashby for quite some time. Now you're here, you just keep your ears open. I bet you'll hear everything you want to know and a whole lot more. Plenty around here have leaky lips, loose jaw hinges."

I labored up out of the little chair, resisting a strong urge to argue. Why risk offending an ally, obtuse and infuriating though he was? I would have to get to the bottom of this another way. "Maybe it would help if the committee spent some time at Thornwood. I'd be happy to have you all come for a visit."

"Couldn't hurt, I suppose. A few of us have been there but not recently."

"How's Thursday for dinner? I can show you around, give you a better feel for the property. Some wonderful work has been accomplished there. It would be a shame if the colony had to be closed for good."

"True, all true. And I'm hoping it won't come to that, believe me. But you know how people can get stuck worrying about old news that doesn't even matter anymore. Filling their brains so full of nonsense it's tough to find room for anything else."

"Tough. Not impossible." I offered my hand again. This time he gave it a moist, flaccid shake.

"I'll check out Thursday night with the others and give you a jingle later on."

"Thanks."

I took the long, scenic route back toward the colony. Lazy ribbons of road wound past thriving apple orchards and rambling quarter horse farms bordered by miles of whitewashed post-and-rail fence. I passed an eighteenth century clapboard church and a vintage one-room schoolhouse, now painted cliché red and open to public viewing for a nominal admission charge. At intervals, vacation homes rose from the bucolic landscape like weeds: cookie-cutter condominiums, stark A-frames with smoked glass facades, soaring cedar contemporaries backed by free-form pools, dog runs, and satellite dishes.

The last thing I needed was more uncertainty. After my father's death, the Berkshire Federation had jumped at the chance to take over Thornwood. When Aunt Lizzie told me they'd changed their minds, I assumed money was the issue. I'd come armed with a folder full of reassuring numbers. But now there was another invisible "concern" for me to battle. And I was about out of hands.

CHAPTER 10

BY THE TIME I turned in through the colony gate, the day had settled in a rippling haze of oppressive heat. The sky was brushed steel striped with smudges of polished copper and sunburn pink. The trees wavered in a halfhearted breeze and made a sound like paper crumpling. A flock of misplaced gulls fluttered in lazy formation overhead.

I spent a restless afternoon waiting for my prearranged meeting with Lynch. My mind was fogged with exhaustion, my temper spring-loaded and threatening to explode. I kept myself at a careful distance from Granny and the children, watching the normal play of events from the padded cell of my own failing control. By the time we had agreed to meet, I was a raw, crackling nerve.

I found him sitting on a stiff chair at the desk, tapping his sunken, sallow cheek with a pencil eraser. His sad eyes were frosted with private issues. I noticed that the sheet of rag bond curled into his portable Smith Corona was a long, accusing blank.

He had transformed the cottage overnight, repositioned the furniture, softened the walls with a few strategically-placed framed posters, strewn a couple of design and cooking magazines on the nightstand.

"Nice," I said as he stood to greet me. "I'd hardly recognize the place." There was a sprig of wild daisies arranged in an artful ellipse in a coke bottle vase on the nightstand, a leather-bound diary set at a careful angle beside the typewriter on the desk.

He plucked the blank sheet from the carriage, stuffed it in the top desk drawer, and sighed. "One of those useless days that drag on forever, I'm afraid. Worth celebrating the end of. Would you care for some tea, Miss Archer? Or perhaps you'd prefer something a bit stronger?"

I turned him down and watched as he fashioned himself a chemist's dream of a cocktail from an extensive array of miniature fixings he had tucked into the small board-and-brick bookshelf in the corner. He had brought a two-burner hot plate, a small electric percolator, two complete place settings of fine china, and scrolled sterling flatware. All the comforts of almost home. He motioned for me to follow him out onto the patio.

I sat on one of the webbed lawn chairs while he ducked back into the cottage to retrieve a glorious platter of fresh fruit and melon slices surrounding a runny wedge of rich, pungent cheese. He set it down on a makeshift cinderblock coffee table and sat beside me.

"You didn't have to go to all this trouble, Chief," I said. "I feel like I'm imposing on you as it is."

He took a fastidious sip of his drink. Gave an approving little nod. "You're hardly imposing, Miss Archer. In fact, you are performing a most generous, valuable service, allowing me to perform any service at all. Did you know that uselessness is the third leading killer of the human spirit in this country?"

He reminded me of one of those trick boxes. Open one and find another inside. And another. Each smaller, darker, and more intriguing than the last.

"Where do we begin?" I said.

"At what seems to you to be the beginning. That's the important thing, to find the very beginning. The mistake many investigators make is not digging deep enough. Afraid to hit something they weren't counting on, I suppose."

"The beginning . . ." I stared at the grainy sky, searching for inspiration. The day was dying a slow, lazy death, descending like a temperamental, hand-drawn curtain on an amateur stage. A band of strident crickets was tuning up for the nightly concert. There was a vague blush of Crayola pink smudged over the horizon. Red sky at night . . .

"A birth?" he suggested. "A death?"

"You mean my father's death?"

"If you think that's the starting point."

"I don't know, Chief Lynch. My father was on a long, slow physical and mental decline for many, many years. Since my mother died, in fact. So I can't say his death was much of a surprise. But I was surprised by certain things I found out afterward."

"Such as?"

". . . His financial situation, for one thing. I always assumed he was very well off, but when his lawyer settled the estate, there was nothing left to support the colony. Strange for him to be so broke, considering the astronomical commissions he used to earn."

The chief shifted in his chair and recrossed his legs, taking care not to disturb the precise crease in his silver gray trousers. "As I understand it, though, he hadn't done any significant work for many years."

"True. But keeping Thornwood going meant a great deal to him. According to his lawyer, there were trusts, complicated investments he'd worked out to keep the colony solvent indefinitely. . . . Then, for some reason, he started raiding the accounts the last few years until there was almost nothing left. I can't imagine him putting Thornwood in financial jeopardy. Not voluntarily at least."

"Then you think someone was stealing from him? Extorting money? Or might the sudden spending have been a symptom of his illness?"

I felt the helpless pit deepen in my gut. "Hard to say. Hard for me to say anything certain about him. He was surrounded by so many locked doors, Chief Lynch. I hardly knew the man. In fact, I thought nothing about him could touch me anymore, much less surprise me. But I was surprised to find out his estate was nearly bankrupt. That's why I had to contact the Berkshire Federation and ask them to take the colony over."

"Hmmm," Lynch said and scratched a note on a pocket pad with an engraved ball-point pen. "Interesting. Anything else?"

". . . The whole business with the Berkshire Federation. I don't know if you'd call it strange or just exasperating but when I first spoke to them about managing the colony, they were all thrilled with the idea. Next thing I know, they've suddenly changed their minds. Everything's on hold because of some deep, dark secret no one's willing to let me in on. Something to do with my father. That's all they'd tell me."

He scribbled again, nodding. "All right, then, I believe we have our starting point."

"We do?"

His face registered a modest crumb of self-satisfaction. "We must begin at the beginning, as I said, Miss Archer. Do you see it?" He downed the last of his cocktail, plucked the cherry from the bottom of the glass, and nipped it from the stem with a set of broad Chiclet teeth. "Do you?"

"My father's death? The bankrupt estate?"

He folded his hands and narrowed his eyes to thoughtful slits. "Walk backward along the path. Close your eyes, if you will, and envision the string of events. Then trace them back to their logical beginnings. Find the place where things first went awry."

I forced my eyes closed and ran the reels of my bumpy past in fast reverse. Back. Further. Events aligned in neat, logical progression. There. I thought I could see the beginning. If you could call it that.

"My mother's death?"

"Excellent, Miss Archer. You have the makings of a fine detective."

My eyes locked with his wistful pair. "I don't think so, Chief. Part of me needs to understand what happened to my family. But another part is scared to death of what the truth might be."

"Precisely the way any good detective feels. Being terrified is standard issue: shield, weapon, jelly legs. Lose that edge and you've lost everything. . . . Everything." His face darkened. He stood, buttoned his navy linen blazer, and tugged his crisp yellow bow tie into perfect position in the starched center of his stark white shirt. His eyes were vague. "Believe me. I know."

Bearing his empty glass and the remains of the cheese tray, he started toward the cottage.

"What's next, Chief? Where do we go from here?"

He turned suddenly brusque and businesslike. Rid his face of any stray trace of emotion, cleared his throat. "Why don't I look into the matter of your father's finances, Miss Archer. You can go to the hall of records and check out the facts surrounding your mother's death."

"But I already know the facts."

"That may be," he said as he backed through the squeaky, wood-framed screen door. "But I must caution you, facts have an odd way of changing when you hold them up to the light."

CHAPTER 11

SIX MEMBERS OF the federation board had managed to clear their calendars. I was grateful for the distraction, eager to forget everything else and concentrate on getting the Berkshire group to take over the colony. Then, I tried to reassure myself, I would be able to walk away.

They arrived in a caravan: a green wood-paneled Chevy wagon in the lead followed by a late-model blue Volvo sedan and a flesh-toned panel truck. Doors opened and slammed in harsh chorus. A motley assortment of bodies assembled on the lawn. Ralph Brindley, Jr., led the stone-faced procession in a thunderous assault on the porch stairs and rang the bell.

He introduced me to the petite, athletic Gott sisters, Monica and Trish; Leonard and Penelope Satenstein, an ebullient, well-tended pair clad in matching blue cotton fatigues and woven white sandals; and Beth Wilkinson, a tall, bone thin, ageless mouse of a woman with stooped shoulders and a lazy eye.

I led the group into the living room and offered them seats on the ring of upholstered chairs I had set around the square, marble-topped coffee table. Chief Lynch offered to fix drinks while I retrieved the prepared platters of cut vegetables, pâtés, and cheese wedges from the kitchen counter.

Granny had taken the children out for a picnic supper at the Town Park lake. "You'll have enough dealing with those . . . types from the federation, think they own the world," she told me with a contemptuous sniff. "We'd only be underfoot."

In the few minutes I was out of the room, the group had settled in a fidgety silence. While Lynch passed frosted glasses of gin-and-tonics, wine spritzers, and diet sodas, he made several unsuccessful attempts to press a conversational trigger. Finally, he connected with a question about the history of the Berkshire Federation. All six leaped into an instant animated debate over how the organization was started and when, why it was founded and by whom. It would not have surprised me if there were some serious disagreement over whether "Berkshire" was spelled with a lowercase or capital B.

"Well, Grandmother was one of the founders," Monica Gott whined. "We should know, shouldn't we, Trish?"

"Of course, you should," Brindley squeaked. "You two girls are the world's foremost authorities on absolutely every subject, after all."

"Now Ralph, no need to be your usual unpleasant, overbearing self so soon," said Penny Satenstein in a lazy southern drawl that hinted of the south of Brooklyn. "We've just met Miss Archer and Chief Lynch. Let them get acquainted awhile before they have to see you at your insufferable worst." She caught my eye and flashed a sultry smile jammed with blinding white caps. "I hope you'll forgive our dear Ralph, Miss Archer. He does have a teensy bit of trouble now and again with his personality.''

Brindley's ears reddened. The chief stepped in and moved the conversation to higher ground. ''May I offer you some cheese, Miss Wilkinson? Miss Gott? We have a lovely English stilton. A nice Danish havarti. And a delightful, tangy cheddar—from Vermont.''

The silence gathered again. It was broken by scattered scraps of necessary small talk. Munching. Ice clinking against locked teeth. I suggested we take a tour of the colony before darkness descended—inside and out.

We filed out and strolled in a ragged double line toward the cottages. Chief Lynch joined me in extolling the virtues and proud traditions of the colony. He was well versed in matters of Thornwood lore, knew several things about the colony I had never heard.

''. . . Two hundred years before Ashby was founded, this property was a monastic retreat. After that, it was a bird sanctuary for a time, until the state moved it to a larger facility. Miss Archer's father researched several sites for his colony and finally settled on this one because of its fortunate spiritual pedigree.''

''Now there's Wild Hill for you,'' Len Satenstein said. ''Spiritual pedigree. Hah.''

''It's your privilege to be skeptical, of course, Mr. Satenstein,'' said Lynch. ''But the fact remains that Thornwood's record of achievement has been outstanding. More honors and awards have been granted to works undertaken or completed here than at several of the other most prestigious artists' colonies combined.''

''Could be simple coincidence,'' Len Satenstein said. ''Or a very picky selection process. This place sure hasn't been fortunate for everybody.''

''Could be,'' said the chief. ''I used to suspect simple

coincidence myself until I did a little investigating. Turns out that many of the same artists have been here and at some of the other major colonies: Strassdale, Carmenton, even the exalted Windsor Manor where you have to be the god of a major international religion to get accepted. Still, none of those places have Thornwood's track record. Curious."

"Yes," Brindley chirped. "Curious."

"Very," said Beth Wilkinson, smoothing the full blue skirt of her cotton shirtwaist. Her voice was a low, smoky haze.

Trish Gott wrinkled her pert little nose. "Come on, now. Bottom line is we're in the art business. It's not for us to decide whether Thornwood is some kind of Lourdes for creative underachievers. All we have to figure out is whether this project makes sense for the federation. Period."

"Good point, Trish," her sister said. "I, for one, am concerned about those . . . other things Link told us. And I am not impressed by awards."

"You would be if you ever got one yourself," said Penny Satenstein. "Too bad there's no prize for obnoxious, Monica. You'd win hands down."

The chief kept his face and voice in neutral. "I must say I have mixed feelings about awards myself, Miss Gott," he said. "But they do have a way of furthering careers, building credibility for both the winners and their champions. And, of course, there are the other benefits, the grants and such."

The group fell in a respectful hush, ruminating on the magic word: grants.

"You're certainly right about that, Chief," I said. "Over the years, Thornwood has been awarded a number of large grants after colonists did prizewinning work here.''

''Very large, I imagine,'' Lynch said with a surreptitious wink.

''Depends on what you consider large, Chief. As I recall, there were several in the six figure range.''

''Six figures,'' said Ralph Brindley with a low whistle. ''Now is that so?'' He smacked his lips as we turned and headed back in the direction of the main house.

''Six figures,'' Beth Wilkinson breathed. ''Do tell.''

I told, recounting what I could remember of the colony's proudest moments. Most were bits and pieces reported as background details in tabloid exposés about my father. Over the years, I had been as morbidly fascinated by the exploits of the crazy, reclusive artist, Hillard Fowler, as the rest of his distant fans.

The mood was brighter at dinner, and I was awash with gratitude for Chief Lynch's offer to help prepare the meal. Granny had insisted on leaving one of her ubiquitous casseroles. She produced three basic varieties: beige, brown, and red, though all tasted identical. Her cooking was a small child's dream, everything soft, starchy and flavorless. She topped her creations with a layer of edible camouflage: potato sticks, Chinese noodles, canned onion rings, bread crumbs asphyxiated in melted butter. And she finished each gluey concoction with a happy face rendered in vegetable sticks and fruit slices with a fringe of parslied hair.

I had waited until she drove off for her picnic with the children to hide her oversized beige company offering in the den. The chief accompanied me on a hurried trip to the I.G.A. to buy the fixings for more suitable fare.

Lynch, who had humbly described himself as an amateur cook, marinated the steaks, whipped up a perfection of steamed baby vegetables and wild rice, fashioned a mouth-watering herbed cheese bread, and worked a masterful Caesar salad at the kitchen table after excusing himself on the pretense of having to make a phone call. I watched as he slicked the cut edge of a garlic clove over the deep wooden bowl, fashioned a light blend of olive oil, lemon juice, capers, and anchovies to pour over the greens, and bound it all with a froth of egg yolk drizzled into the mix at the last minute. Finished, he tossed and served with deft motions, wiped his thick, ropy hands on a dish towel, and slipped back into his impeccable, navy linen blazer. He removed his apron, flicked a microscopic lint speck from his cream-colored gabardine slacks, and returned to take his assigned place at the head of the dining room table.

"Delicious," he pronounced as he took a fastidious bite of steak. "Done to perfection. You are an excellent cook, Miss Archer."

"But—"

I caught his cautionary look. This was Ashby, after all. Chiefs of detectives, even the retired kind, did not cook here, at least not indoors, and not even outdoors—not unless they had slaughtered the food personally, preferably with their bare teeth. Moreover, in Ashby, respectable mothers of three did not major in carry-out Chinese or pizza, as I so shamelessly did. We were trying to make an impression, after all.

"Thank you, Chief Lynch," I said. "It was nothing. No trouble at all."

Our visitors sipped the full-bodied Cabernet Lynch had selected and sated themselves on his superb cuisine. He'd worked a giant blueberry soufflé for dessert, an airy golden chef's hat accompanied by a gossamer lemon sauce that managed to tickle everyone's palate, including the steel-beamed Gott sisters.

Brindley downed a large second helping and pushed back from the table to accommodate his inflating midsection. "Wonderful meal, Miss Archer."

"Wonderful," Beth Wilkinson echoed. "You must give me your recipes. I love to cook. Especially desserts." She and Brindley exchanged a seething, wall-eyed gaze.

Trish Gott petted her taut, little abdomen and bounced up on her sneakered feet. "We enjoyed the dinner, Miss Archer. Now, if you'll excuse us, we have to be up early in the morning. We jog." Monica hopped up next to her sister. They extended a matched set of small, crop-nailed, muscled hands in my direction.

Penny Satenstein planted her fists on the table and fixed them with a killing look. "You two are something else, I swear it. Here this nice woman all but stands on her head to show us a good time, and you act like she's running a training table. Eat and run. Worse, eat and jog, for godsakes. Didn't your parents teach you any manners? Now sit down."

"It's late, Penny," Trish whined.

"Well, it's going to get later. So sit. And shush."

Ralph Brindley squeaked his throat clear. "We really should offer Miss Archer some of our feelings on the project before we go, girls. It's what we agreed to do."

Len Satenstein shook his polished head up and down. "You want my vote? I say we forget about that other . . . business and go ahead. Thornwood could be just the shot in the arm the federation needs. I don't care what Link says."

"I agree," Brindley piped in.

"So do I," said Beth Wilkinson with a toss of her

straight, hay-toned hair. ''It's a wonderful opportunity. Just as you said, Ralphie.''

Brindley flushed and ran a hand through his tight cap of greasy waves. He folded his puffed pink hands in front of him. ''That leaves you girls. What's your opinion, Trish? Penny?''

Trish Gott fiddled with her demitasse spoon, cracked a knuckle. ''I'll be honest. I have mixed feelings. There's still that other . . . business. But sponsoring an artists' colony is an exciting idea. I assume federation members would be given priority to come here and work if we wanted to apply?''

''Now what would you do at Thornwood, Trish?'' Penny purred. ''Write a how-not-to book?''

''You're all forgetting something,'' Monica said as she tugged down the sleeves of her warm-up suit. ''Link's objections aren't the only issue here. This place is going to take work. A lot of work.''

I saw the volley of glances as the pack of them looked around. Granny and I had worked for hours trying to hide the bulk of the clutter, but the improvement was not encouraging. The walls were badly in need of painting. And there were still cartons everywhere, drawers too full to close, a suffocating glut of things.

''Oh, please,'' I said in way too big a hurry. ''Don't give that another thought. I'm planning to have the place painted. And all this will be cleaned out before I leave.''

''Well, that's good to hear,'' Monica said. ''We just got finished renovating our new headquarters and I don't think any of us are in the mood for more cleanup or decorating.''

''Look, if all this is settled, I really need my eight hours beauty sleep,'' Trish said, springing up again.

"What you really need is to sit down and shut your mouth," Penny said.

"No matter what we all think, there are still the others to convince," Len said. "I think Fay Richmond will go along with whatever the group decides. But the Brownleys are behind Link, two-hundred percent. Our charter calls for unanimous agreement of the board on an undertaking as big as this. You want the colony, you'll have to get Link to agree."

"And that's going to take some doing," said Brindley with a sorry little grin. "Link is not one to change his mind easily."

"Chain link, that's what we should call him," Beth Wilkinson said with a hoarse giggle. "Man doesn't give."

"Let's stow it, shall we," said Trish Gott. "You have something to say to Link, say it to his face, Beth. You're not such a big hero when he's around, now are you?"

"Shut up, Trish. Nobody asked you," Brindley said.

"Oh, goodie," said Penny Satenstein. "I love it when we have one of our little brawls. It's so awfully dull when we're pretending to be civil."

"You are one strange person, Penny," Trish said.

"Why, thank you, darling," she crooned. "Aren't you just the sweetest thing to say so?"

I stood and began clearing the table. Penny Satenstein insisted on helping. She trailed behind me into the kitchen. My head filled with the heavy lavender and musk of her cologne and the clamorous jingle of her jewelry. Both pale, plump arms were cuffed with a profusion of gold bangles, and the squat, crepey neck was bound in masses of thick, gold chains. I counted four gilt hoops and a large diamond freckle in one of her pendulous earlobes. She set her stack of dirty dishes in the rubber drain and hissed into my ear. "Run the water."

I did. She inclined her puffed mane of blue-black hair toward the door, listening through the rush of water for approaching footsteps. Satisfied that we were not about to be interrupted, she turned and whispered in my direction through a set of blinding white caps. "You have to go see Link, Emily. Convince him we should take over the colony. He's the ball game."

"All right. I'll call him. Make an appointment."

"No." She gave me a disgusted look, fluttering her false lashes. "You don't make appointments with Link. That's not the way the man operates. Just go . . . see him." She scribbled an address on a soiled cocktail napkin. "Drop in."

I squinted at the address. It was a building near the center of town. "Who is this Link person, anyway?"

"Lincoln Marshall. Federation president. Fine artist in his own right. Gorgeous, impossible man," she hissed and peered toward the door again. "Len is jealous to death of Link. With good reason. . . . Anyhow, Link was away, working on a job in Paris, when we agreed to take over the colony. He all but blew his beautiful stack when he heard about it."

"Look, I'll go see Mr. Marshall if you think it'll help. But I don't understand. What does he have against Thornwood? And why all the secrecy?"

Her face tensed. "It's a long, long story. Maybe we'll talk about it someday over drinks. Lots and lots of drinks. Right now I'd best be getting back to the others. Before they get suspicious."

I folded the address and slipped it in my pocket. "Thanks, Mrs. Satenstein. I appreciate your help."

"Penny," she mouthed and breezed toward the door.

She stopped at the threshold and gave me a long, penetrating look. "Call me after you see him," she mouthed. "I want to hear all about it. Everything."

I nodded, more anxious than ever to have the business of the colony resolved.

The door swung shut behind her, and I started to put the remaining dishes in the sink. I heard a squeak, the door opening again, and turned to the sight of Penny Satenstein's disembodied head, poking into the room. "I forgot to warn you, Emily. Be careful. Link is . . ."

"Link is what?"

A shadow crossed her face. It was replaced in an instant by a glint of mischief. "There I go, getting carried away with myself. Link is Link, that's all. Don't you worry. He's no problem when you know how to handle yourself. You do know how to handle yourself?"

I turned back to the dishes, trying to shake the uneasy feeling that Penny Satenstein had just told me more than she wanted me to know.

But not enough to keep me out of trouble.

CHAPTER 12

LYNCH AND I sat on the porch, watching the taillights beat a bumpy retreat down the colony drive. I took several slow, measured breaths, trying to shake the strain of the evening and the thick smog of sleeplessness weighing on my mind.

The chief's voice was a soothing chant. "It went as well as can be expected, I think."

"I guess."

"But you're not satisfied, are you, Miss Archer?"

I kept my eyes fixed on the black emptiness. "I'll be satisfied when all this is over, when they agree to take over Thornwood."

He sipped his coffee, spoke through the puff of steam. "Will that solve things for you?"

A bitter lump settled in my throat, and I felt a threatening swell of tears. "I hope so."

I could feel his kind, brown eyes, trying to peer inside my head. "Is there something else worrying you, Miss Archer? Something we haven't talked about?"

I was relieved to hear the rumble and crunch of Granny's approaching car. Lynch was cutting too close to the bone, and I was starving for a sympathetic ear. I had told him more than enough already. I couldn't let him or anyone know what I feared about Rachel. I hurried down off the porch and walked across the lawn to greet the children.

David and Adam were fast asleep in the backseat of her battered gray Chevy Nova, tangled together like old clothes. I prodded Adam awake enough to walk and lifted David's sweaty little bulk in my arms. Rachel was stonefaced. Silent. Her hair was a shaped mountain of stiff black curls, her eyes rimmed with dusky purple shadow. She hugged Granny and moved in a trancelike glide out of the car and into the house, refusing to acknowledge my existence. I shrugged, pretending not to care. "It really was better for the children not to be here, Granny. You were right. Thanks."

Her voice poked through the darkness like an accusing finger. "Well now, I know those federation types, dearie. Hardly the kind to enjoy having little children around. Don't care for anything or anyone but their own big deal selves. Can't really imagine you'd want them to run your father's colony now you've seen what a dreadful bunch they are. You're better off if they decide not to go ahead and take over the place. Take my word."

"They're my only choice, I'm afraid. Anyway, they wouldn't have much to do with the colony's day-to-day operation. They'd hire someone to run things in the house. And a committee processes the applications."

"Suit yourself," she snapped. "Don't know how your dear father would feel about it. Then, I suppose that doesn't matter all that much to you, now he's gone."

"Good night, Granny. See you tomorrow."

"First thing," she said. She gunned the cranky engine

and chugged out toward the access road, trailing a wake of dust and cross-eyed tail beams.

I took the boys upstairs and got them changed and into bed. From Rachel's room I heard the angry thump of doors, drawers slapping shut. After a few minutes, she flopped down on her bed with a jarring squeal of the bedsprings.

Lynch was still down in the kitchen, drying the last of the dishes.

"Please, let me. You've done way more than enough already. Dinner was wonderful."

"A pleasure," he said as he buffed the white ceramic platter to an unnatural gleam. "A genuine pleasure. I enjoy cooking, always have. But it's so difficult to prepare anything for one. Nothing tastes quite right."

I wiped the scarred, Formica counters with a sponge. "You live alone?"

"No," he said. "By myself."

"Interesting way to put it."

"The only way," he said with a wistful smile.

Everything was cleaned and put away, but the chief made no move to leave. Not all that ready to fight the losing battle for sleep myself, I offered him a brandy.

We took the drinks out on the porch and stared awhile at the polished ebony sky. A soft, pine-scented breeze lightened the air. Lynch's rocker squealed in shrill refrain as he buried his nose in the giant snifter and inhaled.

"You were very persuasive with the federation people, Chief. How is it that you know so much about Thornwood?"

His face registered unconvincing surprise. "Did it sound that way? I don't really know much about the colony at all. Only what I've read in brochures and such."

He began rocking in earnest, humming a nervous tune. So there was something he wasn't telling me as well. Interesting.

He stood abruptly and set his snifter down on the wicker table. "I'd best be running along, Miss Archer. Rest well."

"You too, Chief Lynch. Thanks again, for everything."

"My pleasure, Miss Archer. I mean that sincerely."

I watched him lumber down the stairs and across the front lawn where he was stolen by a deep slash of dark shadow. I stared into the black void until the lights flashed on in his cottage, casting a diffuse lemon glow over the peaked tile roof.

The house was crackling still. I climbed the stairs, searching for any welcome signs of impending unconsciousness but felt none. Too many disturbing thoughts were holding me awake. The mysterious Link Marshall, the inscrutable Chief Lynch, the skeletons we might begin to unearth tomorrow.

I looked in on the boys. They were hard asleep, faces flushed. A musty talcum scent mingled with the damp heat in their room. I smoothed David's rumpled cotton blanket and tucked Bruce, his beloved one-eyed stuffed monkey, under a floppy arm; kissed Adam's dewy forehead and moved him away from the precipitous edge of his bed. He muttered an angry, incomprehensible protest and bashed his fist against the mattress.

Rachel's door was closed. Locked. The knob twisted halfway and stuck with a harsh sound like angry fingers snapping a command.

I undressed in the dark and slipped into bed. Clenched

my eyelids, searching for the elusive comfort of oblivion. Desperate for a decent night's sleep, I struggled to slide past the crowd of nagging concerns. There had to be logical, rational explanations for everything. With Lynch's help, I had a feeling I would be able to find them.

If only I could sleep. Now, the thought of that odd, dead letter nagged at me. How could I allow myself to be taken in by my own foolish superstitions, bitten by the toothless threats? First thing, I should have gotten rid of it, tossed it away and out of my mind. There were too many real issues. I couldn't allow myself to be distracted by such nonsense.

I dragged out of bed and went downstairs, determined to rip the foolish thing in little pieces. Be done with it.

I flipped the switch in the kitchen. Blinded by the harsh flood of light, I groped my way down the counter, found the right drawer, and felt for the envelope. My hand touched a cool metal church key, a set of bottle caps, a tea strainer. As my eyes adjusted, I searched that drawer and the others in turn. Frantic, I knelt and dug through the clutter of pots and bowls in the cabinets below.

The letter was gone.

I searched the same drawers and cabinets over and over again, staring into the clutter until a tidal wave of weariness washed over me.

Forget it, Emily, I told myself. The letter didn't matter. It was nothing but an antique fluke of a letter lost for years in a dustbin. Thirty years ago it was probably sent as a hoax, a ruse to part some superstitious fool from his money. I had gotten the thing by sheer coincidence. Nothing more to it than that.

Trying to keep a firm hold on myself, I slid the drawers closed, shut the cabinet doors, and went upstairs. So the letter was gone. So what?

But why would anyone want that weird thing? I couldn't imagine a reason. Maybe Granny had thrown it out by accident. Or maybe I had misplaced it somehow. No matter. There was nothing for me to do now but forget about it, put it out of my mind.

Flopping on the bed, I felt my thoughts slipping out of focus. The soft flame of light from Lynch's cottage filtered through the slatted blinds over my window, slicing my world into slim, even pieces. His words echoed in my drifting brain. We would start tomorrow, at the beginning.

And we would get to the bottom of things.

CHAPTER 13

HAVING PROMISED THE federation board I would get the house in shape, I spent the morning on the phone calling painters, painting contractors, paint stores. The few live voices that answered informed me, without attempting to conceal their pompous amusement, that every painter in the area had been booked for a year or more for the busy summer season. I was on my own.

Fast Freddie Fiske sold me the necessary supplies: rollers, sable brushes, gallon cans of generic latex paint. For no extra charge, he threw in several wooden mixing sticks, a painter's hat, and some gratuitous advice. "Hope you know what you're doing, missy. Painting's one of those things only looks easy." That said, he returned to mining between a pair of decayed bicuspids with the whittled tail end of a wooden matchstick.

I dropped my purchases in the rear hatch of the Jeep and walked the two blocks up a gentle incline to Aspen Lane. South Avenue was clotted with meandering tourists, searching for bargains in the rear bins and overflow racks of Ashby's prosaic little shops.

Lincoln Marshall's address was a slender, three-story carriage house done in chlorine-blue aluminum siding with ivory and black satin trim. On the ground floor was a shuttered coffeehouse festooned with hand-lettered fliers heralding poetry readings and an upcoming psychic fair. The front door was locked. A neatly folded subpoena was tucked behind an oversized brass knocker shaped like a broad, bulbous nose.

Halfway down a narrow side alley littered with a dust-caked motorcycle, broken lawn furniture, and large rubber trash barrels, I found an unlocked metal door and stepped inside a square, dingy cell of a lobby. A scrawny calico cat was curled in a sleepy ball in the corner beside an ancient wicker baby pram with a bashed side and two missing wheels. Tinny Chopin sonatas drifted down from a cheap radio overhead. There was the sorry aroma of boiled cabbage poorly masked by a sweet citrusy room deodorant.

Determined to have this uneasy visit over with, I climbed to the first landing and knocked at one of four identical apartment doors. A frazzled child-woman opened the door to the limits of a flimsy chain. She carried a soiled, feverish looking infant astride her boxy hip. The little one wailed in a hoarse G major and rubbed at the swollen pink puffs of her eyes with a dirty fist.

"Yeah?"

"I'm looking for Lincoln Marshall."

An ax blow of a voice came from a back room where TV images danced in eerie silence. "Who'zere?"

Fear crept into the young woman's expression. "It's nobody, hon," she called over her shoulder. She made a desperate face and rasped at me in a gritty whisper. "Link lives upstairs. Now go. Please. Marv hears that name he'll have a fit."

My feet clanked against the bare metal steps as I continued to the top floor. The stairwell was dim and airless, the handrail gritty with rust and flecks of peeling paint. A heavy, steel-faced fire door at the top opened out to a small, dirty, dark landing. I paused and pressed my ear to the solitary apartment door. There was a harsh, rhythmic scraping sound like a desperate, caged animal trying to claw its way to freedom.

From below, the baby's cries had turned frantic. The ax voice bellowed for silence. I ordered the rude hammering in my chest to stop; drew a deep, incendiary breath; and knocked.

The scraping continued, and I forced myself to knock again. Louder this time. There was the harsh abrasion of chair legs against raw wood. Footsteps. The door creaked open.

He was tall, tanned, naked from head to the low-slung waistband of a pair of skin-tight, color-bleached jeans. His eyes were opalescent, mouth full and well-defined like a hopeful child's drawing. A slight bump from an old break saved the nose from cuteness. Ropy veins trailed the lean, muscled length of his arms and lined the thick span of his neck. He had a lush patch of curly brown hair on his chest, perfect foil for the lush curly thatch of overgrown chestnut hair on his head, the dense eyebrows, the line of curly strands that meandered down from chest to belly and disappeared below the thick brass buckle. There was something familiar about him I could not bring in clear focus.

''I'm looking for Lincoln Marshall.''

''You found him.''

''I'm Emily Archer, Mr. Marshall. I hope I'm not disturbing you. I wanted to see you, to talk about the Thornwood Colony.''

"Talk, then."

He led me into a gigantic glut of unbroken space. The ceiling soared to metal roof beams exposed between a dozen hazy skylights. At the far end of the room was a wall-wide span of plate-glass window. The decor was flophouse modern: a folding card table inset with mock green leather, an overstuffed green tufted chair spewing clumps of liberated foam. A king-sized mattress fitted with a cloud bank of pillows and a rumpled gray-white sheet occupied most of the far end of the studio. A folding screen in the corner was available to hide the makeshift bathroom: a lidless toilet, a sink, and a bare shower head protruding from the wall like a headless neck.

Large sculpted stone and marble figures were everywhere, in varying stages of completion. There were coffee cans stuffed with chiseling tools and picks, crisp charcoal sketches tacked to the scarred ivory walls.

"I'm sorry to barge in on you like this, Mr. Marshall. Penny Satenstein thought I should come to see you in person, to find out why you're so against the federation taking over my father's colony."

He squinted at me. One side of his mouth curled in amusement. "You look like your old man." I could feel his eyes tracking the length of my body like seeking hands. "Around the eyes."

A hot rash of anger was creeping up my chest. I held myself in a careful noose of control. "I'm sorry you couldn't join the rest of the federation board for dinner at the colony. They all seemed in favor of taking the place over. It seems you're the only one with any serious objections. Maybe if you tell me what they are, I can put your mind at ease."

"Funny, you don't look like a priest."

"Please, Mr. Marshall. This is very important to me."

He flashed a slow, lazy smile and lit a hand-rolled cigarette that smelled like barbecued broccoli. "It's not going to happen, lady. The federation is out. Forget it."

"Why is the federation out? What do you have against Thornwood?"

He flicked away the smoke and stamped out the glowing end with a booted foot. The floor was littered with butts, crumpled scraps of paper, marble dust.

"Drink?" he said, and without waiting for an answer, he poured large measures of syrupy red wine into a pair of cloudy tumblers. "To you, lady, whatever you said your name is."

"Emily Archer."

"To you, Emily Archer. To the rest of your life. After you give this up."

"Why are you against the project, Mr. Marshall?" I asked again and set down my glass on the onyx pedestal of a reclining female nude.

"It's not the project, lady. It's your old man. What he was. What he did." He lit another smoke, mumbling under his breath.

Fury bubbled up in my gut. "Who are you to judge my father? What gives you the right?"

He leaned against a towering torso of a corpulent old woman and stared at me. "You're missing the point, lady. Right's got nothing to do with it. You asked why I'm against taking over the colony. I'm telling you. I don't want to get my hands dirty. Simple."

His eyes dug too deep. I avoided them. Stared around him at the sculptures. The figures were lush. Lines and planes so dense and rich I felt like an intruder, felt as if my fingers would burn if I touched a rise of the cold marble flesh.

"They're yours?"

"I made them," he said without a trace of proprietary pride.

I walked from piece to piece, entranced by the power of his work. The stone was alive, pulsing with raw emotion. The flush crept up my chest and settled in the hollows of my cheeks. "They're . . . you're very good."

He sucked hard on the cigarette and breathed his words through a cloud puff of pungent smoke. "Go on, touch it. It won't bite."

I pushed away the senseless fear and ran a finger over the hips and buttocks of a twined pair of alabaster lovers. My insides were melting. "It's beautiful."

He had crept up behind me, stood so close the warmth of his breath played along my spine like a deft musician's fingers.

"I'm not as good as he was. Not yet."

I stepped back in a reflex of defense. My breath came in short, shallow stabs. "There's no contest. You're an original. So was he."

"He was an original, all right. But I don't come close to your dear daddy. Not in a lot of ways. And that's fine."

"So that's the problem. You're jealous."

His laugh was dark, angry. "Right, lady. All I ever wanted in life was to be like that wonderful man. How'd you guess?"

I forced myself to lock eyes with him. "I'll leave you to your power trip, Mr. Marshall. We're not getting anywhere."

His eyes drilled into my back as I walked toward the door. I bit back a strong urge to throw something at him, bash my fists against his bare chest until my bones cracked. I was overflowing with mindless, inexplicable rage.

The door stuck. I pulled against the cold metal knob, swallowing a rising scream of frustration. He swaggered over, placed a hand over mine, and nudged the door open with a strategic tug.

"Never works to try too hard, Emily Archer. You have to just let things happen."

"That's not my way, Mr. Marshall."

"Never was."

"What's that supposed to mean?" Our eyes connected again. Something eerily familiar. But what?

"You'll figure it out. If you want to."

"What are you talking about? Damn it, would you stop playing with me? If you have something to say, say it."

His face slackened and went blank as he sipped his wine. There was a lazy insouciance that brought my blood to a slow, rolling boil.

"You want to see something, you'll open your eyes. You don't, that's okay, too. Everything's okay, lady, as long as you're doing it to yourself."

"Good-bye, Mr. Marshall. If you're ever ready to give up your little games and have a grown-up discussion, let me know."

His eyes danced with laughter. "No matter how long you wait, some things never change. Isn't that right, Emmy Lee?"

I was halfway back to the car before the fury stopped pounding in my head. Infuriating man. Obnoxious, impossible . . .

Enough.

There was no reason to allow that dreadful excuse for

a higher life form to crawl under my skin. If necessary, I would find a way around the outrageous Mr. Marshall. Or through him.

My shirt was glued to my back by a torrent of angry perspiration. On the last block to the car, I slowed to a stroll and took a lazy, deliberate look at the shop windows. Ashby's merchants made a comical attempt to blend the insufferable trendiness of the summer vacationers with the devout endless-sameness of the locals. One display had a mannequin garbed in a chintz housedress and high-top Reeboks in a screaming bubble gum pink. Another depicted a plaid-mad Ashby type lolling in a jute hammock reading a copy of *Field and Stream* through a pair of mirrored Vuarnet sunglasses.

Parched by my fit of rage, I stopped for a quick iced tea at Doreen's luncheonette on the corner. I sat on a padded, green-capped stool at the ice cream bar; caught my tight, absurd image in the broad plate mirror; had a long, difficult discussion with myself which got me nowhere.

By the time I was ready to go back to the colony, the shade of a large Japanese maple had slipped off the Jeep, leaving it to bake in the blasting sun. I noticed, as I approached the curb, that I had left the rear door ajar. Cursing under my breath, I hoped that didn't translate into a light left on and a dead battery. Perfect end to a perfectly terrible beginning of what was shaping up to be another one of those days.

I slid onto the scorching front seat and held my breath as I turned the key and waited for the verdict. There was an asthmatic chug of reluctance but, as I stomped down hard on the accelerator, the engine caught and came alive.

Relieved, I leaned across the back seat to close the offending door.

Then I saw it.

My hand was caught in a paralysis of shock. The image registered first as a swell of sour bile in my throat. My stomach heaved. A dizzy wave of black emptiness washed over me as my mind tried to close out the horror. I struggled to breathe.

There was a mangled animal on the rear floor of the car. Blood oozed from the near severed head which was folded under the eviscerated carcass. The rear leg was bent at a crazy angle and a length of cracked white bone poked through the clotted fur.

I fought back the nausea as I dug two mixing sticks out of the bags from Fiske's Hardware and walked around the car to get rid of the thing. My legs were dead rubber; my mind racing in dumb little circles, trying to figure out what this was supposed to mean. A threat? A revolting kid's prank?

Gently, I worked the flat stirrers under the mashed body. The thing twitched in a death reflex, and I jumped half out of my mind, dropping the dead creature at the side of the road in the process.

I could see the head now. A cat's head. The face slack, mouth curled in a dreamy, frozen grin. With a shudder of revulsion, I emptied the paint cans from one of the large brown bags and worked the stiffening little body inside.

The rubber floor mat was puddled with congealed blood and caked with dried entrails. I lifted it by the edges and deposited it in the nearest trash barrel beside the paper sack.

Still shivering, I opened the windows wide and drove out through the center of town toward the colony. I was nearing that bottom point that Lynch had talked about.

Nowhere to go from here but up?

CHAPTER 14

I HAD SKIRTED the wide hoop of shade cast by the hanging tree and come halfway down the rutted road to the farmhouse when I spotted Granny's gray Nova in the rearview mirror. She was trailing a city block behind me, hunched low in the driver's seat, clutching the steering wheel as if she were trying to squeeze the life out of it.

Her car belched and sputtered to a stop as she pulled up and parked beside the Jeep. The air filled with a quivering plume of oily exhaust followed by a harsh volley of backfire.

As I was unloading the paint supplies from the Jeep's backseat, Adam and David clambered out of her car and hurled themselves at me headfirst like a pair of blond bowling balls. They were jabbering in wild, incomprehensible bursts of enthusiasm.

Rachel slid out of the front passenger side, cradling a small bundle swaddled in a terry towel. Her expression was an odd mix of mischief and murderous distrust. Slashes of dirt striped her pink sundress and stippled the pale surface of her slender forearms.

Granny stepped out on her side of the car and bumped the door shut with a quick thrust of her considerable hip. The wig du jour was a Dutch bob the color of New England clam chowder topped by a dense, creamy flap of brow-length bangs. There was a plush carpet of glittery amethyst eyeshadow on her upper lids. She pursed her lips. ''There now, darling. Show your mama what you've got.''

Rachel hugged the squirmy bundle to her chest and cast a pleading look at Granny. ''But what if she says no?''

''Now, now, dearie. Not to worry. What did Granny tell you? It'll all work out. You'll see.''

''It's a puppy,'' Adam said. ''Show Mommy the puppy, Rachel.''

''Lookit a puppy,'' David chortled. ''S'a puppy, Mommy!'' He forced a guttural laugh. ''S'a puppy.''

Rachel flashed them a menacing look and slid back the towel an inch or so to expose the miniature white muzzle, the black jujube nose. I spotted one round, black eye and a frantic twitch of movement at the tail end.

''Aren't you a cutie?'' I said and scratched behind a cocked white velvet triangle of an ear. ''Where'd you come from?''

Rachel pivoted the dog out of my reach. ''Granny bought him for me. He's mine.''

''Now, now, dearie. The dog is for all of you to enjoy. Remember what Granny said?'' Her smile was a clenched fist of faded teeth framed by hot pink lip gloss and a sharp slash of crimson pencil. ''Let me explain, Emily, dear. I took the children into town for lunch at Doreen's. A little treat, I thought. Hope you don't mind.''

Doreen's. I must have just missed them there. Lucky

thing. None of the children needed a chance encounter with a mauled, bloody cat. "No, I don't mind, but—"

She pressed a finger to her lips to squelch the rest of my objections. ". . . Let me finish, dearie. We were walking past the Pet Palace down on Lyman Road when we spotted this darling fellow in the window. Show your mother the little tail, Rachel. Looks just like a feather quill, now doesn't it? Keeps right on wagging it all the time, friendly little thing. You ever see anything so irresistible?"

"The problem is we live in an apartment house that doesn't allow pets, Granny. Rachel knows that. She should have told you."

The coal eyes narrowed to angry, blazing slits. "You can just go to hell, Emily. I don't give a damn what you say. I'm keeping him."

"That's enough, Rachel. Being fresh and obnoxious is not going to get you anyplace. You know we aren't allowed to have pets. I can't change that."

Granny rolled her eyes and sucked the tip of her tongue against her palate. "Temper, darling. Mind your temper like Granny told you. . . . Course, I understand about the apartment and all, Emily. We talked all that over and Rachel agrees he'll stay here with me in the country when it's time for you to go back to New York. Keep me company. All of you can come by and visit the pup often as you like. Now isn't that what we decided, darling? Works out neat and simple."

Rachel was stroking the squirming little bundle, refusing to look in my direction. "Yes, Granny. Max will stay here with you, but he'll still be my dog. And I can come visit him anytime I want. I can take a bus if she won't bring me."

I looked from Rachel to Granny, wall to wall. "All

right. If you understand he can't come home with us, I guess you can keep him while we're here. But he's going to be your responsibility. A puppy needs a lot of care and attention.''

''I know that, Emily. I'm not stupid.'' She gave me a sharp, ugly stab of a look and carried the dog inside.

''Hope it's all right with you, dearie,'' Granny said. ''Rachel spotted him in the window and fell right in love with the little fellow. Not that you can blame her, seeing that precious face and that sweet little tail. . . . Anyhow, seemed to me a pet might be a real good thing for the child, what with her being so high-strung and all.''

''You should have asked me first. It's going to be very difficult for her to give him up.''

She flapped a hand at me. ''Oh, now, dearie. You worry way too much about the child is all. That's why she's so all-fired worried about everything herself, I bet you.''

''In the future, please check with me before you give her anything.'' I hefted the sacks of paint supplies and started walking toward the house.

She called after me. ''If you don't need me for anything, I'll be running along home now. I'm feeling a little worn out from this heat, to tell you the truth. Think I'll put my feet up awhile.''

''Sure. Go ahead.'' I watched as she settled herself in the car, smoothed the soot black skirt of her dress, checked her paint-caked face in the rearview mirror, and angled out of her parking space. ''Don't hurry back.''

Rachel had settled the puppy in a small cardboard box lined with the shredded sports section of the *Ashby Gazette*. The tiny creature scampered across a landscape of dismembered cheerleaders and a headless, one-handed basketball player frozen in the middle of a long lay-up.

Adam and David were kneeling beside the carton, scrutinizing the pup's every move in mute, bug-eyed fascination. Shrill bursts of enthusiasm and curious, grabby little fingers were bound to follow. And a swift detonation of Rachel's temper was bound to follow soon after that.

"How would you guys like to help me do some painting while the puppy takes a rest?" I said.

"Yeah, go on, you dumb babies. Get lost. You keep staring at Max like that you'll drive him nuts," Rachel said. ". . . And you'd better not go near him without my permission. I'll kill you both if you do, I swear it."

In the kitchen, I gave them each a dry paintbrush and put them in charge of the base cabinets while I climbed the stepladder and began coating the faded crown moldings near the ceiling.

Nice, mindless rhythm. Brush dunked in the silver can, excess slapped against the metal sides and squeezed across the notched rim for good measure before the paint-laden bristles were drawn in a careful caress over the dingy woodwork.

"Mommy's painting, Adam's painting, David's painting," Adam chanted.

"Addie painin . . . Daybit painin."

Rachel was in the den, crooning at the puppy in a syrupy sweet voice. "Good boy," she said. "Such a gooood boy."

A broad stream of daylight showcased the expanding fresh white surface. Fast Freddie's pronouncements aside, this wasn't difficult in the least. A few days and the whole mood of the place would be lifted. Maybe that would convince the great strident majority of the Berkshire Federation board to ignore the obnoxious Lincoln

Marshall and his mysterious objections to my father's colony.

"Come here, Maxy Wax," Rachel said and made a series of kissing noises. "Come on. Come to Mama."

I edged the peaked tip of the brush into a difficult corner space and started working on the long, faded soffit above the cabinets, brushing a slim line around the edges I could fill in later with a quick sweep of the roller. Easy.

Below me, the boys were engrossed in their imaginary efforts, making grand sweeping strokes over the cabinet doors. "Mommy painting . . . Addie painting."

That strange sound I heard was calm. Peace. I could get used to that. No problem.

"Come here, puppy wuppy," came Rachel's candy-apple voice from the den. "I love you, Max."

Finished with the trim on the soffit, I climbed down to get the roller.

"Addie painting . . . David painting."

I froze at the sight of paint dripping a trail from the end of Adam's brush. "Adam, no!"

Too late. The walnut cabinets were smeared and spattered, the pebbled linoleum splashed with paint and caked with a ragged trail of little sneaker-shaped footprints. I caught David as he was about to dip his paint-coated thumb into his mouth.

"No."

I lifted the sticky pair of them and deposited them in the double porcelain sink. Tugging off their shoes and tube socks, I realized this job was beyond the scope of the little faucet.

I set them down on the floor again. "Stay right there. Don't move." I passed Rachel, still staring into the carton where Max had fallen over in an exhausted swoon and was sleeping with all four paws tipped skyward like an upended turtle. "Adam and David got in the paint, Rach. I'm going up to grab some towels and clean clothes for them, and then I'll take them out under the hose. Keep an eye on them for a second, will you?"

She rolled her eyes. "Stupid little jerks."

"Please watch them for one second. I'll be right down."

I collected the necessary things and hurried back to the kitchen before they could do any more major damage. Adam had run his paint-smeared fingers through his hair and traced a wiggly line of white latex down the center of his face. His hands looked gloved.

Rachel was sitting at the kitchen table reading the back of a cereal box.

"Outside, you two," I said and followed them to the yard where I stripped off their paint-soaked shorts and shirts and positioned their plump, squirmy bodies within easy range of the hose.

"Hands," I said, and Adam turned his up to catch the sunlit spray. I angled the hose in his direction and pressed the trigger on the brass nozzle to increase the stream.

At the first sprinkle, he flushed a furious scarlet and started howling like an irate coyote. I dropped the hose and knelt in front of him. "It's okay, sweetie. I just want to clean you up. Look, you're all spotted."

He spoke between whimpers. "It's hot, burning."

The water still dribbled from the mouth of the nozzle. I tested it with my finger. Scalding hot. But how? I traced the hose back to the house connection and from there, spotted where the water lines snaked into the basement. The thick, black hose had been shifted from the silver fitting to the bright red, hot water pipe.

Adam's hand had already quieted to a vague, innocent pink. But the horror of what might have been hammered in my head.

I took them back inside and up to the hall bathroom, ran a tepid tub full of water in the ancient chipped claw-foot, and started to rub away the paint traces with a soapy cloth. As I knelt there, the realization crept up my spine like a poisonous insect.

The switched hose, the dangerous spray of scalding water, all of it was no accident. And there was only one person who could be responsible.

"Rachel!"

I had to call several times before she gave up her selective deaf act and came trudging upstairs and down the hall to the bathroom. A satisfied little smirk played on her lips as she watched her brothers splashing in the soapy water. In defiant slow motion, she turned to where I was standing and faced me down with a look of unadulterated loathing.

"What do you want, Emily? I was busy doing something."

"I know what you've been busy doing. You get to your room, Rachel. And you stay there until I say to come out."

"What in the hell are you talking about?"

"You switched the hose outside. I know you did it. Don't bother to lie."

"I didn't do anything to any damned hose, and you'd better not go around accusing people when you have no proof."

"Go to your room, Rachel. Now."

"No. I don't have to listen to you. You're not my goddamned mother." With a haughty toss of her hair, she walked out of the room and slammed the door shut behind her. I heard the furious clump as she ran down the stairs. The screen door whined, and there was a brisk clatter of footsteps across the porch and down the steps.

"You gonna go find her, Mommy?" Adam said, accustomed to our routine chase scenes by now.

"No, sweetie. I'm going to let her go. She's better off by herself for a while."

I leaned against the sink and watched the two of them playing in the water. Simple pleasures: naked, soap-slicked bodies tickled by a gentle riot of bubbles, the delight of slapped water sloshing in a tub, private tunes hummed in innocent, off-key chorus.

Memories of Ruth Messenger's assurances battled against my growing doubts. "There are no wicked children, Emily. I'm convinced of that. Rachel has had a bad start, bad circumstances, bad luck if you believe in luck. But deep down inside, there is a sweet, loving little girl. All we have to do is find her."

All we have to do is find her, I thought.

Before it's too late.

CHAPTER 15

RACHEL REFUSED TO come downstairs for dinner. According to Granny, she'd stormed back into the house while I was meeting with the chief. Without a word to anyone, she'd carted the puppy, box and all, up to her room and locked the rest of the world outside.

"Child was in a giant lather of a temper, Emily. All red in the face and mumbling under her breath, you know the way. Can't imagine what's got her in such a froth." She wiped her soggy hands on a woven dish towel and shook her head. "Anything happen you know of?"

I decided not to tell her about the switched hose. Something warned me she would manage to see the whole incident from Rachel's point of view, and I might be moved to commit some offense that would earn me unsavory headlines. "She'll get over it," I said. "Whatever it is."

She poured almost an entire bottle of cloudy Italian dressing on the salad and began tossing the greens like a crazed symphony conductor. "Seems to me the child's just looking for attention, if you don't mind my saying. Must be hard on her what with you working at the university and all, and so busy with the little ones when you finally get home you probably can't find much time to spend with the girl. Mothers today . . ." She shook her head and puffed out a breath. ". . . Expect children to raise themselves, I swear it."

"Rachel gets plenty of attention," I said. "Maybe too much." I took the pitcher of lemonade from the refrigerator, restrained myself forceably from hurling the contents at Granny, and carried it into the dining room along with a pair of plastic cups for Adam and David.

Granny followed, fussed over the napkins, and rearranged the silverware in military rows. "Now, now, Emily. Don't tell me you're one of those sensitive types who can't stand a friendly little suggestion now and again. I only meant . . ."

Lynch's arrival was timed to perfection. Granny lapsed into a strained, tight-lipped, welcome silence as soon as he walked through the front door. She gave him a killing look and went to call the boys in from the backyard for dinner.

I helped her serve. Tonight's casserole was brown. Beneath the usual camouflage, there was a clotted mass of hard-boiled noodles and chunks of greasy meat in a dilute cordovan gravy. Small, army-drab orbs and chunky, gelatinous, red masses floated in the muck, clinging to stray noodle tendrils for dear life. I took a polite serving, confident that I could tuck what I couldn't stomach under the lettuce leaves for discreet disposal later on.

Lynch's face twitched with the effort to conceal his distaste. He ladled a minuscule portion near the rim of his plate and passed the ceramic casserole toward Granny.

She eyed his spartan dish and puffed her contempt. ''Bet you didn't grow those built-in sidecars picking at your food like that, Mister Fancy Pants. You one of those bachelor types thinks a balanced diet is pretzels with your beer and olives with your martinis or what?''

''Rest assured, you need not concern yourself with my eating habits, Miss Prom. My dear mother sent me out on my own decades ago. And I have managed to muddle through.''

''Can't say as I blame the woman. If I was your mother, I'd have sent you out a darn sight sooner than that I bet. Would have been nice for you to pick up some manners along the way is all I'm saying.''

The chief's expression tensed. ''And just what is that supposed to mean, madam?''

''A person goes to all the bother to cook you a lovely meal, you could have the manners to eat it. That's what it means.''

Lynch managed a tight little nod. ''Of course, you're absolutely correct, Miss Prom. And should anyone prepare a meal such as you describe, I will be certain to demonstrate the proper appreciation.''

Granny clutched the edge of the table, rose half out of her seat. The cords in her crepey neck were throbbing to a tropical beat. ''And what's that supposed to mean, buster?''

''If you insist on pursuing this unfortunate line of discussion, I'll have no choice but to tell you. I would hardly call this a lovely meal, Miss Prom. In fact, I could characterize this meal in a wide variety of ways, and the term 'lovely' would never so much as cross my mind. Not even at a considerable distance.''

"I happen to be an excellent cook, mister. Ask anybody. Why, I'll have you know I won first prize at the eighty-two county fair with my tuna casserole."

"Four-legged judges, no doubt," Lynch said and dabbed at his lips with the edge of his napkin.

"You'd better shut that fat mouth of yours unless you'd rather I shut it for you, mister." She was flushed a deep, unhealthy crimson. "You think you can do better, be my guest." In a furious huff, she got up, collected the food-laden plates, and went to the kitchen where I heard the clatter and crash as she took her rage out on the hapless stainless steel and stoneware.

Lynch looked sheepish. "My apologies, Miss Archer. I hardly ever indulge in mouth-to-mouth combat, especially at the dinner table."

"Don't mention it, Chief. You're human. I like that in a person."

Granny bustled in, carrying a stack of small bowls and a gallon tub of fruit-studded ice cream. She scooped and distributed until everyone but Lynch had a plate. "Don't suppose you want any, Mister Critic. Don't suppose you'd lower yourself to eat anything from a cow."

"That would depend on the cow, Miss Prom," Lynch said.

Granny's ears reddened and a lick of spittle flew off her lip when she spoke. "You're asking for it, Mr. Mouth. You're gonna get it. Take my word."

Lynch took a deep, deliberate breath and wove his fingers in a tight little ball. "Please, Miss Prom. I do not see the need for any further unpleasantness this evening. Let's pretend to be adult and civil, shall we? No matter how difficult that may be for some of us?" He stood, slid his chair under the table, and said good night to each of us in turn. ''Young men. Miss Archer. Sleep well.''

Granny's words stopped him at the door. ''You rest up real good, Mister Smarty Pants. Can't wait to see what kind of a dinner you're going to put together for everyone tomorrow night. Now that'll be a stitch.'' She bent low over the table, nearly dipping her dense bosom like twin ladles in the stew, and spoke in a stage whisper. ''. . . Don't you worry, dearies. I'll bring the Tums. And the sandwiches for later so no one'll starve. We'll all have our fill of laughs, that's for sure.''

Lynch made a deep, dramatic bow. ''It will be my pleasure to prepare the evening meal tomorrow, Miss Prom. You'll have to forgive me though if I don't attempt to equal your legendary tuna triumph. My other faults aside, I am cognizant of my limits.''

She waited for the door to swing shut behind him and sniffed the air. ''Now you see? That's much better. Here I picked up this foul smell, and it was only that Mister Lynch person. He leaves, and a person can breathe again.

''. . . Guess I'll be running along then, too, dearies.'' She ruffled the boys' hair and waggled her large fingers at me. ''You be sure and tell Rachel Granny said sweet dreams, will you? Tell her there's plenty of stew left over if she gets hungry later on. It's good cold, tell her. Good night, all. Hope you have a good rest.''

I got the boys ready and tucked into bed and was on my way downstairs when I heard the flurry of squeaks and light scratches from Rachel's room. Odd pattern. A wink of calm and then a frenzied rush of motion. I knocked at her door, turned the knob when she didn't answer, and peeked inside.

She was lying on the floor on her belly, chin cupped

in an upturned palm, face blank as stone. With her other hand, she held the little puppy by a short length of rope looped around the slim, furry neck like a noose. As I watched, she tossed a piece of a soda cracker beyond the dog's reach, waited for him to scramble after it in a frantic romp, and then gave a sharp tug on the rope so he was stopped dead and nearly strangled in the process. "Stay, Max."

"Stop that, Rachel. Cut it out." I pried the rope end loose from her stubborn fingers and lifted the weightless little pup in my arms. I could feel the shiver of fear, the heart racing at a wild, impossible pace. "Look at him. Poor thing is terrified."

She took her lazy time sitting up cross-legged on the floor, arranging her pink cotton nightie in a prim circle around her knees. Satisfied with the pose, she batted her eyelashes at me as if she couldn't quite bring me into clear focus. "You shouldn't just barge into my room, Emily. I'm entitled to my privacy, you know."

"I want to know what you were doing with the puppy. If that's your idea of how to treat an animal, I'll take him back to the pet shop first thing in the morning."

"It's none of your damned business," she spat, her eyes flashing fury. "He's mine and you can't tell me what to do with him."

"Oh, yes, I can, Rachel. And I will." The little heart was still bumping wildly against the slim rack of ribs. I set the pup down in the carton and carried it out of the room.

"You bring that back, Emily. Max is mine. You have no right to touch him, damn it. Bring him back!"

Her voice climbed to a wretched squeal of frustration. As I walked downstairs, I heard the sound of her hurling things at the wall, feet stamping their outrage on the hard plank floor.

"There you go, Max." I stooped to place the box in a warm, cozy corner of the kitchen near the stove and flipped out the lights.

The phone rang as I was on my way to the stairs. I groped through the darkness to find the receiver.

". . . Em? Hi. I'm at Kennedy. I thought I'd catch you before my flight. You sound breathless. Everything okay?"

"Fine, Will."

"The kids?"

"Everyone's fine." A strident voice was barking flight announcements in the background. . . . "Announcing the departure of TransContinental golden wing service to Atlanta . . ."

"Rachel's settled in all right then?"

"Sure, no problem." No problem unless you count trying to parboil her brothers and drive the rest of us, including the dog, crazy. "She has her moods, as always. But I'll handle it, Will. I told you I would."

Deep sigh. "Whatever. Listen, I have a minute or two. Let me say hello to Rach."

"I think she's . . . asleep."

"No, I'm not."

I startled at her sudden appearance. The child had quite a knack for sneaking around, doing the unexpected. "Here she is," I said. "Have a good trip."

"Thanks, Em. Take care. You know where to reach me."

She moved like a floating shadow across the room. Her fingers slithered around the neck of the receiver and wrenched it out of my grasp. "Hi, Daddy. You're leaving now? Please, can't I come? I miss you. I can fly by myself. . . . No, it's awful, terrible. I don't know what the hell she's talking about. I hate it here. And she's being mean to me. . . . Real mean.'' Silence. ''But . . . All right. I'll try.''

She jammed the receiver down in its cradle and knelt down beside the box to stroke the puppy. ''I want Max to sleep with me. I'm taking him.''

The dark room was bristling with uneasy silence. I struggled to find the right answer, one I could trust. ''Can I count on you not to hurt him?''

''I'm not stupid, Emily.''

''No, you're definitely not stupid. But I need you to promise me.''

The voice was a cold breeze. ''I promise.''

She lifted the sleeping pup from the box. Her hand worked over the downy coat. ''You lied to Daddy,'' she said. ''You told him everything was fine here. Why didn't you tell him the truth?''

''It's between us, Rachel. There's nothing your daddy can do about our problems all the way from the city much less from London. You and I will have to work things out together.''

She was a silent statue in the inky darkness, trying to figure me out. ''We'll see,'' she said finally, turned and left the room.

''Yes, we'll see,'' I echoed in the prickly aftermath of her leaving. ''I'm afraid we will.''

I checked the doors, went upstairs, and listened for a minute at her room. No signs of mayhem.

I flopped on my bed, enjoying the cool tickle of the soft pillowcase at the back of my neck. A glorious flood of warm weariness filled my bones. Maybe I'd actually be able to get some sleep for a change.

I picked up one of the novels on the fall syllabus for

my Freshman Humanities seminar and started rereading it as I'd promised myself I'd do over the summer. *Madame Bovary.* Poor woman. A hundred and thirty years old and she keeps making the same fatal errors.

My eyes refused to work in concert. The words danced on the page and ran together in a senseless jumble. I set the book on the vacant half of the bed and let the anvil weights of exhaustion push my eyelids closed.

I sank in a dense, dreamless fog of oblivion, crawled deep in a padded unconsciousness where I could hide for a healing while. Get lost for a few wonderful hours. Dream in technicolor fluff. Lovely.

And then I heard the scream.

CHAPTER 16

THE FIERCE URGENCY of it shocked me awake, starting a sick, horrid pounding in my chest. I followed the piercing shrill to Rachel's room and raced inside.

She was sitting bolt upright in bed, eyes bulging in horror, shrieking in breathless bursts of hysteria. Her voice was flickering hoarse, dying with abuse.

"Rachel, what is it?"

I sat beside her and took her in my arms. She was shaking with terror. I felt the tremors race through her skinny little body like a flock of startled birds. "Ssh, Rach. What is it? What happened?"

She was still screaming, pointing at the window. I followed her shock-vacant gaze out to the starless, charcoal night.

"Ssh. Tell me, Rachel. What happened? Did you have a nightmare?"

Her voice was dying. Dead. Still, she kept opening her mouth beyond human limits, straining with a force that twisted her face in a grotesque mask of horror.

Nothing came but a harsh rasping sound like air rushing from a flat tire.

"Stop it, Rachel. I'm here now, sweetie. Tell me." I turned her toward me, pressing her in a hug. For once, she didn't stiffen or pull away. She was a foreign object in my arms. Strange and uneasy.

Her nose and chin were pressed into my shoulder. I held her in a firm grip, trying to still the tremors. The voiceless screams were growing fainter, fading away. Her tears were a warm, spreading stain on my shoulder.

The pulsing stilled at last. I pulled back and looked into her swollen, red-rimmed eyes. "What happened, Rach? What is it?"

She wrenched herself out of my grip, then ran her slender fingers over her arms to wipe away the traces of my touch. Her breaths still came in short, shallow stabs. Her voice was a shadow. "You . . . don't care. Why should I . . . tell you?"

"Please, Rachel. I do care. You know I do."

She stared at me, turned, and blew her nose with a loud, theatrical flourish. When she met my gaze again, her stony composure was back in place. "It was the monster again. The same one who tried to get me in the car that day. But you don't believe me, anyway, so just forget it."

"Where did you see him?"

"There." She pointed to the center of the empty night sky. "Out there."

"Let me check, then," I said and walked to the window, raised it full open, tugged up the swollen wood frame of the screen and leaned my head out to look around.

A cool fluff of mist weighted the air and settled in a dull film over the waning vanilla moon. The field was illuminated by a pale wash of light from Lynch's cottage in the distance. Working so late? Then I remembered his talk of a pair of useless days, the kind that beg redemption.

"I don't see a thing, Rachel," I said. "Maybe it was a bad dream. A dream can seem so real, so terrifying. I have plenty of those myself."

"It was no goddamned dream, Emily. He was staring in at me, watching. He was trying to get in here and kill me. I know he was."

I closed the screen and sat at the end of her bed. "Think about it, Rach. How could that be? There's no way for anyone to get up here without a ladder. And there's no ladder. You can look out and see for yourself. You were dreaming, sweetie. That's all."

She slipped under her covers and curled in a tight, fetal ball. "I'm tired. I want to go to sleep now."

"That's a girl. You get a good night's sleep and everything will look better in the morning." I tucked the covers around her and set a light kiss on her moist forehead. Her breathing was deep and regular. Thinking she was already asleep, I tiptoed toward the hall.

"He's going to kill me, Emily," she said. The voice was dead clear and matter-of-fact. "He may even kill us all if we don't find a way to get him first."

"No one's going to hurt any of us. Please, try to put all that out of your mind and get some sleep."

Her words followed me as I stepped into the hall and pulled her door shut. "It's all right, Emily. You don't have to believe me. If I have to, I'll take care of him myself." So offhanded, she could have been commenting on the weather. "I'll kill the damned monster myself. There are plenty of ways to kill a damned monster."

CHAPTER 17

TOWN HALL WAS located at the foot of South Avenue opposite the Ashby town park. I felt a hard tug of nostalgia viewing the ornate iron gate at the park entrance and imagining the steep, winding road beyond it that led past the playground and picnic area, the softball field and tennis courts, ending finally in a precipitous dip to the edge of the park lake where Ashby families gathered to spend their hard-earned leisure.

I plunked a quarter in the parking meter at the curb and crossed to the long, brick, Federal-style building from which the town conducted its municipal affairs. The entrance was flanked by delicate iron railings and capped by a spotless glazed fanlight above a broad pair of polished mahogany doors.

Inside, public notices were tacked to a corkboard in what had been a gracious drawing room. The high plaster ceiling was adorned with flowing raised garlands, sheafs of wheat, and replica Grecian urns in a circular motif. A carved marble fireplace now served as storage for years of back issues of the Ashby annual budget. I followed a small sign and an arrow on the far wall that pointed to the hall of records.

My steps were cushioned by a worn, peach-toned Oriental runner as I strode the length of a long, gloomy corridor. The gray-blue walls were hung with pencil renderings of two-hundred years of Ashby mayors: somber, bespectacled men who shared a common pinched expression as if they'd been forced into undersized, overstarched shirts. At intervals were oval and octagonal rooms in an assortment of chalky pastels. Once used to house visiting dignitaries, they were now occupied by eager Ashby bureaucrats hunched over outsized, drab-gray metal desks burdened with the fine print and endless technicalities of Ashby existence.

The record room was a converted galley kitchen at the end of the hall, dim and musty. The glass-fronted, burled maple cabinets were jammed with upright racks of tabbed manila folders. Additional lines of folders were set in rectangular metal frames on a series of converted harvest tables. I took my place on line behind a young couple with infant twins and a square-jawed, toothy woman who held her oversized briefcase like a battle shield.

The clerk was an aging adolescent with a taffy-pulled body and a face unburdened by personality or intelligence. His pimpled cheeks were adorned with random coarse sprigs of whiskers like onion grass. He had mastered the local two-step and poked through the stacks of folders in a motionless motion that defied several of Newton's fundamental laws.

"Gotta be under K," said the twins' father as he bobbled one fat, pink child in his hands like he was shaking a cocktail. "Kelso. With a K," he said.

"Could be an H," the mother said. "You could try

looking under Helso. We've had that happen before, Ethan. Remember that time in the drugstore?''

''Shut up, Reneé. The boy's having enough trouble already. Don't confuse him.''

The woman with the briefcase bubbled her stringy lips and sputtered. ''Would you hurry up, young man? I haven't got all day.''

The clerk lifted his bristly face and blinked. ''Be with you in a minute, lady,'' he said. ''You got an emergency, go to the hospital, why don't you? Emergency's right out back.''

''I'm going to report you. I swear it. I'm going to march right into the mayor's office and report you.''

The boy's grin was a crooked mass of cracked teeth. ''You do that, ma'am. And you tell Daddy his boy Richard said 'hi.' ''

He found the Kelso file at last, fanned himself with the folder, and printed out the next woman's request in a square, clumsy hand. ''You want a copy of your marriage license, ma'am? So someone married you then?''

''Hurry up, now,'' the woman barked. ''This is getting ridiculous.''

''You want jet service, try the airport,'' the boy said and ran his fingers along a row of tabs raising a sound like cards shuffling.

The woman sucked at her teeth, making loud sighing noises. ''Well, I never . . . Can't get anything done around this one-horse town, I swear it.''

The boy came back and shot a paper across the desk at her. ''There you are, ma'am,'' he said with a gloating grin. ''Express service. Just like the railroad.''

''Express my foot.'' She turned and barreled out of the room, clipping my leg with the loaded briefcase as she went.

The clerk turned to me and spread his lips like a fan. ''Richard Whitecomb Collier at your service, ma'am. Hatches, matches, and dispatches.''

''Hatches?''

''Births, ma'am. Hatches, matches, and dispatches. Births, weddings, and deaths. Covers most everything when you come right down to it.'' He tipped his head toward me. A shock of stick-straight, mud-brown hair flopped over a dull chartreuse eye. ''I'm just working here for the summer, but I could see hiring on full time after I graduate from the high. Never dull around this place. That's for sure.''

''That's nice.'' I made an involuntary step backward. His breath was a sorry blend of salami, chocolate, and nerves. ''I'm looking for a death certificate in the name of Rebecca Fowler.''

''Ef, oh, double-you, el, ee, are. That right?'' He turned the sheet of paper toward me to check.

''Yes. Fowler. Rebecca spelled the usual way.''

He frowned, clamping his lower lip in a chipped vise of faded teeth. ''Are, ee, bee, ee, see, ay, aych?''

''No,'' I said. ''Two Cs and an A.''

He crossed out, erased, copied the whole thing over on a fresh sheet, and held it out for my inspection.

''Right. Rebecca Fowler. A death certificate.''

He nodded. ''I'll go check the dispatches,'' he said and disappeared in the back rows of files.

For once, the local slow motion was fine with me. I was in no hurry to see the hard evidence of my mother's sudden death. The thought of the whole, horrid incident still had the power to turn my mouth to blotting paper and my bones to gelatin, even wrapped in so many years of distance.

One day, I was a normal child, living a normal child's

life with all the accessories: home, school, friends, hurts, wishes, frustrations, and fears.

Blink, and I was torn away, hurried off on a sudden, extended, frenetic trip with Aunt Lizzie. Blink again, and I was enrolled at an exclusive, secluded girls' school in upstate Connecticut where life was laid out in a fat, printed handbook detailing a world of stringent rules: manners, elocution, homework, dress. Thou shalt not chew gum, utter profanities, look at two-legged males, call thy home without prior permission from the headmistress.

No problem for me. There was no home to call. All I left behind was a familiar landscape gone suddenly dark and hostile.

I had passed through an empty, echoing tunnel to this alien other side. My mother was dead. My father was transformed into a dead-centered, unrecognizable eggshell of a person who suddenly wanted no part of me. Pushed me away. Scared me to death.

Aunt Lizzie called when she could; came to see me at school for brief, uneasy visits; brought me back to Thornwood for an occasional, well-orchestrated weekend. She tried to explain, to lay it out in simple, easy terms. ''Your mother died of pneumonia, Emmy. Terrible, sudden thing. And your father couldn't take it. Poor man fell to pieces. Happens that way sometimes. I know it's hard to take, but you're going to be fine. You're a strong little girl, after all.''

Strong enough, it seemed. I made peace with the rules, the change, the permanent empty place in my gut. But I always pined for the missing pieces. The lost, familiar, comfortable spots in my life were an ache, a phantom limb.

Try as I did, I couldn't persuade Aunt Lizzie to fill in

the blanks. She had taken me away so my father could rest in total peace and quiet, she said. No, there was no mystery, nothing in particular we were running from. Nothing at all had happened but a tragic illness. I would simply have to accept things as they had come to be: my father's normal self slipping out from under me as if I'd hit a sudden deadly slick of ice.

Did I really want to know the rest after all these years of working to make peace with Lizzie's reassuring, uncomplicated, unconvincing version of the truth?

"Sorry, ma'am. Got no Rebecca Fowler in the death records. Checked under the ayches, too, in case."

I felt a mix of relief and annoyance. "It has to be here. She died in Ashby. It was . . . about twenty-five years ago."

He cleared his throat, diverted his eyes, and began fussing over a row of tabbed folders. "Sorry. 'Fraid I can't help you, after all. We got no death records before 'Sixty-five. . . . There was a fire in the old town hall that year. Burned up all the dead folk for a hundred years and more."

"You mean, there's no way to check on all those deaths?"

" 'Fraid not. Fire destroyed all the records. Now we keep backup files, microfilm, all that. But back then they only had the originals. . . ."

A slender, pinch-faced girl had come up behind me. "I don't mean to butt in or anything, but you could try over at the *Gazette*. I'm working there as a summer intern. It's not the *Times* or anything, but they do keep records. And the paper's been around forever."

"Thanks," I said. "Good idea."

The records clerk shook his head and shot a stream

of sour salami breath. "Doubt you're going to get anywhere at the paper," he said. "Tru Cunningham's in charge of the record-keeping, and he's one of those that's too heavy for light work and too light for heavy work."

"Well, it's worth a try," the girl said.

"Up to you," said the clerk. "But you're not gonna get anywhere with Tru Cunningham. Waste of time if you ask me."

A chill whip of rain was starting to fall. I fed another quarter into the parking meter and ran across South Avenue and up the three blocks to Larkin where the *Ashby Gazette* staff labored in a converted lumber mill.

I stepped into a frenzy of activity in the barnlike newsroom. The work was tuned to the deafening mechanical drone of the antique press operating in the rear. I was ignored by a row of disheveled reporters in adjoining pressboard cubicles thunking their stories into print on a collection of ancient, infirm typewriters.

"Shit," one said as I passed. "How'm I supposed to write the stupid piece without the stupid space bar?"

"What's it to you, Herlihy? You're not getting paid by the word."

Several times, I tried to call over the racket but got no further than a quick, smoky stare of disgust from one of the typesetters. Giving up, I went from desk to desk and then station to station, checking the nameplate and identification badges for Tru Cunningham. He was nowhere to be found.

I reverted to my useless shouting, trying to get a response from one of the line of fierce worker bees toiling in a frenzied swarm over the week's issue. "Where's Tru Cunningham? . . . I'm looking for Tru Cunning . . ."

The cavernous plant went dead silent. I cupped my ear, thinking I'd gone deaf. There was a relieved whoosh of breath from one of the layout crew.

"That's a wrap," came a bouncy little voice. "Good work, everybody. Let her roll, Harry. Last section on its way."

The press started cranking up again with a discouraging squeal followed by a rhythmic rush of gears. The woman behind the bouncy voice came over to me, pointed an accusing finger at my blouse, and shouted above the din. "You don't have a badge."

I knew that. "I'm looking for Tru Cunningham. I have to ask him something. It's about a death record from twenty-five years ago."

"Oh," she mouthed. "I guess it's all right then. Tru's down in the tombs." She pointed to a rickety flight of wooden stairs at the end of the floor.

I followed them down to a concrete-walled, dingy cell of a basement lined with factory-gray metal shelving bearing countless cardboard boxes of photographs and files. A solitary, grizzled old man sat on a folding chair pitched back against a shelf pole so I could see the sizable holes in the bottoms of his black oxford shoes. One was shaped like New Jersey and revealed a long span of dull brown argyle sock. He was reading a vintage "Archie" comic. I cleared my throat to draw his attention.

"Yeah?" he said without raising his eyes. "What?"

I told him why I'd come, tried to flatter him with a reference to how indispensable he must feel, being in charge of all these important records.

He squinted at me. His eyes were the color of cigar ash, skin a crumpled cigar-wrapper tan. "Whaddya want, miss? Speak right up, will you?"

"I need information about a death. Rebecca Fowler's death, in the early sixties."

He snapped his fingers. "Oh, sure. Simple. I'll just run over and pick it right out for you. Only have about a million papers to look through. Only take me about a year or so. Maybe two years. Hope you're not in a big hurry."

A fresh weight of helplessness settled in my gut. "But there must be some way, Mr. Cunningham. I need to confirm the circumstances of her death, my mother's death, that is. It's very important."

He let the chair clunk down on the cold concrete slab floor, then stood with a soft groan and a crackle of discontented joints. "All's I can do is give it a try, miss. You leave your number, I'll call if I find anything. There's a log book down near the stairs. Put down the particulars, I'll see what I can do."

I entered the details of my inquiry in the moldy log book. There was a long row of requests before mine. Nothing at all had been entered in the column marked "disposition." I climbed back into the noisy pressroom and made my discouraged way out through the tight line of desks and tables to the dismal afternoon.

The sprinkle had accelerated to a driving downpour. As I raced on the gentle downslope toward the car, I felt the cold slick of rain work through the thin cotton of my blouse, penetrate through to my sorry bones. My hair was a soggy mass of mop strings beating against my neck.

I ran across the street to the car, folded myself inside, and listened to my breaths roaring in the cryptlike silence. The rain played in soothing rhythm over the windshield. A shiver of a chill ran through me as I started the engine and was treated to a rude blast of icy air conditioning.

This was the way it had happened. Records or no records, I knew how she'd died. Aunt Lizzie had told me the story a hundred times. My mother liked to keep fresh flowers on the dining table, she told me. So every few days she'd go off to gather the wild blossoms that thrived along the sunny perimeter of the colony and down the adjacent dirt road. A peaceful, innocent routine.

But this particular day, a violent, unpredicted storm caught her half a mile away from the warm shelter of the nearest cottage. She raced to get out of the rain and caught her heel in a gopher hole.

It was hours before anyone noticed her missing, went out looking, and found her lying unconscious, soaked to the skin and chilled a bloodless blue.

She came down with pneumonia. The medicines weren't what they are now, Lizzie always said at that point in the story. Then she'd shake her head as if to dislodge the awful images and fill her chest with a greedy tank of air.

I shivered. Even now, thinking of my mother lying helpless in that vicious, unrelenting storm, catching her literal death, I felt a thrill of fear. I was the only little girl at Miss Adam's Country School willing, make that eager, to wear rubber boots and carry an umbrella on rainy days. Even now, so many years later, I had an odd prescient sense of doom when the weather caught me unprepared. We were so vulnerable, at the mercy of so many evil, unpredictable forces.

Stop, Emily. Cowering in the shadows was no way for a grown, intelligent woman to behave. I flipped off the air conditioning; turned the radio to light, lilting jazz; and drove off toward the colony.

CHAPTER 18

THE KITCHEN WAS not large enough to contain Lynch, Granny, and the giant force of their mutual antipathy. There was a charge of angry current in the air, hot enough to singe an innocent bystander. I changed into dry clothes and went downstairs to referee.

Adam and David were playing with their matchbox cars in the corner near the back stairs. Rachel, I was told between the volley of grunts and snide remarks, was off gathering the wild strawberries that grew beside the pond. She'd taken Max along with her.

"Child has a wonderful sense of responsibility," Granny told me. "Been taking the little pup out every hour on the hour, trying to get him trained. Most children her age wouldn't be bothered."

"That's nice to hear," I said and found myself wondering, with a flicker of shame, what nasty mischief she might be up to now. Responsibility had never been Rachel's strong suit.

"It sure is nice, dearie. There's plenty of people go around taking on jobs they got no right to take on. You know how that can be.'' She cast a tight, sidelong glance at Lynch who was chopping vegetables with a cleaver to stir fry. ''Like when a person claims he knows how to cook when all he really knows is how to make a god-awful mess out of someone else's kitchen, and then he probably expects someone else to clean it up. Which she will not, under any circumstances. Looks like who-did-it-and-ran around here, I swear it.''

Lynch chopped harder. His ear twitched. ''If, despite your incessant critiques and interruptions, I am able to complete these preparations, it will be a miracle, madam.''

''You make a meal anyone but goats could stomach, it'll be a miracle all right.''

A little smirk played over Lynch's lips. ''Whatever you say, Miss Prom. No one would question your knowledge of the feeding preferences of your fellow barnyard creatures, to be sure.''

She menaced him with a soup ladle. ''You mind that mouth if you don't want it to lead you into a world of trouble, mister.''

Lynch rechecked his preliminary preparations. Thin, uniform strips of chicken breast were soaking in a soy-based marinade. There were precise matchsticks of zucchini and carrots, neat florets of cauliflower and broccoli, dried black mushrooms rehydrating in a small glass bowl, cellophane noodles.

''Looks wonderful,'' I said.

Granny sniffed. ''Each to his own, I suppose. I happen to prefer food when it doesn't look like someone's already chewed on it and spit it out.''

Lynch rinsed his hands in the sink, wiped them on a length of paper towel, and hung his barbecue apron on a hook in back of the broom closet. ''If you've a moment, Miss Archer, there was something I wanted to discuss with you.''

I could see it in his eyes. He had news. And it wasn't good.

''Of course, Chief.'' I tried not to let the worry register in my voice. ''Will you guys promise to be good for a few minutes while I take a walk with Chief Lynch?''

''Rrrrroar . . .'' Adam said and ran a tiny checkered racer along the floor. ''Vooom.''

''We'll be right back, Granny. In a few minutes.''

She scowled at the regimental row of bowls and plates beside the stove. ''That's it, Mister Know-It-All? That's your idea of getting a meal fixed?''

''Please, Miss Prom. I can assure you everything will be complete and ready to be served in exactly one hour.''

''And ready to be tossed in the trash fifteen minutes after that, I'll bet you.'' She chuckled and stuck her head into the refrigerator. A soft halo of cool mist settled around her cherry-blond curly wig. ''Not to worry, dearies. Granny fixed a nice tuna salad for later on.''

The air was heavy with spent rain, the ground freckled with mud slicks and murky puddles. Silver spikes of clear sky had worked their tentative way into the dense masses of smoky clouds. From the road came the jarring squeal of brakes and the angry, clashing voices of a pair of warring drivers.

I walked beside Lynch, impressed by the force of his stride, the quiet dignity in his bearing. ''You found out where the money went?''

''I did and I didn't, Miss Archer. That's the problem.''

''I'm afraid I'm not very good at riddles, Chief.''

He smiled. "My apologies. I didn't mean to sound mysterious. I found out where your father spent the money. But . . ." His feet smacked like lips in the leafy undergrowth as we walked toward the pond. He took me by the elbow to warn me past a large, camouflaged puddle.

"But?"

"But I couldn't find out more about the organization he so generously supported. It's called the Edmund Foundation. Your father wrote a series of checks to this group in precisely the amounts withdrawn over the last several years from his trust accounts for the colony. The total amounts to almost ten million dollars."

I sidestepped a wriggling mass of earthworms, and came down in a sodden patch of rain-soaked earth that glued my foot momentarily in place. "The Edmund Foundation? I never heard of it."

"Nor have I, Miss Archer. Unfortunately, neither has the editor of the *Directory of Associations* or the Attorney General's office or the Internal Revenue Service or any of the other various agencies I contacted. If this particular group is a legitimate charity, they have kept an astonishingly low profile."

"You think my father was swindled then? But how? How could a phony charity convince him to give so much?"

"I'm not in a position to speculate on either of those questions, Miss Archer. With your permission, I intend to dig further over the next several days. Any organization with assets in the millions of dollars has to be recorded somewhere, legitimate or not. There must be bank accounts, employees on the payroll, holdings."

"Of course, go ahead and see what you can find out. I hope you have more luck than I did." I told him about my visit to Town Hall and the *Gazette* building. ‘‘I don’t think there’s much hope of getting any information there,’’ I said. ‘‘Tru Cunningham, the man in charge of the paper’s records department, is not the type to knock himself out looking for an ancient obituary. He’s too busy reading comic books on the job.’’

Lynch nodded. I spotted a twinkle of mischief in his eye. ‘‘Not to worry, Miss Archer. Something tells me Mr. Cunningham might be persuaded to extend himself. I’ll pay the gentleman a visit tomorrow, if you don’t object.’’

‘‘No, that’s fine, but I am worried about your spending all this time helping me, Chief. You’re here to work on your book.’’

He edged me away from another hidden puddle. ‘‘The book is nearly written, Miss Archer. I’m in no particular rush to be done with it.’’

‘‘But that’s why you’re here.’’

‘‘That’s one of the reasons. Yes,’’ he said and gazed off in the distance, lost for a time in some personal reflection.

‘‘Why else did you come?’’ I said finally, trying to prod him loose. The man would open up a tantalizing crack only to swing shut like a door in a wind. ‘‘Why is Thornwood so important to you?’’

He peered at his watch and pressed his lips together. ‘‘. . . We’d best return to the house, Miss Archer. I have the rest of my cooking to do.’’

In silence, we retraced our steps through the thickening dusk, staring at the ground to avoid the slimy puddles. I was so intent on each footstep that I didn’t hear her approaching. She came charging at us in a mad rush and plowed into me, breathless and pulsing with hysteria.

"Rachel. Take it easy."

She struggled wildly in my grip. The pup was curled under one slender arm like a rolled newspaper. Poor thing struggled and squirmed as she did, kicking his tiny paws at the empty air.

"Stop," I said. "You can't hold Max that way, Rach. You're going to hurt him."

Her eyes were wild. She was breathing in short, desperate gasps. "Let . . . go . . . of me."

"What happened, Rachel? Don't tell me you saw your monster again?"

She whirled her free arm, caught me off guard, and smashed me hard across the nose. I reeled backward, punched by a hot fist of pain, and tasted the sweet, metallic rush of blood at the back of my throat.

Lynch placed a firm, restraining hand on her wrist. "Take a deep breath now, young lady. Calm down. Are you all right, Miss Archer?"

"I'm fine. What is it, Rachel? What happened?"

An odd mix of fear and fury warped her face. "Why the hell should I tell you anything, Emily? You don't believe me no matter what the hell I say."

I felt a trickle of blood over my lip and wiped it away with the back of my hand. "Why don't you tell Chief Lynch about it, then? He's an expert detective. If there really is a monster, the chief might be able to help us track him down, get him locked away where he can't upset you anymore."

She rocked the puppy in her arms, staring at the ground. "He won't believe me, either."

Lynch's tone was a gentle salve. "Perhaps I'll surprise you, young lady. In my line of work, I've come across quite a number of despicable characters, to be sure. All sorts of monsters. Tell me about yours, won't you?"

In a toneless drone, she described the monster as she had to me: bumps all over, crazy eyes, fat pendulous lips. She lowered her voice to an ominous grunt and imitated the sounds he made. Her monster didn't speak, she explained. But a person could tell he was determined to kill her, hack her body in bloody little pieces and deposit them in trash cans all over town. He managed to get that across without words.

Lynch touched a thoughtful finger to his lips. Looked properly grim. "How old would you say this monster might be, Rachel?"

"Hard to tell," she said. "Medium, I'd guess."

"Hmmm," he said. "And of medium height, would you say?"

"Shorter than Daddy. About like you I guess, but a lot fatter. He has all this disgusting fat hanging off him, even on his neck."

Lynch took out his pocket notebook and made a couple of brief entries. "Any other distinguishing marks? Tattoos? Moles? Scars? That sort of thing."

Rachel's face tightened with concentration. "Just all these disgusting bumps," she said finally and looked up to meet Lynch's kind brown eyes. ". . . He's fat and he wears this plaid shirt and baggy old jeans. It says Coca-Cola on his belt buckle and he has on blue high-top sneakers. Do you think you can find him? Make him stop following me around? Please. He's so creepy."

"I'll do my best, young lady. And your mother will help me. Won't you, Miss Archer?"

"Yes," I said. "Of course, I'll help."

Rachel linked her free hand through Lynch's cocked elbow and managed a near smile. "I know you're going to find him, Chief Lynch. You're going to find him and shoot his goddamned brains out.''

The meal was perfection: stir-fried chicken, sautéed vegetables and a garnish of light, lovely sauce arranged in an artful spiral on each plate beside a tidy mound of mouth-melting wild rice with almonds. Lynch had done a masterful job with the table as well, fan-folded the linen napkins and set a row of spotless crystal goblets before the adult plates. For the children, he'd squeezed an ambrosia of fresh tropical fruit juices into a series of little glasses topped with orange slices and sprigs of fresh mint. Adam was duly impressed.

''So fancy, Mommy. It's like a restaurant for your birfday.''

Granny took a grudging bite and made a sour face. ''These vegetables are near alive, I swear it. You bother to cook them at all or just held them over the water and said a little prayer?''

Lynch seemed not to hear her.

She prodded a morsel of meat with her fork tines. ''Sad to think some poor chicken gave up its life and has nothing more than scraps and strings to show for it. Must've wasted mostly the whole bird, and here half the world's starving.''

''Miss Archer? May I offer you more rice?'' Lynch asked and held forth a delicate china bowl.

''Thanks.'' The children accepted second helpings, too. Granny was satiated for the time being, filled to the brow with her own jealous bile.

''You call that rice? Looks like warmed-up playground dirt if you ask me. What're all those little black things look like ants crawling on the plate?''

Lynch's look was benign. ''Miss Prom. I am most

distressed if I haven't pleased you, to be sure. Do feel free to excuse yourself at any time if you find the meal unsuitable. I'm certain no one would be offended by your absence.''

She puffed her lips, rolling her eyes at him. ''As if I'd need your permission to come or go or do anything else that strikes me, Mister Big Shot. Suppose I'll just force down enough to get by on. Waste not, want not, I always say.'' She hefted a heaping spoonful of rice onto her plate and began shoveling giant mounds of food into her expectant mouth as if she were stoking a coal furnace.

Lynch bit back his amusement. ''A noble sentiment to be sure, Miss Prom. Waste not, want not. You certainly do have a way with a phrase.'' He turned to me. ''Which reminds me of one of my more interesting cases, Miss Archer. . . . There was a team of gifted debaters from the local university. Each time they went out of town for a competition, one of them would meet with tragic misfortune. . . .''

''Don't need anyone telling those kind of stories at the dinner table, mister. Ruins a person's appetite.''

Lynch bowed with his head. ''My apologies, Miss Prom. Your delicate appetite must certainly be protected at all costs.''

Rachel was eating with more enthusiasm than I could remember. She seemed almost content, a rare, incredible state for Rachel. I wanted to thank the chief for listening to her with such wise empathy. When he was ready to leave, I followed him out onto the front porch.

''I wish I had your way with her, Chief. I dug in and refused to listen when she gave me that nonsense about a bloodthirsty monster. Your approach is so much better. Humor her until she gives it up on her own.''

He shook his head. ''You misunderstand, Miss Archer. I'm not humoring the child in the least. If there's one thing I learned during my years on the force, it's never to think you know anything unless you know it as a certainty. I truly want to explore this monster business. At least, until I'm satisfied it's without merit.''

I searched his face for traces of irony. None. ''You're serious? You believe there really might be a monster? You don't know Rachel, Chief. She makes up stories. And she has a wild imagination.''

''All that aside. Suppose in this particular instance she's telling the truth. Over the years, I have come across so-called monsters of every form and variety, Miss Archer. And I've observed the tragic damage they can do. Why take chances?'' The question hung in the air as he tipped his hat and set off down the stairs and across the broad meadow toward his cottage.

The night was dead still, colored in subtle shades of deep gray flannel. Cast in silhouette, the cedar copse was a huddled mass of giant demons. I folded my arms in vain defense against a sudden chill.

What if she were telling the truth?

CHAPTER 19

". . . SO TELL ME all about it. Don't leave out a thing."

"Who's this?" I said.

"It's Penny Satenstein, Emily. You went to see Link, right? You were supposed to call me, naughty girl. What happened? I want you to tell me everything. Absolutely everything."

I could almost smell the cloying floral of her cologne through the plastic receiver. "There's not much to tell. I asked him why he objected to your group taking over the colony, and he refused to tell me. Then I left."

"Oh, now," she said in a coquettish little voice. "That's not everything, is it? What did you think about him? Gorgeous, huh?"

"If you want the truth, he's not my type. I prefer the kind of men raised in captivity."

Her laugh was light and good-natured. "Matter of fact, he was raised right here in Ashby, and that's about as captive as it gets. But it's just fine if you didn't take to him, darling. His fan club meetings are already packed to the rafters. And it's hard to find enough bibs to catch all the drool.''

''Can't you please help me, Penny? Tell me what he has against my father?''

Long, difficult pause. She cleared her throat. There was a jangle of jewelry as she fiddled on her end. ''. . . I can't, Emily. I'd like to, but I just can't. I promised.''

''Who did you promise?''

''I can't say that, either. I'm sorry. It's a long, long story.''

Sigh. ''I am so sick of boxing shadows. How am I supposed to deal with all this hush-hush nonsense? Don't you understand, Penny? My father's life work is at stake here. What if you were in my position? Please help me, please.''

''. . . I'll think on it, Emily. That's the best I can do.''

I hung up. Everywhere I turned, doors were slamming in my face.

Sesame Street was over. David shuffled into the kitchen and plunked his head in my lap. He felt like a hyperactive radiator. I picked him up and pressed my lips against his downy forehead. Burning.

''What's wrong? Does something hurt you, Monkey?''

''Daybit tushy hurts.''

''Pain in the tushy disease,'' I said. ''I think that's going around.'' I looked him over. He was flushed, swollen, fuzzy-faced. His eyes dewy and out of sync. I gave him some liquid Tylenol, his favorite stuffed monkey to hug, and tucked him in on the couch. ''There, you and Bruce take a nice rest, and you'll feel much better.''

Adam watched the whole procedure. When David was half asleep, he climbed up at the opposite end of the couch, gave me a sultry, heavy-lidded look, and informed me he was sick, as well. Which he was.

The joys of motherhood.

Granny arrived soon afterward, surveyed the situation, and offered to take Rachel into town for the afternoon. While Rachel was upstairs changing, she fixed the boys some spiced hot lemonade and clucked over them while they slurped and complained.

"There now, isn't that better already? Granny's own little boy always liked a nice, hot lemonade when he was ailing. Fixed him right up."

"I didn't know you had children," I said and realized she talked about little in her past except her literal brushes and puffs with stardom.

"Oh, he's all grown now, busy with his own life, you know the way. But it's nice remembering. Nothing like a little one."

"I suppose."

She primped in front of the hall mirror, stroked her coal-gray pleated skirt, straightened the tie on her pink striped blouse, and tucked an escaped nylon strand back in her pink-ribboned black ponytail. "You boys drink the rest of that down, now. It'll raise a nice sweat, you'll see. Break the fever. Works every time." She crossed to the couch and patted the taut mounds their bodies made under the afghans. "You two'll be like new in no time. Take my word."

Rachel came downstairs wearing a crisp, white cotton dress with a red belt and strappy red sandals. Her hair was slicked back in a headband, her face flushed with anticipation. She'd snuck a trace of red lip gloss and trailed a wavy line of blue pencil across her eyelids.

Beautiful, impossible beast.

"Well, now," Granny said, sucking in a breath, "you

look pretty enough to set right on top of a wedding cake, I swear it. Why, with you looking so special, we'll have to go to a real special place, now won't we? Maybe over to that fancy hotel in Pittsfield.''

Rachel beamed. ''Anywhere's fine, Granny. Wherever you want to go.''

''Now aren't you the dearest, sweetest thing? Child doesn't have a greedy bone in her body, now does she?''

By the time Granny's car chugged out toward the road, the boys were fast asleep on the couch, chests working in light effortless rhythm, the promised healing perspiration already coursing down their flushed cheeks. I went into the kitchen to put the finishing touches on the paint job.

Despite the temporary setback from my overzealous little crew, the place was coming along. The fresh coat of white latex had brightened the room from dismal to almost promising. Nothing but a few missed spots to touch up and I could move on to the den. At least I was making some progress. Somewhere.

I dabbed, streaked, and checked the walls from several angles to make sure I hadn't missed anything. Satisfied, I rinsed the brush under the kitchen faucet. Thing took forever to clean. Traces of paint kept rising to the sable surface and running off down the drain. Endless. The water hissed and burbled as air bubbles belched from the antique pipes. Noisy racket.

So noisy I didn't hear him come in, didn't have any idea he was standing there watching me until I turned around.

''What are you doing here?'' My voice was full of static.

''Watching you clean up after yourself. You always clean up after yourself like a good girl, Emmy Lee?''

There was a dangerous glimmer in his eye. Too knowing. ''You have a lot of nerve busting in here like that, Mr. Marshall. You might have knocked.''

''I might have.'' He was wearing the same low-slung, worn jeans. Gone formal today, I noticed, with a torn T-shirt and clay-coated sneakers.

''What do you want?'' I dried my trembling hands. Put the brush away. ''I'm busy.''

''Right, lady,'' he said and smirked. ''I should've called your secretary for an appointment. So sorry, but I'm not used to dealing with busy, important people such as yourself. Professor Emmy Lee, isn't it? I know all about you. Endowed chair at an Ivy League university. Got tenure and the whole bit. Big deal articles in literary magazines.'' He made a low whistle. ''I'm impressed.''

''I asked why you came, Mr. Marshall. If you're just here to play more of your little games, count me out. I'm not interested.'' I turned my back on him. Wiped out the sink in angry little circles.

I felt his hand on my shoulder, a gentle tug so I'd turn in his direction, stare into those impossible eyes. I pulled away.

''No games,'' he said. ''I came to apologize.''

''Really? Do tell. Somehow, I didn't think humility was your style.''

He stared at me until I felt like something crawling under a microscope. Shook his head and scratched behind an ear. ''You don't let up, do you? Guess I shouldn't expect any different. You always were stubborn as a rock.''

I tried to clear the fog from my memory. ''Where do I know you from? I can't put it together.''

A self-satisfied grin spread across his face. ''You really don't remember, do you, Emmy? But that's because you don't want to. You don't want to go way back there. Maybe I wouldn't either, if I had the choice. . . . But I shouldn't have played with you like I did yesterday. It was nasty."

"You're still playing with me. Tell me what you have against my father. Tell me who the hell you are." The fury edged into my voice and took over. The walls of my control were crumbling away.

"Ssh, Emmy Lee. Relax. Think about it. It'll come. You'll figure it out." He stepped closer, pulled me toward him, and pressed his parted lips against mine. His mouth was warm velvet, scentless as a breeze. The tip of his tongue edged between my teeth like a snake. His hands played in long, dreamy tickles along my sides, stroked the sensitive side of my breast.

"Let go of me." I staggered back as if I'd been pushed. A wave of dizzy confusion took me over. "Get out of here. Now!"

He saluted, smiled with his eyes. "I'm going, lady. I'm gone. I have to admit it's fun playing with you, always was."

Still shaky, I clutched the edge of the sink and listened to the sounds of his arrogant swagger retreating toward the front door and across the porch. I should have murdered him. I should have reduced him to his component parts: guts and slime. Maybe there was some way to refer him to Rachel's monster for appropriate action.

My mind reeled with the effort to place him somewhere back in my life, to figure him out like an irksome pain so I could excise him once and for all and toss him away. But there were so many blanks. So many dead spaces I kept running into and losing my way.

I bashed my fist hard against the counter and welcomed the distraction of the pain.

Determined to put the heinous one out of my addled brain, I went in to check on the boys. Adam was still fast asleep on the couch, but David's side was empty.

"David," I called and listened for him in the bristling silence. The hall clock trembled and jumped ahead with a loud, insistent hiss.

"Davey?"

I checked the tangle of blanket, half expecting to find him burrowed underneath. No one there but Bruce, the one-eyed monkey. I began to search the house, thinking he might have wandered off in a somnolent trance. Once, after a frantic search through the apartment, Will had found him out cold in the bathtub.

"David?" Could he have gotten up and wandered outside? I couldn't remember the sound of the front door slamming, but he might have slipped out while I was running the water. Or while I was otherwise distracted.

I went out front and scanned the broad meadow. A large flock of broad-winged blackbirds were flying in crisp V-formation toward the hazy horizon, towing a line of full-figured clouds. No David.

I walked around back, squinting through the haze. Nothing. I had turned to go back into the house and look again when I heard a flurry of crazed flapping come from behind the barn. Squeals, more flapping. I followed the sound through dense thickets of dead shrubbery. Thorny sticks tore at my skin.

"David?"

The squeals took familiar form, the tiny, desperate sounds he made when he was hurt. I struggled past the sharp edges, the thorns, working my tortuous way closer to the little, wounded animal yelps.

He was smacking at the air in a wild, desperate frenzy. I spotted the darting swarm as I got closer.

Bees.

I picked him up and carried him in a mad rush back through the dense thicket, swatting the stray insects that pursued us as I ran. Through to the clearing. A dead run toward the house. The last of the nasty buzzing faded to an innocent hum in the distance.

He was covered with angry red welts, wailing in a weak shrill of spent misery. He let his brick of a little head flop on my shoulder and whimpered in my ear.

The welts were blowing up, blending together in a scarlet fury. His frantic crying had hushed to a sorry little hum. I grabbed Adam, still locked in a daze of sweaty sleep, and raced to the car.

Berkshire Memorial Hospital was twenty country miles away, the distance stretched by the winding, narrow strands of ill-kempt roads favored by the locals who were rarely in a particular hurry. I blasted my horn and sped past a dozen startled, meandering motorists and one hollow-cheeked chicken farmer in a panel truck boasting designer eggs.

I pulled up under the broad illuminated canopy fronting the emergency room and hurried inside. David's breathing was shallow, his face a dreadful chalky pale. The receptionist took a quick look at him and sent us directly inside.

A bearded gorilla in green scrubs laid him out on a paper-topped table and checked him over. "Wasps? Hornets?"

"I don't know," I said. "Bees, I thought."

He glanced up at me from under an awning of eyebrow. "You must be from the city."

"Yes."

"Thought so. Kid's allergic. Lucky you brought him right in. If Pete Maxon's family had reacted so quick, he'd be here today to tell about it.'' He filled an enormous hypodermic with a rush of viscous liquid from a tiny vial and injected it into David's thigh. Adam cringed and cowered behind me.

''Will he be all right?''

''Good as new,'' he said. ''But you'll have to keep a vial of adrenaline and antihistamines handy, in case. And it's not a bad idea to think about having the kid desensitized. Couple of years of shots, he won't have this problem anymore. Worth thinking about. I told Pete Maxon the same thing, but did he listen?''

I couldn't think about anything. Nothing existed but the inert little boy lying on the crinkled paper slab like a baby ghost, lips the color of an old bruise. His fingers were splayed like a statue's, stiff and defensive.

Dr. Ape hiked up the blue T-shirt and pressed the round metal mouth of his stethoscope against the little chest. ''He's doing fine. Let him rest here for a few minutes till he comes around, and you can go on and take him home.''

''You're sure?''

''Positive. He'll be on the drowsy side for a few hours. That's all. Otherwise, good as new. I'll leave a scrip for the medicine. You know how to give a shot?''

''No.'' The thought turned my knees to tapioca.

''Easy,'' he said with a dry chuckle. ''Fill and stab. Nothing to it. You can practice on an orange if you want. Just be sure you get out the air bubbles. And stick him where he's got plenty of meat; the thigh's good. Or the butt.''

His words were soupy and meaningless. I sat in a tall, rock-hard chair with Adam on my lap until David was awake enough for discharge. In a near coma of anxious exhaustion, I signed the necessary forms and took the prescription forms from the charge nurse.

A snare drum was playing in my head. My stomach was fisted. All the way back to Thornwood, Adam chattered in incessant refrain about David's "stab needles" and how he would be a willing volunteer for the task of sticking his darling brother in the butt. David provided the background music, droning on in a miserable stupor about "Boot," his name for the stuffed monkey who was his comfort and confessor in time of trial.

"Want Boot, Mommy. Daybit want Boot."

"As soon as we get home, sweetie. Bruce is home waiting for you."

"No like a bees, Mommy. No like da bees-man. Want menkie, Mommy." He sucked hard at his thumb.

"Yes, Davey. You'll have your blanket, too."

I would have enjoyed some childish comforts myself. Weariness had filled my bones with quick-setting cement. All I wanted was for this terrible day to be over.

Granny's car was parked in front of the veranda. I pulled in front of it and carried David into the house. Adam followed a half step behind, still absorbed in animated conversation with himself about doctoring his brother.

Rachel was in the kitchen with Granny. She cast a flicker of a look at us but didn't bother to ask about David's fading hives, my sodden fatigue, or Adam's inexplicable mania.

"We had a wonderful time," she said. "Granny took me out to lunch and I went to a movie—all by myself."

"By yourself?"

"Oh, now, dearie, it was one of those kiddie shows so I figured I'd go ahead and let the child watch while I do a few chores. I dropped her at the door, went to fetch her. What could happen, after all?"

I was too spent to argue. This latest no-win discussion would have to wait.

David hung on me like a brick necklace. When I tried to put him down, he stiffened and screamed. Poor baby was still hungry for comfort.

''All right, sweetie. Come on and we'll get Bruce. You can rest with him and your blanket, okay?''

''Get Boot.'' He clutched me around the neck, tapped a foot against my middle as if he were urging a horse to trot.

I carried him into the den where he had left the stuffed monkey huddled in the afghan. I could see the shape of it, swaddled in the length of crocheted cotton squares. Pressing David hard against my shoulder, I bent over to liberate Bruce from his afghan prison.

Reaching my hand inside, I felt the furry, jug-eared head and pulled. With a quick reflex of protection, I turned David's head away and held his face so he couldn't look.

The monkey had been slashed in a dozen places. Tufts of stuffing poked through the puffed face and the love-worn body. A felt ear dangled by a slender thread, and his remaining brown marble eye was sliced nearly in half. There were bloody, crimson blotches on the matted fur. Ketchup.

''Bruce isn't here, Davey,'' I said and stroked the fine blond hair. ''I'll sit with you while you rest, okay?''

''Want Boot, Mommy.'' His voice was growing fuzzy, lids dropping like broken shades. I pushed the ruined toy under the crumpled blanket and sat with him on the couch. Then I sang a lilting tune and stroked my little boy until he was gentled into a soothing sleep.

Lynch was right, after all. There really was a monster. And I knew just who it was.

CHAPTER 20

RACHEL WAS TAKING her sweet time getting ready. I could hear the insistent bass beat thumping from her radio, her feet shuffling in deliberate slow motion over the bare plank bedroom floor.

"Hurry up, Rachel, we're going to be late," I called for the tenth time.

As if she cared. The snail act was just another phase of the protest. "I'm not going to any more damned shrinks, Emily. You always tell me you think Dr. Messenger is so damned wonderful. Why can't I wait and see her when we get home?"

"You will see Dr. Messenger when we get home, Rach, but I don't want it to wait until then. I want you to talk to somebody now, see if you can get your feelings straightened out."

"I told you, Emily. I didn't touch the monkey, and I didn't switch the damned hose. You're the one who needs the doctor, not me. You're always so crazy suspicious. And when I tell you things, you don't hear me. Maybe you're going deaf or something."

"Rachel, get moving!" I screamed with the full force of my impatience. There was a bitter, metallic taste burning at the back of my throat.

She slunk down the stairs. Her face was caked with harsh smears of color: tomato-red blotches on her cheeks, a screaming violet lipstick spread halfway to her nose, streaks of glittery grape and aquamarine shadows on her eyelids. Her lashes were burdened by a dense layer of flaky blue mascara, so heavy she had to work at keeping her eyes open.

"We're not going to a costume party. Wipe that stuff off."

"It's my face, and it's my makeup. Granny bought it for me."

Granny. I took a breath. Held my temper though I could have used extra hands for the effort. "I don't care where you got it, Rachel. You look like a clown. Go wash it off. Quickly."

"And you go to hell," she said. "Quickly."

Control, Emily. Sinking to her level was not the answer. Deep breath, nails embedded in fist. "All right, have it your way. You want to look ridiculous, I suppose that's your privilege. Let's get going."

She sat in the back, set her Walkman earphones in place, and stared out the window. I flipped on the radio and tuned to the local news.

Ashby was to host the upcoming Southern Berkshire Mini-Marathon. Stephanie Hutt, graduate of the Ashby High School Class of '86, had been named to the dean's list at the University of Massachusetts, Amherst campus. The Concerned Citizens' Alliance was launching a petition drive in their continuing battle against the proposed residential facility for the mentally handicapped. A chicken supper was planned for Friday night at the

Episcopal Church. Admission was five dollars for adults, two for children under twelve. There would be a curbside trash pickup on Saturday, all trash was to be neatly bundled . . .

Dr. Barton Havenick's office was in a narrow, beige, Cape colonial wedged in a tiny triangular plot on the corner of Mason Street and McPhee. A polished brass plaque beside the door instructed us to enter and wait in the well-appointed front room. It was furnished with posh upholstered sectional sofas, Oriental rugs topped with protective plastic runners, and rows of bright lacquer occasional tables strewn with a far-ranging assortment of current magazines. I picked up the latest issue of *People*. Rachel selected a *Ranger Rick* and occupied herself with scoffing at the contents.

"This is so goddamned stupid. Can you imagine a whole story about a hippopotamus who falls in love with a giraffe? People who write this stuff must be dumb as rocks."

A stocky, middle-aged man with black-framed glasses and a benign smile poked his gleaming bald head into the room. He was wearing a rumpled white shirt drawn tight over an inflated middle, baggy tan slacks, and a striped brown on brown bow tie. "Mrs. Archer? I'm Dr. Bart Havenick. And you must be Rachel."

She shot a killer glance at him, curled one corner of her mouth, and looked down again at the magazine as if he were of no more interest than the "dumb stories."

"Listen to this, Emily. There's a whole page of recipes for bird food. Is that sick or what?"

"Come along with me, Rachel," Havenick said. "I'll show you my office."

She blinked. "What for?"

His smile didn't waver. "We can discuss all that once

we get inside. Come along, now.''

She tossed the magazine on the couch, checked her makeup smudges and smears in the glass fronting a still life of fuzzy summer fruit, and followed Havenick through a polished ebony door. He bobbled when he walked like a wind-up toy on a downhill lie.

Not a very impressive soul, I thought. Then Ruth Messenger's associate had recommended him with high praise. And I did not have a particular wealth of choices.

Waiting for the session to be over, I flipped through a dozen magazines. Through the wall, I could hear the drone of their discussion, the substance without the words. Havenick's soft wash of a voice peppered by Rachel's harsh pronouncements and indignant whines. He had to get through to her, had to. I shuddered at the thought of what other terrible things she might be capable of doing if she weren't stopped.

They reappeared together. The doctor set a pale, proprietary hand on Rachel's shoulder and passed a crisp nod in my direction. ''I have an hour open day after tomorrow at eleven, Mrs. Archer. Is that good for you?''

''Yes, fine. All right, Rachel? You'll come back and see Dr. Havenick on Thursday?''

A coy little smirk spread her lips. ''You know I'm not busy Thursday, Emily. I'd like to come, unless you don't want to drive me. Or if you think it's too expensive.''

''It's fine, Rachel. You don't have to worry about that.''

''Oh? Good then. I'll see you Thursday, Dr. Havenick.''

''Yes, dear. And remember, you have my number. Call if you need me.''

On the way out, she turned and smiled at the man,

raising her fingers to her lips as if she were about to blow him a kiss. "Thank you."

The car seats were searing hot. I tossed a blanket from the trunk over the upholstery to spare the backs of our legs. "Sit in front, Rach. I'll put on the air conditioning."

She got in and pulled the seat belt tight around her spare middle. In the harsh daylight, her paint-caked face took on a used, dissipated look.

"You liked him, I see."

She shrugged. "He's all right."

"Did you have a good talk?"

She hummed a bright, staccato tune, stared absently out the window. "It was fine. Really just what I needed."

I angled the Jeep out of the tight spot on Mason and turned onto South Avenue. Halfway up the block, the line of traffic came to a dead halt. I rolled down the window to see what had happened and heard doors slam, threats and accusations hurled like stones.

"You some kinda cowboy or something? You coulda killed somebody."

"You kidding? I was just about standing still. You backed right into me with that fat jalopy of yours."

". . . Look, I saw the whole thing. All of it. They oughta take your license away, mister. That is if you have one in the first place."

There was a distant wail of sirens. The Ashby police to the poky rescue. Knowing how things moved in this town, I pulled into an angled space and turned off the engine. "Doreen's is two blocks up," I said. "Let's go have something to eat while they clear up this mess."

Rachel lagged a few steps behind me. When I slowed,

so did she. Not willing to be seen fraternizing with the enemy, I supposed.

I passed the accident. Three late-model sedans were strewn across the road like discarded toys. The street glittered with shards of shattered glass and ran with a rainbow-capped stream of spilled gasoline. The drivers were squared off across dented fenders, exchanging license numbers, flashing clenched teeth and insurance cards.

Crossing Tyler Street, I noticed a small group gathered in front of the luncheonette. At their center was a metal folding table strewn with circulars. A tall, square-jawed woman presided, chattering on in a relentless lecture voice and tapping a long sheet of lined paper with the tip of a sharpened pencil.

"You, there." She motioned at me. "You interested in keeping Ashby safe for your little girl?"

I picked up one of the hand-written flyers. It was a rambling diatribe against the mentally retarded. A paragraph of wild, unsubstantiated text was followed by a row of bulleted statistics claiming that outrageous percentages of rapes, kidnaps, child molestations, and murders were committed by mentally handicapped people. There was a dotted line over a tear strip that said, "As a concerned citizen of Ashby township, I call for a stop to the opening of the proposed Center for the Mentally Handicapped. My children's safety is at stake." It was followed by a signature line over the Concerned Citizens' Alliance logo: hands clasped supposedly in friendship, though they might just as well have been trying to strangle someone.

I crumpled the flier and deposited it in the trash barrel at the curb.

The square-jawed woman charged out from behind

the desk and shook a long, threatening finger at me. "It's obvious you don't understand what can happen if this so-called group home is allowed to open, miss. There were two little girls raped in Westchester County last month alone. Both no more than a mile from one of these places. People like that can't be trusted to control their sexual urges, you know. It's been proven. And you can't imagine what it's going to do to the property values around here."

"Right," I said and tried to walk around her. She blocked me like a determined guard under the backboard.

"Isn't that your little girl? Would you like to see something terrible happen to her? Of course, you wouldn't. A child her age gets molested, raped, she's scarred for life."

"Please, excuse us," I said and tried to brush past her.

She kept stepping in my path. "You let her wear all that makeup, you're asking for trouble as it is. Do you know the teenage pregnancy rate was up nearly thirty percent last year? Thirty percent. And who's supposed to pay for all those babies? You tell me that."

"Excuse us," I said and made a wide, deliberate circle around her, fencing her off with an outstretched hand and an expression as off-putting as I could manage in the melting heat. "Leave us alone."

She was not deterred, but followed right behind me, practically stepping on my heels. "You'll see. The likes of you will come around to my way of thinking, but it'll be too late. Way too late. By then Edmund House will be full of those raving, uncontrollable lunatics, and our poor little children won't be safe walking the streets. None of us will. We'll have to keep our doors locked, get burglar alarms. And guns.''

With a disgusted look, she turned and marched back to her post behind the folding table.

I followed her. ''The Edmund House, you said? Is that the name of the new residential facility?''

''Thought you weren't interested?''

''Now I am. Is the Edmund House being run by a group called the Edmund Foundation?''

''That's them. Bunch of meddling do-gooders. They want to live near those dangerous maniacs, that's their privilege. They don't have to shove it down our throats, now do they? Let them all move to another place where they're wanted.''

''Can you tell me who's in charge of the Edmund Foundation? Please. I have to speak to them.''

A sharp slash of a smile tightened her shoe box chin and narrowed her eyes to slits. ''Now that's the spirit. You go tell them you're not going to see your precious little girl put in danger. Not by a bunch of bleeding hearts with deep pockets and empty heads.''

''Where do I find them? Where is the foundation headquartered?''

Rachel was tugging at the back of my skirt. ''Come on, Emily. It's hot as hell out here. I want a soda.''

''One minute.'' I turned back to the woman. ''Do you have their address?''

She lifted a huge clear plastic satchel full of folders onto the metal table and started thumbing through. ''I may have it here, somewhere. It's a little group. Hardly worth the bother they're causing, that's for sure. Came in from somewhere in the midwest a few years back, I think. They don't have a permanent headquarters or anything.''

''But you have the address?''

"I don't know. I'm looking." She leafed through the folders, ticked her tongue, and dumped the contents of the satchel out on the table. I listened to Rachel's complaints for the five minutes it took the woman to determine she didn't have the information I wanted.

"Give me your phone number, why don't you? And here's mine. If I can put my hands on it, I'll give you a buzz," she said. "There's a whole trumped-up board of directors, officers. But it seems the whole organization comes down to one family. We had a private eye track it down awhile back. Point is, the group itself isn't important. People like that don't listen to reason. We have to deal with the mayor and such. Convince the town bigwigs that we can't have people like that around here. It's not safe."

"Who was the private eye?"

"Someone down from Boston, fast with the bills, slow with the information. That type. I don't honestly remember the name, but it wouldn't do you any good if I did. When we tried to contact him for some follow-up, his phone had been disconnected. There was no forwarding number."

More dead ends. "Your group must be very serious about blocking this facility."

"Serious isn't the word for it, Miss . . ." She looked at my name on the slip of paper I'd handed her. ". . . Archer. We are not going to stand back and let our town be overrun by crazy, uncontrollable freaks. Ashby's a nice, quiet, safe little town, and we intend to keep it that way. We'll take this thing to the Supreme Court if we have to."

"Just one question," I said as Rachel started dragging me bodily toward the entrance to Doreen's. "Where do you suppose these so-called crazy freaks should go if they don't belong in Ashby? You know, every one of those people is someone's child. The only difference between them and any one of us or our children is a little luck."

"Well," she huffed. "I don't have the slightest idea in the world where they should go, Miss Archer. But it's not going to be Ashby. I can tell you that."

"Suppose one of them were your child?" I said. "Suppose one of them were you?"

She narrowed her eyes and glowered at me. "Point is, they're not, Miss Archer. Point is, it's not my problem."

Rachel thought my fury was hilarious. She sat opposite me on a padded green banquette near the counter stools at the ice cream bar. "That woman's just a dumb jerk, Emily. Why should you let her get to you like that?" She took a long slurp of her strawberry soda and dabbed at her lips with a rumpled napkin.

"I just can't stand that kind of blind bigotry. I used to work in a summer camp for retarded kids. And sure, I felt a little uneasy at first, not knowing what to expect, but when you got to know them, you realized they were simply kids. Some were funny, some shy, and yes, some were pains in the butt. But they were people. And certainly nothing to be afraid of."

Her face was thoughtful. She took a dainty bite of her grilled cheese. "A lot of them are weird, though," she said. She took another bite, chewed in broad, lazy rounds. ". . . There's this class of retarded kids in my school. You see them all together, it's hard not to laugh. I mean, there's a big fat boy with hair like a dust mop, a sort of midget with these little triangle teeth and a tiny little pointy head. One girl's got white hair and googly pink eyes, and there's this other one who drools all the time.''

A smile lit her face. ''. . . Then there's this one boy, Tony, who's really a riot. He's got these real long gorilla arms and he walks all hunched over with his head down, staring at the floor. But whenever he passes me in the hall, he says, 'Hi, toots,' in this really deep, funny voice. It's like he can see me without looking, like he's got radar or something.''

''They're just people, Rachel. All they want is what everyone does: love, health, fun, security. Acceptance.''

She shrugged. ''They sure look weird, though. I know they can't help it, but they do.''

The woman was still collecting signatures when we finished our lunch. She opened her mouth as if to say something, changed her mind, and let her lips flutter together like butterflies in love.

For once, Rachel did not turn on the radio or hide under her earphones. As I drove, she looked out through the side window, tapped her fingers in sequence on her thigh. ''Maybe I'll work in one of those camps like you did one summer.''

''If you'd like.''

She giggled and dropped her voice to a grainy bass. ''Hi, toots.''

CHAPTER 21

LYNCH HAD BEEN to see Tru Cunningham at the *Gazette* and come away empty-handed. ". . . But not discouraged, Miss Archer. I have a very strong feeling Mr. Cunningham will manage to find the information we seek as soon as he possibly can. I believe I was able to make the gentleman understand how strongly we feel about this."

"I hope you're right, Chief. Not that I think we're going to find out anything unexpected about my mother's death. She died of exposure, pneumonia. It was a tragic accident, not a mystery."

"The greatest of mysteries often come disguised as certainties and absolutes, Miss Archer. We mustn't be reluctant to lift the corners and look underneath the veneer of our firmest beliefs."

Not reluctant, I wanted to say. Terrified.

He was intrigued by my chance encounter with the box-jawed, bullheaded woman from the Concerned Citizens' Alliance who might be able to provide us with more information about my father's favorite charity: the

Edmund Foundation. Lynch took her name and resolved to follow up on the lead. His omnipresent vest-pocket notebook was already more than half filled with his impeccable entries.

He stood and extended a gallant hand to help me up from the wicker rocker. "We are getting closer and closer to the answers you seek, Miss Archer. I can sense it."

"I hope so." Or did I? We walked across the porch and into the farmhouse. A cloying, pungent smell weighted the air. Lynch wrinkled his nose and made a tent with his fingertips. "Miss Prom's portion of the meal appears to be well underway. It would seem the soup du jour is a nice creamed bisque of athletic apparel."

"I must tell you I considered it a stroke of diplomatic genius when you suggested that the two of you split the cooking," I said. "Granny's food leaves more than a little something to be desired, I'll admit, but she's not easy to turn off. And I guess she means well."

"As, no doubt, did the gentlemen who built the *Titanic*, Miss Archer."

I followed him into the kitchen. Watched as he retrieved his large, canvas apron from the broom closet hook and fastened it over his razor-creased, gray, tartan plaid trousers. He turned up his shirt sleeves in crisp folds nearly to the elbow and conducted a long, surgical scrub at the sink.

"Hope what you're planning goes with mushroom barley soup, Mister La Dee Da," Granny sniffed. "Things you cook are so all-fired fancy, it's hard to know what to put beside them other than a roll of Tums and one of those little airsick bags."

He peeked under the domed lid of the soup kettle. "I

see no problem here, Miss Prom. Anything prepared in a nice dishwater stock is most versatile.''

''You watch it, Mister Cheeky Big-Mouth. I've warned you. One more crack out of you and I'll . . .''

Lynch held up a hand, working his face into a kindly, conciliatory smile. ''Please, Miss Prom. If I have given offense, do accept my humblest apologies. I'm afraid I am not familiar with the social conventions of your particular species.''

She made a furious face as she plumped her ginger bouffant wig. ''You'll get yours, mister. Mark my words.''

The boys were coloring at the table. Adam's face was tight with the effort to stay inside the lines, tongue working in his cheek like a drill bit. David held a fat blue crayon in his fist so the point stuck out the wrong end. He made giant blue circles that started on the paper but extended over to the tabletop and ticked the front of his T-shirt in a rash of blue blemishes.

''Easy, Monkey.''

Rachel had locked herself in her room as soon as we got back from town, emerging only to squire Max on several short walks around the side of the house. She had gotten him trained to the lead so the tiny fluff ball moved at a brisk, bouncy trot at her side, plume tail flapping like a fan.

I could hear her outside, addressing the dog in a crisp, authoritarian tone. ''Hurry up now, Max. Do what you have to do. I haven't got all day.'' Pity she wasn't born to another time and circumstance. The child would have made a wonderful Fascist general.

When she went back upstairs, I slipped into the den and put in a call to Dr. Havenick. He answered himself on the third ring.

"Rachel told me you had a good talk," I told him. "I wanted to thank you."

"I'm glad to hear she felt that way, Mrs. Archer. Will there be anything else?"

"No. I guess not. I was just wondering if you wanted to tell me anything about your discussion."

Brusque annoyance edged into his tone. "It's unethical for me to betray my patient's confidence, Mrs. Archer. I assumed you understood that. If Rachel wishes to confide in you, she will do so."

"I didn't mean—"

"No, I'm sure you did not. If there's nothing further, then." There was a rude thump and a jarring click on the other end.

"No," I said to the empty air and saluted. "Nothing further, Dr. Havenick, your honor, sir." What had become of the gentle man with the unwavering smile and the patient, even demeanor?

And what was wrong with my asking? Ruth Messenger called from time to time and made periodic appointments to keep Will and me posted about Rachel's progress. There was no worry there about breaching confidences. When Ruth helped Rachel identify a sharp, troubling truth, they agreed together that Will and I should be told about it. Dr. Messenger helped Rachel agree, if necessary. The child was a child, after all.

All right, Emily. This Havenick person is temporary. No need to make a federal case over annoying details like the man's officiousness or complete lack of manners. Those were probably the very qualities that endeared him to Rachel.

I set the table while Lynch and Granny cooked-off at the stove. Finished, I posted the boys' masterpieces on the refrigerator door; scrubbed David's accidental mural off the tabletop; got them washed for dinner.

Granny and Lynch appeared to have settled in a tacit truce. She stirred while he whisked and basted, peeled while he sautéed and parboiled. They worked with cocked elbows poised to define their respective territories. Grim-faced and rock serious, they turned, at last, in concert to announce that dinner was ready to be served.

Rachel was in a wonderful mood. She chattered on about the puppy and how smart he was, ate hearty portions of Granny's tepid, taste-free soup; Lynch's succulent butterflied leg of lamb with creamed squash and dilled new potatoes; Granny's overdressed hearts of lettuce and soupy wild strawberry parfaits; Lynch's luscious, lemony madeleines.

''That was great,'' Rachel said, wiping away the cookie crumbs along with the final traces of smudged violet from her lips. The makeup had faded until she resembled a near normal little girl again. ''I'm stuffed.''

''Well, I'm glad you enjoyed it, dearie,'' Granny crooned. ''You can afford to eat all you want, lucky girl. I so much as look at sweets and the pounds come rolling on. Just thinking about ice cream is enough to put another inch on these hips of mine. You know, I haven't seen hide nor hair of my ankles since spring of 'Seventy-two. Keep promising myself to sign up for one of those aerobics courses, but you know how it is.''

Rachel stood and slipped her arms around the old woman's considerable shoulders. ''You're not fat, Granny. I think you're just right.''

She complimented Lynch on the lamb, tossed a crumb of a smile in my direction, even deigned to give each of the little ones a light love tap on the head as she passed to take Max for another walk. ''You guys have a good night,'' she said. ''After I take him out, I'm gonna go upstairs and read or something. I'll bring Max down to sleep in the kitchen before I turn in. I figure he'll get spoiled if I keep him in my room every night. Don't you think so, Emily?''

''Makes sense.''

While Granny and Lynch cleaned up in the kitchen, I bathed the boys, told them their favorite new-age child story about Beauty and Bruce Springsteen, and tucked them into bed. They both seemed over their colds, nothing remained of David's hives but a few vague pink dots on his back. At the drugstore that morning, I'd armed myself with a powerful insect repellent to douse him with before he went outside, the prescribed antihistamines and adrenaline in a series of tiny, self-injecting glass vials, a dozen practice hypodermics with which to assault my citrus fruit, and a cunning little booklet on insect allergies. It assured that, ''Deaths from stings are not nearly as common as you might assume.''

After Granny and Lynch left for the evening, I went into the den and tried sorting through a few more of my father's cartons. One was packed with a jumble of snapshots. Most featured people I didn't recognize, smiling little knots of strangers in stiff poses. A few were of my father, then a young, dangerously handsome man with intense features, ice-blue eyes, and a sly, knowing smile. He seemed to come equipped with a variety of fawning, stylish young women, draped around his neck like living scarves.

A second box was full of dog-eared novels, purchased at remainder tables for nickels and dimes. I read through some of the titles: shoot-em-up westerns, bodice-ripper romances, gothic horror tales, all of which seemed to be set in the same mist-coated stone castle. None of them was the sort of thing the father I remembered liked to read. I began to wonder if everything in this house was the product of some entirely different person, one I couldn't recall because I'd never begun to know him in the first place.

A third carton held old mail order catalogs and a layer of newspaper clippings. At the bottom, I found several of my ancient dolls, dirty, loose-limbed, and bedraggled. The names came back to me: Lillie Ann, Tonette, even my beloved Millicent who had kept me company when I was at my desolate, desperate worst.

I cleaned them off at the sink with the gentle wipe of a soapy cloth and went up to knock at Rachel's door.

"Yeah?"

"Can I come in, Rach? I found something I wanted to show you."

"I'm busy, Emily."

Good old Rachel. "It'll only take a second. I think you'll like these."

Rush of impatient breath. "All right, then. Come on in."

She was sitting at the maple vanity, staring into the oval-framed mirror she'd tipped to catch the light from the overhead frosted glass fixture. An array of tubes and tiny boxes were strewn on the polished surface. Her head was angled toward the glass, so close her breath left a circle of fine mist in the center of her reflected face.

She was smearing a frosted grass-green powder over her eyelids with a green-stained fingertip. Her cheeks were lost behind garish greasy pink ovals, lips outlined in a wavy red pencil and caked with ruby-colored gloss. She had extended her eyebrows with a harsh ladder of short brown slashes that stretched from temple to nose.

"Having fun?" I said.

"My makeup got all worn off. I'm fixing it."

"Rach, you don't need all that. Remember what Granny said? You're a natural beauty. You really are. And anyway, you're much too young for all that gunk."

She wrinkled her brow, set her mouth in a disapproving scowl. "My eyes are spread too far apart, like a frog's. And I have lousy color. I look sick all the time. Gross."

"No, you don't. Who told you such nonsense?"

"And my teeth are disgusting. They're all crooked, and they stick out, and my mouth turns down at the ends. When can I go for braces?"

"Rach, what is it? What's bugging you now? I thought you were feeling happier today."

"Nothing's bugging me. I just don't like the way I look. That's all. My eyes are ugly, and I have these fat, ugly bags under them, and my hair stinks. It just hangs there like a dead, stupid mess." She grasped it in a fist and pulled it up on top of her head, so tight her eyes were narrowed to diagonal slits. "It's straight as sticks."

I stood behind her, tried to imagine what she saw in the mirror. "Everyone feels like that sometimes. I used to call them my ugly days, when I was so disgusted with the way I looked I wanted to hide. Believe me, Rach. You're a very, very pretty girl. And you don't need all that junk on your face."

She blotted her lips together; drew a fat, irregular brown line above her eyelashes. "I hate my ears. They stick out like Dumbo's. Can't they be glued down or something?" She pressed them against her head and made a face at the mirror.

I was getting nowhere in a hurry. "I'm sorry you're not liking yourself right now, Rach. I brought these up to show you. They were my favorite dolls when I was a little girl."

"Well, they're all messed up and dirty now," she said and returned to her dabbing and smearing.

I felt a tug of disappointment. Foolish. What had I expected her to say? "I guess they are. It's been a long, long time."

"And I'm too old for dolls, anyway, Emily. You know that."

"I just thought you'd like to see them. . . . Good night, now. And please wash off that stuff before you go to bed. It's not good for your skin."

She squinted toward the mirror, clamped her eyelashes in a metal curler and pursed her lips. "I'm too young for zits. And anyway, neither of my parents had any. . . . My real parents, that is. Good night, Emily. And close the door, will you?"

Night was the enemy. I was tossed from terror to terror, torn between my growing dread of sleep and a deadly plague of exhaustion that fogged my brain and dragged on my body like an iron yoke. It was morning before I was able to sink into a deep, silent, black crypt of healing sleep. Lost. Drifting . . .

I awoke after nine, middle of the day in my normal life. A crisp fuzz of sunshine streamed through the slatted blinds. I took the lazy luxury of stretching myself awake in stages.

I could hear David and Adam chattering downstairs with Granny. Everything under control for a change.

I took a quick, bracing cool shower, wrapped my hair in a thick terry towel, and sat in my robe at the tiny writing desk under the window. Seizing the moment, I took one of the gossamer blue overseas mailers I had put in the center drawer and wrote a breezy, upbeat note to Will. I folded and sealed the thing before some of my nagging doubts and insecurities found a way to insinuate themselves between the lines. Plenty of time for him to draw a bead on that side of things when he came home.

His London address. I thought I'd stashed it in the center drawer with the mailers, but the slip of paper wasn't there. I opened the tiny side drawers in turn.

My throat closed as I saw it lying there, at the top of the second drawer: the dead letter.

I picked it up and read it again, felt the same icy chill scaling my vertebrae. "... Suffer the torment of my stricken child for all eternity." Rachel must have taken the letter from the kitchen drawer and stuck it here.

Why?

Silly question, Emily. Why did Rachel do any number of things?

I read the letter again in a clear, flat voice, tried to dismiss it with Rachel's cynical eye. The thing couldn't possibly have any meaning for me, couldn't possibly hold any personal threat. Still, I couldn't bring myself to rip it in pieces and throw it away like the silly nonsense I kept telling myself it was. Why take unnecessary chances when a little prudent, irrational superstition would do just as well? I folded the letter and put it back in the drawer.

My hair was almost dry. I combed it through, put on a pair of shorts and a T-shirt, and went out into the hall. As I passed, I heard an insistent pulse of a whimper coming from Rachel's room. Must be Max, I thought, then remembered that Rachel had planned to have him sleep in the kitchen. She must have fallen asleep and forgotten. Now the fuzz ball wanted out. I turned the knob and stepped inside the dark, musty room.

No Max.

The whimper was coming from the bed. Rachel was

enshrouded by her blanket so the sound of her cries was a muffled shrill.

"What is it, Rachel? What's the matter now?"

No answer. She slid further under the covers until her body was a tight, trembling mass. "Get out of here. Get the hell away and leave me alone."

"What's wrong, Rach? Tell me."

"I said get the fucking hell out of here. Now!"

There was a sharp blade of panic in her tone that kept me from screaming at her, kept me from leaving, also. "I'll go when you tell me what happened. Not before."

Her body heaved in silent spasms of grief under the covers. I sat on the edge of the bed and put a hand over the sharp rise of her shoulder, made soothing circles on the pulsing surface of her back. "What, Rach? Take a deep breath and tell me what happened."

She tried to shake off my touch and raised a wild, keening sound. "I'll kill him. I'll fucking kill him, I swear it."

"Calm down, Rachel. Get a hold of yourself."

"Look what he did to me!" She wrenched the covers off her head and turned to show me the stump of her ponytail, severed at the scalp line so nothing remained but a bald patch of bloody stubble. The rest of her hair hung in a matted, stringy mess around her tear-streaked, grief-swollen face. Her voice was heavy with anguish and fury, eyes round with horror.

"He cut my goddamned hair off while I was asleep. I woke up and saw him with the scissors, but it was too late. He climbed out the window before I could catch him. Fat, ugly creep could hardly fit through. I tried to scream, but I couldn't get it out. My voice was stuck in my throat. Just stuck there like a goddamned knife. It still burns."

I saw the large, polished pair of kitchen shears beside the bed. Hair scraps traced an irregular path to the pillow where the banded clump of her ponytail lay like an amputated limb.

I held her against my chest and stroked her back to calm her. She was drenched with perspiration, her thin, pink cotton gown glued to her shivering flesh. "It's all right, sweetie. Ssh."

". . . He was going to cut off my ears next and then my nose, and then—"

"Stop, Rachel. Stop it."

". . . Then my fingers, one at a time. Snip right through them at the bone. Cut them off . . . snip . . . snip, so I'd have nothing but bloody holes on my hands. Snip and I'd have blood running all over the place like juice. You have to help me find him, Emily. You have to stop him, have to. He's a fucking maniac."

"Ssh. Please, Rachel. Stop. There's no one here. No one's going to hurt you."

"If you don't kill him, I'm getting the hell out of this place. I'll run away so he can't find me and neither can you."

I left her lying in bed and went to the bathroom for a cool, damp washcloth. She seemed to relax as I stroked her face with it, running it across the back of her neck and over her slender wrists. I dabbed at the sore spot where the hair was cut to the skin, the ring of scalp raw and angry.

". . . He had this mean, disgusting laugh like he was enjoying every minute of it, Emily. He may be a sicko, but he knows just what he's doing. Fucking maniac has the whole thing planned. He wants to kill me a little bit at a time. Wants to watch me suffer. It's part of his goddamned game."

"Come on downstairs and have something to eat, Rachel. You'll feel better."

I helped her up out of bed and guided her downstairs by the elbow. She seemed like a frail, disconnected invalid, lost and trembling, her voice a disembodied breeze.

"After my fingers, he'll cut off my toes. Snip. Snip. Snip. Snip. And then my hand. He wants to do it in pieces so I'll suffer longer."

"Stop, Rachel. No more."

Granny was sweeping the kitchen with a straw broom. She looked at Rachel and frowned. "Well, now, what happened, dearie? You try playing beauty parlor? Heh, heh. I remember when my sister's boy gave himself a little trim one time. That what happened here?"

"Seems that way," I said. "Sit down, Rach. I'll make you some cereal."

Her voice was a pinched whisper. "I don't goddamned believe you, Emily. I didn't cut my own hair. I told you. I told you it was the monster . . ."

"All right, all right. Stop. It's not important."

"Course it isn't," Granny said and clicked her tongue. "Nothing that can't be fixed in a jiffy." She combed through the remains of Rachel's hair with her fingers. "No harm done, dearie. Granny'll trim it up for you, and it'll look just grand. You'll see. Short hair's much more comfortable in this heat, anyway, that's for sure. And it'll grow in right in time for the winter if you want it long again. Young hair like yours grows like weeds. Now, isn't that so?"

Rachel sniffled and perched on the stool as Granny slipped comb, spray bottle, and scissors from her canvas tote. "There now, dearie. Let Granny shape it up. It'll look real cute once I get it even. You'll see."

"I'm going to kill that goddamned monster, Granny. I swear I am."

Granny sprayed a fine mist of water on Rachel's hair and combed the moisture through. Her scissors made a bright, clicking noise, and scraps of shiny black hair rained over the pebbled linoleum. "Well, of course you are, dearie. You're not going to let any mean, old monster get the best of you. You're a big, strong, beautiful girl, after all."

Rachel's eyes were glazed with fury. She seemed to enjoy the taste of the words. "I'm gonna kill him."

Granny snipped and combed, humming a bright little tune under her breath. "There now, dearie. That's much, much better. You leave it to Granny. Granny can fix everything."

CHAPTER 22

PENNY SATENSTEIN HAD called and urged me to make an appearance at the annual student art show to be held that day at the Berkshire Federation building.

I arrived less than an hour after the opening, but the parking lot was already packed to capacity. An off-duty Ashby cop was directing the overflow of cars to the few remaining spaces on the blacktop of the former school playground and past that to the littered, weed-choked, softball diamond. I edged the Jeep into a tight spot between third base and home.

Federation headquarters was festooned with twisted lengths of bright red crepe paper streamers and clusters of oversized helium balloons. There was a refreshment stand outside the building's main entrance featuring foot-long, flesh-toned hot dogs and a poison-green beverage bubbling in a murky vat. Len Satenstein was busy ringing up sales on an antique cash register.

Ralph Brindley, Jr., dressed as a carnival barker in straw hat and barber-pole blazer, stood in the doorway, held a megaphone to his skinny lips, and announced the show's events in his most commanding chirp.

"... Judging in the minimalist sculpture category will be held in ten minutes in room three-twelve. Hurry on in, folks. Wouldn't want you to miss the big moment. . . . And again, our congrats to Myrna Algus who placed first for the third year running in the found object collage category. Way to go, Myrna."

Beth Wilkinson, dressed to her oversized teeth in a taffy-pink, lace-trimmed dress, was collecting admission tickets in the lobby. The Gott sisters, garbed in matching black and gold nylon warm-up suits, were in charge of the raffle booth. Between customers, I could see their tight little muscles working through a surreptitious series of isometric exercises.

Penny Satenstein emerged like Moses from the milling sea of spectators and wrapped me in a generous, cloying floral hug. "I'm so delighted you could make it, Emily. Come on with me, I'll take you around and introduce you."

She led me from room to room, pointing out federation members and suggesting which particular works I should make it my business to admire at the top of my lungs. "Smile pretty, darling. That's Rose Linkmartin over there. She knows or owns just about everybody in town."

Between introductions, she filled me in on her plan in a tutti-frutti-scented whisper. "Len and I have called for a members' referendum on the question of taking over Thornwood, Emily. I don't think it's ever been done by anyone in the federation, but it's all legal. Right there in the bylaws. Len's a lawyer. He likes to read things like bylaws on the potty, bless his greedy heart." She lifted a manicured hand, twiddled her fingers at a tiny bald man who twiddled back.

". . . Anyhow, it seems that when the board doesn't have unanimous agreement, a majority of the entire membership can decide on a project like the colony." She tossed her head, fluttered her lashes. ". . . Well, hello there, Philip darling. You must meet my dear friend, Emily. Emily, say hello to Phil Glotzer."

I did and waited for him to move on. ". . . That's wonderful, if you think the membership can be persuaded."

"Oh, they can, they can. You just follow me and pucker up. Nothing makes the lot of them come around faster than some good old-fashioned ass kissing. Trust me. . . . Now is that Rhonda Cattell? Well, would you look at you! I hardly recognized you, darling. You're skinny as a rail. The grapefruit diet, right? Just how much weight have you lost?"

I trailed behind her, sporting a stilted smile and a collar of embarrassed impatience that was drawing ever tighter around my neck. "Is all this really necessary, Penny? Thornwood is a worthy project for any arts organization. I don't see why we have to—"

". . . Mary and Dick Klingman. Come on over here, you two. I haven't seen you in an age. . . . I want you to meet my dear friend, Emily."

I nodded. Managed a few civil words. Swallowed hard.

"Now, you listen to me, young woman," she said in a tense whisper she forced through a taut, laminated smile. "Len and I have gone way out on a limb for you on this one. Link is spitting mad that we've refused to see things his way. He's ready to have my hide. Not that I'd altogether mind if he did. . . . Anyway, I know how the tiny minds in this town work. You want them to vote to take over the colony, do as I say."

"I'm trying."

"It's the only way, darling. Honestly. Link won't budge on this one. I've tried to persuade him. Lord knows, I've tried. But it's no use. Your only chance is to go for a majority of the member votes and approval of the legal committee. . . . Oh, hi there, Gwendolyn. Don't you look just marvelous? I swear, you get younger all the time. Emily, this is that darling woman I told you so much about. Would you believe she has a married son? Looks hardly old enough to be married herself."

My face felt tight enough to crack. When Gwendolyn drifted off, I felt it sink like a failed soufflé. ". . . I'll try. But I don't like it."

I followed after her, swimming upstream through the sea of grinning strangers, shaking my head a great deal until I felt it start to wobble on its own. When she led me into the dim, quiet room at the end of the hall, I was overcome by a momentary rush of gratitude. A welcome break. "Thanks, Penny. If I had to say one more hello . . ."

Then I saw him.

He was slouched against an abandoned chunky wooden teacher's desk, puffing on a vegetable stick, blowing out the smoke in long trails of broccoli-scented fog. Spidery lines framed his frosty eyes. His mouth stretched in a smug, infuriating grin. "Well, well, look who's here. Little Emmy Lee Fowler. Thanks, Penny. I owe you one."

The sight of him set fire to the short tail on my emotional fuse. "Good-bye, Mr. Marshall." As I turned to flee, I saw Penny slip back out in the hall and pull the door shut behind her. The lock turned. I hammered hard on the wood frame and jiggled the doorknob. Turning, I faced Lincoln Marshall with a scrupulous mask of calm. ''Open the door.''

''I just want to talk to you, lady. Don't worry. I won't hurt you. I'm a good guy. A regular prince.''

''I don't happen to share your high opinion of yourself, Mr. Marshall, and I don't find you cute in the slightest. I have no interest in playing any more of your games.''

He grinned, tapped his fingers on a desktop. ''I know that, Emmy Lee. You're too busy playing your own.''

''Look, if you have something to say to me, say it. I'm in a hurry.''

He walked toward me. I backed up until the cold metal of the doorknob bit into my spine.

''I told you, Emmy Lee. Don't worry. All I want is for you to take one more good look at me. A long, hard look. See if you can remember. Try hard.''

My heart was pounding at my ribs like a crazed prisoner. ''Leave me alone. And stop calling me that. Where did you get that name?''

He ran a gentle finger over my cheek, his touch was boiled velvet. ''I want you to remember me, Emmy Lee. I'm tired of being back here on Memory Lane all by myself. It's lonesome.''

My heart was squirming like a beached fish; the blood roaring in my ears in mad, deafening waves. ''I . . . don't know you. I don't know what you're talking about.''

''Yes. You do. Think, Emmy Lee. Think hard.''

I tried to work through the dense, dark webs of confusion clouding my memory. There was a flicker of something. But not enough. ''If you want so badly for me to remember how I know you, just tell me.''

"No, that wouldn't be the same. You have to get there by yourself, Emmy Lee. Think. Who do I remind you of? When you look at me, who do you see?"

"No one. I don't see anybody or anything. And I don't want to look at you, Mr. Marshall. You make me sick."

He held up his empty palms and sighed. "Go on then, Emmy Lee. Fly away home. That was always your way, wasn't it? Run and hide. It doesn't work, lady. Not forever." He pulled a ring of keys out of his pocket and opened the lock, flung open the door, and stood back to let me pass. "Sweet dreams."

I picked my way through the milling crowd. Ralph Brindley was barking the results of the mixed media competition. ". . . Third place goes to Samantha Gold for her 'Logs and a haystack.' Bouquets to you, Sammi. . . . And our second runner-up is Ray Worley. Buckets to you, too, Ray. See, buddy, and you said you had no talent."

I raced outside and across the playground to my car, gunned the engine, and turned on the radio, welcoming the distraction of the noise.

As I pulled out of the crowded lot, I spotted a trio of young children jumping up to grab the strings of the helium balloons tacked to the window frames and popping them underfoot in a joyous frenzy of mischief.

Now there was a memory. I could conjure the feel of the cool, taut skin of a filled balloon pinched between my fingers, my lungs bursting with anticipation. I could hear the jarring pop. The rise of giggles and that wonderful rush of mindless satisfaction as my friends gave me the nod of approval. I could see the bunch of them: Teejay, Dinky, Meryl the leech, crazy Jerome. Not a

Lincoln Marshall in the crowd. Not a single little face that my imagination could grow and translate into that hideous, obnoxious man.

None of them.

Think about it, Emmy Lee. Who do I remind you of? When you look at me, who do you see?

I turned out onto the road and edged into the line of traffic leaving the art show. The cars were moving at a maddening crawl, raising a shimmering trail of exhaust and short tempers. An impatient someone several cars ahead leaned on the horn. Others joined in, filling the torpid air with a mournful chorus of honks and bleats. Barbra Streisand made a valiant, nasal effort to be heard above the din. ". . . Peeeepulll. People who need peeeee-pullll."

I crept along in the jerky crush, trying to sort through the confused tangle in my mind, working to make sense of Link Marshall's taunting, infuriating words. Who do you see when you look at me?

Who do I see? I'll tell you, Mister pompous, infuriating, self-important, supercilious Marshall. I see a giant pain in the butt, that's who I see.

And who did he remind me of?

No one from the top of the evolutionary ladder. No one I wanted to be reminded of, that was clear. I didn't want to have anything to do with anyone or any memory vaguely connected to that dreadful creature.

But the truth was, he did remind me of someone in an exasperating, impossible way. The answer was an invisible gnat teasing at the edge of my mind. If only I could dredge it up. Get a firm grip on it so I could squash it and throw it out of my mind for good. Who was it?

The realization crept over me like a sick fever. So clear, I don't know how I had managed to deny it this long.

I knew exactly who I saw when I looked at Link Marshall.

CHAPTER 23

My mind was reeling. I could not bring myself to go back to the farmhouse. Not yet. Not until I could find a way through the suffocating fog.

I turned back toward town and drove for a time in large, aimless circles: through the traffic-clotted, tourist-ridden commercial district; past neat, level strands of unassuming little houses and square-cut lawns; out onto the deserted scenic Route 23 where the Jeep seemed to pick up a rush of dizzying speed on its own. I rolled down the window and offered myself to the heady power of the wind.

Better.

Straps of hair lashed at my face, and seeking fingers of cool, calming air crept beneath the soft cotton of my blouse, making it billow like a spinnaker.

Fly away home. His words crawled under my skin, stuck there in a rash of invisible burrs.

I pressed harder on the accelerator, felt the engine growl and leap in response. The Jeep whipped past a regimental row of top-heavy trees and power poles strung with long cat's cradle webs of shimmering line. Past giant rocks thrust upward through the flat plain like still, gray giants napping in the empty afternoon. I felt as if I could go on forever, until the road dead-ended at the perilous edge of the world.

And beyond.

Run and hide, Emmy Lee. That was always your way.

Faster. I strained my foot against the accelerator. Felt the steering column shiver and scream. My fingers cramped, calf fisted in an angry spasm from the effort to hold steady on the gas as the car bucked over potholes and frost heaves in the neglected pavement. The speedometer needle inched in its trembling ascent toward sixty-five . . . seventy.

The road was a long, polished metal slide. Beckoning, winking at me. A sun-slicked dare.

Who do you see, Emmy Lee? Who?

I was a puffed balloon, floating. Soaring. Nothing but me and the speed.

Free. Pure exultation. No tethers to the impossible earth. No end to it. Slash through the straightaway. Melt in the soft bosom of the curve. Whip around the corner cradled by the gentle bank of the road.

I felt a bubble of a crazy laugh surging up from my toes. Spreading through me in a warm, liquid rush. Nothing more heady than a tiny bit of a reckless risk. The road was empty. Mine.

The playful sun was poking me in the eye. Slick around another curve. Toss of cool air like water from a bucket. Yes.

You were always like that, Emmy Lee.

Round another turn, the road was reduced to a narrow, wiggling line of pebble-capped pavement. There was the sharp ping of gravel against the Jeep's sides. A biting crunch under the tires.

The car teased toward the edge of the blacktop, wavered in a dangerous little dance. I clutched the headstrong wheel. Slammed hard on the brake. The Jeep skidded with a sick, jarring squeal that tossed me to the roof of the car like a rag doll. I slammed my head and bit down hard on my tongue, the pain shooting me into a cold, steely terror of fresh reality.

Turn into it, Emily. I forced myself to go with the skid, let the crazed vehicle have its head. The world spun wildly out of focus. The car wrenched and bucked like a sick, mad animal; landscape melted to a dizzy green-beige stain. I closed my eyes to force it away. Teased at the brake pedal. Prayed and tried to steel myself against the expected end. Every muscle drawn. Tensed in a fist of boiling pain. Trying to still the vicious knocking in my chest.

The car tensed. Slowed. I drew a deep, burning breath, allowed my screaming muscles to uncoil. Pressed harder at the brake.

With a tooth-jarring squeak, the Jeep slipped into another crazy slide. The world was a gut-wrenching blur. I shut my eyes against the rushing stream of sun and leafy shadow. Under me the car heaved and shuddered over the stony, uneven ground. Lurched off the pavement and surged up a rutted incline. There was a straining whine of springs. Squealing rattle of jolted metal parts. Thumps and breath-stealing pockets of empty air . . .

A sick, reverberating thud. The harsh clink and clatter of parts settling. A crisp, metal crunch like a flimsy tin can in a giant's fist.

Silence.

I slipped up a cautious inch at a time. Kept my lids clenched. The eerie stillness enveloped me. A silence still as death. In a frozen panic, I passed a trembling hand over my face. My fingertips came together in a gentle ring. Felt and fell apart. With enormous care, I ran a hand over my left leg, toe to thigh. The sensation was too good. Almost painful. The other leg. An arm.

Bumps. Bruises. Nothing serious. I opened my eyes a tentative sliver. The sun had gained force, the air sweetened with a breath of pine. Hot, dismal tears stung my eyes and slopped over. Even the pain was good. A bloody purple bruise throbbed on my swollen knee. The top of my head was sore and pulsing in insistent rhythm. There was a tingling soreness in my tongue.

What the hell is the matter with you, Emily? You trying to kill yourself or what?

I forced open the door. The lock was bent. It came undone with a sorry thunk. Standing on rubber legs, I checked the condition of the Jeep. A few small dings in the dull, maroon paint. The right rear tire was scuffed, the rubber chafed to a chalky gray. A taillight hung suspended by black strips of insulated wire and twisted aluminum guts. I forced it back in position like a dislocated limb.

Torrents of sweat coursed down the sides of my face, and I was caught in a violent spasm of a shiver. Amazing that I wasn't badly hurt. Killed. In a too vivid image, I saw myself strewn in a grisly horror of bloody, torn fragments across the highway.

How far and fast could you run from yourself before there was no turning back?

I had almost managed to find that out the hard way.

CHAPTER 24

THE CAR LIMPED along the highway, jerking and complaining, wheels jolted out of alignment. I urged its shaky progress until I spotted a grassy strip of a rest stop fitted with a redwood picnic table, a metal mesh trash basket, and an ancient pay phone mounted on a broad wooden slab. Turning in, I rolled to a bumpy stop beside the phone and fished in the bottom of my cluttered purse for change.

Granny answered on the third ring in a breathless huff. She agreed to stay with the children for another couple of hours. If I was sure it was absolutely necessary, she said. If I was sure there was positively no other time for me to take care of whatever it was that was so all-fired important (of course if I didn't choose to tell her, she was certainly not the type to snoop). The children weren't any bother at all, she said with too much vehemence. Nothing like children, she assured me. In fact, she couldn't understand for the life of her why some mothers didn't seem to want to spend any time with the dear little ones and always had to be running around like headless chickens. Not that she had any particular person in mind, of course.

I could hear Rachel and the boys in the background, jabbering questions at her, vying for attention as they always did with the phone. Granny's voice bristled with unsatisfied curiosity and a sharp trace of annoyance I pretended not to notice. I thanked her for the reluctant favor, climbed back into the cranky Jeep, and edged onto the road, heading toward town.

I drove up South Avenue and angled into a vacant spot half a block from Doreen's. My mind was ice clear, churning out clean, simple solutions that had somehow eluded me until now. I could see the way out of the maze, the direct route from here to daylight. Something terrible had happened at Thornwood, an unthinkable something that had stolen my home, my parents. And I was about to find out what it was.

My knee ached in dull, pounding waves, and there was a sharp, misplaced pulse in my scalp. Ordering the pain out of my consciousness, I forced a commanding energetic stride up the avenues toward Fiske's Hardware.

The Fiske family had settled in Ashby six generations earlier. One of my ancient, intact recollections was of a birthday party for little Fast Freddie in the Fiske's large pine-paneled museum of a family room, showcase for a dusty collection of Fiske memorabilia: antique muskets, crudely-rendered genealogies linking Fast Freddie to foot soldiers in the Revolutionary War, a wear-beaten family bible crammed with generations of jotted Fiske milestones, and a row of round, wire-framed spectacles, one with a bullet-shattered lens. If anyone had a handle on Ashby's past, it would be Freddie Fiske.

A smooth wooden wedge held the door to Fiske's half

open to admit the stingy, exhaust-scented breeze. A swirl of grainy dust followed me inside, and a bell pinged as I tripped some hidden trigger in the worn plank floor. The overhead fan hissed as it revolved, chasing a mass of warm, dust-laden air around the store. A biting aroma that blended turpentine with lawn fertilizer stung my nose and made my eyes water.

Fast Freddie was just inside the storeroom door, grinding a duplicate key from a shiny aluminum template. I caught the side view of the graying mahogany hair draped over his flat forehead like a soggy towel, the cracked lip caged between the crooked rows of brown-edged teeth, the dull face tight with concentration. Metal sparks shot from the grinding machine in a brilliant haze, but Freddie's were not the sort of features to take on much in the way of illumination.

I waited for him to finish. Watched him contort his head and urge his thick, flat-topped dirty fingers to echo the contours of the key's bumps and indentations. Every move was so worm-slow and deliberate. I felt my body prodding his fingers around the curves, straining to hurry him along.

Done at last, he wiped his hands on the broad bib of his dusty denim overalls, ran a batch of soiled fingers through his hair. Turning in my direction, he extracted a rumpled yellowed hankie from his pocket and made a grand honking sound with his formless nose. ''Well, would you look who's here, whatsername?''

''Emily Archer. Hillard Fowler's daughter? Remember?''

He made a fold in the hankie, mopped the back of his neck with the fresh surface. ''Course I do. Yours was that little girl who passed out in the car. You ordered a quart of Parker's sudsy lemon ammonia last time you were in. That right? Don't think it came in yet. You got a minute, I'll check." He turned to amble back into the storeroom.

"Please. I didn't come for that."

He stopped. Gave me a bleak, uncomprehending look.

"I need your help. I have to find out about something that happened at Thornwood a long time ago. You said you remembered me as a little girl. . . ."

He flashed a crooked, embarrassed little grin. "Didn't mean to insult you about having link sausage arms. You weren't real fat or anything. Pleasantly plump is all."

"I'm not insulted. I think it's wonderful that you remember. What about other things from that time? Do you remember my mother, Mr. Fiske?"

The grin faded. He cleared his throat and seemed to be inspecting something on the floor. His voice was edged with gravel. "Nope. . . . Don't believe I knew your mother. Only knew Wild Hill by reputation, to be honest, not personal-like or anything. Folks at Thornwood kept to themselves mostly. Colony never was really part of the town." He gave an emphatic toss of his head, shaking out the thick flap of hair like a picnic blanket. "Nope, not likely I'd have anything to tell you about way back then."

I tried to keep the impatience out of my tone. "Please try to think back, Mr. Fiske. Something must have happened at the colony around the time my mother died. Aunt Lizzie took me away on a sudden trip. We wandered around for months, stayed with one after another of her relatives until it was time to enroll me in boarding school. She told me all the running around was because my father needed peace and quiet. But now I'm sure there was more to it than that. She was trying to keep something from me."

He scratched at the salted stubble on his cheek. Cracked a knuckle. Then he stared at the ceiling as if trying to read a cryptic message printed in the stained acoustical tile. Anything to keep from looking my way.

His eyes darted from ceiling to floor. He stooped to retrieve a ten-penny nail that had worked its way under the counter, stood with a soft groan, and started sorting through the nail bins. ''Nope. . . . Can't say anything occurs to me at all. Course, I was just a small boy at the time. My father, big Fred, couldn't abide gossip, wasn't much for any kind of talk, to tell you the truth. Used to sit with me nights, and we'd look at *Popular Mechanics* together. 'Fred Junior,' he'd say. 'An idle brain is the Devil's workshop. Better to fill yours with U-bolts and copper tubing, Son.' Never was any gossip in the Fiske house, so it's no wonder I don't remember anything, ma'am. Not a thing.''

''But there must have been talk among the children. In school . . . You must have heard something.''

He shook his head, fiddled with a speck on the countertop, kept his guilty face diverted. ''Nope. Not that I remember. Like I said, I never was much for gossip. And not so hot in the memory department, either. You're talking about a long, long time ago.'' He shrugged and recleared his throat. ''Long time.''

I left, triggering the bell again on the way out. Fast Freddie was lying. And lying was not one of his particular talents.

But why?

I deflected the thought. Fiske's motives weren't important. There had to be plenty of Ashbyites left over from that era whose minds were not full of back issues of *Popular Mechanics* or muddled by deceit. Someone had to be able to help me to fill in the blanks.

Doreen's was jammed with a noisy lunchtime crowd. I walked in past the tight line of couples waiting for a booth and took the single vacant stool at the ice cream bar. Without success, I tried to catch the attention of a sour-faced waitress with sharp features and a tangled mop of dynel-blond hair. She was hauling filled orders off the slim conveyer belt leading to the kitchen and tossing them at the startled customers with a rude clatter and an expression that said, "screw you and your cheeseburger deluxe" with an eloquence that obviated the need for words.

It took her ten minutes to work her rude, clamorous way around to my section and finally, my place. She poised her Bic pen over her order pad and cracked her gum as a signal that it was time for me to speak.

"I need to see Doreen. Is she here?"

She nudged the gum with the tip of her tongue until it was wadded in her sunken, powdered cheek; fanned me with a flutter of her cocoa-caked lashes and expressed her displeasure in a whoosh of syrupy breath. "Who wants to know?"

"I do." I was in no mood for her gun moll imitation. My knee was feverish and achy. A matching ache had settled in the dull hollow behind my eyes. "You can tell her it's Hillard Fowler's daughter." My father's name had a way of arousing irresistible curiosities.

I waited ten minutes more, trying to avoid my strained, sodden reflection in the broad mirror behind the counter. My hair was summer wild, eyes sunken in dusky purple bruises of fatigue. A large woman on the adjacent stool kept me busy passing sugar packets, salt and pepper shakers, bottles of reluctant ketchup, tiny paper napkins from a jammed metal holder.

The blond reappeared at long last. "Doreen says

okay,'' she said with a fierce gum crackle and a haughty toss of her Barbie hair. ''Come on.''

I followed her to the back of the luncheonette, through a thick, scarred wooden door marked ''Emergency only—alarm will sound.'' It didn't, and we passed in single file through a cramped storage room lined with crude metal shelves. They were stuffed with enormous tins of green olives and pickle slices; ten gallon jars of generic mayonnaise and mustard; powdered milk, eggs, and gravy mixes; industrial-sized cereal boxes; soap flakes; hamburger buns.

She rapped her knuckles against a narrow door at the far end of the room, and the voice of a Romanian bullhorn directed us to enter.

The Doreen, recognized high priestess of Ashby's burgeoning commercialism and flourishing tourist trade, sat behind a delicate Regency writing desk, counting her way through a giant stack of fresh bills.

She was a tiny woman, beige-haired, ruddy-cheeked, and brimming with visible, restless energy, at least eighty years old, I knew, though her bearing was decades younger. Her leaf-colored eyes twinkled as she motioned me to a Louis XIV chair with an inset hand-tapestried seat. She pushed a polished silver trayful of filled chocolates in my direction. ''Hand-dipped,'' she said in a dense accent. ''Heaven.''

''No, thanks.'' I shook my head. My stomach rebelled against the sugary smell and I took a deep, cautious breath through my mouth. ''I appreciate your seeing me. I'm trying to find out about something that happened in Ashby about twenty-five years ago, and I thought if anyone knows this town, it's you.''

She beamed. Her smile was filled with tiny child's teeth, a row of tightly strung, faded pearls. ''Like the back of my hand. What is it you're looking for?''

I was starched with tension. Held by stiff, invisible wires in the chair. Our eyes locked. ''Something terrible happened at Thornwood all those years ago, something that turned my life inside out. I need to know what it was.''

She blinked hard, pressed her lips in a tense seam. ''Thornwood? Now that's a different story. I don't know a thing about what goes on at the colony. Those people keep to themselves. . . . Have a chocolate, really. You'd be doing yourself a favor.''

''. . . Whatever it was, there had to be talk in town. Rumors.''

A flicker of discomfort crossed her face. She stared into the candy dish and ran a gnarled finger like a Ouija probe in the air above the chocolates. ''Did you know there's a code on each piece that tells you what's inside? This curlicue means a cherry; and the squiggle there is caramel. You know how many caramels I spat out over the years before I learned that? A sin.''

''Please. This is very important to me.'' I forced the shrill edge of exasperation out of my voice. ''Please tell me what you know.''

Her expression hardened, slammed shut like a sprung trap. ''I don't have any idea what you're talking about, Mrs. Archer. Take it from an old woman, you're better off not poking around in the ashes. Nothing ever comes of that but trouble.''

''That may be. But I have to know.''

She lifted the thick stack of bills and passed her index finger over her tongue to moisten the tip. ''Good luck to you then. . . . You'll excuse me. I'd better get back to work. I'm up to my ears. And tonight's canasta.''

She was lying, too, with no more finesse than Fast

Freddie. I felt a sharp stab of frustrated rage. "I'm going to find out what it was, whether you're willing to tell me or not."

She was hunched over her bankroll, absorbed in a counting trance, refusing with every shred of her considerable will to acknowledge my continued presence.

Defeated, I turned and retraced my steps through the storage room, through the luncheonette, and outside to face the discouraging blanket of glare and heat shrouding this lifeless, airless, useless day. I was getting no place. Hitting wall after wall and running headlong into an endless string of blind alleys.

Now the way was littered with lies. Ashby's good citizens banding together to keep their shameful secrets from the prying eyes and seeking hands of the outside world.

But these were my secrets, too. My past was buried in this small-minded, stubborn little town, and I was determined to find a way to dig it up.

CHAPTER 25

LYNCH FOLDED HIS arms across his chest and tipped back in the wicker rocker. He faced a flat, black-flannel sky, dead blank except for a scooped sliver of a dull-edged moon inching up from the dark, hilly horizon. The cottony sounds of his breathing mingled with the ruffle and hush of a crisp night wind. He was lost in thought, face striped with deep lines of grim concentration.

"This is how it often goes, Miss Archer," he said at last. "You seek answers and find questions, seek solutions and find yourself knee-deep in fresh perplexities. Let's go over it again, shall we? Perhaps there's something we've overlooked."

"But what, Chief? I keep turning the pieces around and around, but they refuse to come together."

His sigh was a low, mournful breeze. "Then perhaps we don't have all the right pieces. It takes time, Miss Archer. You are dealing with distant history here, faulty memories, recollections colored by the playful brush of time. It's hard enough to get at fresh events. Don't be discouraged."

I looked out over the porch rail, seduced by the possibilities: cool, black emptiness, silence. Oblivion. ''I'm trying not to be. But these people are building walls faster than I can climb them, Chief.''

''Then we must find a way around them. Bear with me, Miss Archer. I assure you, this is how it's done. Slowly, methodically.''

My patience level was dipping into emergency reserve. ''The more we find out, the less we seem to know. It's so aggravating.''

''I understand, Miss Archer. But the truth often suffers from stage fright. We must coax it out of hiding.''

''But how? This town is afflicted with an epidemic of voluntary amnesia. How are we going to get at the truth if the people who have it refuse to give it up?''

''Patience, perseverance. You will have your answers. In time.''

''. . . It has to be soon, Chief. This place, the whole thing is getting to me.''

He placed a thick, reassuring hand over mine. His warmth penetrated my bones. ''Perhaps you'd rather put this aside, Miss Archer.''

''That's exactly what I want to do, Chief. That's why I have to keep digging.''

''Certainly. It's your decision.'' He bit his lip, seemed lost a moment in a private argument. When he looked back at me, there was a trace of pain in his eyes. ''Forgive me if this sounds presumptuous, Miss Archer. . . . You have a fine family. A satisfying career. A bright future. Don't allow the past to grow larger and more important than it deserves to be.''

''I won't, Chief,'' I said. He was so dear, so solid. The father I had always wished mine could have been. ''Thanks for worrying.''

''Not at all, Miss Archer. Worrying is what I do best.''

He strode across the lawn toward his cabin and was sucked into the dense shadows fronting the cedar copse. I slipped into the dim, somnolent house and closed the door behind me.

The boys had gone in early without a syllable of protest, their energies spent from hours of trudging all over Thornwood in the brutal heat with Granny, searching for a wild blackberry patch she appeared to have misplaced.

Rachel hadn't said a word during dinner. Just sat with a dreamy look on her face and downed an enormous serving of Lynch's sublime veal and peppers, Granny's spaghetti in white paste, Lynch's delectable Caprese salad, Granny's lumpy liquid brownies.

After the meal, she had asked to be excused, walked Max, and tucked him into his bed-box in the kitchen before going up to turn in herself. '' 'Night, everybody,'' she said and floated out of the room like a pint-sized Loretta Young.

Was it my hopeful imagination or had she gotten past the worst of the storm? Not a word today about her googly-eyed, grunting monster. Not a trace of garish makeup on her face, not a hint of festering subcutaneous rage to harden and warp her delicate features.

The house was drawn in long webs of shadow, crackling with an expectant hush. The silence was pure except for the puppy's light whistle-snore, the snap and groan of the floors shifting and settling, the wind-whipped branches rapping at the windows in the den.

Perfect night for covers to the chin, a good book. I flipped off the porch light and climbed the stairs by the spare glow of the meager moon. A pleasant fog of fatigue was working its way up my neck, spreading behind my ears. As I went, I could almost feel the cool, beckoning softness of the sheets, the fluffy cloud of down pillows plumped under my cement-block head.

I had worked my lazy way to the top landing when I heard the knock.

Lynch must have forgotten something, I thought with a yawn and gripped the handrail to guide my way down the darkened stairs. I crossed the gloomy foyer and was about to open the door when an odd feeling stopped me with my hand on the cold, polished knob.

"Chief?"

No answer.

"Who's there? Is that you, Chief?

". . . Granny?" A knot of fear was drawing tighter around my neck, making it hard to breathe. I reached out to secure the old, unused dead bolt, lock whatever it was outside. But the bolt was jammed. Stuck.

Silence.

I gripped the door handle and held it fast with the total force of my mounting terror.

"Who is it? Who's there?"

A startled bird trilled in the distance. There was a sudden rush of wind. No answer. But I knew something, someone was still standing out there. Someone up to no good. I could feel the evil presence like a biting surge of frigid water through my bones.

I struggled again with the lock. It made a harsh, rattling sound like a throat clearing. Refused to turn.

There was an eerie, electric silence. My fingers were cramping, and I shifted to grab the knob with my other hand. It shuddered in my grip, twisted in violent spasm. The silent visitor was trying to get in.

"Who's there?" Fear closed my throat, reduced my voice to a foolish squeak. I held on with all my strength, muscles screaming with the effort. ‘‘Who is it?’’

The door shot open. I was shoved backward, knocked off-balance, and sent sprawling into the shadowy hall. ‘‘Who?’’

A nasty chuckle. ‘‘Who do you think, Emmy Lee?’’ His leering grin glowed in the darkness, and there was a sick glint of mischief in the frosty eyes.

I struggled back to my feet. Fury replaced the lost force behind my words. ‘‘You get the hell out of here, Mr. Marshall. You have no right barging in here like this.’’

He lit one of his hand-rolled vegetable smokes. The match light leapt and cast his face in ghoulish shadow. He blew it out and spoke through a dense, smoky fog. His words ran together in a drunken blur. ‘‘Did I scare you, Emmy Lee?’’ His tongue clicked. ‘‘So sorry, lady. The last thing I want is for you to be afraid of me. I want us to be friends. Real good friends.’’

‘‘Get out of my house. Now.’’

He walked toward me in cocky, unsteady, slow motion. I turned and raced into the kitchen, grabbed a large carving knife from the drawer.

He sniffed in contempt, watching me from the doorway. ‘‘You wouldn’t hurt me, Emmy Lee. Now, would you? You can’t hurt me now that you know who I am.’’

The knife was shivering in my hand, the long blade glinting in the reflected haze of light from Lynch’s cabin. ‘‘I don’t give a damn who you are. . . . You come a step closer and you’ll find that out the hard way. Stay away from me.’’

His face was etched with menacing planes and angles. Eyes gleaming mad, unblinking. He kept inching soundlessly toward me. Coming closer. I raised the knife. Pointed the glistening tip at his chest. ‘‘Stay back!’’

Still, he came at me. Moved in teasing, tormenting, slow motion. "I won't hurt you, Emmy Lee. I want us to be friends. Real good friends. I want to know all about you, lady. Everything."

The knife blade danced in my trembling hands. I worked to keep it steady, cramped my hands into boiling fists. "Get away."

He moved a step closer. Another. "There now, Emmy Lee. Relax. No one's going to hurt you. You know I'd never hurt you."

The knife was a frozen weight, my fingers locked in a paralysis of horror. Time was running out. I would have to stab him. I would . . . have to. I forced the knife higher. An inch. Two.

Suddenly, he lunged at me. Caught my wrist in a hot metal vise. Squeezed with inhuman strength until my grip released in a wrenching spasm and the knife fell to the linoleum floor with a clamorous clunk. The puppy whimpered and barked a shrill protest.

"That's better, Emmy Lee. Much better . . ." He caught me around the waist, forced me against him. I felt his chest mashing against my bosom, the insistent probe of his hardness. He was breathing in shallow, animal breaths. Holding me so tight I couldn't move, so tight every struggling inch of me stroked against a straining muscle, a seeking hand.

"Let . . . me . . . go!" I was shot with cold fury. The man was crazy drunk, capable of anything. I swallowed back the rising swell of terror and forced myself to stay in control. "Let go of me."

He held me against him, pressed his mouth over mine. His tongue probed between my locked lips, worked over the surface of my teeth. My head filled with his scent: booze and fury.

I couldn't break his grip. He was steel. Muscles pumped from all the years of shaping stone and metal. Arms like my father's arms. Like my father . . . I had to find a way out, some way to distract him.

He ran an insistent hand over me, rubbing my back, the sides of my breasts, pressing hard enough to burn. There was a low moan coming from deep in his throat as he ground himself against me. I would not let this happen. There had to be a way out. Some way . . . I tried to go limp, to let him think I was giving in. Maybe he would let his guard down. Just long enough . . .

The light flashed on in a blinding, fiery rush. She was standing with her back pressed against the wall, arms folded. "Christ, Emily. What in the hell do you think you're doing?"

Startled, he eased his grip, and I broke free, filled my screaming lungs with a desperate breath. I stepped between her and Link Marshall. "Stay there. Don't come any closer." I stooped quickly to pick up the knife, keeping a wary eye on him. I wouldn't trust the animal anywhere near Rachel. The phone was within arm's reach. I could call the police, have him locked up.

But no. My mind raced through the possibilities, and I saw a better way. Much better. I would take care of this myself, get what I was looking for in the bargain. Finally, I had the upper hand. I held the knife out, pointed at his throat. "You get out of here right now, or I'll have you arrested."

He flashed a satisfied grin, raised his eyebrows, passed his tongue over his lips in a lazy arc. "Sure, Emmy Lee. I'm going. Whatever you say."

". . . If I ever see you around here again or anywhere near me or my family, I'll press criminal charges against you, I swear it. I'll put you where you belong—in a cage.''

''Right, lady.'' He winked at Rachel, blew a kiss in my direction, and swaggered out of the house. I held my breath until the door slammed shut behind him, and I heard the thunderous catch of his engine and the puttering roar of his motorcycle retreating toward the distant road.

A tremor of relief and exhaustion ran through me. ''That man's crazy, Rach. If you hadn't come in . . .''

She made a snide face. ''Sure, Emily. Right. If I hadn't come, you could have gone on slobbering over each other all night, couldn't you? After all, Daddy's not around to see anything.'' Her cheeks were blotched with fury.

''No, Rachel. You don't understand. It wasn't that way at all. He forced his way in here. He could have . . .''

She pressed her hands over her ears. ''I don't want to hear it, Emily. You save your bullshit stories for Daddy.'' Her voice was a rasp of fury, eyes narrowed to slits of rage. ''You're a goddamned whore on top of everything else, aren't you, Emily? A goddamned whore.''

''Stop it, Rachel. That's not true. It wasn't what you think.''

She spat her contempt at me. ''Daddy's too smart to believe your stories, Emily. You'll see. I'm going to tell him everything. Everything.''

''You don't understand, Rachel. Let me explain.''

A wicked little smile curled the edge of her mouth. ''You explain everything to Daddy when he gets home, why don't you? And then we can get the hell rid of you and your stupid, precious babies. Once and for all.''

She ran up to her room, slammed and locked her door with a noisy clatter of the key. There was the dull thump and thwack of objects hurled against the wall. She was taking her rage out on everything she could lay her hands on: books, shoes, wooden hangers. The sounds hammered in my head like furious fists.

I leaned over the sink and tried to wash away the traces of him. Scrubbed my hands and rinsed my mouth again and again with the hottest water I could stand. The imprint of his body clung to me like a bad stench. I could feel him pressing against me . . . probing.

Rachel was still at it. Beating out her frustrations. Crash . . . thump.

I wanted to go to her, to try and help her understand. But it wasn't going to be easy after what she thought she had seen. This was Rachel, after all. At the very least, I'd have to wait until she was as calm and rational as possible. It would be hard enough getting through to her then.

No time to worry about that now. I would see to Rachel when she'd cooled off. Right now, I had other things to take care of. This wasn't over yet. I had to make sure he couldn't come back and try again. Not tonight. Never.

I fished through the kitchen drawers for tools to fix the frozen dead bolt. There was a screwdriver tucked in with the silverware, a hammer in the tiny corner drawer where Aunt Lizzie kept the gadgets. I needed a pair of pliers. The bolt was rusted shut, paralyzed with disuse.

A mounting sense of urgency was hammering in my chest. What if he came back right away? I could almost see him stopped at the edge of the road, puffing on a smoke, letting me dangle like a hooked fish until the little girl went back to bed. Planning to finish what he'd started . . .

Waiting.

I abandoned the search and took the hammer and screwdriver to the front hall; flipped on the lights, inside and out, to dispel the menacing shadows. Prying with the blunt tip of the screwdriver, I tried to nudge the bolt free.

The knob wouldn't budge. All I had to show for my frantic attempts to unfreeze the mechanism was a series of sharp nicks in the oval brass surface.

I jammed a chair under the doorknob and hurried back to check the cabinets. Aunt Lizzie always had an odd sense of order, a tendency to stash things in places you'd least expect. Flour in the refrigerator, cereal under the sink.

I threw open door after door, trying to think past the horror thumping in my head. Checked between the stacks of plates and the china cups suspended from a regimental row of sharp-edged hooks. My ear was trained to the access road, tuned to pick up the first sounds of approaching menace.

No pliers.

I took a damp, woven dish towel from under the sink and went back to the foyer. With an end wrapped around the stubborn knob to keep from denting it and making things worse, I hefted the hammer and brought it down with all my might against one edge of the metal oval. It yielded with a sick squeal. Another vicious smash of the hammer, and the lock was freed. With a giddy sense of elation, I flipped the knob and felt the bolt slide securely in place.

In fast forward, I worked my way through the deserted rooms, forcing the stiff window locks. The back door had been replaced, and the bolt fastened with a soft, satisfying click.

That would do for the time being. Lincoln Marshall had been quick enough to back off when Rachel showed up. He wasn't about to blow down the house to get to me. That wasn't this little piggy's style. Tomorrow, I'd take care of the rest. Tomorrow I would be finished with Lincoln Marshall for good.

The thumping sounds from Rachel's room had stopped. I walked back through the kitchen and paused to slide the drawers closed and shut the cabinets. The place looked like the aftermath of a dangerous storm.

With everything back in order, I walked over to Max's box and picked up the little fur ball, more for my comfort than his. He snuggled in my arms with a contented sniff, licked my hand, regarded me for an instant with his clear, black-marble eyes, and issued a broad, squeaky yawn. Then he plunked his weary muzzle on my arm and nodded off to sleep.

For a minute, I stood holding him, gentling my breaths to the quiet, even rhythm of his, stroking his silky fur. Even in sleep, the plume tail twitched from time to time, tickling my forearm.

"Sleep tight, sweet prince," I said and stooped to settle him back in his box. He sighed once and flopped his muzzle down between his tiny paws. His eyes fluttered shut.

Feeling calmer now, I left the lights blazing on the porch, the foyer light on for good measure, and climbed the stairs clutching the butcher knife like a favorite toy.

The boys were fast asleep. Oblivious. Rachel was silent at least. I listened for a minute at her door. Nothing.

Overwhelmed with exhaustion, I headed toward the

beckoning comfort of my bed and set the knife on the vacant pillow.

In my room, the blind slats had been angled to admit the lost daylight. I shivered at the thought of what else they might let in. Prying eyes. Crossing to close them, I noticed that the light was still glowing in a cloudy haze over Lynch's cabin.

I suppressed a mindless urge to run across the hazardous, dark meadow and seek the comfort of his paternalistic caring. Nothing would have felt better than to bare my soul to the chief, to let him soothe me with his firm reassurances.

But no, I couldn't tell him about what had happened tonight. I would not. This was between me, Lincoln Marshall, and the Berkshire Federation. This was one more unpleasant piece of business I'd have to see to myself.

CHAPTER 26

RACHEL WAS HER usual, sullen self at breakfast. Scanning her face, I detected no hint of extraordinary trouble. Nothing but the standard traces of hostility and blind hatred I had come to expect. She seemed to have set last night aside, saving it for Will no doubt, savoring the delicious damage she thought it might do.

Maybe this was what she'd been looking for all along: a wedge she could try to drive between us. A way to excise me from the family portrait like so much dry rot. Poor Rachel. I was about to deny her that particular pleasure. Lincoln Marshall would be done and declawed soon.

Adam and David munched in lazy chorus on their corn flakes, still socked in by a dense fog of leftover sleep. Granny bustled about the kitchen, fixing a top-secret main dish for the evening meal which, she declared with a crisp, confident nod, was guaranteed to put "that Lynch creature" in his place. I suspected Granny saw the chief's proper venue as the bottom of a fetid sewer swarming with plague-ridden rats. And Lynch, ever the gentleman, would have been more than pleased to offer Granny his intended spot in the squalid muck.

Their attempts at a culinary compromise had degenerated into bare-toothed snarling and unbridled competitive rage. Like chronically warring nations, each labored under the unshakable conviction that the other had no clear right to exist. When they were both in the kitchen, I kept a wary eye on them, fearful one might snap and do the other in with a garlic press or a soup ladle.

Sipping at a mug of scalding coffee, I rehearsed the scene I intended to play at the Berkshire Federation. I could picture the board gathered around the conference table in the old principal's office after Ralph Brindley called the emergency meeting. Link Marshall would swagger in like a Clint Eastwood parody, oozing misguided confidence. He wouldn't expect what I had to say, certainly wouldn't expect me to skewer and roast him in front of his fawning underlings. The man assumed he could get away with anything, take whatever he wanted like a greedy child. But not this time. I would tell all of it, everything. With pleasure. Every revolting detail: his slobbering, drunken advances; his threats. Then I would wonder aloud how the news of their dear president's arrest would affect the future of the Berkshire Federation. I couldn't help but smile at the thought of his face falling like a failed soufflé, his stammered defenses when I mentioned the sordid charges: breaking-and-entering, attempted rape. I sipped again. Nice. Nothing sweetened a cup of coffee like a spoonful or two of revenge.

When she finished eating, Rachel went up to dress for her appointment with Dr. Havenick. Granny headed back to her house, overwrought as always about the massive weight of her endless, unnamed obligations. She promised to return in time to watch the little ones while I took Rachel into town.

I waited until she was halfway to the cedar copse before dialing Ralph Brindley's home number. He answered after three rings in a somnolent squeak.

"Mr. Brindley? This is Emily Archer. I hope I didn't wake you."

"Wake me?"

"I wouldn't have called so early, but this is an emergency."

"An emergency? What sort of emergency?" The word seemed to nudge him back to life.

"It's not something I can discuss over the phone. I need to meet with the federation board—today."

"Oh, my, Miss Archer. I don't know if that's possible on such short notice. We all have outside jobs, you know. Federation work is gratifying, but it doesn't put food on the table."

"I understand, but it has to be today. This morning at eleven, in fact. Please arrange it, Mr. Brindley. And please make sure Lincoln Marshall is there. It's urgent."

I hung up, leaving no space for his protests, and went upstairs to put on my most commanding outfit: crisp navy linen suit, silk blouse, pumps that added height without reducing me to a two-legged aspic.

Rachel was waiting in the front foyer, anxious for her meeting with Dr. Havenick it seemed. Not surprising. Think of all she had to tell him. The details of her whore stepmother's misdemeanors alone could more than fill the hour.

She was costumed for the performance, all fresh-faced innocence in a starched pink sundress edged with ruffled lace, ankle-wrapped white sandals that emphasized her slender delicacy, a pink ribbon threaded through her cropped, shiny hair and tied at the top of her head in a prim double bow.

"Where the hell are you going all dressed up like that?" she said.

"I have a meeting at the Berkshire Federation while you're with Dr. Havenick."

"Yeah, sure." She rolled her eyes in disgust. "Right."

We drove through the clot of downtown traffic toward Havenick's house. Ashby's annual Summer Sales Days were under way for the extended weekend, and shopkeepers had set up jammed rolling racks and display bins on the sidewalks. Tourists and locals alike had gathered in teaming swarms to rummage through the shopworn remainders. In the oppressive heat, tempers flamed and cranky tongues were joined in mortal combat. At a crawl, we passed knots of tight-faced strangers feuding over the rights to a variety of improbable bargains. Rachel flipped up the volume on the radio to drown out the unpleasantness.

By the time we pulled in at the curb fronting the doctor's office, I was running late for my meeting at the federation. I dropped Rachel off with orders to wait in the outer room if she was finished first. She walked toward the house in a prissy stride befitting her sweet-little-girl disguise and went inside.

Driving as fast as my wobbly wheel allowed, I made it to the federation building at eleven-fifteen. There were seven cars scattered across the parking lot. I recognized the Satensteins' Volvo and the Gott sisters' flesh-toned panel truck. There were two wood-sided wagons, Ralph Brindley's and clone, and an antique forest-green MG. At the far end of the lot, a late-model, white Chrysler convertible and a flame-red Hyundai were huddled together in the scant puddle of shade cast by an elderly, balding oak.

My pulse quickened as I crossed the lot to the building's side entrance. The thought of confronting that creep . . .

Stay calm, Emily. You're ready for him.

My heels clacked on the hard, polished floor as I passed the eyeless banks of bright metal lockers and the long string of darkened classrooms. There was no one in the front hall or the common area in the main office. I went to the door labeled, "Berkshire Federation, Conference Room" in creaky calligraphy, and knocked.

Ralph Brindley invited me to enter.

I found Brindley, Monica Gott, and Penny Satenstein planted at careful intervals around the long, faux-walnut conference table. Penny was brushing a clear topcoat on her square crimson talons while Brindley ruffled through a dense computer printout and Monica pored over a formidable volume of tiny type and severe line drawings entitled *Modern Holistics.*

The three of them set aside their separate amusements and studied me as I took the vacant place at the head of the table.

"So?" Monica said with no attempt to conceal her impatience.

"So?" Brindley echoed. "What's the big emergency, Miss Archer?"

"I'd rather wait for the others." I cast a nervous glance at my watchless wrist. "When will they be here?"

"I'm afraid we're it, darling," Penny crooned with a hitch of her plump, freckled shoulders. "Len's in court this morning and Trish couldn't possibly miss her five-K run, now could she? Poor thing would perish without her little races, after all.''

''Beth had to be at her boutique—for the sale,'' Brindley said. ''She sends regrets. And the Brownleys couldn't close their gallery. There's an opening today—the Romanowitz collection. And Fay Richmond's psoriasis is acting up—''

''What about . . . Lincoln Marshall?''

Penny gave me a sultry look, several months pregnant with significance. She fiddled with the puffed sleeve of her off-the-shoulder peasant blouse. ''Link couldn't make it. He wanted to but he was all . . . tied up this morning. You understand.''

''I understand perfectly, and being busy has nothing to do with it. Your Mr. Marshall thinks he can get away with what he's done by avoiding me. But he's wrong. Dead wrong.'' Fury wavered in my voice. ''You tell him that.''

''Now, now, Miss Archer. I'm sure he's not avoiding you,'' said Brindley. ''Link's a very busy man.''

''You bet he is. You want to hear what keeps your wonderful president so busy? He goes around breaking into people's houses, trying to force his . . . attentions on them.''

Penny's laugh was a throaty cackle. ''Now come on, honey. You don't expect any right-minded person to believe Link has to force himself on anyone. Man has a three-year waiting list, for godsakes. And that's for standing room. He has to beat the ladies off with a stick.''

''Now you're exaggerating, Penny,'' Monica said.

Penny waved her away. ''Just a whip then, Monica. Let's not pick nits, shall we?''

''This is not a joke. Last night Lincoln Marshall broke

into my house, he threatened me. He—''

''Now, Emily. Let's not let our morbid little imagination get the better of us,'' Penny said.

''Imagination! That drunken creep was all over me. I should have called the police right then and had him locked up but—''

''But what?'' Brindley said.

''. . . But I thought you might prefer to take care of him yourself . . . without destroying the reputation of the Berkshire Federation.'' There. The threat was on the table. I looked at them in turn. They were expressionless. Taking it in . . .

Laughing. Brindley's face reddened, and mascara-tinged tears of mirth streamed down Penny's cheeks. Monica Gott's nose wiggled like a bunny's, and her steel belly pulsed under her runner's mesh-and-nylon T-shirt.

''I don't see anything funny about this. Not a damned thing.''

They took a few minutes to collect themselves. Penny was the first to find her voice back in working order. ''Forgive us, Emily. We're not laughing at you. It's just the thought of worrying about Link Marshall ruining the federation's good name.'' She lapsed into a last gasp of hilarity. ''He's done it all, darling. That's the whole point.''

''What are you talking about?''

Monica flipped up her palms. Empty. ''Link doesn't have to play by the rules. He's an artistic genius. And there's nothing more romantic than a naughty artistic genius, especially one who looks like Link. It was romantic when he enlisted in the Marines, decided he hated it, and went over the hill; romantic when he got kicked out of art school for boffing the headmaster's wife. It was even romantic when he got busted in Paris for drug possession. Soft stuff, of course. A brilliant sculptor—locked up in a foreign prison. Suffering, lonely. Delicious.''

''Then you know the man's got the social conscience and moral fiber of a radish. How can you associate with a person like that?''

''Every arts society needs its folk heroes, Miss Archer,'' Brindley said. ''Where would we be without the bad-boy mystique of Link Marshall?''

''Mystique! You think attempted rape is romantic, too?''

Penny rolled her eyes. ''No comment.''

In a blind fit of rage, I stood and raced out of the conference room, ran down the deserted corridor toward the parking lot. Their impossible words swarmed in my head like crazed insects. What was wrong with those people? How could they turn everything upside down like that? How could they?

I was halfway through the exit when I felt the hand clamp on my arm.

''Wait, Emily.''

Penny Satenstein was gasping for breath, her face blotched with exertion. Beige-tinted sweat was dripping in a steady beat down the puffed front of her peasant blouse. ''Please . . . wait.''

''I've had enough, Penny. Way more than enough. I'm getting out of this place.''

''Don't take it all so seriously, honey. That's Link's problem, too, everything's so damned deadly serious.''

''Link has deadly serious problems, all right. And I'm going to make sure he doesn't take them out on anybody else. If you won't take care of him, I will.''

Her face tightened. ''Now, Emily, don't be hasty.

We'll never convince the members to vote for the colony if you declare war on Link. He's their hero."

"Hero my foot. That man belongs in a zoo—with his fangs and certain other dangerous parts removed."

"There's nothing dangerous about Link, I swear it. True, the man can't hold his liquor, but you tell him 'boo' and he'll back off in a second. You don't need to be afraid of him."

"That's not the point."

"Then what is? Think, honey. You won't get anyone around here to back you up. It's your word against his. You'd be cutting off your own pretty little nose. And for what?"

Reality settled on me like a stone. Rachel certainly wouldn't corroborate my story. Worse, I was Wild Hill Fowler's daughter, hardly worth paying attention to in the best of circumstances.

"I can't let him get away with it. He . . ."

She wrapped me in a soggy, scented hug. "I know, darling. I know. It's aggravating. Drives me wild how you can't just get out your car and run over anyone who pisses you off; or mow them down with a nice little submachine gun. Real life is such a drag."

"He is the most disgusting, hideous, impossible—"

"Listen to me, Emily. Revenge is lovely, but you have to decide whether that's what you're after. Think what you want to get out of all this, honey. That's the main thing."

I was overcome by a bitter swell of angry frustration. ". . . I want to kill the sonovabitch. That's what I want to get out of it," I confessed into the plump, perfumed swell of her bare shoulder. "I want to take him to the vet and have him neutered."

"You want his family jewels, that's your prerogative.

But you've got to go after them the right way. Think it through. Be sensible.''

She took me by the wrist and led me into the girls' room, a dull beige square with dull beige tiles and cracked, dull beige fixtures to match. While she repaired her streaked makeup, I splashed icy water on my face.

''There, darling. Isn't that better?''

''Not much,'' I said and frowned at my image in the mirror. Nothing was ever near as simple in life as it was in theory.

She crossed to the door, peeked out in the hallway, closed it again, and flipped the lock. Turning back toward me, she clamped a finger over her lips. ''I have something for you. Swear you won't tell anyone.''

''What is it?''

''Swear first.''

Penny had a staggering number of ways to make a person dizzy. ''All right, I swear.''

''Good. Come with me then,'' she mouthed and led me to the last in a long row of narrow beige-metal toilet stalls.

I followed her inside, refusing to imagine what she might be up to. Cramped in the tiny cubicle, she slipped her hand up under the side of her voluminous square dance skirt, pulled out a sheet of folded paper, and handed it to me.

''What's this?'' I tried to get enough light and space to look at the thing.

''Not here,'' she hissed. ''Don't open it anywhere near this building. Swear.'' Her eyes sparkled with fright. Not like her.

''All right, I'll wait. But—''

''Sssh. I'm risking my neck showing you this. It's my only copy, so you'll have to give it back to me when you're through with it. The pack of them are scared witless, took a blood oath not to tell anyone. This town has more secrets than people to keep them, I mean it.'' She set her glossy mouth in a grim smile. ''. . . But hell, no matter what the rest of them think, you've got a right to know what's going on. It's your father's place, after all.''

''Yes, it is.''

Fear crept in to replace the grin. ''But you can't let on to anyone from the board. They'd skin me.''

''No one will find out. I promise.'' I stuffed the paper in my suit pocket and pushed on the cubicle door, starving for a breath of unscented air. The perfumed heat was making my head spin.

She clutched my elbow. ''Swear, Emily.''

There was more than simple fear in her eyes. ''I swear, for godsakes. Now let me out of here before I faint, and you have to fish me out of the little bowl.''

Late again. Rachel would be waiting. I hurried to the Jeep and drove toward Havenick's office. The day was darkening, preparing to storm. There was a guttural growl of thunder in the distance, a dead weight of muggy mist in the air.

The rain caught up with me as I slipped into the curb fronting Havenick's Cape colonial. Cool, pelting drops soaked through the thin fabric of my suit on the short run to the front door, chilling my bones.

Inside, I found Rachel perched at the edge of the plush sectional sofa, hands folded, slim legs glued together at the knee. Her face was set in a devilish hint of a nasty smile.

''Sorry I'm late, Rach. I got held up at the meeting.''

''Sure you did, Emily.'' She stretched out the words like lengths of Turkish taffy. ''I know all about it.''

''Let's get going. It's starting to pour.''

She cocked her head. ''Dr. Havenick would like to talk to you . . . If you have the time, that is.''

Surprise. Dr. Tightlips was going to talk to me, after all. ''Sure. I'll call and make an appointment.''

A slow, lazy shake of her beribboned head. Mouth edges warped upward. ''No, you don't have to do that. He's waiting for you now. His twelve o'clock appointment canceled. Isn't that lucky?''

Lucky me. All I needed today was more disturbing news.

I went through the door at the end of the waiting room and found myself in a short, bright corridor fitted with a tiny powder room, bifold doors that contained the Havenick washer and dryer—now in use—and knocked at a final door marked ''Dr. Barton S. Havenick, M.D., Ph.D., P.C., Inc.'' He ordered me inside in a voice bristling with rude displeasure.

''Rachel said you wanted to see me?''

He was hunched over his desk, writing copious notes in a manila case folder. Despite my impatient presence, he kept up his scribbling for a few minutes, stopping at intervals to search the empty air for a thought. I was about to remind him who was paying whom when he looked up from under his dense, black-framed glasses and fanned a pale hand toward the visitor's chair.

''Please, sit down, Mrs. Archer,'' he said. ''I have something to tell you, and I'm afraid it isn't going to be easy.''

''Why? What's the problem?''

''Give me a moment. Please. I need to work one last thing through before I explain.''

He stood and seemed to be shopping for words as he paced the office, a narrow rectangular room done in soothing silver-gray tones with liberal touches of burgundy and plum. As he walked, the soles of his scuffed black oxfords sank in a quicksand of burgundy shag carpet. His careworn face was illuminated by harsh splotches of light from a series of lamps that dangled from a long, metal track in the ceiling. With one soft, freckled hand, he kept stroking the top of his bald head as if to summon a genie.

He moved in an edgy orbit between his desk and the long span of varnished wooden shelves under the broad bay window. They were filled with puzzles, board games, inkblot and IQ tests, recording equipment, anatomically correct dolls laid out like the spent principals in a Roman orgy, their correct little plastic anatomies staring me right in the face.

Waiting for him to collect his thoughts, I allowed mine to slip away from his disheveled pacing and back to my useless, infuriating meeting at the Berkshire Federation. There had to be some other way for me to get Link Marshall. I wasn't about to give up because of silly obstacles like reality or the dictates of good sense.

"No. That's it," Havenick said suddenly. "There really is only one way to handle this." He flopped down in his chrome and burgundy swivel chair, shook his ovoid head from side to side as if a gnat were buzzing in his ear, and sucked in an expectant breath. "I'll give it to you straight, Mrs. Archer. Your little girl has accused you of committing serious abuses."

The word would not sink in. "What?"

He nodded. "Abuses. Beatings, to be more specific. She says you hit her . . . often . . . with a baseball bat. A Louisville Slugger, to be precise."

A nervous giggle escaped me. "A baseball bat. Leave it to Rachel."

''She says you tie her to the bed at night, with leather belts, and refuse to let her up, even to go to the bathroom.''

''That's ridiculous. . . .''

He silenced me with a hand. ''. . . And she says there are times you refuse to let her have anything to eat. Sometimes for days. . . .''

''Come on. She can't expect anyone to buy a crazy story like that . . .'' A terrible thought stopped me, coiled around my neck like a snake. ''. . . You don't believe her?''

He stood and started pacing again. ''I'm sure you know my duty in cases like this is clear, spelled out letter for letter by the state authorities. I'm supposed to report all such instances immediately—to the police and the child welfare department. No exceptions.''

''But—''

''But, no. I don't believe her.''

I felt a swell of relief. ''Good. Because it's all a bunch of nonsense.''

He blew out a breath as he eyed the ceiling. ''The problem is, I'm caught in the middle here. If I don't report this and something happens, I could be disciplined. Maybe lose my license.''

''But nothing is going to happen. Rachel and I may not have the best of relationships, Dr. Havenick, but I would never, never do anything to hurt her.''

He sat again, faced me with folded hands, forehead pleated with worry. ''I know that. The problem is not you, Mrs. Archer. It's Rachel. I believe she is capable of going to great lengths to make you look bad, even to the extent of making sure it appears that you actually do abuse her.''

I felt a sick wave of dizziness. All of her insane meanness came flooding back: the scalding hot water in the hose, David's stuffed monkey slashed to hopeless ribbons, the tiny puppy trembling in terror after her cruel teasing. And what about the other things? The mangled cat I found in the Jeep? Rachel was in town that day with Granny. Could she have slipped away for a minute . . . ?

His voice was full of foreboding. "What if she hurts herself and blames it on you? What then, Mrs. Archer?"

"You really think she would go that far? How could she hate me that much? Why?"

He stroked his chin and below, training an invisible beard. "In my opinion, it isn't hatred at all. Rachel is afraid. Afraid to get close to you, terrified of risking another loss after what happened to her mother."

Now there was a feeling I could understand. "But there has to be a way to make her know I'm not going to abandon her, no matter what. I'm committed to that child, even though I'm beginning to realize that 'committed' may be the operative word here. She's my daughter, now and forever, no matter what she does. Christ, I've been in labor with that child for five years already."

"She has to come to believe that on her own terms, Mrs. Archer, at her own pace. In the meantime, we have to deal with the immediate problem. What to do about these charges of hers."

". . . Maybe it's best if you go ahead and report them to the proper authorities, Dr. Havenick. The whole thing is absurd. I'm sure they'd see through it just as you did."

His mouth curled in distaste. "I'm afraid I've seen too much to share your confidence in the system. At one time, nothing a child said was taken seriously. It was a field day for abusive adults. Now, the pendulum has swung so far in the other direction, an accusation like this might well land you in court, or even in jail. At the very least, you would lose custody of Rachel until the matter was thoroughly investigated and resolved.''

''That's terrible . . . impossible.'' I tried to sort through the incomprehensible mess, but everything was tangled together, tipped with dangerous thorns. ''Why is she doing this? I don't understand.''

Havenick settled back in his chair and pressed his lips together. ''My guess is she feels terribly threatened, Mrs. Archer. Rachel sees herself as responsible for her mother's death.''

''Dr. Messenger has suggested that, too, but it had nothing to do with Rachel. Her mother died in a car accident. It was a freak thing, nobody's fault. Rachel has been told that a million times.''

''I'm sure that's so. But it happened on the way to a custody hearing, a hearing held on Rachel's behalf. She bears enormous guilt about it. As I said, I think she's afraid to take you or anyone on as a replacement. That would leave her exposed, vulnerable.''

I tried to put it all in place. ''So she'd rather destroy me?''

''She doesn't see it that way,'' Havenick said. ''This is not about you as far as Rachel is concerned. It's about Rachel—her desperate need to protect herself.''

More dark alleys. ''But why now? Why this way? She's gotten so much worse since we came to Thornwood.''

''Rachel is in crisis, Mrs. Archer. Coming here has left her without her usual support system: father, friends, familiar surroundings.''

Will's words. "Then I'll take her back to the city. We can go now, today."

He issued a sorry little sigh. "It's not that simple, I'm afraid. She'll have to work this through wherever she is. Going home at this point might only prolong the process. She finds herself having to confront her own worst enemy—herself."

Her own worst enemy. "Is her imaginary monster part of all this crisis, too?"

He stroked his scalp again, then shook his head. "Yes. I think so. Many children have trouble separating their nightmares from reality. Their fears can be manifested as beasts, monsters. Rachel is a very bright, imaginative child. Her terror is more vivid than most."

"Then at least there's no real monster. Chief Lynch was worried that some lunatic might actually be after her."

He threaded his fingers together, lowering his eyes. "Yes, there is a real monster, Mrs. Archer. A pretty, bright, eleven-year-old girl monster. And she threatens to make enormous trouble for us all."

Rachel hadn't budged. When I emerged from the inner office, she gave me a sly, sidelong look.

"Come on, Rachel. Granny's waiting."

Hanging back, she moved in an aimless shuffle toward the car, oblivious to the drenching downpour. Waiting for her, I turned on the engine and watched the windshield wipers dance in frenzied rhythm across the rain-splattered glass. In the instant of clearing, I caught a blink of her expression—cold as granite. Bloodless, inhuman.

Now I would have to find a way to control her, keep her from whatever unspeakable acts she might be capable of committing. Horrors I could not predict or imagine.

It was that or invite the authorities into our private nightmare, chance the impossible consequences.

The incurable optimist in me clung to Havenick's final, hopeful possibility. "You're going to have a rough time, I'm afraid, Mrs. Archer. But you might come out of all this with a changed Rachel. Sometimes it takes a crisis like this to break a child out of a dangerous, destructive pattern like the one she has been hiding in."

Sometimes, I thought as she opened the door and slipped into the seat beside me. There was a wicked, knowing fire in her eyes, a grim, deadly set to her mouth. She knew what she was determined to do. And how.

There might be peace at the end of this long, black tunnel of crisis. Or this might be one of those other tragic cases, where it doesn't work out that way at all.

I angled the Jeep out of the parking space and headed toward the colony. The rain was coming down in driving sheets, casting slick, dangerous swirls on the oily pavement. My visibility was reduced to near zero. I would have to feel my way along.

CHAPTER 27

BY THE TIME we reached the colony, the rain had gentled to a fine, bracing spray. Rachel went directly into the kitchen, retrieved the slumbering puppy from his box, and announced that she was going to take him out for a long walk.

Seizing the opportunity, I went upstairs and searched her room, determined to confiscate anything she could conceivably use to injure herself: the scissors, a box of colorful thumbtacks, a tape dispenser with a sharp, serrated edge. Even as I slipped the obvious offenders into a shopping bag, I recognized the futility of what I was trying to do. The most innocent objects could be distorted into hazardous weapons with enough warped determination: belts, shoelaces, pencils that could be sharpened to razor points and poked into desperate eyes. I would have to keep a close, careful watch on her. And even then . . .

My only vague consolation was Dr. Havenick's firm assurance that Rachel would not do herself any serious harm. "The worst she'd do is try to raise a few bumps and bruises to support her allegations against you, Mrs. Archer. I'm positive she's not capable of serious self-abuse. If I thought she was, I'd insist she be hospitalized. Right away.''

In the top, center dresser drawer, I found the ancient, leather-bound manicure set Granny had given her in solemn ceremony. It was the one she'd used ''on the road,'' when, as a young woman, she'd traveled as part of the retinue with various celestial performers (who would remain nameless because, after all, Granny was not the sort to brag). Now, I saw the metal file, clippers, and probes as vicious tools of potential destruction. I slipped the entire case into the shopping bag and tried not to consider the temper storm that was sure to break when Rachel found several of her prized possessions missing.

My ear caught the beat of her delicate stride on the porch steps, Max's paws clicking in a fast shuffle to keep up. I made a final, frantic survey of her room and stole across the hall to my own. Working to still the harsh thumping in my chest and force the guilty flush from my cheeks, I heard her down in the kitchen fussing over the dog. ''Such a sweet Maxy Waxy. Such a goooood puppy.''

Chair legs scraped over the linoleum, and I pictured her sitting at the oak table, sipping iced lemonade and scoffing at the mundane headlines in the *Gazette*. I had a clear image of the cropped satin hair draped over her pale, porcelain brow, the ebony eyes wide with wicked brilliance.

Rachel's moods were as fickle as the tides. Maybe Havenick was wrong to take her accusations so seriously. Maybe all this abuse business was nothing more than another of her terrible, inexplicable jokes. By tomorrow, she might well drop this hideous scheme and turn her attention to a fresh torment.

I stashed the shopping bag in the back of my closet and set out a dry pair of jeans and a sweat shirt. The soggy silk blouse was plastered to my back, and the suit was drying in odd puckers and pleats. My stockings were mud-spattered, shoes swampy and soaked out of shape. Peeling off the damp layers, I felt the forgotten bulk of Penny's mysterious paper in my suit pocket. The latest horror had knocked that adventure right out of my mind.

I wished for the will to rip the page to confetti and throw the thing away. Enough for today. Enough for a lifetime.

The sheet was water-stained, wrinkled. I sat on the end of the bed and peeled open the sodden folds. Moisture had made the ink run so the tiny writing was buried in dull-edged streaks of blue-black fog. With enormous care, I blotted around the print with the tip of a Kleenex until enough of the excess ink was absorbed to make the words readable.

"This is my final warning. Take over the Thornwood Colony and every one of you will pay. You will suffer the torment for all eternity. You must not deny me if you value your future, your lives, and the lives of your children. You must tell no one if you value your safety."

. . . This couldn't be. The writing, the words. On rubber legs, I crossed to the writing desk and extracted the dead letter from its worn envelope. My eyes flashed in horrified disbelief from the ancient lost missive to this anonymous threat.

Could she possibly be capable of such diabolical viciousness? Forgery? The borrowed words? The threats?

My mind sifted through the meager possibilities. Incredible though it seemed, it had to be Rachel. No one else knew about the dead letter, the tiny handwriting.

The handwriting. I looked again from the original to the copy. The new version was shakier, the slant more irregular. But it was a decent imitation. Then Rachel did have artistic ability, an unusually good eye. I remembered the cover of a report she had done on the Declaration of Independence, the first words copied with all their grand swirls and flourishes.

Incredible, but it all fit. It had to be Rachel. Who else had any reason to try to ruin things with the Berkshire Federation? At least now I understood some of the board's unspoken objections. At least now the enemy had a name, a face.

I waited until I had a firm grip on my temper and went down to the kitchen. Granny was polishing the company silver, confident that her mysterious special dinner entrée deserved the fanciest of appointments.

David and Adam were playing a favorite game they called ''gas station.'' With ear-splitting enthusiasm, David hurled the matchbox cars in turn off the cliff edge of the oak table. Adam, as mechanic, retrieved each wounded vehicle as it hit the floor and rapped it back in good working order with a bent knuckle or bashed it with all his might against the pebbled linoleum. ''All fixed now. Next!''

''Nudda one comin','' David announced and let fly a tiny flame red Mazda. ''. . . Nudda one.''

''Drive it right in there, mister man,'' Adam said and prodded the vehicle toward one in a row of imaginary service bays. ''Adam Jason Archer, at your service. I'll fix your car right up, good as new. That'll be two dollars. . . . We take Visa Card and American Distress.''

Rachel was, as I'd imagined, perched in a demure

pose at the table, flipping through the latest issue of *TV Guide*.

"Come with me, Rachel. I need to talk to you—alone."

She cast a disinterested eye in my direction, made a sour face, and went back to her page-flipping.

"Now, Rachel."

"I'm busy now, Emily," she muttered without bothering to look my way.

"Right now. Or I'll be forced to discuss this here, in front of everyone. And I'm afraid you might find that very embarrassing."

She fluttered her lashes at me, puffing her lips in disgust. "All right, if it's such a big goddamned secret." Kicking off her dangling sandals, she followed me barefooted out to the backyard. I wiped off the webbed chaise, sat down, and motioned her to take the woven lawn chair beside me. She hesitated a moment, swiped the beads of water off with the side of her hand, and flopped herself down with a loud, contemptuous rush of breath.

". . . None of this is going to work out the way you expected it to, Rachel. I want you to know that. You aren't going to get anywhere playing cruel jokes or telling ridiculous stories."

She curled her mouth in an ugly smirk. "What the hell are you talking about now, Emily? I swear, you don't make any goddamned sense sometimes."

I let out my words a spare inch at a time. "No one is going to believe your lies about my beating and starving you, for one. Or that bull story about being tied to the bed at night."

Her eyes flashed fury. "It's none of your business what I tell my doctor. None of your fucking business."

"... And it's very fortunate that no one will believe you because if they did, you'd be taken away and placed in a foster home, or a children's shelter. You wouldn't like it in a children's shelter, Rachel. Not at all."

She twirled a length of hair between her jittery fingers. "Anything would be better than this goddamned ugly place."

"No." I kept the tone flat calm. "You're wrong. There are much worse places. Children's shelters among them, and certain foster homes. But no one is going to believe your stories, so you'll be lucky enough not to find out how wrong you are the hard way."

She got up. "I'm going inside. It's time for *General Hospital.*"

I grabbed her by the wrist. She struggled for a second and went limp. "Just one more thing. I know about the threats to the Berkshire Federation, too. The board had a good laugh when I told them you wrote the letter. Mr. Brindley said to tell you he thinks you're very, very smart. He said if you'd learn to use that good brain of yours the right way, you could really make something of yourself. Something we'd all be very proud of. Something you'd be proud of yourself."

She struggled again in my grip. I let go of her and watched her rub away the traces of my touch. "Now you're talking nonsense again, Emily. I didn't write any letters, and I don't know anyone named Mr. Brindley. You know, I think you must be cracking up, going nuts like your father did. I bet Daddy didn't figure you for some kind of a nut case when he married you. He'll probably have you locked up on a funny farm when he finds out."

I caught her eye and gave her a long, meaningful look.

"Give it up, Rachel. None of it's going to work. It's over."

"You're over, Emily. That's who's over." She turned and stormed into the house, letting the screen door clatter shut behind her. I waited until she had time to clump her angry way through the kitchen to the den and went inside also.

Granny was grinding black pepper into her secret concoction. Her face, half hidden behind by a dense riot of vanilla curls, was drawn in tight folds as she metered the slow revolutions of the tall wooden mill. David and Adam were hunched over a military row of rehabilitated vehicles, playing traffic jam or some absorbing variation on that familiar theme. They were communicating in giggled whispers.

I spotted Rachel in the den, lying on her side in front of the television, slim arms drawn tight across her chest as if she were using them to hold herself together. The images on the small screen held her rapt attention and magnified the fire playing on the taut, angry canvas of her face.

I couldn't predict how she might react to my direct accusations. But I knew I had no choice. She had to be put on notice. She had to know that I was on to her and her hateful games. There was no physical way to watch her every minute, prevent any damage she was determined enough to do. My only choice was to stay a step ahead.

There was the harsh squawk of angry voices from the TV set. I caught a glimpse of a mannequin-faced, raven-haired woman sparring with a muscle mountain of a man whose craggy features were set in a mask of obvious evil intent. As I watched, he raised a huge, ropy hand and smacked the woman hard across her high-boned cheek. The camera zoomed in for a close-up as the cheek began to purple, and the first bitter tears rained from her enormous azure eyes. There was a swell of eerie organ music as the focus shifted to the man's expression: smug, satisfied, murderous.

Rachel's back pulsed in a light giggle.

Blind rage; senseless, sadistic violence. Now there was my little girl's idea of fun.

CHAPTER 28

LYNCH WAS LATE for dinner. I had hoped to have a few minutes alone with him before the meal, to fill him in on the latest episode in the continuing nightmare. But our conversation would have to wait. He came through the front door in a short-winded rush just as Granny was beginning to fume aloud over his tardiness.

She assassinated him with a look and continued ladling hefty portions of her prized concoction onto the polished plates. The dish resembled a turbulent, muddy sea afloat with tiny, square, brown-timber rafts. At intervals, transparent onion bits bobbled to the surface like schools of jellyfish. There were perilous glaciers of undercooked white potato and sodden corn kernel buoys tangled in deep-green, kelplike webs of unidentified floating vegetable matter. My stomach knotted in rebellion.

Lynch took a forkful, chewed in round, exaggerated motions.

"So what's the verdict, Mister Big Shot?" Granny said.

He gave her a vacant look, seemed to be searching through a long, awkward pause for his place in the conversation. "... It's fine, Miss Prom. Most ... unusual."

She snorted like a bull in a temper. "Heaven forbid you should admit you really like it or anything I fixed, Mister Hoity Toit. Now that'd be a shockeroo."

He poked his fork tines into the gravy's taut, suntanned skin. "I'm sure all this took extraordinary effort, Miss Prom. So many ingredients."

"Always was a favorite in my house," Granny said with a grudging smile. "Friends called it Alma's Ambrosia. You like it, I'll give you the recipe, seeing as you're such a hotshot cook and all. It's a fuss, but then you do get the whole meal in one pot."

"One-pot ambrosia. Clever, Miss Prom. Truly."

Her eyes narrowed, darkened. "Are you putting me on, mister? Cause I wouldn't go putting anybody on if I was an ex-nothing from nowhere like some people, that's for sure."

Lynch took another forkful and chewed in broad, lifeless rounds. "I am not putting anyone on, Miss Prom."

Granny hefted the giant casserole, menacing each of us with it in turn. "Who's ready for seconds? There's plenty. You, Emily? You can afford it. Got no extra meat on those bones of yours."

The chief was far away, distracted. No matter how she tried, Granny could not lure him into one of their regularly scheduled bouts. She couldn't fan a spark of temper or raise a bristle of pique. Here she was, aching to start a nice, neighborly conflagration, and she couldn't for the life of her manage to locate the man's fuse. By dessert, her frustration level had risen to a screech.

"You poach these peaches in gasoline or what, Chief Boyardee?" She turned to me, holding one of the dripping cling peach halves aloft for emphasis. ''You'd think the old coot would bother to make something decent for dessert after all the trouble I went to with dinner. Might as well have thrown some stale cookies at us—from a bag.''

His face took on a spare hint of remorse as he nipped a genteel taste of raspberry-glazed fruit from his dessert plate. ''. . . You know, Miss Prom. I do believe I've used too much lemon. Yes. You're absolutely correct. Please, don't force yourself to eat it on my account.''

''Last thing I need is you telling me what to do, Mister Know-It-All. Mind your own beeswax, why don't you? I need advice, I'll write to Dear Abby.''

After dinner, she stormed into the kitchen and responded with a sharp smack of the door when Lynch offered to help with the dishes. He hitched his shoulders in a noncommittal shrug, and I motioned for him to follow me out onto the porch.

He sat in the wicker rocker, folded his arms, and forced a brave, unconvincing smile. ''Lovely night, don't you think, Miss Archer?''

''What happened, Chief? What did you find out?''

His eyes made a broad sweep of the skyscape. He passed a finger through the air, searching. ''Look there. You see the single fast moving star beside that cluster of four? I forget the name.''

''Please, Chief. Whatever it is, tell me.''

He pressed his lips together, dropped his eyes to meet mine. His were weary and brimming with sadness. ''It's nothing, Miss Archer. That's the problem. There is absolutely nothing to tell.'' He met my gaze with a look of abject apology. ''Twice today I thought I was on the brink of discovery, but it all came to nothing.

''. . . I went to see Mr. Cunningham at the *Gazette*,

certain I could convince him to locate your mother's death certificate. A little threat often goes a long way with slackers and malingerers, I've found.''

''But?''

He sighed. ''But it seems his slacking and malingering has been more thorough than most, Miss Archer. All those file boxes are filled with nothing but old comic books. When pressed, Mr. Cunningham simply showed me a portion of his remarkable collection. Worth quite a fortune, it seems. Far more, in Cunningham's own words, than 'those danged records nobody cared about.' ''

''You mean he just threw everything out? How could he?''

''Without a bit of difficulty, I gather.''

I felt a sinking sense of disappointment. ''. . . You said there were two things.''

A listless nod. ''I went back to the building site for the Edmund House, and this time I managed to get hold of the construction foreman. I was able to persuade him to tell me what he knows about the Edmund Foundation.''

''And?''

''And unfortunately, he has no useful information at all. Communications and payments have been made by mail and channeled through a numbered Swiss account and a South American lawyer. The foreman has tried to reach the Edmund Foundation board with questions, but even he isn't able to contact them directly. The organization has been arranged as a complex maze of dummy entities. I'll be frank, Miss Archer, I'm running out of ideas.''

''You said it yourself, Chief. It takes time, patience.''

''True, Miss Archer. But it also takes a keen eye, an

acute, predatory instinct. I fear mine have gone dim and moldy.'' He leaned forward, hung his head. ''I'm afraid I've failed you.''

''Don't be silly. You haven't failed me at all. You've been wonderful.''

His head shook in a sorrowful arc. ''Not wonderful. Hardly.'' He looked up at me. ''I'm afraid Miss Prom is right. I am an ex-nobody from nowhere.''

''That's not true. Please, Chief. All this isn't necessary.''

He held up a hand. Dabbed at his eyes with a corner of his hankie. ''Yes. It is necessary. I want you to know the truth about me, Miss Archer. You deserve to know.''

I took his hand, felt the salve of his solid warmth. ''I already know the truth about you. You're a fine, sensitive, intelligent gentleman. And a good, caring friend. That's more than enough.''

''No. It isn't. Please hear me out. . . . My wife, Lorraine, died twelve years ago. She was ill for quite some time. So unjust. She was such an active, vital person. A wonderful woman.''

''I'm sorry to hear it.''

He shook his head. ''All she wanted was for me to take care of our daughter, Pamela. Those were her final words: 'See to Pam, Augustus. You know she needs looking after.' ''

A well of tears filled the hound eyes; there was a tremor in his voice. ''. . . Our daughter was a difficult young woman, always had a tough time of it. Emotional problems. I knew she needed a great deal of support, but after Lorraine died, I was so desolate, so lonely. I immersed myself in work, all but ignored the girl.''

The tears spilled over, tracing an erratic path down

his sallow, sunken cheeks. "I got the call in the middle of a big investigation. Pamela had taken tranquilizers, sleeping pills, enormous quantities. The ambulance took her to Michael Reese, but it was too late to save her. . . ."

He buried his face in his hands, pulsed with silent grief.

"I'm so sorry, Chief."

"It was all my fault."

I thought of my father, of Rachel. Raging seas with no predictable tides or currents. "She was ill. You mustn't blame yourself."

He mopped his eyes. Bound himself in taut ropes of control. "But I do blame myself. I should have been there for Pamela. I should have seen what was happening to her."

"It's done, Chief. No amount of guilt is going to bring her back."

He sniffed and took a breath. "I know. There is no reconciling with the past. Still, I'm compelled to keep trying. . . . That's the reason I came to Thornwood. Pamela was writing a novel when she died. She started it here, at the colony. I wanted to finish it for her, to do something . . ."

"So you will, Chief."

He lowered his eyes. "I don't seem to be able to finish that or anything, Miss Archer. I'm a foolish, old man. I should go back to the pasture where I belong."

"Nonsense. You belong right here. At least until you finish your work. Anyway, you can't go. You promised to help me find out what happened to my family. We're not licked yet. We'll find some way to trace those dummy corporations. We'll think of something. . . . Besides, if you leave, the kids and I would have to make do with

Granny's cooking. You wouldn't want that on your conscience, now would you?''

A flicker of a smile. ''You are too kind, Miss Archer. Of course, I'll stay on, if you insist.''

''I insist.''

He drew a deep breath. ''Then I suppose I'd best get a good night's sleep, try to clear this foggy old mind of mine and come up with some fresh ideas. Good night, Miss Archer. Pleasant dreams.''

''Good night, Chief Lynch. I hope things look better in the morning.''

''Perhaps they will.''

''I bet they will.''

''So good night, good night already,'' Granny said as she bustled out of the farmhouse, wiping her hands on her black dirndl skirt. ''No need to make a federal case out of it. You say good night, you go home. Period. Going, going, going. Comes to going—staying. Never saw such a fuss.''

She clunked and wobbled her way down the stairs and toward her cottage. Near the cedar copse, she was redrawn in shadow, converted to a large, lumbering beast, stalking its prey. Lynch followed at a determined distance.

I was haunted by his story. All that pain and guilt borne with such quiet dignity, faced with such candor and directness. The least I could do was face my own demons, confront them head on.

Upstairs, I forced myself to walk directly down the dim hall and throw open the door to my father's room. I would not panic, would not turn back like the last time. I kept my breathing slow and even, ignored my heart's frantic tap dance. My head filled with the musty odor as I flipped on the light.

Amazed, I kept looking from wall to wall. I tugged open the drawers and walked into the deep closet. Nothing. The room was stark empty. There was not a single trace of the man who spent his final years hiding here in terrified exile.

Still, an uneasy feeling worked its way under my skin. I was assailed by flashes of remembrance; echoes of desperate, panicked voices; a shattering blast; deep, cryptlike, terrifying silence. Something about this room.

But what? I could not bring it into focus. It was too distant, wrapped in too many dark, impenetrable layers. Chilled to the bone, I shut the light and closed the door hard behind me.

Tied in knots of tension, I soaked awhile in a neck-deep, bubble-salted tub, let my mind move with the lazy, floating currents.

There had to be a way through the tangle, a logical route I hadn't thought to follow. Lynch's words drifted through my mind. Walk back along the path, Miss Archer. Follow it back . . .

How was I going to break through the stone walls of my own memories and this town's conspiratorial silence? If one more person told me that Thornwood was a separate world . . . not a part of the town at all.

Then I had lived on an arts colony, if only as a little girl. And the fact was, it did have a separate existence, a tone and character of its own. It was distinct from Ashby, had to be. That was the point of a colony, after all: getting away, shedding mundane intrusions like so many stifling layers of extra clothing.

It was like that at all the colonies. I remembered Aunt Lizzie comparing Thornwood to Strassdale, Carmenton. She knew those other retreats in an intimate, family sense. They were all connected in a way, joined in their deliberate separateness.

The water sloshed, slopped a trail over the edge of the clawfoot, and spattered on the irregular tile floor.

All connected.

Of course.

The revelation was a cool rush of energy. I stepped out of the tub and into my white cotton robe. It was not too late to call and make an appointment.

Tomorrow, I would have my answers.

CHAPTER 29

I WAS DRESSED and down pacing my eagerness over the pebbled linoleum long before Granny arrived for her daily dawn patrol.

She made no secret of her annoyance when I told her in a breathless rush that I had an important errand to run and would be back in about an hour. With luck, it wouldn't take any longer than that.

"Can't tell you what to do, Emily. You're a big girl, after all. But all this running around you do does make a person wonder."

A person would have to cope with the wondering, I thought and hurried outside, trailed by her muttered protests. I decided not to stop at the cottage and tell Lynch about the trip, hoping I'd have something to surprise him with when I returned.

Tracking a maze of narrow back roads laid out like spider legs on the Ashby map, I made decent time to state highway 46 and drove through the town of Great Barrington. The main road was flanked by countless strips of motel rooms whose flashing neon signs boasted air conditioning, cable television, and vacancies. There were ramshackle antique shops and family restaurants, a miniature golf course where players could shoot their practice balls like bullets through the empty eyes and down the throats of smiling, garish clown faces.

At the outskirts of the town, I turned off the main thoroughfare and followed a trail of faded, hand-lettered signs along a series of dirt-strand roads. I passed trailer parks jammed with long motor homes on cement-block foundations and enclaves of shabby ranch houses settled like Monopoly pieces on the patchy landscape. A rangy Irish Setter came bounding out from one weed-choked backyard, barking at the Jeep's wobbly progress. He followed for several blocks until he was forced to drop off in a standing heap of exhaustion, ribs flaring like air-starved nostrils, long tongue flapping like a flag.

A final sign, carved to resemble a gloved hand pointing a finger, directed me down a winding, wooded camp road. The Strassdale Colony for the Furtherance of Arts and Letters (founded 1952) was nestled at the dead end. It was fronted by a stark white picket fence and a row of wooden wine barrels planted with marigolds and petunias.

The Jeep bucked over deep ruts and rises in the pebble-capped road. Here, the cabins were set in a broad circle around the main building, strung together by trampled footpaths and empty clotheslines.

Lou Devaney, the colony administrator, had promised to arrange a meeting for me with Strassdale's cook, Ingeborg Larson, who had been a constant fixture at the place since its inception.

The blue-stone drive ribboned around the large, brick-faced colonial main building and terminated in a black-topped oval fitted with a tall, green dumpster and the colony's twin, black panel trucks. I parked in the tunnel of space between them and went in through the rear door to the kitchen.

A tall, slender, uniformed woman with braided gray hair was stirring in a large copper kettle, raising a cloud of onion-scented steam. There was the delectable aroma of sweet pastry, a rush of fragrant warmth from the glowing wall oven.

"Miss Larson?"

She gave me a curious look and instructed me to sit at the long, polished pine table. "I know why you've come," she said simply. "I figured you would—eventually."

"Mr. Devaney explained, then."

"He didn't have to explain. He said Hillard Fowler's daughter. I could guess the rest. . . ."

"Then you can help me." I felt the tension spreading through me like an electric fever. "You know what happened at Thornwood."

The kettle hissed and raised a low, keening wail. She filled a metal tea ball with fragrant, brown leaves and set it to steep in a delicate, porcelain mug. Her face was tight with worry. Deep lines furrowed the pale forehead and the slim lips were drawn in a determined seam. "A thousand times, I told her. 'The girl has to know, Lizzie,' I said. 'You can't keep it from her forever.' But she loved you like a mother, Emily. She wanted to keep the ugliness away from your life. She tried."

Ugliness. "You're a friend of Lizzie's, then?"

She pulled up the tea ball by its fine metal chain and took a tentative sip. A haze of steam rose from the mug in misty tendrils. "Poor woman. To think of all she had to bear. All the terrible secrets."

"Tell me," I said in a choked whisper. "I have to know."

She looked deep into my eyes, beyond. "Yes, of course. You know this is not going to be easy to hear."

I felt a rush of fear. "Yes, I know."

She hesitated, seemed to be ordering her thoughts. ". . . Your mother died under what the police called—suspicious circumstances. There was an investigation, a flurry of rumor in the town. Then they dropped it."

"What kind of suspicious circumstances?"

She made a sorry shake of her head. "According to Lizzie, your mother was dusting off one of your father's guns when it went off by accident, fired at her head. She died instantly."

Hot sparks of disbelief were singeing my mind. "But that makes no sense. My mother hated guns. My father kept rifles for skeet shooting, and they argued about them all the time. She didn't want them in the house, insisted he keep them in a padlocked case. She would never go near them. Certainly not to dust. Never."

She nodded. "That was common knowledge. Many people, the police included, believed Lizzie made up the accident story to protect your father. But they didn't have enough evidence to take to a jury. Not that time—or the others."

"Others? What are you talking about?" I was in a cold, clammy sweat, thoughts undulating like images in a fun-house mirror.

Her eyes were filled with sadness. "It's hard. I know. Take your time with it, Emily. Don't try to absorb it all at once."

I tried to force air past the thick swell of nausea rising in my gut. ‘‘I’m all right. Please, go on.’’

She cleared her throat. ‘‘Your father was known to have had several . . . women friends. Over the course of the next few years, several of them died in a series of tragic . . . accidents, too. A drowning. A deadly fall. An automobile that went out of control on a steep hill. All of them were labeled accidents. All impossible to prove otherwise.’’

‘‘You’re telling me you think my father was responsible for all those deaths?’’

She ticked her tongue, blew out a breath. ‘‘I have no proof, only feelings, rumors. There was never anything to go on but Lizzie’s word, and she was unshakable, swore your mother’s death was an accident, that she saw the whole thing. Swore she was with your father at all times during the other incidents, that he was never out of her sight. She was your father’s alibi.’’

I shivered. ‘‘That’s an awful lot of coincidence to swallow. All of the victims involved my father? All killed in suspicious accidents?’’

‘‘Yes, it is an awful lot. The people involved in the investigation were more than suspicious, but they couldn’t prove anything. They were forced to accept Lizzie’s testimony supporting your father.’’

‘‘But I can’t imagine Aunt Lizzie covering up a murder. I can’t accept that.’’

‘‘It’s hard, I know, Emily. But there’s no other way to make sense out of what happened.’’

‘‘It can’t be, Miss Larson. There has to be another explanation.’’

‘‘The only other bit of evidence was dismissed after a while, as a child's prank.''

''What was that?''

She stared into my eyes, trying to gauge my reaction. ''Each time there was an . . . accident involving one of these young women, the police found a doll hanging by the neck from the large maple at the colony's entrance. Local children took to calling it the hanging tree. It's the sort of peculiar, quirky business that usually draws public attention to a case, catches the eye of the press. But not at Thornwood.''

The rest of it settled on me in a suffocating mass. All the lies and evasions. ''. . . Because the whole town of Ashby conspired to keep the case their dirty little secret.''

''I'm afraid that's true. Mass murder is not what you'd call a tourist attraction. Ashby was coming into its own after decades of difficult economic struggle. Your father opening the colony there helped, and outsiders were finally accepting the place as a reasonable alternative to West Stockbridge and some of the other, more well-known Berkshire towns. The last thing Ashby wanted was a nasty scandal.''

''But why didn't people stop coming to the colony? They must have heard the rumors.''

She cocked her head, sipping again at her tea. ''People hear what they want to hear. The pull of Thornwood has always been stronger than sense. They came for the magic. They still do.''

''Magic?''

''It's there. And here, too.'' She closed her eyes briefly. Inhaled. ''It's here.''

I felt her watching me as I tried to sort through all the incomprehensible horror. Every situation had its rules. There had to be a thread of sense in all this I could find if I forced myself to dig deep enough, looked with the proper eye.

Or maybe I'd done too much looking already.

CHAPTER 30

I'M RUNNING. PUSHED by the slick, insistent fingers of a frozen wind. Racing on legs turned to screaming metal strings that shiver dangerous octaves above high C. The terror brands searing holes in the surface of my lungs, stings my naked mind. Can't stop now. They're after me.

Coming close.

Closer.

One by one, they slip their bonds, dribble out of their nooses as if their heads had gone liquid. Free, they drop down from the tree with a hallow clunk and move toward me. There's a long, ragged line of them now, chasing after me. Pointing. Taunting with their dead, bony fingers. Laughing faces etched on cold sheets of dried rubber. Mouths drawn back in grotesque smiles. The eyes smile, too. Empty knowing smiles I can see through. Tunnel smiles that draw me down, under.

I have to stop. Can't go on. But the first of them is gaining on me. Closer now. So close the sweet, metal, dead scent fills my head. I'm inflating, expanding with each icy breath of terror. Straining for release. The scream starts at the pit bottom of my fear, builds to take me over. I am the scream. Help me, help! . . .

I was wrenched awake. A rioting crowd was stampeding inside my chest, trampling my brain. In the sooty darkness, I tried to find my lost place in the blind span of reality. The dream was fading like the salty, hushed aftermath of a tidal wave. But there was still the scream.

"Help me! Oh, God, no! No!"

The desperate shrills drew me down the cold, shadowy hall. Downstairs.

"Help!"

I flipped on the overhead kitchen light and squinted through the rush of glare. The screams were hidden by the counter, coming from the corner near the stove.

I found Rachel huddled there beside the puppy's carton, her body curled in a tight question mark. Her slender back was pulsing, hands cupped over her eyes, trying to block out the horror.

The fur ball was whimpering in a powerless, near-silent shrill. There was blood everywhere: splattered on the fresh carpet of shredded papers, the sides of the carton. Blood mottled the silky fur in an oozing, scarlet rash.

Fighting back a sick swell of dizziness, I spotted the bloody scissors, the near-severed plume tail dangling like a broken twig.

Shivering with disgust, I checked the site of the wound. The bleeding had stopped, clotted in a fiery bubble. Lifting the pup, I wrapped the blood-crusted tail in a clean dishtowel tourniquet and called the emergency veterinary clinic in Pittsfield.

I explained what had happened, my revulsion growing as I painted the horrific incident with words. A bored, sleepy voice asked a batch of mechanical questions: How much blood? How deep was the cut? How old was the puppy? Did I know how to make a pressure bandage? No, it wasn't necessary for me to bring the dog in, certainly not tonight. Keep an eye on it, the voice yawned, and if there were any signs of infection, they'd have a look tomorrow or the next day. Chances were, it would heal right up on its own. No big deal.

We might have been talking about the price of dog biscuits, for all the concern or interest in the voice.

Rachel was still kneeling over the bloody box, head twisted over her shoulder, watching me. I cradled the dog and held up a bowl of cool water until he poked out his tongue and took a halfhearted slurp. Searching through the drawers, I found the necessary wad of cotton, paper-wrapped gauze pad, and surgical tape. As instructed, I slathered the wound with antiseptic salve and wrapped it in a fresh bandage. With a damp cloth, I dabbed at the bloody patches on his coat. Then I sat on one of the ladderback chairs at the table and gentled him like an ailing infant with soft strokes and chanted reassurances. "Ssh, Maxy, old boy. You'll be okay, buddy. You'll be fine."

I couldn't bring myself to look at her. Fury was a perilous live wire sizzling in my gut, threatening to erupt in licks of uncontrollable flame. How could she do such a thing? How could she?

A low, keening moan escaped her. She drew a dramatic breath and started to cry, arms stretched like bandages around her wavering back. I tried to find a morsel of understanding, a crumb of human empathy. But I couldn't feel anything for that wretched child. She had turned my blood to ice water, forced polished rods of cold, steel hatred through my bones.

Her cries stilled to a tremble; a silent, syncopated pulse. Slowly, she uncoiled and stood to face me with blood-ridden eyes, face swollen and tear-streaked, lips puffed and wavering with deliberate traces of leftover remorse. High drama.

"Is Max going to be all right?" she sniffed.

I was caught in a violent shiver of rage. "Go to your room, Rachel."

"Is Max all right, I said?" The words climbed in an indignant shrill. "Is he?"

"Why do you want to know? So you can start thinking about better ways to hurt him? Maybe kill him next time? Go to bed, Rachel. Get out of my sight."

The puppy stiffened and yelped. I hushed my voice and soothed him back to sleep.

Her eyes bulged. "Are you fucking crazy? I didn't do this. I'd never hurt my own dog."

"I don't want to hear it. None of it. Get out of here. Now!"

Her words were tight, desperate. "It wasn't me, goddamn it. It was the monster. The noise woke me up, and I came down here. He saw me and went running out the back door. His hands were all bloody, and he had this crazy look on his face. If I didn't show up, he might have killed Max altogether. I told you to get us away from that goddamned monster, but you wouldn't listen. This is all your goddamned fucking fault."

"Get out of here!"

She stared at me, through me. "I'm taking Max up to sleep with me. I can take care of him better than you."

"Over my dead body." In a spasm of rage, I stood and carried the dog up to my room, locked the door to keep her out.

He curled up on the towel I laid out for him on the

opposite side of the bed and drifted off in a slack heap of exhaustion.

"Poor, sweet little fur ball."

Propped against the pillow, I watched him breathe, placed a careful hand over his ribs to monitor the rhythmic swell of his tiny chest, the steady butterfly flutter of his heartbeat. I went cold at the sound of Rachel's angry footsteps on the stairs. She was mumbling to herself, swearing at the silence. "I'm getting out of this goddamned place. I'm running the hell away, once and for all." Her door smacked shut with a furious thud.

Where was it going to end? How much more could I allow this child to do?

Dr. Havenick was wrong. There was only one way to handle all this, one certain way to keep her from doing any more damage.

And I intended to see to it first thing in the morning.

CHAPTER 31

HAVENICK WAS NOT answering his phone. I dialed for what felt like the hundredth time and again heard the exasperating drone of his message tape. . . . No, I would not like to leave a message. No, I did not understand that he was unable to come to the phone right now, and I did not accept his honeyed apology. No, it was not all right if he got back to me as soon as he could. If I ever ran into the person who invented answering machines, I wished it could be with the front tires of my Jeep. Not all Penny Satenstein's notions were sound, but four-wheel-drive justice did have a certain irresistible appeal.

All right. I would have to do this without Havenick's help. With a shudder of resolution, I looked up the number of the High View Psychiatric Hospital in Great Barrington and got through to the medical director of the children's unit.

I recounted the whole sordid tale of Rachel's deteriorating behavior during the past hideous week. I forced myself to sound clinical, to leave out loaded words like "wicked" and "vicious" and stick to presentable psycho-babble. ". . . She's obsessed with this so-called monster of hers," I concluded. "And I'm very concerned that she might be capable of doing some very serious damage to herself . . . or someone else."

There was a long, onerous pause. Dr. Eileen Slattery came back on the line and asked me to hold for another of her extended minutes. I could hear the timbre of her garbled voice through the palm she held over the receiver. Maybe she was explaining things to a colleague, making arrangements to admit Rachel.

It was the only way. I was convinced things were worse, far worse than Havenick had imagined. And far more dangerous. Next time it could be Adam or David. Next time the damage could be permanent.

Slattery climbed back into the conversation. Her tone had chilled by several degrees. "Sorry to keep you waiting, but I'm afraid there's nothing we can do for you here at High View. Our children's unit is filled at the moment. And more important, if Bart Havenick doesn't think your daughter needs to be hospitalized, I'm sure she doesn't. As you may know, Bart is president of the local child psychiatry association. He's very well respected at High View and in all the mental health facilities in the area. Believe me, Mrs. Archer. If your daughter's problems were that serious, Bart would be the first to insist she be admitted. He's very cautious."

"But he didn't know about the dog. He didn't know she was capable of anything like that."

Now she turned coy. "Oh, now, Mrs. Archer. I'm sure Bart took everything about your child into consideration. You know, if we hospitalized every youngster who did something reckless or foolish, we'd have to close our schools, roll up our playgrounds. Rachel is probably just acting out. Wait until Bart gets back, and he'll help the two of you work through the whole business. You'll see. You'll have a good laugh about it all."

"A laugh? No. I'm afraid no one could possibly convince me there's anything amusing about vicious, mindless violence, Dr. Slattery. Not even . . . Bart."

Her tone was dry ice. "Well, then, why don't you discuss all this with Dr. Havenick Monday, after he gets back from the conference. I'm sure he'll help you determine the best course of action."

"Conference?" I was sinking. Havenick had mentioned a meeting, said he wouldn't be able to see Rachel again until after the weekend, but it hadn't penetrated.

"Oh, yes, didn't he tell you? Bart was selected to attend the APA national leadership conference in the Bahamas. Quite an honor, huh? I told you he was well thought of, Mrs. Archer. He's a very bright, capable person. Do yourself a favor. Listen to Bart."

I tried the other two psychiatric hospitals in the county. Same dismal result. If Havenick thought she needed hospitalizing, he'd say so. Wasn't I being just a trifle hysterical? This was rather a drastic step, after all.

Ruth Messenger's backup was no better. He listened, made sympathetic noises, and told me he was convinced this could wait until Ruth returned in the middle of the week. No, he was not at all concerned that Rachel might turn on her brothers. Apparently Dr. Sorley's crystal ball came with a strong warranty and a very powerful remote receiver.

I tried Cornell, the children's units at several other New York hospitals. The best anyone could offer was a complete evaluation. Perhaps they could fit her in at the end of next week. No, this did not qualify as an emergency. Well, yes. If she actually did physical violence to a small child, that would qualify. But she hadn't, now had she?

There had to be a way. I couldn't allow my little boys or anyone else to be jeopardized by legions of irrational medical minds.

Maybe Lynch could help. As police chief, he'd had plenty of experience with dangerous people and volatile situations.

Granny was in the kitchen with the boys, beating on a lump of bread dough as if she held a particular grudge against it. Adam executed a perfect parody, thumping with wild abandon on his English muffin while David, who had battered his beyond recognition, gnawed on a flaccid slice of American cheese.

Rachel was still asleep or pretending to be. I settled Max down in the fresh box I'd fixed for him, offered Granny a vague, deliberately misleading explanation about how his tail came to be wounded. I told her I was going out for a short walk and asked her to keep a close, careful eye on the little ones.

"Now, Emily. I was watching children long before you were even given a mouth to insult people with."

"I didn't mean to insult you. It's just especially important that you keep an eye on them today."

"Well," she sniffed. "Lucky thing I'm not touchy like some people."

A timid sun was inching up from the edge of the earth, fitting the top-heavy cedars with long trails of spidery shadow. My sandaled feet slogged on the dewy, rain-drenched ground, and my head was packed with the musty stale aroma of things left soaking too long in the dark.

I walked at a fast, determined clip across the broad meadow, shivered as the morning chill slipped through the flimsy cotton of my camp shirt and insinuated its cool, willowy fingers up my spine.

Lynch's cottage was a hazy, charcoal smudge in the distant mist. Wishing for the welcoming beacon of his lights, I decided to wake him if need be. This could not wait.

Outside the cabin door, I stopped for a second to draw a decent breath. From within came the insistent beat of a leaky faucet, the strident ticking of a travel alarm. I rapped at the door.

Nothing.

I knocked again and opened the door a cautious crack, not wanting to startle him if he were still asleep.

The bed was made, the cabin in pristine order. I looked around several times before I spotted the folded note bearing my name propped against the Smith Corona.

He had left before seven to make the two-hour drive to Boston, he wrote. An old friend on the force there would help him dig into my mother's death and the other freak "accidents" involving my father.

After my visit to Strassdale, I had told the chief I could not accept Aunt Lizzie covering up for my father, allowing him to go on killing people. I didn't know or understand the stranger my father had become, but I did know Aunt Lizzie. That woman wasn't capable of such evil deceit. There had to be another explanation.

Lynch promised to get right on it, to find out if any part of the ancient damning rumors could possibly be true. In a manic rush, he'd set out a whole new plan of investigative attack. But Rachel's craziness had forced all that to the distant hollows of my mind.

According to the note, Lynch expected to be back by midafternoon. Nothing to do in the meantime but wait and make sure the little ones were safe.

Granny was having what appeared to be a cleaning fit. Armed with several long-stemmed mops and brooms, a thick mound of rags and a bucket jammed with cleansers, she lumbered from room to room, assaulting the dirt with a grim expression and a series of guttural grunts.

I tried to read the boys a story, but she kept spraying and grunting, scratching the broom against the wooden floors until the sound settled under my skin like a rash of splinters.

"I can do the rest, Granny. There's no need for you to stay."

"Oh, now," she huffed. "So you don't care if I come or go, is that the way? All you care for is your crock of a Sherlock, after all. Been that way ever since Big Chief Blowhard showed up. . . . Fine then, I'll go. Wouldn't want to be underfoot, now would I?"

"It's just not necessary for you to do all that. The place is clean enough."

She swatted me away like a pesty gnat. "No need to explain, Emily. I know when I'm not wanted. Always did." Muttering under her breath, she tramped out of the kitchen and butted her way through the front door. There was the buffalo charge of her furious footsteps down the wooden stairs.

I listened to the retreat with no small sense of relief. At times, that woman felt like something stuck between my teeth.

Rachel still hadn't come downstairs, avoiding me as long as possible, I assumed. The boys were playing in the den. They had draped one of Aunt Lizzie's cotton afghans over the kneehole in the desk and crawled underneath, giggling in wild abandon at their infinite cleverness.

''The star warriors can't see us,'' Adam said in a pneumatic whisper.

''No theeyus,'' David lisped. ''Ssh.''

A vicious headache was pounding behind my eyes. I found a tin of aspirin in the cabinet beside the sink and took out a glass. As I ran the faucet to let the water cool, I spotted Granny's ring settled in a ceramic dish. She must have taken it off to do the cleaning and forgotten it in the heat of her snit.

Rachel hadn't stirred. If I hurried, I could probably deliver the ring and get back to the farmhouse before my resident monster decided to face the day. That was a far more appealing scenario than having Granny drop by to get it herself, and probably stay. And stay.

Declaring a temporary cease-fire between the boys and their invisible adversaries, I was able to lure David and Adam out of their crocheted encampment for a quick hike to Granny's cottage.

A blazing flame of a sun had baked the earth dry and polished the air to a blinding sheen. I forced a rapid stride, and the little ones raced to keep up, trailing a step or two behind like obedient ducklings. The heat had raised a rash of creature tempers. A haze of cranky mosquitos shimmered over the pond; toads croaked in hoarse complaint. A broad-winged crow dipped and squawked its strident message across the empty air.

''M'firsty, Mommy,'' David said.

''All right, Monkey. We'll get some water at Granny's.'' I slowed and wiped the shimmer of sweat from his forehead. His face was flushed and bothered.

''Daybit firsty.''

''Okay,'' I said. ''We'll be there in a minute.'' I quickened my pace, anxious to be done with this and back to the relative comfort of the airy farmhouse. We trudged past the cedar copse, trooped across the last parched ribbon of dirt road, and passed under the shady bower of the hanging tree. I shivered in the earthy coolness, hurried away and toward the colony gate.

At the road's edge, I stopped and took firm hold of a pudgy hand in each of mine. In tandem, we set out to walk the last hundred yards to Granny's tiny stone cottage, our rhythm set by the now relentless back beat of David's complaints. "M'vewy firsty. Vewy."

"We're almost there, Monkey. See? That's Granny's house."

"Gammy hout!" He broke loose and took off at a mad tilt toward the cottage, plump legs churning, arms flailing with a surge of mindless enthusiasm.

Fear gripped me as I imagined a carefree Ashby tourist careening around the nearby curve in the narrow pavement, mowing him down.

"David, stop!"

He kept hurtling along the road's edge, but Adam was frozen solid by the edict. In the second it took me to pause and scoop him up in my arms, David had swerved in from the road, traversed the tiny span of unkempt grass toward the cottage, and climbed the three worn, wooden steps to Granny's front porch. I caught up just as he started slapping his hands against the splintery frame of the patched screen door. "Gammy!"

"Ssh," I said. "Take it easy." I demonstrated a sedate knuckle rap and waited in the smoldering heat, trying to force air past the hot lava welling in my lungs.

There was the slow, approaching thunk of footsteps,

the inner door screeched on rusty hinges. Granny's considerable silhouette loomed behind the locked screen. All the heavy cabin drapes were drawn, stealing all but a few scattered slivers of daylight.

"Yes?"

"You left your ring at the house, Granny." I fished for it in the pocket of my shorts and held the rutted, gold circle up for her to see. "I didn't want you to miss it and worry."

"Oh. Well, thank you, dearie. You can just leave it out there in the milk box. I'm not dressed."

"Sure. No problem. Come on, guys. Let's go."

"Daybit firsty!" He mounted his famous siren scream, starting at a low warning shrill that escalated in a steady swell until the morning's calm was shattered and the air pulsed with the considerable might of his indignation.

I shrugged at the silhouette. "Could he just have a little water?"

She sputtered. Her mouth worked open and closed like a straining fist. "All right. Stay there," she said finally and disappeared into the shadowy recesses of the room.

David was still wailing when she came back. I heard the metallic clank of several chains, locks flipping. She held out a jelly glass full of water and wrenched the door shut again, nearly trapping several of my fingers in the process.

"Thanks," I said and handed the glass to David who miscalculated in his overeagerness and slopped most of the cool liquid down the front of his shirt and onto his sneakers.

He screeched as if he'd been burned and held the glass out for refilling. I rapped again at the locked screen. Waited. David's cries were shattering the slim remains of my patience. I knocked again. Harder this time.

Granny's disembodied voice came from behind the closed door. "Well, what is it now, Emily?"

"Could we please have a little more water? David spilled his."

She registered her impatience in a furious whoosh of breath. "All right, I suppose." I heard her plod across the room, run the tap. The disembodied hand poked through the screen, holding forth another glass. Before it was sucked again into the void, I placed the empty jelly jar into the oversized palm and slipped the ring on the first knuckle of the thick index finger. As she was about to reel the hand back into the shadows, the ring slipped off and rolled through a crack in the plank floor of the tiny painted porch.

"Now look what you've done!" Granny burst out through the screen and crouched to peer through the crack. She was dressed after all, wearing her worn, brown linen dress and ubiquitous, black patent pumps. But she was barely recognizable without the overgenerous makeup and flamboyant wig. Her real hair was a wispy, air-pollution gray, fine enough to show broad patches of scaly, dry scalp. It was drawn back in a thin rubber band aided by a trail of shiny, black bobby pins. Bereft of makeup, her features were softer, like fabric laundered and soaked until it had surrendered its sheen and sizing.

"That tears it," she said. "Now what do I do?"

I knelt beside her, and stared into the discouraging blackness. There was a spare opening at the far side of the stairs. "I'll crawl underneath."

"No," she said in a panicky shrill. "You go on home,

now. You've done enough already . . ." The door squeaked again. Her head shot up and her voice narrowed to a reedy shriek. "Get inside now! Get back in the house."

I followed her gaze to the cottage. There was a shadowy figure huddled in the doorway. It seemed to shrivel under Granny's verbal assault.

"Get back inside, I said. Now hurry up!"

"Who's that?" I shielded my eyes, trying to hasten their adjustment from the glare to the inky darkness.

Adam cowered behind me, pointing a pudgy, trembling finger at the shadow. "Make him go way, Mommy! I'm scared."

I wrapped him in a hug and stroked his back. "What is it, sweetie? What's wrong?"

"Make the pond man go away!" He was shivering in fright, breathing in small, whimpering pulses, still pointing at the image.

"Ssh."

"Jesus Christ, Teddy," Granny said. "Can't you do as I say? Get back now. Get inside the house this minute." She stood and started moving toward the door, menacing the shadow with a raised club of a fist.

The door swung open. The dark figure lumbered out onto the tiny porch, emitted an ungodly grunt, and pointed back at Adam. "Eh, eh," he said and tugged his cracked lips into an eerie grimace. "Buh!"

Paralyzed with shock, I took in the crossed eyes, the complexion pocked and bubbled with severe cystic acne, the saggy pouch of a double chin, the sack of flab around his middle. Even the way he was dressed: baggy worn jeans; wrinkled, blue plaid shirt; thick, brown belt fastened with a brass buckle inset with the Coca-Cola logo; blue, high-top sneakers.

Rachel's monster.

"Who . . . who's that?"

Granny's eyes were round with fear. "Now please, Emily. Don't get excited. Let me explain."

". . . That's Rachel's monster. She described him exactly. You knew about it all along. You knew she was telling the truth."

Her face went cheesy pale. "Now, now. You don't understand. Let me explain about Teddy. Please."

I clutched a chubby wrist in each hand, took a step backward, kept the boys close within the shade of my protection. "Go ahead. Explain."

She walked over to the grimacing figure, raked her splayed fingers through his greasy, mud-brown hair, tucked his rumpled shirt down tighter in the pinched waistband of his jeans. ". . . Teddy's no monster, Emily. He's my dearest boy . . . my good, sweet little boy, just like those dear little cherubs are to you."

"But he chased Rachel, he . . ."

She sucked in a breath and nodded. "I know what the little girl said. I'm sure she was just scared is all. Problem is, Teddy's not much to look at. Has to do with his illness and all. Boy can't help the way he looks, now can he? Poor thing always has had this way of giving people a fright till they get used to him."

A flush of anger was climbing my cheeks. Adam was still pulsing with terror. "She was not just scared. What about all those things he did? He cut her hair, and the dog's tail . . . and all the rest of it." The gruesome truth washed over me in a dizzy wave. Poor Rachel. I'd refused to believe her, accused her of all those terrible, unspeakable acts.

Granny bit her lip. Her face crinkled in a taut

mask of pain. She tugged at Teddy's crinkled collar, rubbed at a lick of soil on his pimply neck. "You are a good boy, now aren't you, Teddy, darling? You're Mama's good, good boy." She turned to face me, her voice stretched with pleading. "Teddy's a little . . . slow, Emily. He doesn't always understand what's right."

"Then someone has to control him, make sure he stays out of trouble. You can't let him go around menacing people, doing these awful, dangerous things. Why didn't you warn me? How could you let me go on thinking it was all Rachel's fault?"

Her lip quivered, head drooped until the cupcake chin rested near the plump swell of her bosom. "I was afraid," she said in a tiny voice. "I'm sorry."

"You were afraid! What about Rachel? And what about the rest of us? We all could have been hurt. God knows what else he was capable of doing."

She came toward me and clutched my hand like a starving mendicant. "Please, please. You can't tell anyone about this, Emily. Last time they put him away in one of those institutions, they all but killed my baby boy. He was beaten up by one of the aides, neglected. Poor thing caught a death of a flu, and they left him to lie there in his own filth. If I hadn't come to visit . . . Oh, God. Please. I'll keep a closer watch on him, make sure he takes enough of his medicine. I promise."

She dropped my hand and walked over to Teddy. He was watching the proceedings with what appeared to be mild curiosity. ". . . Tell her you'll be a good boy, won't you, dearie? No more sneaking out on your mama. And tell her you'll take your medicine like a good boy. Now won't you?" She turned toward me, her voice stretched thin with desperation. ''You can't tell anyone, Emily. You just can't.''

I held the boys close to my sides. Adam's shivers had stilled. ''You can't keep this a secret. He's dangerous.''

''No, he's not. Not when his medicine's working.'' She tucked a stray hair behind his pendulous ear. ''Teddy's a lamb most of the time, never has a problem during the day. It's the fits make him act up, sneak away during the night and do naughty things. The medicine usually takes care of it, but every so often, something changes, and the dose needs adjusting. Now, isn't that right, Teddy? I bet that's the whole problem, isn't it, dearie? Your pills aren't doing what they're supposed to, now are they?''

''Ah guh.''

''You see?'' Granny said. ''He said, 'I good.' Yes, you are, darling, a very good boy. Why, all those times I came to help you out, Teddy stayed right here like he was told, never moved a step out of the cottage, did you, dearie?'' She held out a trembling trough of a hand. ''I always keep the door locked when he's here alone. And I make real sure he has his pills right on time, Emily. I've always done everything I could for him. We'll get the medicine straightened out. You'll see.''

Teddy clapped his hands, rocking back on his heels. ''Guh buh!''

''There, you hear that? Yes, Teddy's a good boy. And soon, he's going to a nice, new school. Isn't that right, darling?'' She filled my eyes with her pleading. ''They're planning to open a wonderful new place in town, Emily. Soon as it's ready, Teddy'll move in where they'll have folks to keep an eye on him all the time, help him learn how to take care of himself, maybe how to read. Now wouldn't that be nice?''

The Edmund House. "I understand all that. The problem is right now, Granny. I'm sure Teddy doesn't mean to hurt anyone, but he's done some awful, dangerous things. We're lucky there hasn't been more serious damage. I won't take chances with my children's safety. You can't expect me to do that."

"Oh, God. Please, Emily." Her face was twisted with grief, her voice reduced to a mewling whimper. "You mustn't tell anyone. There's no other place for Teddy to go until they open the new building. I have to keep him here with me, I must. Don't you see? If they put my baby back in one of those institutions, he might not make it. He's all I have, Emily. Everything. . . ." She buried her face in her hands and collapsed in a spasm of grief.

"Gammy kyin," David said and shook his head in firm opposition. "No ky, Gammy. Ssh."

"It's all right, Monkey. Granny's worried, that's all." I waited until she regained her composure, using the time to set my thoughts in order.

"Please, Emily," she sniffed. "I'll make sure he doesn't get out at night. I don't know what more I can do."

Teddy stood beside the door, face stretched in his odd grimace of a smile. He kept trying to engage Adam in a game of his own invention, imitating my little boy's every move: crouching when Adam did, hiding behind his cupped fingers, shrieking "mama" and darting behind Granny's back. For all his evil actions, he was an innocent. A child.

I found myself smiling at his antics, forgetting for an instant what he'd done. . . .

"I'm going to pack up and take the children away

from here, today. I can finish up my business with the Berkshire Federation over the phone. I'll explain things to Chief Lynch. You concentrate on Teddy, keep a close watch on him until the new facility opens. That's the best solution.''

A fresh glint of panic crept into her teary eyes. ''No, you can't leave yet, Emily. Not till you've settled things and finished getting the house in order. That won't do at all. Don't you worry, I'll keep Teddy here at the cottage. He won't get anywhere near the colony. On my life, I promise. Please don't go. Please.''

There was no point in discussing this further. After we were packed and ready to leave, I would stop by with the children and say a quick good-bye. ''Everything will work out. Don't worry about it. Listen . . . we'd better be getting back to the house now. I left Rachel sleeping.''

I forced a wavering smile in Teddy's direction. He lifted a thick, callused hand and warped his lips in a gargoyle smirk. ''Bah . . . buh.''

''No, darling, you're not a bad boy,'' Granny said. ''You're my sweet angel. It's just the pills aren't working.''

I hurried the boys toward the colony. We retraced our path through the pocked wooden gate, under the broad bubble of shade cast by the hanging tree, down the rutted access road toward the farmhouse. My thoughts were bumping over the perilous, new terrain. Who knew what brutal acts Teddy was capable of committing when he was caught in the blind power of his ''fits''? And who could tell when the next one would strike? Granny's assurances aside, I couldn't wait to have everyone safely away from this place. There were far worse perils, I knew, than unresolved childhood questions.

''Where we going?'' Adam said, troubled by my urgency. I had tugged them at a near-run past the cedar copse and onto the gentle meadow fronting the farmhouse.

''We're going home, Addie. Back to New York.''

''Ayyy . . . lub Noo Awk,'' David chirped in dissonant parody of his favorite commercial.

''Good, I'm glad you love New York. We'll be there soon.''

''Home, Mommy?''

''Yes, Adam. I don't think I have the strength for any more peace and quiet.''

We straggled over the final stretch of grass, climbed the broad porch steps, and walked into the musty, cool foyer.

''Rachel?'' I called up the stairs. ''Rach? I have to talk to you. Are you up?''

Nothing doing. She was going to stay buried in her room until something forced her out. I hurried up the narrow flight, anxious to tell her about Teddy, to begin making things up to her. ''Rachel?''

Her door was locked. I jiggled the knob and called again.

Remembering Aunt Lizzie's trick from the days when attempting to disappear was a favorite act of mine, I pried up the two long brass bolts holding the hinges and pulled the door off its fittings.

The room was empty. Her bed still smooth and made from the day before. On the spread was a note rendered in minuscule block print: ''I'm never coming back,'' it said over Rachel's wavering skull-and-crossbones logo.

''No, not now.'' My head was spinning. How could

she pick this of all times to carry out her threats?

I had to find her, get her and the little ones far away from this place before one of us became its next tragic victim.

CHAPTER 32

A POWDER BLUE patrol car turned into the colony minutes after I made the call, a probable violation of the local two-step law for which I was overwhelmingly grateful.

A single uniformed officer snaked out of the car. He was plump and copper-haired with algae-green eyes and a massive, russet walrus moustache. One ruddy cheek bulged with a huge chaw of tobacco, and he paused every several words to spit in punctuation.

"You say you got a"—spit—"missing person?"

"My daughter, Rachel. I think she's been gone all night. Her bed wasn't slept in. She left this note."

He twisted the pointed edge of the moustache, spat. "How old?"

"She's eleven. We have to find her quickly. She was very upset."

"She ever run . . . away before . . . ?"

"No. I mean, not more than hiding around the house. She's threatened to—but."

He made an entry on his clipboarded form. Spat.

"Any idea . . . where she might . . . go?"

I rummaged through the spare possibilities. "We've only been in Ashby for a little over a week. She's been downtown, to Pittsfield. That's about it."

His eyes swept the property. "Plenty of . . . places for a . . . little kid to . . . hide right around . . . here."

"I've checked the house and the cottages. I know all the hiding places around here. She's not at Thornwood."

He shrugged, checked his watch. "Okay. Guess that's . . . it then. We'll get started on it . . . first thing . . . tomorrow morning." Shooting a final spurt of muddy saliva, he ambled toward the patrol car.

For an instant, I was frozen in disbelief. I found my voice as he was ducking out through the door. "Tomorrow morning? What are you talking about?"

He twirled half his moustache in a tight coil, made a sucking noise. "Rules say . . . she's not missing . . . for twenty-four hours, she's not . . . really . . . missing."

My temper was rolling to a boil. "She's really missing, Officer. She's gone. Believe me."

"Not till it's . . . for twenty-four hours. Rules are . . . rules."

My face was on fire, gut churning. I lowered my voice to a studied, conciliatory lilt. "All right. Tell you what. You write down that she's been gone since ten yesterday morning. That's twenty-four hours, so you can start looking right away."

He bobbled his head from side to side like a mechanical toy. "Sorry . . . gotta be . . . twenty-four hours . . . from now."

"You mean to tell me the rules specify *which* twenty-four hours my child has to be missing? You mean to tell me just any twenty-four hours won't do?"

He smiled. "That's right . . . ma'am. Glad to see

you . . . understand. Rules are rules.''

''I do not understand, 'rules are rules.' I understand missing is missing. What in the hell is wrong with you people? My child could be in terrible danger, and you're worried about your stupid rules? Get away from here. Go hug your rule book. I'll find her myself.''

He gave me a peculiar look, raised an eyebrow. ''I'll be on my . . . way then.''

''Right, you go on. You're wasting my time.''

He curled the edges of his lips, fluttered his fingers at the boys, got back into his car, spat a final shot out the window, and drove away.

''Where's Rachel?'' Adam said.

''Rayshoe awgone,'' David said and popped his thumb in his mouth.

''Come on. We'll go look for her.''

He started to whimper. ''Daybit firsty, Mommy.''

I bit my tongue, tried to stay ahead of my fury. ''All right. You two stay right here. I'll go get drinks to take along.''

''And snacks,'' Adam said.

I raced into the kitchen and grabbed the pitcher of lemonade, the last of the oatmeal cookies, a batch of paper cups, and napkins. Max was fussing in his box. I set out a fresh bowl of water and gave him a fast scratch behind the ear. ''I'll find her. Don't you worry.''

I planned to go to South Avenue first, look around the stores, stop at Doreen's and see if she'd been there. The child had to be hungry by now.

I called out through the door for the boys to get in the car. As I juggled things to free a hand to turn the knob, the phone rang.

I answered on the vague chance that it could be the Ashby idiot patrol, having second thoughts. They didn't inspire much confidence, but they could provide very welcome extra eyes.

It was Penny Satenstein.

"I can't talk now, Penny."

"Not even to hear good news, darling?" Her words curled up at the end. Teased.

"What?"

"Ralphie and I took an informal count. The federation votes on the colony tomorrow and, barring any complications, it looks like they're going to go for it. Isn't that marvelous?"

"Yes, but—"

"Link is fit to be tied. I figured I'd take my little self over to his place and see if I can't find some way to soothe those fabulous feathers of his. What do you think?"

"I think I have to run, Penny. Thanks."

We had driven halfway down the access road when I spotted Granny's car angling through the colony gate. All the delays had fired my sense of urgency. I was a raw nerve, in no mood for any more useless discussions.

"Hold on, you guys," I said. The gray Chevy was bearing down on me now. I swerved off the dirt road and onto the grass, angled out far enough to skirt the unwelcome intruder. Granny flashed a look of surprise, mouthed a few angry words, tipped her determined brow nearer the wheel, and swung out onto the grass to head me off.

Twisting the wheel hard, I forced an even broader circle, gunned the engine to shoot past her before she could change her trajectory again. We were almost clear when the car started to shimmy, then vibrate, then took to bucking like a crazed mechanical bull. I struggled with the wheel, stomped hard on the brake pedal, and screeched to a wild, trembling stop.

Granny pulled up beside us, jerked up on her brake lever, and climbed out of the Chevy. She made a sorry shake of her head so the hastily donned blond-froth wig wavered on its own as she ticked her tongue in sympathy. ''That tire of yours is about fit to fall off, dearie. Lucky thing I came along before you got out on the road and had some real problems. Where're you all off to in such a hurry, anyhow, if you don't mind my asking?''

Desperate to begin the search, I told her about Rachel's disappearance, the note. ''I have to find her, Granny. She was very upset when I accused her of cutting Max's tail. I can't stand to think of her out all night by herself. Angry, frightened—''

''Oh, now, dearie. I bet you she's just fine, bet she'll come strolling back here any minute, pleased as punch with herself for giving you a good fright.''

''I have to find her.''

Granny frowned, blinked hard. ''Well, all right then. But you'd better take my car. Yours is in no condition to go anyplace. And you can leave the little ones with me. It'll be easier to get around.''

Yes, it would. ''But what about . . . Teddy?''

She forced a tight-lipped smile. ''I told you, dearie. There's never any problem in the daytime. Teddy's home, coloring in his favorite book. Keep him busy for hours. Boy loves to color. He's very artistic. Like his father was.''

''All right, then, if you're sure. When Chief Lynch comes back, please tell him what happened. I'll check with you in a little while.''

She handed me the keys. I slipped onto the red vinyl-coated front seat, waved to Adam and David, and started to roll away.

"... Try the Town Park lake, dearie," Granny called after me. "Bet that's where the girl would go. Child fell in love with the place when we went there on our picnic."

"Good idea," I called. "Thanks, Granny. You guys be good."

As I drove, the relentless sun beat on the dull gray finish of the little car and baked through the dust-caked windows. I cranked open the sunroof and aimed the front triangle flap of window glass to shoot the hot breeze at my face.

I decided to follow Granny's parting suggestion. The Town Park had always been a favorite hiding place for miniature Ashby runaways, groping adolescent lovers, lust-driven Ashby elders panting through their small-town peccadilloes under cool cover of the brick barbecues and scraggly hedgerows. Perfect place to run away: peaceful, shady, dim, a tonic mood set by the playful lapping of the crystalline water, the darting birds, and ash-brown squirrels foraging for picnic scraps in the leafy scrub.

I angled the car down South Avenue and into a tight line of traffic. Sale days were still in progress, clotting the street with reckless pedestrians willing to risk life and safety for a discounted treasure spied on the opposite side of the jammed thoroughfare. Cars were double- and triple-parked, reducing the traffic flow to the sorry trickle of a hair-clogged pipe.

I tapped my impatience on the steering wheel, leaned on the horn. As I crept along the avenue, I scanned the hordes of shoppers until my eyes ached, searching for one petite, delicate, dark-haired, wounded little girl. Several times, my breath caught as I thought I'd spotted her. But the child in question would revolve to full face or step out from the shadows cast by a striped store awning, transformed into someone else's daughter.

I inched past Fiske's Hardware. Fast Freddie was propped against the counter, dull eyes trained on the locust swarm of frantic shoppers. Past Doreen's. The booths and counters were packed with foot-worn bargain hunters seeking rest, revival, and the sale days' salad-and-sundae special at two-ninety-nine plus tax. Mothers and children were gathered in cozy, connected groups.

No Rachel.

Leaning harder on the horn, I spotted a possible escape route. If I could thread the car through the tight corridor between the traffic lane and a silver Mercedes parked with two wheels on the sidewalk, I'd be able to sneak the tight remainder of the way down the avenue to the park entrance.

The sky blue Buick in front of me edged forward a few inches. I turned the wheel hard and drifted out of the traffic line and toward the spare noose of space beside the Mercedes. Breath held, I poked the Chevy's nose into the perilous void and lifted my toe a tentative notch off the pedal. The car coughed, lurched forward. I caught a flash of the Buick's driver's crimson face, spread with shocked indignation as the metal side panels of our cars came close enough to embrace. He shouted a prodigious stream of obscenities based on female body parts and raced his engine in a sooty tantrum.

I tensed, sucked in every possible muscle as if my shrinking could set a proper example for the car. It wavered forward another inch and another. My eyes held straight ahead, unblinking. The Buick's driver had escalated his assault to male anatomy and procreation curses. Hot, furious words bumped at the shimmering air and fell away like spent bullets.

Another foot to go. Inches. The rear fender set a tender kiss on the Buick's rubber-coated front bumper and I was through.

Free.

With a cool breath of relief, I eased my toe off the brake and allowed the gentle grade to tug the car down the remaining stretch of steaming pavement. The tight line of stores yielded to low, modern office buildings and row houses. The crowds were replaced by occasional Ashby gentleman farmers plucking weeds from their postage stamp lawns and apple-cheeked Ashby toddlers swarming like termites over their metal-frame backyard swing sets and plastic wading pools.

No Rachel.

I turned the car through the scrolled black-iron gate fronting the Town Park. Inside, the road ribboned through pockets of shaded grass and dirt-floored playgrounds fashioned from mountains of treadless tires. There were cracked, all-weather tennis courts bound by failed, chicken-wire fence; picnic areas fitted with redwood bench-and-table sets; and open metal grills littered with unfired charcoal briquettes, lost chunks of charred meat, crumpled cigarette boxes.

My progress was slowed by clusters of speed bumps and the glacier tips of enormous boulders heaved up through the road surface by the winter frost. As I inched along the shaded car path, I searched for Rachel, working to place her among the sun-slicked bodies splayed on army blankets, the packs of girls playing double Dutch in the shade of a towering elm.

Where could she be?

The road bent left, narrowed, and dipped down toward the long, winding, tree-shaded incline to the water. I kept my foot on the brake, attention tuned to the hooks and fickle angles in the slender lane. Leafy patches of speckled shade worked my eyes through a jolting series of tricks, stealing the road in places, sending it coursing off in improbable directions. The knots of tension drew tighter around my neck.

The path floated over a playful bubble of a rise, settled for a moment on a level straightaway, then sagged into the final precipitous approach to the lake. Squeezing hard on the brake, my body arched back against the harsh pull of the downgrade. Pressing hard. Harder.

A sudden snap. The pedal lost force. Gave way. I pumped a desperate foot against the useless metal flap. The car was gaining speed, plummeting toward the end of the world. Hurtling in mad abandon. One hand strained against the trembling wheel. The other groped madly, searching for the hand brake. I felt the cool rod and tugged up with the full force of my terror. There was a jarring screech. The lever caught for an instant and broke loose, wobbling like a boneless limb in the steel vise of my desperate grip.

No!

The world was running together, racing past in a wild fury. I couldn't see through the dizzy rush, couldn't see a way out.

Plunging. Plummeting toward the black emptiness. The lake winked, beckoning. A slick gleam of mischief in the cosmic eye.

My mind shifted, raced ahead of the screaming tires. Refused the dizzying pull of oblivion. I felt for the door handle, squeezed. Pressed out against a charging wind that won out with its greater force, slamming the metal plate hard against my straining hand.

The water was rushing closer, reaching up to swallow me whole. I released the wheel, pulled myself up through the slim rectangle of the sunroof. The hot metal bit into my hands. Straining, I forced through the narrow opening, felt my flesh squeezed, burned by the impossible pressure. Almost through.

The car trembled at the water's edge, surged forward like a muscled diver from a springboard. I grabbed a breath, pressed my feet against the roof of the car and lunged away.

The Chevy went under with a thunderous splash and was lost beneath the surface, reduced to a lazy trail of large bubbles and wide, concentric circles spreading rapidly to a certain end.

In a shocked daze, I swam to the side, pulled my sodden, shaky self out of the chill water. People were running to me, shouting. Odd, rubber-faced people swimming toward me through the fiery air. Their words were muffled. Garbled bursts of foolish noise.

I was far away. Drifting.

Letting go. Drowning in cool, black, lovely oblivion.

CHAPTER

33

I OPENED MY eyes to a bristling, inky stillness. Listening hard, I caught the low, pulsing thunder of my heart beating; breaths shot in hollow wisps. My stiff limbs crackled with the tiniest movement, working on tight, rusted hinges.

Where was I?

Straining to focus, I caught a distant tinkling sound, droning muted mechanical voices. There was a thick, flowery scent. Footsteps. All so far away from my padded edges, the tingling tips of my near-dead senses. I was entombed.

Floating away.

Lost.

Heavy, thudding footsteps, doorknob twisted with a harsh, metallic rattle like chains dragging on cement. A sudden blast of light jolted me full awake.

"Who's there?"

Granny stood in charcoal relief against the blinding splash of light from the hall. "Well, now, the sleeping beauty's awake. How're you feeling, dearie? Better now? No more chills?''

It all came flooding back: the failed brakes, the desperate escape from the drowning Chevy. ''. . . I'm sorry about your car, Granny. The brakes.'' My words were woven together, blurred at the borders.

She slapped the air. ''Now, now. Don't give it another thought. Car was nothing but an old heap of metal and scraps, after all. People are all that matter, dearie. Not things.''

''Aunt Lizzie always said that.''

She came toward the bed, blotted at my still-damp hair with a fluffy towel, turned the sodden pillow so I was settled in a fresh pocket of cool softness. ''There, that's better, isn't it now? . . . Your Aunt Lizzie was right, Emily. Things can always be fixed, replaced. You lose a person, take away a person's chances, there's no going back, now is there?''

I tested my gelatinous limbs. Bend . . . flex. There was a sharp stab of soreness in my pre-bruised knee, a knuckled fist poked in my lower back. Nothing serious.

''What about Rachel? Did Chief Lynch find her? Is she . . . ?''

''Hush now, Emily. Doctor said to be sure and keep you calm. You just concentrate on getting over the shock, dearie. Everything else will work out, you'll see.''

''No one's found her? I have to get up . . . have to keep looking.''

Granny stroked my cheeks with the cool, damp towel, lifted my brick of a head, and wiped the back of my neck. ''The girl will be fine, dearie. Believe me. Chief Lynch and the police are out looking for her right this minute. I told the chief not to dare come back till he finds her. No need for you to worry. Here, swallow this."

"But . . ."

She set a tiny round pill at the tip of my tongue, pressed a glass full of icy water against my lips, and tipped it up until I was forced to swallow or drown.

"What was that?"

"Mild sedative, dearie. Doctor said it'd help you rest."

"I don't need to rest. I need to find Rachel."

"Hush, now. Don't trouble yourself. You've been through a terrible trial, Emily. Gave everyone quite a fright, if you don't mind my saying. To think of that car sliding to the bottom of the park lake, and you nearly trapped there inside." She fanned herself with a cupped palm, rolled her eyes. "Just the idea."

"I don't understand what could have happened. The brakes were fine one second—then . . ." I tried in vain to snap my slackened fingers.

"Never did trust machines. Hard enough finding people you can count on, I'll tell you." She wiped down my limp arms in turn. My legs. I was a sorry heap of mush. "There, now, dearie. Isn't that much better?"

My tongue had put on weight, flopped against the floor of my mouth like a dead fish. "I can't just lie here, Granny. I have to go look for Rachel . . . have to." I struggled to sit. The room wavered out of focus, and the bed tried to throw me like a horse in a temper.

She clacked her tongue, tossed her cherry curls from side to side. "Now, now. You're not being a good girl, Emily. Doctor insisted you have a couple of days rest. Mustn't underestimate a shock to your system like you had. You wouldn't want to come down with something serious, now would you?"

"But she's been gone so long. I'm terribly worried."

She smoothed a palm over my forehead, hovered over me like a rain cloud. "Course you are, dearie. Course you are. She's your child, after all. Every mother worries buckets about her child."

I was sinking again, trying to stay above the surface. "So tired."

". . . That's the girl, Emily. You rest now. I'll see to the little ones and all. I'll stay right here until you're back to yourself. Don't you worry."

Sinking. Struggling to push back against the rising, engulfing wave.

Every mother worries buckets.

"There, dearie. Everything will be done and settled before you know it."

Settling deep, deeper.

"That's the good girl, Emily."

You're a good boy, Teddy, aren't you?

Surrendering to the warm, irresistible weight.

Mama's good, sweet, darling boy.

Drifting, sinking to a calm, undulating peace.

He's a lamb most of the time, a regular lamb.

Can't let go. A hot, electric probe is teasing at the cool, black silence. Something I have to get my drowning mind around. Something wrong . . .

Never any problem in the daytime, Emily. Teddy only has his fits at night.

I try to struggle back, but I can't. Cannot. The darkness is too heavy, too deep.

It's the fits make him do those terrible, naughty things. I'll watch him, Emily. I swear it. Don't tell anyone, can't tell anyone.

The puppy yapped in the fuzzy distance. I heard the light giggles, Adam and David getting ready for bed.

Ready to sleep. Sweet, open, vulnerable, velvet baby boys. Soon they'd be curled in their beds. Asleep, where they wouldn't hear a thing. Wouldn't see the danger coming.

The medicine's not doing what it's intended. Poor Teddy's slow, doesn't understand what's right.

Poor Teddy.

Teddy.

If Granny was here, then Teddy was home.

Alone.

CHAPTER 34

THE CLUMP OF his certain footsteps on the stairs cut through the penetrating fog. I tried to force open my eyes, but an anvil had been fixed to each lid. Someone in cement boots was standing on my limbs. Useless to try and struggle back. Not yet.

The sound of his voice poured through me like warm soup. "Miss Archer?"

I tried to answer, but nothing worked. My lips were rubberized and tipped with powerful epoxy. My voice a furry mole tunneling deep in the muffled hollows of my throat. If only he could hear my grateful thoughts. I'm so glad you're here, Chief. So relieved.

"Miss Archer? Are you all right? I came as soon as I heard."

The steady slap of his footfalls beat inside my head like sweet, clean sheets airing in a brisk, summer breeze. Lynch would take care of everything. Lynch would make sure nothing happens to the children. He'd see to them. And Teddy.

I felt myself uncoiling, settling in on the rhythmic

waves of drugged unconsciousness. Tingling with the easy wash of playful images.

Crash! My drugged peace was rent by a brutal, heart-wrenching explosion. The silence torn by a clamorous rush of furious sound. Mad grunts. Furniture tossed and shattered. Fists smashed against sorry flesh. Sick crackle of bone on wood. Shocked rush of breath.

Then nothing. A terrifying void.

I felt the oily, invisible presence. There was a crisp, expectant crackle in the silence. The harsh, acrid scent of inhuman evil. I opened my eye a spare centimeter. On the ceiling, a broad mass of shadow wavered and moved toward me.

My mind was shocked alert. Ice clear. I caught the scream rising in my throat. Held it. Felt the etch of its bitter acid, tasted the bloody swell of my own fear. Whoever it was had knocked Chief Lynch out, nothing worse. I could hear the indignant rasp of his breathing, see his crumpled form in the far corner of the room.

There was a vague shifting sound, the overhead shadow trembled again and stretched. He was coming closer. . . . Closer. A careful, cushioned step at a time.

Another.

I had to let him think I was sleeping. Surprise was my only weapon. Had to find the right split second. Wait until he came at me. Catch him off-balance. Lunge at the last instant and get away.

Wait.

My muscles were coiled, trembling lengths of white-hot wire. Heart squirming in frantic spasm. My lungs ached for a decent measure of the air I allowed in a hot, cautious bit at a time.

Had to wait.

My eyes were open a spare sliver, trained on the ceiling. Watching the shadow's every move as it slithered and snaked its menacing way across the room. Slowly. Deadly slow.

Not yet.

The shadow swallowed the reflected spokes of the brass footboard, climbed over the foot end of the mattress, began sliding its mean fingers up my legs.

I caught a burning breath, tensed in a paralysis of fear. My nostrils filled with the bloody scent of my own terror.

Almost.

I was being eaten alive, the shadow engulfing me like a seeking, hungry mouth. A clammy, cold rash of sweat climbed my body with the threatening darkness. Over my hips now. Slipping like a vile caress around my waist. I clenched hard against a threatened tremor, felt the sick rumble of horror in my gut.

Closer. Close enough to smell the sour warmth of his breath, the oily scent of his skin. A coarse, splayed hand inched out of the mass of shadows, angled toward my throat.

Now!

He lunged at me with a guttural grunt, all teeth and groping limbs. I rolled out, away from the suffocating mass of his weight. Pushed with all my might against the forward press of his body. Caught off guard, he wavered and fell backward. There was a plodding thud as he slammed against the wooden floor. He flopped down with a shocked whoosh of breath and a sorry little giggle.

I felt a flicker of relief, took a step in the darkness toward the fallen image.

Suddenly, he sprang to his feet. Came at me like a

crazed animal, clawing at the air and screaming in vile, ear-splitting pulses.

I backed away, tried to duck aside, but my leg was caught in the tangle of bedding, and I lost my footing. Staggered into the inky corner.

"No!"

He was all over me, grabbing at my wrists, holding my legs under the suffocating mass of his weight. I was caught in the impossible steel vise of his mindless fury.

"Let go of me!"

One hand eased off my wrist, reached down. Came up clutching the long, metal shears. Clicking in the air. Aiming at me.

Snip.

I grabbed the thick wrist holding the scissors, struggled the hand back . . . away. Trembling with the effort, I felt my muscles straining, threatening to rip. The scissor was coming closer. Blades snapping their vicious way toward my neck.

Snip . . . snip.

"No, Teddy," I said. "Stop."

Snip. My hand was giving way, shivering, letting go. I forced the last lick of strength into my failing grip. But he was gaining, getting the better of me.

There was only one way, one chance.

I forced myself to let go. With no resistance, he sprang toward me. I veered, jerked out of the path of the plunging scissors. Off-balance, he was propelled toward the corner, and bashed his forehead with a sick thud. The long, polished blades stabbed and caught in the plaster wall.

Behind him now, I clasped my hands in a makeshift club and brought them down hard at the base of his skull. He wobbled on his heels, let out a low whoosh of surrender, and crumpled in an unconscious heap.

Trembling with horror, I flipped on the wall switch. Teddy was unconscious, curled in a tight, fetal ball. He was facing the corner like a naughty child doing forced penance.

I crouched beside him, felt his wrist. The pulse was strong, regular.

He could come around at any minute. I hurried to the phone and called the Ashby police, gasped out the necessary details of my deadly emergency.

Lynch was huddled like a rag doll in the opposite corner. I knelt beside him, shook him gently by the shoulder. ''Chief? Can you hear me? Are you all right?''

He mumbled, chewed the empty air.

''Chief Lynch?''

His face registered serious distaste. Still unconscious, he straightened the knot of his tie and brushed off his trousers.

''Please, Chief. You have to wake up. We have a prisoner.''

''Prisoner?'' His eyes shot open. He forced himself up on an elbow and fixed me with a misty, uncentered gaze. ''Miss Archer? What's happened? Prisoner, did you say?''

''It's Teddy, Chief. Granny's son, Teddy. He was the one who changed the hoses and slashed the bear. All of it was Teddy.''

''Teddy?'' His head was wavering, eyeballs dancing in uncertain rhythm. ''Teddy bear?''

''No, Chief Lynch. Teddy. Granny's son. He has fits.''

''Teddy bear? Granny fits?'' His voice was a soggy towel. He cocked his head like a curious dog. ''If you'll excuse me, Miss Archer. I do believe it's time to retire. Been a long, long day.''

I caught his head as it began to sink and lowered it gently to the floor. Lynch was not ready to go ten rounds with reality. Not yet.

Nothing to do but wait for the police. I tugged the scissors loose from the wall. Held them and sat on the edge of the bed, listening for the approaching swell of sirens. Watching.

The taunting tick of the clock was the only break in the relentless silence. Why didn't they hurry?

Teddy was starting to stir. He grunted, and rolled over. I held the scissors tighter, slid open the blades.

I forced past the swell of revulsion. Forced myself to look at him. His skin was a gleaming span of angry welts, the hair a porcupine swell of greasy brown spikes. The neck . . .

What was that on his neck? Morbid curiosity drew me closer. Clutching the polished shears, I bent over the hulking body. The skin on his neck was divided in two distinct bands of color. A grimy tan near the face, gray-pale below.

Closer still, I saw the odd raised welt of skin between the color stripes. I extended a trembling finger, touched the edge of it.

The thing had a weird, rubbery feel. I recoiled in disgust and drew back my finger. The welt puckered and pulled away.

Forcing myself to look, I saw the pale, wrinkled skin underneath.

He groaned, tossed his head from side to side. The rubbery skin peeled further away, lifted off in a slick curl.

Swallowing back the bilious lump rising in my throat,

I pinched the corner and tugged. The thing surrendered with a smacking sound, the welts, the scarred pockets of flesh. Pulling further, the hair lifted off in a piece. Underneath, fine gray wisps covered a broad span of patchy, pink scalp.

It was Granny.

She blinked open her eyes, fixed me with a blank, eerie, unfocused gaze. One eye was her own ash-toned circle, the other was covered by a hard, gleaming milky bubble, the iris painted off-center, drifting toward the nose.

I fought off a wave of dizziness, stared in shocked disbelief. ''You. You're the monster.''

She raked her fingers hard over her face to remove the dried pebbles of glue, tugged at the corner of her eye until the lens bulged and popped out like a bursting pod.

With practiced fingers, she smoothed her eyebrows, pinched color into her cheeks, slicked the sparse wisps of hair behind her ears. Finished primping, she tried to sit. A lightning shock of pain ran through her. Her face twisted in agony, and she slumped down flat a moment to catch her breath. One hand worked in soothing circles over the broad swell of her hip. Groaning with the effort, she rolled up on the opposite wavering elbow and faced me down with a look of raw hatred.

''Oh, now. I'm no monster, dearie. All I want is what's right for my boy. That's all I ever asked.''

''What are you talking about?''

She coughed, wiped a lick of spittle from her lower lip. ''I'm talking about your father. Your darling genius of a father. All he knew was taking. Had no idea about paying back, not even when it came to his own son.'' Her eyes were wild, sparkling with rage.

I clutched the cold, metal shears. "What son?"

"My boy, Teddy, is your father's child. Same as you. But all these years the boy's had to live in the shadows, never had near what you had. Little privileged princess, you were, off at your fancy schools, wearing your fancy clothes with your fancy la-dee-dah friends. Only the best for little Emmy Lee, while poor Teddy had to struggle by on wishes and air."

The thought snaked and darted out of my grasp. "Teddy is my father's child?"

A trail of furious spittle strained from the tight corner of her mouth. "I know what you're thinking. No, Teddy's not movie-star handsome like your father was. But Hillard wasn't so fine on the inside. Man was full of the devil. He knew how to crawl up under a girl's skin, that one did. Told me he loved me, promised he'd always take care of me. . . ."

Her laugh was a dead, dry cackle. "He took care of me, all right. Got me in a family way. Disgraced my people so bad they threw me out, refused to have anything to do with me. But Hillard said not to worry, he'd see to everything.

". . . He got me a job with one of his Mister Big-Shot friends, a theatrical producer. Man was taking a play on a South American tour and offered me a good salary to come along and see to the star's hair and makeup. Sounded just right, your father said. I'd be back months before the baby was due. He'd have gotten your mother to agree to a divorce by then, and we could be together. Only . . ."

She tried to adjust her position, but the shock of pain sucked the blood from her face, stole the power from her voice. ". . . Only it didn't work out like that. The show ran way over budget, the crowds stayed away in droves. Mister Hotshot producer cut his losses and stranded the lot of us in Colombia. The others scattered. I wrote your father, told him I was near out of money. . . .

"While I was waiting to hear back, waiting for money to get home on, I had a bad fall. The baby came early. Too early . . ."

"That's why Teddy's retarded?"

She was straining against the pain, trying to get up. ". . . Teddy's that way because of your sonovabitch father. I couldn't get a decent place to stay, couldn't afford to pay the good doctors. Had to have Teddy seen at a lousy clinic. Child was so weak and sick he almost didn't make it at all."

"I'm sorry."

"You're sorry." She raised her eyes and spoke to the ceiling. "You hear that? She's sorry." She started to laugh in earnest now, a mad, hysterical, rolling laugh dredged from the black, bloody depths of her fury. Her belly heaved, and tears streamed down her cheeks. She spoke through the breathless sputters. "That's just what your father said, 'I'm sorry, Alma. Forgive me.' "

She turned off the laughter, lowered her voice to a grainy whisper, narrowed her eyes to smoldering slits. "But I told him it was too late for sorry. Way too late. He had to pay with all he had, everything."

Her mouth warped in a grotesque grimace. ". . . It's taken us years to get this far. So many years." She cocked her head, a trace of mischief teased into her tone. "It was easy getting rid of your dear mother, but we had to track down all the others. Figure out who they were. We had to sniff them out, one by one."

My mother. "You arranged all those . . . accidents? You murdered all those women?"

"Not just me, dearie. Me and Teddy. It was his revenge, after all. You wouldn't expect the boy to sit idly by while his mother settled his scores, now would you? My Teddy's not that kind of a boy, Emily. He knows what's right. Not like some."

"No. Teddy's just an innocent. It was all you. All the horror."

Her face spread with glee, eyes fogged with lunacy. She poked her manicured index finger at the air, counting the ghosts. "One . . . by one . . . by one, we found them. Sneaky devil, your father was. Told all his girls the same story. Got away with the same line over and over. Left a trail of illegitimate children all over the country. Favored light-eyed brunettes, he did. All of us could've passed for sisters in those days: your mother, me, Lilly Marshall."

"Link Marshall's mother."

Surprise flashed in her expression, faded away. "Clever girl, aren't you? Poor Lilly had a terrible accident. Freak thing, it was. Lilly used to work for your father. She quit after the baby was born, but she'd come back to visit. She even brought the little boy to play with you. Isn't that sweet?

"Worked out real perfect, as far as we were concerned. We wanted you and the boy to know. Wanted you to suffer the way Teddy did. The pair of you were up playing in your father's room when the accidents happened. The time your mother was shot. And when poor Lilly drowned. Poor thing went for an innocent little swim in the pond. She just slipped in, got stuck in the bottom weeds. You were there to hear the screams. Served the lot of you right."

Adam's near-brush with disaster flashed through my

head. The ‘‘pond man’’ he kept talking about. ‘‘You held her under?’’

‘‘Used a plastic straw for breathing. Simple. Heh, heh. Police around here are so all-fired stupid, they couldn’t figure out any of the killings. Couldn’t prove a one. They thought maybe your father was responsible. Your Aunt Lizzie thought he was guilty, too, but she made excuses for the sonovabitch, which suited me just fine, kept everyone wondering. Lizzie loved Hillard, too, you know. All those years, she wanted him for herself.’’

Aunt Lizzie. ‘‘No, that’s not true. Lizzie was a friend, that’s all.’’ I caught something in her expression. ‘‘Lizzie didn’t go to see any sick sister. What have you done with her?’’

She rolled up onto her good hip, waggled a finger at me. ‘‘Oh, now, dearie. Can’t expect a girl to give away all her secrets, now can you?’’

I lifted the shears, slipped the blades apart. ‘‘Where is she?’’

Her lips stretched in a beatific smile. ‘‘All right, if you must know. Your Aunt Lizzie is fast asleep and far, far away. Eternal rest, they call it. Isn’t that nice? Anyway, not to worry. She had a nice end. Granny and Teddy tucked her in real nice and cozy.’’

I was trembling with rage and anguish. ‘‘You crazy, vicious, old witch. That woman never hurt a soul. I ought to—’’

‘‘Now, now, you’re not going to hurt us or anyone, Emmy Lee. You’re such a very good girl. Always were. Such a good, sweet, pretty, obedient little girl. Your daddy’s favorite, now weren’t you?’’

She was rising like a wave, sitting now, biting through the pain. ‘‘Nothing like a little girl, Emily. Your daddy always preferred girls, now didn't he? If only Edmund had been born a girl. . . ."

"Edmund?"

"That's Teddy's proper name, Edmund Hillard Fowler. Always called him Teddy, but Edmund'll be more seemly after he comes into his inheritance."

Her madness was a sick fever raising dangerous, bloody patches in her cheeks. "After the Berkshire Federation turns you down, I'm taking your father's will to court, dearie. Have it declared invalid. Edmund's older by six days. Thornwood belongs to him. Your father knew that. It took some convincing, but I made him realize that he owed everything to the boy. That's why he donated all the money he had for the new school we're going to open—Edmund House. I explained it to Hillard until he came around to my way of thinking. 'See all it's costing, Hillard,' I told him. 'How much more blood do you want on those hands of yours?" At first he didn't believe me about the murders, but later he came around. Your dear father didn't want any more killings, so he gave all his money to the foundation, made it so no one knew, and I had complete control over how all the money'd be spent. That was how it had to be. It was only right, Emily. You can see that."

"You're a lunatic."

She waved me away. "Never mind what you think. Point is everything belongs to Edmund. Not you. And not to that precious little girl of yours, either. Another greedy little princess, now isn't she? Wants to take what doesn't belong to her. Well, that's not going to be."

She was working past the pain, rising straighter, pushing up on her knees.

My hand tightened around the shears. Careful, Emily. Nothing could happen to Granny, not until she told me what she'd done with Rachel. ". . . That's fine," I said. "Let the court decide. No one else has to be hurt."

She was up on one foot. Muttering to the pain, brushing it aside like a mild annoyance.

"Teddy's such a good boy. He could have been an artist, you know. Boy loves to draw, loves clay work. Has real talent, if I do say so. Comes by it natural, after all. Takes after his father."

She was crouching on both feet. Pulling up to stand. Madness fogged her expression. ". . . Soon he'll be ready for his own show. Just a few more pieces and his agent'll arrange something in New York. Art world is waiting for Edmund Fowler. Been waiting too long." She grunted like a wounded beast as she took a faltering step.

"Take it easy, Granny. Stay back."

She took another step toward me. Shook the injured leg and smiled. "Time to tidy up, Emily. All's left to take care of is you, Chief Bigmouth, and the little cherubs. Fast asleep like angels, they are. I'll see they stay that way—-permanently."

I caught the vague wail of distant sirens. A few more minutes. I had to distract her, keep her mind off the children. I tuned my voice to a low, reassuring hum. "Tell me more about Teddy's show, Granny."

Her smile broadened, she fluffed her hair. ". . . Probably have it in one of those fancy Madison Avenue galleries, I betcha. Champagne reception and all. Think I'll get a long dress, maybe a nice silk jersey . . ."

She seemed to be wrenched awake, narrowed her eyes, waggled a finger at me. "Now, dearie. You're trying to get me off the subject, aren't you?"

"No, I—"

"Don't waste your words, Emily. They're the last

ones you're going to get." She lunged at me with coiled fingers, face twisted with rage.

Adam cried out in his sleep.

"You two and then the sleeping angels, Emmy Lee." She was closing in on my neck, pressing her thumbs against my larynx. Electric flames leapt in my head, the room exploded.

Floating in the last puddle of dim, blue awareness, I brought up the shears, forced them up. . . .

Snip.

CHAPTER 35

I CAME TO in a bright, frenzied rush of activity. There were swarms of police, paramedics. A dour man swathed in wear-polished black mohair strolled around the room taking notes as if he were cataloging a museum collection. Everyone was talking at once. Unconnected remarks were tossed and caught like plastic Frisbees in a fickle breeze.

My throat was flaming sore. I tried to speak but could manage only a toad-croak of a whisper. A towheaded, fresh-faced female officer caught my static and bent over me. "They'll get to you in a minute, miss. You all right?"

"Yes. The chief?"

"He's fine. He came around as soon as we showed up. Quite a character, that one. You should have heard him with the old woman. 'Admit it, Miss Prom,' he said to her. 'You are not now and never have been an actual member of the human race. Confess, Miss Prom. Your alleged tuna casserole is being tested by the National Security Agency for possible use in our country's strategic defense.' I wish our chief had a sense of humor like Chief Lynch. The only thing funny about Chief Errol Rubin is his face."

"Is Granny . . . ?"

She shook her head. "The mind is a terrible thing to lose."

"Is she going to die?"

"Die? Hardly. You gave her a tiny scratch on the cheek, that's all. But she's been carrying on like crazy about her precious complexion. You'd think she was a Hollywood starlet or something." She scratched her head, tucked her hair up into her cap. "The old girl confessed to everything. Her complexion's not going to matter a whole lot where she's going."

I pulled myself up, took a sip of the water she offered me. Steel knuckles were pounding inside my head. "My kids?"

She smiled. "Cute little guys. All this commotion didn't even wake them up."

"But she has my daughter someplace. You have to find out where. Please, she has to be all right."

The officer frowned. "They were questioning the old woman downstairs, but I suspect they've left to take her in for booking by now. . . ."

With a desperate surge of energy, I raced down the hallway and bounded down the stairs. Lynch was staring out the window.

"Where's Granny, Chief?"

"On her way to a nice, cozy prison for the insane, Miss Archer. God willing, she'll not be assigned to work in the kitchen."

"I have to talk to her. She has Rachel!"

"But she said the child was upstairs sleeping. She said . . ."

Outside a car door slammed. There was the ponderous roar of the engine catching.

"No. Wait!"

I raced out and ran after the car as it bumped down the narrow drive. They were halfway across the meadow before they spotted me screaming and flailing in the rearview mirror and rolled to a reluctant stop. Lynch ran up behind me, breathing in desperate gulps.

Granny was sandwiched in the back seat between a pair of grim-faced cops. She gave me a curious look, as if she couldn't quite remember the face.

I leaned in through the window, spoke in a harsh, breathless rasp. "Where is Rachel? Where are you keeping her?"

"Rachel?" She blinked, pointed an accusing finger at me, and turned to the officer on her left. "You see there. That girl could be real nice-looking if she'd take more care with herself. Put on a little lipstick, do up her hair. Girl has to make the effort, is all I'm saying."

"Granny. Where is Rachel? You have to tell me."

"Tell us where you've kept the girl, Miss Prom," Lynch said. "It'll go easier for you if you're cooperative."

". . . She'd look real sweet in a nice braid pulled up in the back, don't you think? Did one like that for Greta once."

"Where is Rachel? Tell me, and I'll make sure Teddy's taken care of. You want someone to see to Teddy, don't you?"

She turned to look at me. Blinked hard several times as if a flying insect were buzzing at her nose. "You'll see to Teddy? Now that'd be real nice. Tell him he's a good boy, dearie. And tell him his mama had to go to the store, will you? Don't want the boy to worry."

''Where's Rachel?'' My voice had risen to a shriek of frustration. ''Where is she?''

''Tell us, Miss Prom,'' Lynch said. ''Tell us this instant, or I'll use my influence to see to it you are deprived of all cosmetics during your incarceration. And I will arrange to have your correct age printed on the front page of the prison newsletter.''

Granny flapped a hand at him, ticked her tongue. ''Oh, now, Mister Hot Air. Don't get yourself in an uproar. The girl's fine. I left her with Teddy.''

The cop at the wheel gave me a vacant look. ''Time for us to be going now, miss. Gotta take the prisoner in.'' He saluted, rolled up the window, and started to pull away.

''But wait . . . my little girl . . .''

The car picked up speed. Granny's light giggle trailed on the exhaust-tinged breeze. ''Not to worry, dearie. Teddy's a lamb. Most of the time.''

CHAPTER 36

LYNCH AND I raced across the dark meadow, past the solemn ring of huddled cedars. Stones bit the soles of my bare feet, and my eyes were stabbed by mites of grainy dust.

Granny's cottage was a shadowy specter in the distance. We ran past the hanging tree and through the pocked colony gate.

Across the last strip of road, I forced my boiling muscles to keep pumping at top speed. Lynch's face was florid and sweat-slicked. She had to be all right. She had to.

Gasping for breath, I ran up the three steps to the tiny porch and bashed my fists against the locked cottage door. Lynch motioned for me to stand back and prepared to kick it in. There was a flurry. A chair raked across the floor. I heard the plodding approach of footsteps.

Someone was banging back from inside.

"Teddy, open the door."

"Beh, guh." More pounding. "Buh."

Lynch searched the porch. There was a metal milk

box in one dim corner. Using the lid as a probe, he worked the rusted long bolts out of their cranky hinges. The wooden panel yielded with a groan.

Teddy peeked out in the darkness. ''Bah bah.''

''Where's Rachel? Where is she?''

''Guh.''

Lynch and I pushed past him and into the tiny front room. Teddy ambled to a narrow door and turned the knob. There was a creak of movement from the room beyond. ''Rachel?''

She stepped into view, sporting a flowing ash-blond wig and a bubble-gum pink feather boa. Her eyes were streaked with turquoise shadow, lips coated with a thick glob of strawberry gloss. ''Hi, Emily. Chief,'' she said and turned toward Teddy ''See, Ted. I told you they'd come get us out.''

My eyes worked over her, examining.

''Are you all right?'' the chief said.

She dipped her chin. ''It's hot as hell in this place. And there's nothing good to eat. Otherwise, we're okay.''

''I'm so sorry, Rachel.''

She frowned, shook her head at me. ''I told you I was telling the truth, Emily. You just wouldn't listen.''

''Ha—gee.'' Teddy brought his cupped fingers toward his mouth, poked them back and forth a few times.

''He's hungry,'' Rachel said and aped his gesture. ''That means 'hungry,' in sign language. This guy's always hungry. Come on with me, Teddy. I'll get you a snack.''

She held out a hand and waited for him to take it. With clumsy, bearish motions, he lumbered beside her and wove his thick, ragged fingers into hers like an obedient child. "Hah tuh."

Rachel's laugh was the light clink of polished crystal. "You hear that? He said 'hi, toots.' I taught him that. 'Hi, toots' to you, too, Teddy Weddy."

"I'm so glad you're all right, sweetie. I was so worried."

She made a face. "Not about Teddy, I hope. He may look funny, but he's really a nice boy. Granny was the one who did all the terrible things." Her face fell, and she eyed the ground. "She's a real nut case, I guess. You know she has a whole collection of little dolls she makes that look like real people she knows. She's even got one for each of us. And they've all got these strings tied around their necks. At night, she holds them up and talks to them like they were real. She threatens these stupid dolls like she really hates them. It's weird, I'll tell you. I was wrong about her."

"We were all mistaken about Miss Prom, my dear," Lynch said. "Imagine, I thought her most unforgivable misdeed was her cooking."

"We all make mistakes about people, Rachel. Sometimes it's hard to see the truth." I had to take all this in slow, careful steps. "I'm sorry I didn't believe you. I'm so very sorry."

She hitched her shoulders, pressed her fine lips together, and looked up at me from under her dense flap of dark lashes. "I'm sorry, too. I've been a rotten pain in the butt, I guess."

"I think it's fair to say you haven't been easy."

She turned her attention to Teddy. The corner of her mouth wavered in a satisfied, smug little smile. "Tell them about how you're going to school soon. Listen to this."

Teddy grimaced, worked his mouth. "Guh goo."

Rachel dropped his hand a minute to clap in appreciation. "You hear that? Go school. That's good, Ted. You're really making progress. Try 'hi, toots' again. Say, 'hi, toots.' "

"Ha too."

"Isn't he great? Isn't he wonderful? Hi, toots," she said and giggled. "I just love it."

CHAPTER 37

WE WERE PRESSED against the fat coil of red velvet rope, watching the arriving stream of bedraggled passengers. David sat astride my hip, chubby finger poking at the air, accusing every third man that passed of his paternity.

"Dat's Daddy."

"No, Monkey. That's a stranger."

"Dat's Daybit daddy."

"Nope. Not him, either."

Adam's fingers clutched the tail of my denim skirt. He was still subdued by the earlier arrival of the Concorde. I'd tugged them over to the observation window, pointed out the sleek beauty sliding along the tarmac, only to have him break away and run shrieking bloody horror across the passenger lounge. "Don't let it get me! Don't let the star warriors get me! Help!"

I studied the sea of faces, searching for Will, half afraid I wouldn't be able to recognize him, either. It seemed a raw eternity since he'd left on his brief journey, and we'd embarked on an unexpected adventure of our own.

''There he is,'' Rachel said. ''Daddy!''

He muscled through the tight crush of people and ducked under the velvet rope, drew us all into a tight, loud, smacking, lovely circle of greeting.

''What a trip,'' he said, working us out of the crowd. ''London was the pits: rainy, crowded. And the conference was a crazy house. You guys didn't miss a thing.''

''Sounds that way,'' I said.

''How was the country?''

I winked at Rachel. We'd agreed this was a story worth saving for home. ''Things worked out, Will.''

And so they had. Chief Lynch had agreed to keep an eye on Teddy until the Edmund House's scheduled opening at the end of the month. The Berkshire Federation had agreed to keep an eye on the Thornwood Colony. The Commonwealth of Massachusetts had agreed to keep an eye on Granny Prom permanently. And Lincoln Marshall had agreed to bid the Commonwealth and Ashby a permanent good-bye. According to Penny, Len Satenstein and his shotgun had presented very persuasive arguments favoring the move. Apparently, Len had caught the two of them, as Penny put it, ''in flagrante delicious.''

''Great,'' Will said. ''Then you're finished with the colony? No more worrying about all that?''

''Finished.''

''Terrific.'' He hoisted David and Adam on his hips like a set of airborne bookends and began walking toward the baggage claim area. ''. . . I thought maybe all of us could go out to the beach for a few days, relax.''

The boys raised a chorus of cheers, planted wet kisses on Will's scruffy cheek.

''Sound good to you, Em?'' he said.

''Perfect.''

Rachel was beside me. There was a troubling mist of distance in her expression. I touched the back of her hand with a tentative finger. ''How about you, Rach? You like the idea?''

Her fingers twined into mine like fine lengths of velvet ribbon. I met her dark, hopeful gaze. ''The beach?'' she said.

''Just the family,'' I said. ''Okay?''

A slow smile tugged up the corners of her mouth. ''Sounds great, Emily. It sounds goddamned wonderful.''